fade to
black &
white

I0638300

A novel by Kris Abel-Helwig

"A power shot into the goal that is the life of a high school senior. Very relatable, fun, and an overall great read."
— Erin, Kentucky

"This "young adult" book is a wonderful read for any age. Kris Abel-Helwig is a very talented writer whose characters are well-crafted and engaging. I highly recommend stepping into Joan's world and enjoying the experiences this book has to offer."
— Marianne, Illinois

"This book is refreshing in its approach to young adult topics and has so many entertaining moments. It is surprisingly non-formulaic and witty. I read it twice and have shared it with 3 friends so far. I also read more of the set. The author crafted in them a sense of purpose and interdependence that is unique. I am glad I read these although I don't usually sit down and read books in print. I recommend that you treat yourself also--and added bonus-- play the author's Spotify playlist to set the stage.
— Tracy, Iowa

"I loved their relationship. I loved Joan. I loved being able to relate to a tomboy who, with a little help, figures out that she can be silly, be herself, and be loved for it."
— Kathryn, North Carolina

"Smart, funny, riveting read, that once picked up cannot be put down. Loved Joan Jett, who stayed true to character throughout. I'd say, "hit me with your best shot," but you already did."
— Mary, Colorado

"One of the greatest books I have ever read, and I have read A LOT of books. What I loved about is was that it grabbed you and didn't let go! I stayed up all night last night reading it. It has such great detail about the characters that you really get an image in your head of what's going on. Also I loved how the songs tied into the the story. I listened to a few and it put a different perspective on the story. PLEASE let me know the next time you write a novel because I would LOVE to read it. Thanks so much for the great story!"

— Rachel, Colorado

"Joan Jett is an inspirational main character - she's quirky, personable, funny, tough, and above all courageous."

— Jessica, Pennsylvania

"The author has truly captured the intelligent voices our teens possess. Joan is bright, wickedly clever and finding her way. Glad I got to go on her journey all the while remembering mine!"

— Shel, Florida

"Fade to Black and White is a great story about love and loss and finding life again. It is full of teenage angst as well as the grief of losing a parent and the stress of preparing for college. But this book also includes the fun parts of high school and discovering your true self. I rooted for Joan and all of her relationships. Truly a good read."

— Andrea, Iowa

"I cried. I laughed. I loved it."

— Trish, Colorado

Culicidae Press
PO Box 620647
Middleton, WI 53562
USA
culicidaepress
editor@culicidaepress.com

FADE TO BLACK & WHITE

ISBN: 978-1-68315-060-2

Library of Congress Control Number: 2023945533

Cover photo, art and design ©2014 Kris Abel-Helwig
kris@kahcreative.com • https://kahcreative.com

Our books may be purchased in bulk for promotional,
educational or business use.
Please contact your local bookseller or the Culicidae Press
Sales Department at +1-515-462-0278
or by email at sales@culicidaepress.com

twitter.com/culicidaepress — facebook.com/culicidaepress

Introduction

(Or The Gallbladder – because you don't really need it)

Feel free to jump in and start reading the novel. You can come back after you are done. Go ahead. I mean it.

The Ruptured Appendix: As you are reading and come to a term or quote you are not familiar with, check the page number and look for it in the back of the book.

The Playlist: Each chapter begins or contains songs that set the tone. Download and listen as you read. Weird. I know. I did not receive any compensation from any of the record labels. But music played an important part in Joan's fictional life.

The Blatant Marketing Pitch: if you find something in it that resonates with you, or someone you know, feel free to pass it on, or buy a hundred copies to give as gifts. Your choice.

This book is about healing. Surviving. Thriving. As a breast cancer survivor you may think it is strange that I had Joan's mother die. I did so as a strong proactive plea for everyone to be diligent in your health care and of those you love.

Dedication

Thanks a billion to my amazing beta readers, proofreading posse, and grammar sheriffs whose ages ranged from thirteen to seventy eight. Special shout out to my co-conspirators and co-editors Cori Tanner and Mike Helwig. I love you guys. Cori helped Joan come to life, or more appropriately, find her way back to life. Mike was my sports consultant to "keep it real." Fictionally speaking that is.

Time to download the playlist on Spotify krisabelhelwig titled: FADE TO BLACK & WHITE and get busy reading!

Enjoy!

Playlist

1   "Total Eclipse of the Heart" Bonnie Tyler, 1983

2   "Close To You" Carpenters, 1970

3   "Wind Beneath My Wings" Bette Midler, 1988

4   "I Love Rock n Roll" Joan Jett, 1981

5   "Because You Loved Me" Celine Dion, 1996

6   "I Hope You Dance" Lee Anne Womack, 2000

7   "Hit Me With Your Best Shot" Pat Benatar, 1980

8   "Misty" Leslie Gore, 1963

9   "Just The Way You Are" Billy Joel, 1977

10 "Amazing Grace" Jadon Lavik, 2008

11 "Maneater" Hall & Oates, 1982

12 "Fire and Rain" James Taylor, 1970

13 "Singin' In The Rain" Gene Kelly, 1952

14 "Mean" Taylor Swift, 2010

15 "Impossible" Shontelle, 2010

16 "Forever and Ever, Amen" Randy Travis, 1987

17 "Eye of the Tiger" Survivor, 1982

18 "You Give Love a Bad Name" Jon Bon Jovi, 1986

19 "Point of Light" Randy Travis, 1991

20 "Roar" Katy Perry, 2013

21 "Name of the Game" ABBA, 1977

22 "Larger Than Life" Backstreet Boys, 1999

23 "I'll Make A Man Out Of You" *Mulan*, Donny Osmond, 1998

24 "My Guy" Mary Wells, 1964

25 "This Kiss" Faith Hill, 1998

26 "When We Stand Together" Nickelback, 2011

27 "Can't Fight This Feeling" REO Speedwagon, 1985

28 "Something to Talk About" Bonnie Raitt, 1990

29 "Hero" Mariah Carey, 1993

30 "Holding On To Heaven" Nickleback, 2011

31 "Wide Open Spaces" Dixie Chicks, 1998

1

"Total Eclipse of the Heart"

For three years I was invisible in high school. Easy if you have the determination and imagination. Fair skin, freckles, black dyed hair, green eyes, and slight build made it possible to float like a ghost through the shadows of claustrophobic hallways filled with raging hormonal teenagers.

I was a ghost. The pale version of my mother without her outgoing personality or comfort in her own easy-to-tan skin. In high school she embraced all aspects of the academic, athletic, and social scenes. Later, her natural exuberance for life intensified battling the cancer for over a decade that ultimately won their war.

And then she was gone. And all color went with her. Making my high school experience more like watching a black and white movie of someone else's life. Feeling none of the happiness, fulfillment, or any emotional involvement at all... until that is, the day the son fell out of the sky.

Contrary to Greek mythology, when Icarus flew too close to the sun, thereby melting the waxwings Daedalus had made, he did not plummet into the sea and drown. Rather, like a true, mythical hero he performed a perfect landing, gracefully and beautifully, to become on that eventful day, my next-door neighbor, Jason.

❂

I'm Joan. Joan Jett Bennett. Yes, named after a rock star, and also Joan of Arc. My parents were not only Classic Rock of the Eighties fanatics but also passionate about literature, history, art and education about all of the above. I grew up listening to their music, which is still my favorite. When I got a bit older, they made me watch their best-loved movies during our "family night," so I know the lines to Caddy Shack, Animal House, Princess Bride, and a million other movies that adults a generation older than me would appreciate.

My parents met in college and married after graduation. They got jobs teaching in the city, then bought a house in the suburbs, and would "rock 'n roll all night, and part of everyday" in their spare time as they created their life together. And they laughed. And kissed. A lot. Nauseating at times, even for their young kids. And then she was gone.

I couldn't reside full-time in the solace of my colorless void. Only at school where I was invisible, and had a running conversation in my head, observing the bizarre socialization of my peers living their lives. No, at home I had to hide my despair to help my father survive the collapse of his world. Losing the love of his life so young and having a mini version as a constant reminder could have driven him off the ledge, but he rallied for my sake and that of my older brother, Jon.

Named after another rock legend, Jon (Bon Jovi), he lived up to his namesake. Entertaining, easy-to-smile, faithful and true to his passion; in his case, the beloved instrument was a lacrosse stick instead of a guitar. He constantly practiced, would run for miles cradling a ball in the pocket, throwing against any wall. And he taught me to play, letting me use his older, shorter stick. We would run and pass, "it doesn't do any good to stand and throw, you need to be constantly moving, like in a game." We would play one on one and shoot on goal for hours in our backyard. Silent, or smack talking the invisible goalie, it was the best therapy for two kids who had lost the solar power that energized their lives.

Recruited by colleges to play lacrosse, Jon opted to major in Engineering at the University of Illinois, my parent's alma mater, where he could still play on a club team. And I was left, again, but he gave me his old stick, and a few spares he'd outgrown. And that's what I was doing, six weeks into summer after my junior year in high school, shooting on goal, when I heard a voice from over the fence.

"What did that net do to you?"

2

"Close To You"

"What?" I said, breaking my silent concentration and turning toward the sound. There he stood, tall, tan and awesome. Smiling. Either blocking the sun or generating beams of light all by himself. I was awestruck. I shut my eyes and re-opened them, thinking it was a hallucination. But no, there he was. In my backyard. Shielding my eyes to get a grip, "May I help you?"

"Heck yes, you can teach me how to use that weapon you wield like a champion!" He walked over, stuck out his hand, looked straight into my eyes (gasp), smiled a one-sided Kevin Bacon smile (breathe, just breathe) and said, "I'm Jason, your new neighbor."

As soon as I could break my completely awkward, gaping stare, I looked down at his outstretched hand and shook off my lacrosse glove and grasp his warm, dry hand, realizing too late (!) that I was a sweaty mess. He pretended not to notice and shook it firmly before letting it go, sadly, to return to my side, forlorn.

"And you?"

"And I?" I replied slowly.

"You are...?"

A complete idiot, apparently, mentally kicking myself. "Ah, Joan," I flinched.

"Joan of Arc, leader of the French Army?" he said as he motioned to the lacrosse stick in my hand, "Cool."

"No, she was quite hot, blazing, it seems," I said without thinking. I'm used to carrying on conversations in my own head, and yes, frequently, I crack myself up.

"Well yes. Smoking hot," he added with a laugh.

Trying to hide the annoying burning blush on my face regarding the smoking hot reference I blurted out. "Her and Joan Jett, 80's rock legend, I was named after them both."

"You're named after a revolutionary and a rock star?"

"Yes, my parents went a little crazy," I sighed.

"Best naming job ever," he smiled. That smile was a serious weapon that should never be deployed at random. And it seemed that somewhere a choir was singing. Good grief, I'm an idiot. Salvage this!

"What about you, Jason Bourne or Jason and the Argonauts?" I asked. Take your pick, both major studs, once again talking to myself. Hopefully!

"Neither, a family name, just Jason Paul Halsted," he said shrugging his perfect, broad shoulders and shaking his head, which caused the wind to gently tease and flirt with his shimmering sun-kissed locks. Gag. I'm hopeless.

"Well, grab a stick, scoop up the ball and show me what I've got to work with." I rotated to hide my glowing face and focused on the goal, any goal, especially one that could help me quickly rebound from being a totally undignified, ridiculous, star-struck teenager.

We passed the ball back and forth. He threw like a newb – like everybody does when starting out – by not following through on his passes. I showed him the correct way to throw, and although he did follow through, his pass went straight into the ground. "It's all right," I said. "Just release the ball a little earlier." His next pass went way over my head, and I had to run after it, but after a bit, he got the hang of it and was throwing very well, for a beginner. I also taught him to cradle the ball so it wouldn't fall out of the pocket, and then hit his stick to knock it out, because that's legal in lacrosse.

I threw the ball to his left side which is more difficult for a right-handed player to catch, and after a few, he laughed. "You're throwing it to my left-hand side on purpose!"

"Yep. You can catch it backhanded, but if you have the time, try and switch hand positions."

"Like this?" he asked as I threw another pass, and he put his right hand down low on the stick and moved his left hand up high – like a natural left-handed player would do.

"Perfect. Now try and throw the ball back to me left-handed. In lacrosse, you should be able to pass and catch with either hand."

"Says who?" a voice from behind me joined in. I turned and saw my brother Jon's mischievous smile. He was home on break from his summer internship at school. I introduced Jon and Jason, and after the obligatory introductory, "Welcome to the neighborhood – Thank you I'm glad to be here" comments, Jon asked Jason if he had played lacrosse.

"No, but it looks like a blast," said Jason.

"It is," said Jon, "but you have the wrong size stick." Jon went back into the garage and came back with two longer sticks. "These sticks – and the lax bros that use them – are called D Poles," said Jon.

"What is lax? And why are these sticks longer than the other one I was using?"

"Lax" is short for 'lacrosse', and a lax bro is short for 'lacrosse brother," I said. I didn't mind Jon's usurping the attention. It gave me a chance to catch my breath, calm myself and resume my familiar role as a spectator.

"These Poles are about six feet long and are used primarily by defensive players," added Jon. "You look like a defensive player, so that's why I said you had the wrong size stick. A short stick or the players that use them – are sometimes called a shorty – and are used primarily by Attack and Midfielders.

"If you're interested, come watch a game. We're playing tomorrow night up in the city."

"Sure," Jason said.

"I'm hangin' with the bros after the game – can you two take a separate car?" Smooth move, Jon, that's my bro.

He had recovered from our loss better than me. I knew this was a trick to get me out with kids my age, but this time I didn't mind. At all. "Okay then, catch you later," Jon said as he made a quick exit back into the house, with an incredibly smug look on his face. I knew I was in for a grilling later.

As Jason and I continued to play, he kept a running one-sided conversation going. He told me about his family. His dad was a military fighter pilot (of course he was) and they had just returned from a long overseas tour. He went on to data-dump his life history. His mom was ia graphic designer (cool). He had two younger sisters. The oldest, Sofia, was going to be a sophomore and hoped to make the cheerleading squad. "She's a flyer, like my dad" he said, assuming I understood what the heck he was explaining.

I looked at him, wondering what on earth, or sky, bouncing around with pompoms cheering for someone else's accomplishments had to do with piloting a jet.

He must have figured out I was clueless, and added, "that's what they call the crazy ones that climb on top of the cheer pyramids and get flipped and thrown around."

"Oh." How was that for witty banter? Could I sound any more sophisticated than that? Lame. I could just picture Jane Austen rolling over in her grave. To regain a small piece of my dignity, I took a shot at the net, top right corner.

"Sweet!" he said and continued with his monologue. I tried my best to concentrate on what he was saying, but I was crushing so hard he could have been speaking French, might as well have, or any romance language that I could not comprehend. Where was I? Oh, here we go, his youngest sister, Gracie, was small, quiet, liked to draw and read a lot, and "lived in a fictional world most of the time," according to him. I caught up on this note. This comment totally resonated with me.

"That's great."

"Really?" he looked to see if I were joking.

"Yes, reading is a wonderful way to escape into someone else's life when yours completely falls apart..." After this unexpected meeting, my guard was down. I hadn't thought before that comment escaped. And I knew once out, just where it was going... Dark clouds rolled in; the pounding in my head started. My stomach turned. I dropped everything, couldn't catch a breath and gasped, "Excuse me; I have to run." And I did. Left him standing there, beautiful, stunning. Stunned. Mouth dropped open, at my sudden, unexplained, unexpected, desertion.

"Thanks for the lax lessons ..." I heard faintly as I tore open the back door and fled to the darkness of my fallout shelter.

3

"Wind Beneath My Wings"

I hit my bed just before the bomb exploded. The pain, the panic, the shaking, the tears, gasping for breath, clenching my teeth, squeezing my eyes closed, shutting it all out. And then ... her face, her smile, her laugh, her jokes, her shampoo scent, and of course, her stories ... rolling like an old movie across the inside of my eyelids.

She was diagnosed when she was seven months pregnant with me. The cancer was like my twin, taking nourishment from her as I did. She refused any treatment and said it could wait until after I was safely delivered. So as I was taken out of delivery to the nursery she was transferred to a different surgery unit where they did a radical double mastectomy and collected lymph nodes to biopsy.

I had to be fed with a bottle; ironically this was my mother's biggest regret about the whole ordeal, that she couldn't breastfeed me! Determined to bond with me, while sitting in the dark she fed me with the bottle where her nipple used to be. She would rock, stroking my freshly washed, silky copper wisps, and inhale my scent, her scent, a mix of her shampoo and baby shampoo she'd concocted, and sing my lullaby . . ."I Love Rock n Roll."

Soon after they brought me home the chemotherapy started. She told me since we were both mostly bald she would dress us in matching goofy headbands or floppy hats. After getting infused with drugs designed to kill the quick growing cells, hair, skin and of course cancer, she would come home and take a nap, wake up to throw up, and then get up to take me for a stroll to get the toxins out of her system. Once she told me about the time we saw a woman sitting on a park bench with a toddler in her lap, so she stopped to chat. The woman commented on our matching hats-of-the-day and asked what my name was, Mom said she told her, and the woman was aghast.

"You named your daughter after a *rock and roll* performer?" she gasped, incredulously.

"Well yes, we did. When my husband saw she was going to have my copper penny haircolor," she said she had casually lifted her hat to show her scarce wisps, "he asked if we should name her Penny, or Ginger or Autumn. But I told him no; she was already Joan. When he asked, 'Joan Jett or Joan of Arc?' I simply said, both."

"What did he say to that?"

My mother had smiled and replied, "He knelt down on one knee in front of the rocking chair in the hospital nursery, took the bottle from me and gently tapped her on her left shoulder, then her right, and said, 'I dub Ye the Fair Maiden Joan Jett Bennett, may you always strive to go forward on your path to enlightenment and enjoy life and love to the fullest.' And then he kissed her on her forehead, and she smiled for the first time ..." Mom said, as she reminisced.

"Sounds like you married the right man," the woman said, shaking her head.

"And what is your lovely daughter's name?"

"Henrietta, after my husband's mother."

Before she could stop herself, Mom said she blurted out, "Well that must have earned you major brownie points!" then quickly she attempted damage control by saying to the little girl, "Henrietta, it is a pleasure meeting you, may you grow into a strong woman of character, brilliant, and full of integrity." The woman and her baby just stared at her and couldn't get away fast enough!

That was Mom. Always trying to make the best of any situation and look at the bright side of everything. The glass of water wasn't just "half full" it was simply the most delicious water ever, straight from a cool mountain stream, probably one in the Rocky Mountains in Colorado, and you could taste the clear blue skies, and puffy white clouds, and inhale the cool, crisp, dry air with every sip. And then she would digress this way or that, how the colors out west were so vivid since the air wasn't polluted, and even the black and white photography had richer blacks, and grays and whites . . . and I listened to every word, inhaled every scent, tasted every idea, observed all the colors in her world, and held on tight to this strong, magnetic, whirlwind force of nature that was my mom.

She loved the random act of kindness concept, for instance, one time we were on a winding country road and she stopped our car in the middle of the lane, got out, picked up a migrating turtle and took it to the side of the road so it wouldn't get run over. Or the time she paid the toll money for the person behind us who had let us merge into the correct lane in front of them when no one else would, even though we had our turn signal on, just to show she appreciated their thoughtfulness. And when the young couple caught up and waved and mouthed the words "Thank you," she just waved and smiled her glorious smile.

She was my hero. And Jon's too. She adored us both and expressed it daily. She would tell us she loved us at least ten times a day, to the point where she'd look at him and say, "Do you know?" and he'd say, "Yep" and she'd say, "How much?" and he'd casually reply, "Infinite." "That's right, and don't ever forget it," she meant it. And he knew it.

And being four years younger I wondered how I fit in. Once when she asked me "Who's my sunshine?" I answered, "Jon." And she quickly responded, "Yes! But you are too Joan, and always will be." And even though I was only three or four, I felt so happy, and relieved. And I was so proud she was my mom.

I grew up, loving every minute I spent with her, and when I started school and we were apart I couldn't wait to tell her about everything I had done, what my friends had said, and how fun my teacher was and ... on and on and on as she listened patiently.

So as soon as I would see her, I'd run to her. She would pick me up and twirl me around, and we were a whirlwind of copper penny curls spinning in circles, smiling, laughing, glowing, until ... she found another lump.

The cancer had come back, like a hibernating creature emerging from the darkness, hungry, needing to devour the sunlight and everything it touched.

And then it was the race of her life, for our lives. She refused to give up the good fight as she tried to cram a lifetime of lessons learned along with emptying her arsenal of honor, intelligence, compassion, creativity and humor into me, her overwhelmed, adoring, eighth grade daughter. Her last quest was to fortify me so I could face the world without her. And all I wanted was to hold onto her once vibrant body, begging her invincible spirit never to leave me. And she didn't want to. But she finally had to. And I didn't want to. But I finally had to let her go.

As I watched the color drain from her beautiful face, I kissed her gently on her cheek, said "Goodbye" and then slowly, began to fade to black and white ...

4

"Because You Loved Me"

The funeral. The wake. I had to escape. I couldn't listen to one more sympathetic friend, neighbor, or stranger say how sorry they were, how wonderful she had been, how she had helped them with this, or made that for them, or how talented she was ... and then it would come, every time, about how lucky Dad was to have Jon, such a fine young man, and *me*, a mini-version of *her*, constant reminders, my twin and me, of what had been taken from him. An idea came to me, slowly forming in my throbbing head.

I found Jon and asked him to take me away, *get me away*, from all of the well-meaning people. He didn't even hesitate. He grabbed his car keys, and my hand and we were out the door. I had him take me to the drugstore where I bought a box of the black dye that would erase my mother's copper hair and hopefully lessen my dad's pain. When we got home, I went straight up to my room and waited until all the mourners left, and the house was quiet.

I kept the lights turned way down in the bathroom, not able to stand the bright light shining off her hair in the mirror. I put on rubber gloves, mixed the formula, and with one last look, said goodbye to the ghost in the mirror.

The black dye circled the drain in the white sink as I rinsed. It was strangely comforting, watching it descend into the darkness. I wanted to follow. In the dimly lit room I found solace. I finally looked into the mirror again, and *she* was gone. Another ghost had replaced her, slightly familiar, but dark and pale, and secretive. Except for *her* eyes, the green eyes that searched my face, my hair, and then dove deep back into themselves, trying to find something missing. What was it? A point. What point was I missing? That bothered me, some forgotten point, nagged at the dark recesses in my mind ... but it was gone. For now at least it was buried. I think I needed it to be. Wrapped in my dark towel cloak I felt safe. I felt serene, strangely in control. Invisible.

The next morning I braced myself and went down into the kitchen. My dad looked up from the paper, and his look of shock hit me, but he recovered quickly and got up and walked over to hug me for a long time. When he finally let go he held me at arm's length and smiled, tears in his eyes, but smiling nevertheless, and he told me I was beautiful. Searching his eyes, was I looking for – *regret, relief or redemption*?

But to his credit, he supported me, and gave me the space I needed to deal with my life lost. And even though I put on a brave front at home, I suspect he knew when I took off on a run, exactly what I was ran away from, and when I went to school *every day for three years* wearing my invisibility cloak consisting of a black tee shirt, black hoodie, black jeans and black Converse shoes, he realized this was the armor I needed to face my inner demons.

Jon was my rock. He teased me mercilessly, relentlessly, wonderfully, the way only an older brother could. He was a lifeline to hold onto when I felt I was falling into nothingness. He would call from college a few times a week, just to tell me a humorous story, or something fun he had discovered, or what bizarre food they were featuring in the cafeteria. And he would end every conversation with something like, "Still rock'n the zombie look?"

To which I'd respond with some version of, "Still think you can play Old Man? I heard they have a girls' team you can try out for." And we'd laugh and say, "Later" but never, ever, did we say "Goodbye."

5

"I Hope You Dance"

The door slowly opened, letting a triangle of light into my nothingness, waking me out of my self-imposed coma. My dad quietly made his way across my room. I sat up, still in sweats from my workout, and I know my face was a puffy mess.

"Hey sweetie, I brought you some hot tea," he said.

"Thanks," was all I could mumble.

"Was it a bad one?"

"Level ten."

"Ouch, I'm sorry," and he meant it.

"Nothing you can do Dad, it is what it is."

"I know ..." he put the tea on my bedside table. "I met the new neighbor boy Jason."

"Ohhh noooo," I groaned, fell back and covered my head.

"He seems like a nice kid. He brought in all of the lacrosse equipment. And then stopped by to check on you. When I opened the door he looked me in the eye. Always very important. I don't trust a guy who doesn't look me in the eye. It always makes me think he is hiding something. He also stuck out his hand to introduce himself. Impressive. He was worried about you.

"I told him about mom. Thought it would be easier for me to do it. He was very respectful. I like him. He asked about a good running route, and said you could show him tomorrow if you are up for it. It would be nice for you to hang out with someone your age, and he's new in town." He leaned down to kiss my forehead then quietly left the room.

❁

The morning after a migraine was always a train wreck. I finally got up and managed to eat a banana and some peanut butter with a spoon. Toast would have been too crunchy. I not only needed energy for a run later, but also a boost to face my new golden boy neighbor. I showered, threw on a tee shirt and shorts and attempted to capture my mop of dark curls into a ponytail.

Next I had to figure out the best approach to explain my strange behavior the previous day. After rehearsing different scenarios for a ridiculous length of time, I finally gave up and put on my running shoes to go over to "face the music." Taking a deep breath, I braced for his extraterrestrial glow and rang the doorbell. I didn't realize I hadn't exhaled until the door opened . . . and a small dark haired girl with enormous eyes looked up at me.

"HEY!" I practically exploded.

The startled girl almost jumped back.

"Hi," she said, looking at me like I was an escaped convict on her doorstep.

"I'm Joan, next door, well actually, I'm standing here, but I live next door. I met Jason yesterday. I'm your neighbor, but you probably figured that out already thanks to my long, eloquent introduction," I blurted out. Real smooth. I said to myself, grateful at least that I was not babbling incoherently to her glorious brother at this point in time.

Remarkably for one so young, she composed herself, smiled a little, and threw me a bone.

"I'm Gracie, Youngest Sister of Jason, pleased to make your acquaintance, Joan Next Door."

Despite the fact that this intelligent little runt was mocking me, I admired her spunky, pesky attitude and response. It seems I had found a most worthy verbal sparring partner.

"Touché, Youngest and Probably Most Annoying Sister of Jason, is he around?" I requested and bowed.

"Yes, I will seek him, would you like to enter?" she swept her hand into the entry, stepped aside, and suppressed a giggle.

I shook my head and laughed, "No, I'm good, this jester prefers the courtyard, rather than the court," making myself at home on their doorstep. I figured it was better than the possibility of humiliating myself with yet another member of the family.

What was happening to me? My invisibility cloak was slipping and my control-freaky nature was taking a major hit. Internal conversations were in an uproar. I stretched my legs by doing calf raises while hanging on to the railing. Then I took turns rotating each ankle. Going through simple exercises to regain composure and silence my inner thoughts by doing my warm-up routine. Hoping to find my normal, cool, calm and collected self before he showed up. *Breathe. Focus. Exhale. Calm.*

I was back.

"Hey."

I was gone.

Replaced by the very uncool, Not In Control Stranger Joan. "Hey. Run?" I managed to spit out.

"Sure, let me grab my shoes."

As soon as he was ready I took off on a familiar three-mile run; I was hoped to find my old self along the way.

"Three miles okay?" I asked.

"Great," he said, falling in step with my pace.

We ran in silence, outwardly at least, inside the chaos clamored. I pushed my mind aside and concentrated on my feet, which were behaving much better than my brain. At the end of the street, we cut through the baseball fields and entered the trail in the woods next to my neighborhood.

The trees, heavy with lush, green leaves, were a canopy above us, blocking out most of the sky. A slight breeze cooled my flushed face. A creek mimicked the curve of the trail; glancing at it rippling over the smooth rocks soothed my rattled brain. My erratic breathing regulated and I started feeling like myself again.

The only person I had ever run with was my brother Jon; who made me go faster than I'd wanted to. I pushed myself to earn his respect. Now, I realized he carried on Mom's mission to make me confident and self-reliant.

In contrast, Jason didn't rush the pace. Thankfully, he did not carry on a conversation because there were enough of them going on in my head. As we rounded a curve, a fox froze on the trail ahead of us. It had some prey in its mouth, and sized us up for a moment as a potential threat before disappearing as a flash of orange into the thick, dark underbrush.

It must be the "fox" not "ground squirrel" episode on today's nature show because I was rooting for it to make it back to its den for a nice, well-deserved lunch. I glanced over at Jason to see if he had seen it, he nodded and smiled. That smile. *Gasp.* So much for serenity, *hello calamity*, as I stumbled over a non-existent rock.

Jason grabbed my arm and kept me from falling. He let go quickly, *too quickly*, and we continued. It was awkward, but amazing. We finished and looped back to the baseball park.

"Cool down," was all I said, as we slowed to a walk.

After awhile Jason went over to the swings and sat on one. He kicked off and started swinging, so I took the swing next to him and did the same. Eventually, he broke the silence, "Good pace. Do you run cross-country for the high school?"

"No," I said. *I don't do anything for the high school. Except haunt the hallways. I am a ghost there.*

"You should; maybe I'll try lacrosse too, if you can teach me more about the game," he carried on.

Trying, with difficulty, not to think about teaching him how to do anything, I asked, "What sports did you do at your last school?"

"Football, track, basketball. We were on an island military base. I worked out a lot on my own. Running sprints on the beach . . ."

. . . and I was off on an awesome tropical island visual, picturing him running shirtless through the surf as the waves reached out

to caress his feet ... and the seagulls flew in the breeze over him, urging him on, cawing his name ... but wait, back to reality, "... and I did some Functional Fit workouts, you know, push ups, dips, sit ups, body weight exercises."

"That's what Jon does at school. He's tried to get me to now that he is home."

"You should. We could work together, and with your running program we'll be in shape for sports this fall." He rambled on as we approached our street. "Thanks for showing me the trail. Are we on for the lacrosse game tonight?"

Jon's game. *The setup.* "Sure, do you want me to drive?" I threw out *(and fortunately not up).*

"That would be great since I don't have a car!" he laughed. *That laugh.* Again, the choir, starting on the chorus now.

"See you at six," I said, trying to sound casual, hoping my blush would be mistaken for a post-run flush. I turned away and went into my house. Wow. I was definitely entering the *Twilight Zone,* a corny old black and white TV show where the characters start out in reality and then some strange supernatural event occurs and they are abducted by aliens, or attacked by bizarre creatures, and nobody believes them when they try to tell the authorities.

How do I explain my new reality to anyone, let alone myself? I have alienated myself from my classmates and peers for three years. Why? To protect myself of course, from any more pain or loss. Whoever said, "It is better to have loved and lost than never to have loved at all" is a freaking whack job. *Are you kidding me?* How can it be better to have your heart ripped out, your head split open by migraines, the air knocked out of your lungs so when you open your mouth to scream nothing comes out? No thank you. It is definitely *better* to skip all of the above in my very experienced opinion. I had convinced myself if I didn't get close to anyone I would not be at risk of losing anything. In reality, the only thing I had left to lose was myself. *To nothingness.*

This led to my self-imposed separation from friendships. It began the summer after eighth grade before my mom died. I had been busy helping her near the end, and didn't have time to spend casual summer days with my eighth grade friends at the pool or the mall.

Our junior high class was divided and sent to two different high schools. Most of my friends were going to the other one. I was fine with it. It may seem strange that I preferred hanging out with my mom instead of my teen friends, and really, under normal circumstances I probably would have been a normal teenager. But thanks to my "evil twin" I didn't have the luxury.

The typical hormonal roller coaster of a thirteen year old girl was kept on track by our mutual need for exercise and ice cream. If I were the least bit moody Mom sent me on a two mile run. If that didn't fix my "bad-ittude" I was sent to shower or bathe.

That did the trick, knowing a milkshake would be waiting for me after. We mixed our shakes in special glasses. And used favorite spoons for any additions. She'd tell me the story a zillionth time about when she asked for extras in a milkshake as a teenager and the clerk had refused her request "because peanuts might get stuck in duh straw . . . ," my mom would say, with an exaggerated drawl. And she would laugh *that laugh*. With a little snort at the end. Then I would laugh too. And any earlier snit was forgiven and forgotten with the last slurp, thanks to our spoons, from our "peanut-free" straws.

So what has happened to the dark, illusive, hermit-like exile I have maintained for three years? Am I tired of the only conversations I've had *outside* of my family have been *inside* my head? Am I finally *feeling* a lack of something? Anything? Anyone? *Someone*? Am I starting to move again after being cryogenically frozen for so long? It certainly felt like it, especially when I hear Jason's "Hey," or see that one-sided smile, and my heart practically bursts out of my chest beating like a pimped up car woofer.

At any rate, I have only a few minutes until I am going to a lacrosse game with Jason The Golden Boy Next Door. I need a shower and a clue, on what to wear, say, do. I jumped in quickly and washed and conditioned my hair. Put on a clean black tee shirt, black shorts and black Converse, the usual.

But for some reason today it didn't feel quite right. *Too bad, no time to change.* I grabbed my wallet and keys and went to get my Jeep out of the garage. *My Jeep. Wow.* That was the first time I had dropped that so casually. It had been Mom's Jeep, always *hers.* She loved driving it, especially in the summer. We'd unsnap the vinyl top and fold it into the back compartment. We'd drive. Listen to music from the eighties. Look up at the blue sky above us with the puffy white clouds. She was there now. And I was here. In *our* car. Was I finally be on my way back from nowhere?

As I pulled out of the dark garage into the brilliant sunlight, blinded for a second, I put the car in park. When my eyes adjusted, another bright son appeared.

"Whoa! Sweet Jeep!"

"Thanks," I said, and added to myself, *Mom.*

He opened the door, and jumped into the passenger seat. "Figures you'd have my Jeep, Jett. And the all-black look? Are you always this cool?"

Cool? Anything but, good grief, get a grip. If I am going to drive without being a menace to society, I need to get in control. Forget cell phones or the iPod, I now know the number one distraction. I should have a bumper sticker that reads, "Don't Crush and Drive," I shook myself out of it as we sat parked, but not parking.

"Did you just call me Jett?"

"Yes, if you'd have shown up in a '65 Mustang I probably would have gone with an Arc riding on a horse reference," he laughed.

And so did I. I laughed. And smiled. And looked straight into his dark blue eyes for the first time. And stopped breathing . . . . *And his eyes got even bigger, as if that were physically possible,* and he looked surprised, and looked away quickly, probably thinking about how strange I am.

"I like that it has an old school vinyl top," he said, trying to get the conversation back on track.

"Me too," I said, then added without thinking, *(Always a bad idea.)* "It's easier to go topless this way. I mean to take your top off. I mean the *Jeep's roof off*!" Absolutely, positively, stupidest series of embarrassing slip-ups *ever*. Argh.

Putting on my Aviators, I looked over my left shoulder to compose myself, and shifted into reverse, *literally*.

I could not believe he let that open door invitation to totally smoke me go without comment. "Can I put on some tunes?" he asked instead, pulling out his phone.

"Go for it, just keep the volume down so we can hear the purr of the engine," I added, over the roar. As we drove, Jason tapped his fingers on the door in rhythm with the music. It was a beautiful summer evening, warm, but not humid, which was nice for a change. My hair dried and wasn't a frizzy mess. It did get tangled, but I didn't mind.

"How about this?" he said, as he put on Pat Benatar's, "Hit Me With Your Best Shot."

I started to sing, caught myself, mortified. "You like eighties' music?"

"My folks lived it, so they play it a lot. And I've seen all the movies from that decade . . . *Pretty in Pink*, *Sixteen Candles*, *Breakfast Club*, and of course, *Flash Dance*."

"You have got to be kidding me, why?"

"Sisters, remember? We were on an island, not a whole lot to do entertainment-wise. My mom even made me learn all the Kevin Bacon *Footloose* dances."

"You might want to keep that juicy piece of knowledge on the DL." I winced.

"DL?"

"Down Low, Confidential, Off the grid," I said.

"You're probably right."

We made it to Jon's game, and after about five minutes I knew that the lax community had a new convert. Jason loved the game. I could tell he was itching to give it a go.

At halftime, he grabbed Jon's stick and we went out onto the field to throw. I taught him that throwing with a longer stick, a Pole, was different than throwing with a shorty. When throwing with a Pole it was less of an overhand motion and more of a side-armed motion. Unless you were trying to score, in which case, a pure overhand shot was most common. "Wait a minute," said Jason, "Poles can score?"

He had watched the first half of the game closely, and noticed that the defensive Poles rarely crossed midfield and had never tried to score. Even the Long Stick Middies, or LSMs, ran off the field as soon as their team got possession of the ball. *Sigh.* Explaining lacrosse to a newcomer is difficult, and to do it justice would take some time. *Bummer.*

"Poles can score but their longer sticks are easier to stick-check. The best opportunities for Poles are during unsettled situations, like face-offs or immediately after turnovers." Jason pondered that for a while and we watched the remainder of the game.

Afterwards, Jason asked Jon several questions, and Jon invited Jason over to our house tomorrow to further discuss some finer points of the game. I think Jason realized that with Jon leaving in a couple of days he had a very short window to learn from him. After settling on a time tomorrow afternoon, we jumped back in the car to head home.

"How about we go grab some ice cream? My treat," Jason said. I froze. Tried desperately to defrost quickly. *Ice cream. Mom.* However, by the time we pulled into the ice cream parlor I had recovered and went into the shop. I tried to decide what combo to create, as ordering ice cream is an art form. I told him to go ahead and studied the palette of flavors.

He smiled at the attendant, who only had eyes for him. "Could I please have two scoops of vanilla on a cone?"

"Sugar or plain cone?" the server asked, too sweetly.

"You know, a person's ice cream preference tells a lot about his personality," I said, under my breath, for only him to hear as I walked by him.

"Sugar please, and can you add some sprinkles?" he asked, looking sideways at me.

"No worries, Sugar." The scooper lady was fluttering her heavily made-up lashes. After she had managed to unglue them from him, with difficulty, she sized me up and down. No doubt was putting me in the "no competition" category. Terminal friend zone. "And for you?"

"I'd like one scoop of "Everything Dark Chocolate" with a scoop of "Heavenly Raspberry Swirl," peanuts and whip cream, in a cup please," I ordered decisively.

"Perpetually in a conflict between the forces of dark and light, a little fruity and definitely nuts. Fits you perfectly," Jason said smugly, congratulating himself.

"Very funny Vanilla Boy, which makes you pure, plain and yawn . . . ," I countered, with the obvious non-verbal action, covering my mouth.

Eye Lash Lady handed him his cone and left him, reluctantly, so she could go make my order. I noticed he was just standing there holding it, not eating. Quite the gentleman.

I said, "Go ahead before it melts" . . . and then a deliciously evil thought seduced my brain. As he moved it up to take a bite I said, "Wait a second," crinkling up my nose for effect, "does that smell okay to you?" I asked, pointing at his cone.

Like taking candy from a baby. He naively took the bait and moved it to his nose to take a whiff. I seized the opportunity.

Bam. I lifted up on his elbow, thus shoving his cone into his nose. Ice cream face-plant.

"What the?" he choked.

"Oh, my bad, it looks fresh after all," I laughed, nervously. *What did I just do? Sabotaged myself, that's what! Traitor!*

"So that's how it's going to be Jett? Or is it Benatar in this case? Nice shot." He grabbed napkins to wipe off his face and his adorable grin *(whew)*. "Hereby serving notice, you better watch out because revenge can, and will be very sweet," he warned, trying to look serious. Seriously adorable. Then he took a step back out of range before taking his first bite from a safe distance.

Forewarned, I cautiously ate my dark and light, fruit and nutty combo but Jason behaved. Still I knew that there would eventually be payback, and nasty or not, coming from him, I was certain it would be "sweet." We finished up and went back to the car, no doubt leaving Eye Lash Lady behind the counter wondering why he would waste his time with me. And at that moment, and every single moment since that fateful day we had met and from this day forward, *so did I.*

"Can you drive by our school? I've only seen a picture of it on the website. It looks pretty nice. My old one was so small, and didn't have a stadium or track or any of the stuff like the normal schools have here in the States."

As I drove through the neighborhood, he kept a running conversation going, "Do you have your schedule yet? I wonder if we'll have any classes together?" He was looking forward to getting involved in school here, to make up for being out of the country for three years.

In contrast, I had been avoiding any involvement for the same length of time. But to both of us, it had seemed like an eternity, for totally different reasons. I started to think about all of the other aspects of high school, besides the academic, which was the easiest part to deal with, and I felt nauseous, but I had to ask. "Did you have a lot of drama at your school?"

"You mean like, theater classes?"

"No, not theater drama, plays and musicals and such. I mean the daily, obnoxious teenager relationships, class hierarchies, politics and social structures, nerds, partiers, jocks, cheerleaders, you know, that kind of drama," I answered.

"Hmmm, like dating stuff or worrying about what classes to take, scholarships and college placement exams?"

"Not exactly." How do I explain life as a teenager in today's society here in the States compared to that of one on a remote island paradise? I couldn't. Not without ultimately condemning our new friendship to the firing squad or hangman's noose. We didn't fit. Hero gets the girl, not the ghost. So I dropped it. But I knew it was going to haunt me.

"Do you ever run here?" he asked, bringing me back from the grave thoughts.

"Only in P.E., I prefer the woods, better views, less repetitive and not as crowded."

"I know what you mean, but I need to be timed on some distances, do you think you could help me out?"

Umm, a tough decision ... *watching him run around the track, holding a stopwatch ... timing him, wondering how fast he would drop me when school started and he realized what I was really like* ... but what could I say, other than, "Sure, as long as you don't make me race you."

As we drove away, he pointed to the tennis courts. "You play?"

"A little." *Very little.*

"How about tomorrow afternoon? It will take me awhile to find our rackets," he said. *That's when I heard Annie singing "Tomorrow."*

"All right, I'll see if I have any balls," I said. *Argh*. Nice choice of words. Oh well. *Another plan. Another day. Another non-date. What is happening to my non-life?* I pulled into his driveway.

Opening the door he turned, "Can I get your number?"

"Sure," I grabbed my phone out of the glove box *(that's where my dad makes me keep it when I'm driving)* and handed it to him. "Send yourself a text, and then I'll have yours as well." I congratulated myself on matching his smooth move, of course, I was sweating bullets and blushing, so maybe not quite so smooth.

"Here you go, don't forget to add me as a new contact," he said, leaving my phone on his vacant, abandoned, lonely, seat. *Not likely,* I said to myself, as I waited for him to head to his door before backing up into the street and driving to my driveway. When I had pulled into the dark garage I turned off the car, pushed the remote to close the door, and heard the swoosh of a new text. I picked up my phone to read.

(unknown number)
Rest up for your match
You are going to need it
Vanilla Ace

Wow. Clever and can dish it out as well as take it in. *I am in big trouble.* Huge. Suddenly the light went out and I was sitting in the dark, but this time for a change, I was smiling. Using my phone in flashlight mode I stumbled into the house trying to figure out what to save him *(!)* as in my contacts. Golden Boy? Bourne ID? Icarus? Adonis? Sir Lancelot? All of the above? I certainly had the room in my very brief list of numbers. I finally just typed in *jason*, and then for some reason added *gb*. I saved it and slipped it into my back pocket. In hindsight, I *probably* should have left off the *gb (for Golden Boy)*, but we all make mistakes . . . and quite often pay heavily for them later.

The next hour I searched my house for my racket, a can of balls, and *a reason* to play a sport I wasn't very good at with a guy who made breathing difficult. I had to figure out how to play without oxygen, or reduce Golden Boy to human status in order to function, let alone compete.

The following morning was the opposite of the previous one. Had it only been twenty-four hours? This time I knew I was going to see Jason, but looked forward to it. Although the possibility of being a total klutz on the tennis court was high, his easy-going, positive attitude was infectious. He was confident and funny, not cocky or conceited like some of the guys I observed.

At school, I would sit back and silently watch how they would *interact* with each other, and even worse, *overact* around girls. Because I was invisible, they would talk about *everything* and not even notice or care if I could hear. Strange. Discussing pick-up lines and as the girls walked by they ranked them numerically.

No doubt about my score. *Zero, in fact.* But up until now, today, I had never cared about what guys my age thought of me. Or even *if* they thought of me. Until Jason. Now I was obsessed about his first impression. I tortured myself thinking about our meeting in my backyard and my quick exit, but then lightened up thinking about our run. I moved on to being relieved that he thought the ice cream in the face was funny. I had to smile. I was still smiling when Dad walked into the kitchen. *Tactical Error.*

"Hey Sunshine, what's on your mind?"

"Just thinking about how warped I am because of you and Jon."

"What have we done?" I told him about the trick I'd played on Jason. "Gutsy move on the first outing, how did he take it?"

"He laughed and threatened payback."

"I told you he seemed like a nice kid, but be sure to watch your back, you pretty much demanded retaliation." He laughed.

"Will do. You guys trained me well. How about breakfast for dinner?" I asked, changing the subject before he could ask more questions about Jason.

"Sounds good to me," he said, getting out the eggs and waffle mix. "Have you fed Misty yet?"

"No, but I will when she tells me she is ready."

6

"Misty"

Misty was my salvation the fall of freshman year in high school. We had left Jon at his campus for his first year of college and were heading home in the car. We drove in silence for a long time. After a while Dad asked, "How would you like to adopt a kitten from a shelter?" I had wanted a cat forever, but we couldn't have one because Mom was allergic.

"Okaaaay," I said slowly, torn between the thought of getting a kitten, and knowing the reason it was now possible.

At the shelter we learned there had been an outbreak of feline leukemia at the end of the summer. They had to evacuate all the felines for a month so they could bleach the entire facility. They were just beginning to get kittens and cats back in. There were only three kittens, and two had been claimed. The tech pointed to the back of the cage. The three looked similar, but he pointed out the littlest. She was a tiny ball of black fur with flashes of orange and gold. He explained that they called this type of cat a tortoise shell, but she was essentially a darker version of a calico. I stared into her amber eyes, and she stared back into my green ones. Then she meowed. A small but strong "meow." Then she walked right up to me. Done. The tech asked if I wanted to hold her. I said, "Yes, I'll take her."

"Are you sure, she's pretty shy, and we should be getting more litters in soon," he said. *Seriously Dude? Isn't it pretty much in your job description to get people to take them?*

"I'm sure. We're good. She picked me." I reached for her.

"Well okay then, I'll go do the paperwork," Dad said.

I couldn't believe it when the tech handed her to me. She weighed next to nothing, but her meow kept getting louder and louder. I rolled her over on her back, which I'd read is a good way to tell how comfortable a cat is with you. She purred as I stroked her soft belly and up under her chin.

"A good match," the tech said as he led me to the lobby where my dad was waiting. We finalized the adoption and headed to the car. As soon as we buckled in the kitten climbed up my arm and went into my dark cave of curls and fell asleep purring on my shoulder behind my neck.

"We can stop to get some supplies. I'll run in so she can sleep."

As I waited for him, I sat in the dark car looking out into the foggy night and listened to her steady purr. The store glowed through the mist, and eventually I dad emerged with his arms full of supplies. As soon as he was in I said, "Her name is Misty."

He looked out into the night. "Looks Misty to me too."

When we got home I took her up to my room. After setting up her food and litter box in the adjoining bathroom, I sat on my bed with her in my lap. I looked over at a framed picture on my night stand and picked it up and brought it over to my new kitten.

"This is my mom," I told her.

"She died," I said, shutting my eyes and holding her up to my face, burying my nose into her tiny neck. "She would have loved you, but you couldn't have lived here with her. So that's why I have you here now, because she can't be."

"Meow."

"I need you to hang out with me. I miss her so much. I can't talk to anyone about her. It hurts too much, but if I don't let some of my conversations out of my head, it will explode. And I can't talk to Dad because he's in his own personal hell on earth without her. Do you understand?"

"Meow."

"I thought so. You looked like a smart cat, walking up and

talking me into getting you out of that cage. Thanks for waiting for me to make your escape."

"Meow."

I've never had a pet before. I hadn't realized what I was missing. Being able to spill my guts out and not worry about being asked for the millionth time, "How *are* you?" Not having to bite the inside of my mouth or dig my fingernails into my palm to keep from crying. No, now I can say anything I want, or *not* say anything at all. Either way, she was good, as long as I stroked her soft fur and listened to her steady purring.

After that when I was at school and once again watching, not participating, if something triggered a memory of my mom I would inhale and hold my breath. I'd picture Misty in the window seat in my room, content, napping, waiting for my return. A sense of calm would wash over me. I knew I could handle the rest of the day because she waited for me. Granted, as she grew she did become somewhat judgmental, for, after all, she is a cat. If I'm late to feed her *(because unlike dogs, cats can tell time)* she will not let me hear the end of it. Dark, with flashes of orange and gold, she provided a small beacon of hope in the emptiness that sometimes threatened to drown me.

For the past three years she has been my constant. My true friend. An intricate part of my family. She tolerated Dad and Jon, but would not talk with them like she did with me. Jon would pretend to be mad about it when he came home from school. He would accuse her of being sexist, or a snob. But I knew he knew what she meant to me. Secretly he was relieved I had her for companionship and comfort.

Dad, on the other hand was her champion. He was paranoid about her well-being. He considered her a lifesaver ring that he had tossed out to keep me afloat in my sea of despair. He kept her vet records in his office, and knew when she needed updates on vaccinations or check-ups. It was endearing. Such a sweet, caring guy. He must have congratulated himself for getting her for me. It had been a stroke of genius, bringing a little furry spark of light into my dark world. I loved her. I loved him. *And they loved me.*

> (jason gb)
> Ready to get schooled?
> I found my racket, nay, sword
>
> (me)
> Haha Ace. Live by the sword . . .
> But first I have to find my cat
>
> (jason gb)
> Need help?
>
> (me)
> Sure, check your backyard.
> Black w orange and gold spots
> Misty – very shy

I went out in my backyard and started to call her. I looked around the bushes and up in the tree. When I heard the gate open, I turned and saw Jason walking in cradling Misty in his arms. *Jealous.* I couldn't believe it; she usually ran away from everyone else. But there she was, lying content like a well-fed baby in his amazing arms. Can't say that I blamed her one bit.

"Sure cat, make a liar out of me," I said as he delivered her to me. "I'll put her in and meet you out front. I'm assuming I'm driving again?" I asked, reaching for her.

"If that's okay? You take my BFFF, and I'll grab my stuff," he said. Misty meowed as he let go of her, so he scratched under her chin one more time. *How cute is that?* He can even charm my illusive cat. *Figures.*

"Your BFFF?" I had to ask.

"Best Feline Friend Forever." He laughed.

"Ugh. I hope your serves are better than your jokes."

"You're just mad because your cat loves me."

"Ha, love means nothing in tennis," I said, then turned quickly to hide *his* effect on *me*.

"Ouch, that was your first, and probably last, ace of the day." He let himself out of the gate.

And it was. But that was okay, because he was no Federer either. Apparently smack talking was a large part of his game too. We started out just attempting to hit it back and forth. And once again, like when we were running, he surprised me by not trying to be a know-it-all. He didn't tell me how to hit the ball, or recover to starting position, or serve, or anything. He just let me play.

What a concept. What planet was he from? Is he allergic to kryptonite? Where is that remote island they raised him? Did they realize what they had created? A guy who doesn't think he is better at everything, therefore, he doesn't feel the need to impart his vast wealth of knowledge to every genetically incompetent female?

It bugs me when a guy automatically assumes he can "coach" a girl just because he is a guy. I've seen it in PE classes all of the time. One day this guy got partnered with the girls state champion tennis player at our school. He went on and on correcting her form on her serve, but when it was his turn, he couldn't even get it over the net!

I've also witnessed it in basketball, softball, and volleyball, even in dodge ball! "Try to not get hit by the other team." *Really Einstein?* That's what I am supposed to do? Try *not* to get hit in the face? That totally clears up all of those confusing directions the coach just gave us. What a MOTO *(Master of the Obvious)*.

But not Jason. Did he miss that gene in his DNA? I should send his mom a thank you note on behalf of all the teenage females on Earth. She probably also taught him to not only clean a toilet but to put the lid down as well!

But, as usual, I digress in my head. Something I do amazingly well and quite often. In my internal play-by-play action sequence I'd neglected to knock Jason the Golden Boy off his pedestal. On the contrary, I confirmed he deserved to be there! Comparing him to flawed mere mortals made it easier to function around him. Apparently I have accepted his hero status. I can breathe again!

Does that make any sense? *Of course not!* But at least I don't have to worry about fainting from lack of oxygen for the time being. Now all I have to overcome is the rapid beating of my heart, or worse, the breaking of it when this fantasy friendship explodes at summer's end. In the meantime, we decided we were both so pathetic that neither could claim victory. As I dropped him off at home, he said he'd text me tomorrow morning. We were going to start on our "serious training program." Running, Functional Fitness, *(crushing, therefore, blushing)* and ice cream. Yum.

Ugh. Morning. I'm already sore. From tennis. Pathetic. The good news is I'm *hanging out* with Jason today. The bad news is I'm *working out* with Jason today. I looked outside and saw a cloudy day, so I threw on a gray tee shirt, shorts and arrested my hair in a band. After I ate my protein and fruit breakfast, I did chores around the house so I could digest before our training session. About ten I got this text.

> (jason gb)
> Morning Jett, here's the plan for Day 1:
>   1 round equals:
>   5 wall climbs (walk feet up the wall
>   and go into a full handstand,
>   then walk back down)
>   20 body weight squats
>   5 pushups
>   25 sit ups
>   5 pushups
>   20 body weight lunges
>   5 burpees
> Complete 3-5 rounds depending on pain haha

Awesome. This should be grand. And why am I doing this again? Oh, that's right, Hercules asked me too. Totally makes sense. It should be fun. Here goes nothing. I checked the time, grabbed my water bottle and headed next door to Workout Command Central.

And wouldn't you know it, like everything else having to do with my mythical neighbor, it turned out that it wasn't too bad. Figures. This is messing with my gloom and doom philosophy. My running internal conversations seem to spill out into the fresh open air when I am with him. Funny thing is he listens to my rambling, and laughs, or smiles. *(Sigh, haven't totally gotten over that natural wonder in the universe.)* He rarely comments. Weird.

We ended with a cool down walk back to Jason's house and went around to stretch on the back patio. He brought out a hard foam roller, and we took turns rolling out to stretch out the leg muscles and ease the usual soreness that follows a hard workout.

After I finished I gave it to him and laid back flat on my back on the warm cement, absorbing some vitamin D, but hopefully repelling freckles with the help of my sunblock. I had applied extra so I wouldn't burn or get more freckles. *Too bad there isn't a Jason SPF 17.* Ha. *Good one.*

At least I can still appreciate my warped sense of humor. I couldn't believe how relaxed I was, considering my previous inability to function around him just a few days ago. At peace with the world. One with the universe. "Oops," I thought too soon, as I heard the back door open, and a cheerful woman's voice call out to us.

"I brought you guys some water and lemonade, your choice." My first choice would have been to crawl under the nearest rock, but instead I jumped up to my feet. Embarrassed.

"Relax Joan, don't pull a muscle! I'm Jason's mom, Jody. I finished work early today and saw you both out here. Obviously you've had a good workout! Do you want me to put on some music? Jason tells me you are a fan of Pat Benatar." Judging from the grin on her face, she apparently was aware of the now infamous ice cream incident.

"Ah ... sure. Yes. Guilty. Thank you," I responded. Not sure what I was guilty of, liking Benatar or admitting to the unspoken prank, either way, I did, and I was. "It's a pleasure to meet you, Mrs. ... Er ... Ms. Halsted," I said, looking into her smiling bright green eyes.

"Mrs. Halsted, or just Jody, if you would prefer," she replied, answering my awkward greeting.

"Mrs. Halsted works," I said, and it came out pretty smoothly, but then I took a quick sip of the lemonade, and as luck would not have it, the drink went down the wrong pipe and I coughed, sputtered, shook my head and waved her off.

Graciously she nodded and said, "I'll let you get back to your cool down, it's nice to meet you." She mercifully turned and went back into the house so I could spew out the lemonade and catch my breath again. What is it with this family? Why am I such a spaz around them?

The answer dawned on me. It wasn't them *(as glorious as they all were)* it was me *(as reclusive as I had been)*. I was so used to talking to myself I had lost the ability to communicate. Salvaging my sanity had sabotaged my social skills. Say that sentence seven times quickly. It was going to be a long way back to civilization. Fortunately, the scenery along the way had drastically improved. I am on the scenic route. Speaking of awesome views, back to reality . . . and by that I mean my new reality, which is laying on a warm patio, looking up at the beautiful blue sky, in the company of an amazing Golden Boy, listening to awesome tunes. Wow. My new reality actually resembles an unbelievable fantasy, one I couldn't have imagined in a million years.

7

"Firework"

"Do you know what today is?" Jason asked after an easy run, well easy for him. I was nursing sore muscles I didn't realize I had from back to back tennis and funky fit workouts. I tried not to walk like I had just been on a cattle drive for a month. But to answer his question, I had to think: The fifth day in a series of luckiest and most unbelievable days of my life? The day you tell me how you got here from Mount Olympus? The day the answer of the age-old question, *"How many men does it take to put on a new roll of toilet paper?"* is to be revealed? But instead I settled for . . .

"Let me think, the Fourth of July?"

"Yep, so what do people do around here for the Fourth of July?"

"Most people around here go down to the beach on the lake and watch the fireworks."

"What do you do?"

"I try very hard to avoid most people who go down to the beach on the lake and watch the fireworks."

"Why? You don't like crowds, or do you have an aversion to hearing lots of "ooohs" and "ahhhhs" and the '1812 Overture?'"

"No, I definitely avoid them. And yes, some angst, over which to say? Fireworks critique protocol? What constitutes an 'oooh?' How does it differ from an 'ahhh?' Height? Hang time? Color combinations? Boom factor? Or do you simply alternate between the two? It boggles the mind. So much pressure. As for Tchaikovsky's tune, it all boils down to the percussion section. They make or break it. I can't help but feel for the cymbal player who has to have nerves of steel, and hopefully earplugs." I answered aloud but as if talking to myself. I've been doing that a lot lately. Jason looked at me for a second, and then he burst out laughing, which still sounded like the "Hallelujah Chorus."

"Jett, you say the craziest things. Do you have a file cabinet of witty replies in that brain of yours? Don't take this wrong; it's nice for a change to meet a girl who doesn't just spew out slang or the first thing that pops into her head," he said once he quit laughing *(and the choir took a break)*. "Okay, how about this, can you think of somewhere we can go to see the fireworks but not be surrounded by the hordes of ooohers and ahhhhers?"

Paradise popped into my mind, but thankfully I didn't say it out loud. "Well, we could load our old canoe onto the Jeep and go down to an inlet and row out and watch like my dad and Jon and I did a couple of years ago," I responded, trying not to look like I'd just won the lottery.

"That sounds great! I'll grab some sodas and snacks. What do you like?"

You. Pretty much *just the way you are,* should be the name of a song. Oh, it is! First by Billy Joel, more recently by Bruno Mars. Dreamy. Back to Reality. "Coke or Pepsi, nothing diet please, straight up real sugar for me. Pickle flavored sunflower seeds in the shells if you can find then. I'll make some Whirly Pop popcorn."

"Could you try to be more specific? Just kidding. What time should we take off?"

Already have. Singing, "A Boy and a Girl in a Little Canoe . . ." from our family campfire days. "We can load at seven-thirty. That will give us time take the back roads to get around the traffic and launch before dark," I told him.

"Sounds good! See you in a few." And with that he exited Stage Right. *Bravo. Encore, please!*

Dinner. Shower. What to wear? As if. Black of course, so I could slip quietly into the night as we paddle silently out to witness bursts of color connecting the stars on a black canvas sky . . .

"Where are you off to? Ninja meeting with Jason?" Dad asked hopefully. We were sitting at the table eating a variety of leftovers celebrating their independence from the refrigerator.

"Sssshhhhh, it's a matter of National Security, yes. We are going on a reconnaissance mission in our canoe to investigate suspicious explosive devices rumored to have been seen on the beach down by the lake," I whispered looking over my shoulder pretending to make sure no one else was around to eavesdrop on us.

"Make sure you have your life vests on, remember, safety first, always," he said. He couldn't hide the smile of relief that I was doing something somewhat normal again.

At seven thirty I opened the garage and pulled out the Jeep. Jason arrived wearing a gray hoodie, sweat pants and a smile when he saw my all-black outfit. He helped disconnect the canoe from its storage area and load it onto the car, and then put a small cooler in the back with a backpack filled with our snacks.

The back way worked like a charm, and we pulled off the road into a secluded parking area. After getting the canoe down Jason put some soda in the backpack and we hoisted the canoe onto our shoulders for a short walk to the water's edge. I noticed how easy it was to be around him now, and how well we worked together at a task, usually without even discussing how to go about it. Natural. Scary. Super Natural. Super Natural Scary, but nice.

I zipped the Jeep key in my pocket, just in case we tipped over. Then I put a flashlight in a plastic bag and attached it to a seat in the canoe for the trip back to the car. I handed a life jacket to Jason, desperately hoping he wouldn't scoff it off, but as always, or at least so far, he took it without whining and put it on. *Whew.*

I stepped into the front, and Jason pushed us out, stepped into the back and settled in his seat. We launched without difficulty, lifted our paddles and glided into the inlet just as the sun was easing into the mirror lake.

Seriously, just like the Prince and Ariel. I was waiting for some fish to start singing or something. Except of course, unlike the mermaid, I hadn't lost my voice, but reflecting over the past few years, I realized that I very nearly had. *Wow.* Heavy load. Better lighten up so we don't sink.

As we paddled out around a finger of land the water opened up to the main lake. It was amazing how calm the water was. It was a warm night, with a gentle breeze. Just about perfect. No, correction, absolutely perfect. I could hear the rubble of anticipating voices from the crowd across the water and see flashlights flickering like a million dancing fireflies.

When we got out far enough to see the display, but not be under it *(or part of it)* I turned around and nodded, and we glided and put the paddles down. I swung around to face Jason, sighed and smiled. He quickly looked down and reached into the backpack that he had clipped around his seat.

After rummaging around he handed me a soda, and just as I popped the top the first firework exploded over the lake. I jumped and almost tossed it overboard. We looked up. The burst started as red, turned to white and then of course, blue, and faded into its own reflection in the middle of the lake. I looked at Jason and together we said, "Coooool." And then laughed, realizing we had already violated the firework judging system. Rebels. Nonconformists. Revolutionaries.

In between firings we traded sunflower seeds and popcorn and listened to the waves gently slapping the canoe only to be drowned out by the politically correct crowd responses when each new color blast exploded across the dark, smoke filled sky. Just when I thought it was all too good to be true, it was. Smack! Something dropped out of nowhere and bounced, glowing, still smoldering, inside of the canoe!

"Yikes! We've been hit!" I shouted. Jason grappled for his paddle. I dropped the popcorn and grabbed my flip-flops as we both frantically tried to knock the glowing ember out of the canoe. We succeeded, and it sizzled as it entered the water.

Sitting back in our seats, we saw the tossed popcorn floating alongside the canoe. Oops. All of a sudden, out of nowhere, came a flock of ravaging, quacking, obviously starving, white ducks. We laughed which added to the uproar. When we finally got control of ourselves, I heard another noise. People were shouting. Close by people. Not on the shore people.

I looked over and saw a pontoon boat bearing down on us. All of the passengers were pointing at the ruckus the ducks were causing, urging their pilot to hurry over to join the melee. Just when I thought it couldn't possibly get worse, it did. The pontoon had lights on it, and I could see it was a group of teenagers from my school. Popular ones. Mean ones. Rulers of the hallways that I haunted. I knew all of their faces, and instinctively knew none of them knew mine. To them I was invisible. Jason was oblivious and having a blast as he watched the feeding frenzy surrounding us. I sat mortified of attracting the unwanted attention. The pontoon chugged closer and closer.

"Quick Jason! Let's go before we tip over!" I urged. He looked up at the desperate look on my face, and over my shoulder at the charging pontoon, and grabbed his paddle as I pivoted to face forward, and we got to work turning the canoe to head back to our launching cove.

Fortunately it was still calm, and we sliced through the water with even strokes, alternating side to side; thanks to his gray sweats and my black ones we escaped detection as we entered the inlet. We heard the finale of the fireworks above and behind us. Then silence. And darkness. Except for the moonlight. I stopped paddling. So did he. I sighed again, sadly this time, and swung around to face him. "Sorry about that, I didn't mean to freak out."

"Pirates?" he asked with a slow smile. *Dangerous waters.*

"Even more treacherous, Knights. Football Knights and their

Lady Cheerleaders in Waiting. I have always wondered, what were they waiting for back in the day? Was it for their knights to return home from battle or for them to grow up and stop acting like pompous jerks? But back to the present, it's our high school mascot, The Fighting Knights."

"Are you jousting me, get it, jousting!" he cracked himself up. I sat there staring at him. Glorious and goofy. Winning combo. I shook my head as the dread slipped away, and a smile spread across my previously somber face.

"I thought knights were supposed to be good, brave, virtuous and seek the truth," Sir Lancelot *himself* added.

"In fairy tales and ancient realms perhaps. But in the here and now they oppress the peasants and common folk."

"Maybe what they need is for someone to start a Renaissance," he responded as he looked across at me. Choke. Now who's playing the part of the jester? He had better be talking about himself because this distressed damsel is not up for the task.

I looked away, turned and without a word started to paddle again, in silence, until we were about five yards from the shoreline, when all the sudden, he said, "Look there, on the bottom, on your right!"

"What?" I asked, straining my eyes looking down into the dark water. I couldn't see anything. Not even my reflection.

"There it is again, quick look, something shiny, on the bottom! It's . . . it's . . ." he practically shouted. I leaned over the edge, looking down . . . and the canoe lunged to the right . . . . "PAYBACK!" Was the last thing I heard before my face plunged into the water. I was wrong; it wasn't sweet after all. It was wet. And cold. And muddy. But in all honesty, pretty funny. And definitely deserved. Well played. But I couldn't let him know that!

I stood up in the mud, soaking wet, chest deep in water, looking like some swamp monster I'm sure, pointed at him and shouted, "Mutiny!"

"Hardly, who made YOU Captain?" he laughed, sitting all dry and warm in the canoe. With that I did the only thing I could, considering the situation. I fetched my floating flip flops and staggered back to the canoe, reached up with my left hand to be rescued all damsel in distress like, and when he grasped my hand to help me back in, I grabbed his sweatshirt with my other, dropped and dragged him out into the water tipping the canoe on top of me. I let go and popped up under the upside down canoe and felt my way up to the bag with the flashlight and found it just about the time I heard him pop up under it at the other end of the upside down canoe.

"Talk about pirates, that was a nasty trick!"

Even in the dark I could tell he was smiling. Don't ask. It had become a sixth sense by now. I reached the plastic bag, opened it and retrieved the flashlight, turned it on and illuminated the underbelly of the canoe as well as his shining face. We both looked like drowned rats, stupid, grinning drown rats, so I burst out laughing, which considering the close quarters, echoed, and ricocheted back and forth, front and back.

"Stop, Jett, you are going to break our ear drums!" he laughed too, but not so loud.

"Truce?" I choked, trying to stop laughing.

"Yes . . . for now."

We stood up, and lifted the canoe to our shoulders. Fortunately his backpack was still hanging from his bench between us, so he snagged it, looped it on his arm, and we started walking slowly towards the shore. When we were on firm ground we set it down to catch our breath. After a minute Jason put his backpack on and together we picked up the canoe again and carried it back up to the Jeep. Soaking wet, it was a pretty chilly ride back home, but the stars above winked as we drove in silence, and a dry sense of humor goes a long way.

❂

The next day I had plenty of time to reflect on the previous evening's activities as it was outdoor chore day. I had been helping Dad and Jon for the past few years, and after Jon had gone to college, I took over the mowing and trimming. Dad had taken over Mom's organic garden, a small patch behind the house where he would go to weed, nurture and mourn. She had researched it extensively, made him use all natural products and would not allow any pesticides. When it was in full bloom it needed to be harvested daily even though he treated his plants with harmless deterrents; otherwise we would lose out to the typical plant predators. That being said; he harvested the most amazing, beautiful, delicious tomatoes, which you could eat straight off the vine. He would toss me one as I maneuvered our riding lawnmower around the yard.

Ball cap and shades on, sun blocked from head to toe, even though I had to wear shoes, in case the mower somehow turned over *(remember, safety first, always)*. I rode around with my earplugs in, listened to my tunes, and I sang along, my voice accompanied by and concealed by the motor. When I had finished the main mowing, I would switch to a little walking mower, and trim around the trees, bushes and flower and rock gardens that had been lovingly planted, placed and nurtured, just like me.

Biology had been her first love. A study of life, how living organisms were put together: humans, animals, and plants. When she went to college she was inspired by the book, "Silent Spring," by Rachel Carson, 1962, a bold pioneering female scientist who passionately raised the alarm against the effects of insecticides and pesticides on the future of our planet, and who, after she had painstakingly researched and written the book in order to inform the public, died of cancer not long after she completed it.

Mom also loved rocks. All kinds, but especially smooth river rocks. The yellow, gray, red, green, and blues, gold flecks in some, fossils in others. She loved how they looked with water rippling over them. So much so she had managed to convince my skeptical dad that they should put a small waterfall outside their bedroom window. It trickled over stones into a small pond, and would eventually pump back up to continue the cycle. Although the pipes might freeze in the winter months; the calming sound would surely soothe the soul and that would make it all worth it. After four years it still flowed, meticulously cared for by a man whose lonely soul was still in need of continuous soothing.

And what did my soul need? The reawakening of my frozen self seemed to be thawing out in the presence of the summer sun, or more appropriately, the summer son. I pondered the thought as I made smaller and smaller rectangular tracks around my yard. Is that what I had done to get over, around and through my loss? Automatically moving along like I had flipped a switch to autopilot?

What would happen in a month when we go back to school? Would I be strong enough to take back control of my life, or would I crash and burn into blackness again once Jason met other people and found new interests? I couldn't imagine why he would maintain our friendship once he got involved in the school activities he had missed out on and craved so much.

The same ones I had opted out of and avoided. What would happen when he met people *(face it, girls)* who didn't shrink away into the hallways like me? The ones who walked down the middle equally daring and inviting onlookers to not only bask in their beauty but admire their self-absorption. Whoa. Talk about self-absorption. I pretty much have cornered that market at this moment. But still, I wondered what Jason thought of me? For like the millionth time this minute.

Thinking back about the past few days, he did compliment the way I dress, how I thought things through *(over thought things through, to be honest)* and seemed to like *(and share?)* my warped sense of humor. Payback indeed. But then there were the times when I looked at him, and he swiftly looked away, almost nervously? What's up with that? Am I that hard to look at or is it something else?

Three things were for certain; I needed to stop thinking about myself so much, stop obsessing about Jason so much, and start figuring out some positive course of action for my road trip back to civilization. Otherwise, when and/or if Golden Boy flew back out of the picture, would I disappear again? Forever?

Over the next few days, I had ample opportunity to try not to think about Jason as his family went out of town on vacation. He did leave me with a task to work on in his absence though; I was to research what we needed to do in order to go out for a sport at our school. "Go out" being the operative words, as in not staying in my shell, in my dark hermit existence, but instead, visibly functioning in and joining an outside organized activity. And being timed, evaluated, judged. What was I doing? Best not to think about it, or over-think about it, and "Just Do It."

I went on the school website to the athletic teams page and learned we needed to get sports physicals and download a bunch of pages with waivers and promises to act responsibly, make wise choices and exhibit sportsmanlike behavior as representatives of our school. Hmmm, thought-provoking. We also had to get a parent or guardian signature. That promised to be so much fun with my dad. His dream come true. Me, actually getting involved in something at my school.

By the time Jason returned I knew everything I could possibly need to know about going out for a team, except of course, why in the world I was going to put myself through it. That's not true, I knew exactly why *(or for who in this case)*.

(jason gb)
I'm back
Ready to run today?

> We're heading over
> to the high school track
> 10 am ok?

The message greeted me as I got out of bed the last week of July after hearing the swoosh of a text. I had to admit *(only to myself, geesch; a girl has to maintain some dignity)* that my heart did skip a beat. I waited at least twenty seconds before responding.

> (me)
> Suppose so
> I almost can't contain
> my excitement

I thought that was totally in character.

> (jason gb)
> Quit whining
> you big baby
> it will be fun

So like him too, so I texted back.

> (me)
> Like going to the dentist fun?
> We definitely have
> different definitions
> of the notion of "fun"

He quickly texted back.

> (jason gb)
> What teenager uses "notion"?
> Are you just grumpy because
> you missed me?

Busted. Gasp. Must. Retaliate. Immediately.

(me)
Don't flatter yourself
Remember the ice cream?
I don't miss

Whew, not bad.

(jason gb)
Hoisting the white flag
See you at 10

Smile.

(me)
Dealio

On the way to the track I filled Jason in about going out for a team. I mentioned treating my dad for shock after asking him to sign cross country permission papers, then stopping him from heading to the store to buy spikes as he reminisced about his "glory days" running track and cross country in college.

"Where did he go?"

"University of Illinois." And then it came out, slowly, but to my complete surprise, not too painfully, "that's where he met my mom . . ." *careful, take a breath* ". . . she majored in Biology and was a cheerleader there, but they met playing flag football for their dorms against the fraternities and sororities." Gaining speed it continued to spill out and away from the potential panic attack-inducing zone. "That's why Jon went there, and he took an internship with an environmental energy company for the summer, but as you know comes back to play lax now and then. He'll be a senior next year."

"Is that where you want to go too?"

No, too many ghosts, no, that's not true. Only one.

"Ah, I don't think so. It's a great school. Big Ten Conference and all, but I'm looking into going a little further away, to major in

No Mosquitos, Humidity or Poison Ivy."

"I wonder, is that in the Department of Entomology, Meteorology or Botany?" he joked.

"I'm not sure, I may have to do a double or triple major," I said. "In any case, it's not offered anywhere around here, don't get me wrong; it's a lovely place to grow up. However, if you are the constant victim of vampire insects that crave your specific type B+ blood, hair that goes all fuzzy and springs out of your head randomly, and that itchy, inflamed, oozing condition that spreads through your body systemically and requires steroids to be alleviated, it tends to give one pause to wonder if there is a better place to live.

And, more important but by no means no less dramatic, I fell in love with the black and white photography of Ansel Adams and feel the need to experience the natural beauty he captured through his lens first hand," I finished.

"I have to admit you argue a series of valid points Jett, have you ever considered studying law?" Jason said, as he shook his curly, golden, surfer boy locks. Sure, the *Law of Attraction* maybe.

And with that in mind, we started to jog our warm up around the track. I couldn't help but wonder what we looked like to the casual observer. Him, tall, tan and handsome, with his shimmering crown of hair. And me, skinny, pale and forgettable, with my dark curly ponytail bouncing behind me.

But to its credit, running calmed my insecurities as I fell into the methodical, mesmerizing rhythm of our footsteps, side by side in the not-too-hot-yet morning air. After a couple of laps, we slowed down to a walk and then stretched in preparation for some interval work. We worked in silence, individually. Together. Then we started our speed workout, the length of the football field, starting slow and gradually getting faster and faster until we were at about ninety percent of our max speed for twenty yards in the middle of the field and then gradually slowed back down into the end zone.

A slow jog recovery back to the original starting point and then back at it. Ten times. Of course, each time Jason left me in the turf. No kidding, the guy was a machine. A fine *(very)* tuned running machine. But he'd wait until I got to him, and caught my breath *(at least I could breathe around him now)* and then we'd go again. When we had finished, we walked and grabbed our water bottles. Jason picked up his phone and went to the stopwatch mode and handed it to me.

"How about timing me in the 40?"

"Sure thing. Does this have a sundial app?" I joked, as I pretended to examine his phone.

"Ha ha, I'm not going for the land speed record, I just want to see what time I can do," he responded as he lined up in the first lane on the track at the extended end zone line. I walked down the track 40 yards away using the football field 10 yard increments as a guide.

"Okay, you ready?" *Boy, was he.* "On your mark. Get set. GO!" I said and hit the start button. And he was off and running. Flying was more like it. Like on a Pegasus, without the Pegasus. My eyes couldn't help but follow him as he flew through 40 yards. He ran past me and continued down the track for a bit, and that's when I saw him. Someone else watching Jason's flight. Next to the football locker room.

A big guy, in a ball cap and reflecting sunglasses. Reflecting the son. He stood there, mesmerized for a second, and then he stepped onto the field, and headed straight towards me. Pulled towards Jason's finish line. Gravity at work. And as Jason jogged back to me, I felt an eclipse coming. And I was a pale, soon to be obscured, moon.

I had faithfully hit stop as Jason passed by, and then held the phone up for him to see that I had indeed stopped time for him. And he came back to me. Smiling. Not knowing that earth was about to invade our space. I smiled back, and fought the foreshadowing feeling. *Knowing there was nothing I could do to move heaven or earth, and that I, like the earth, was destined to revolve around the son.*

"What was his time?" I recognized Coach Johnson – head coach of the football team. Not a bad guy. Normally. But I knew what he had in mind when he saw Jason.

"Um . . . 4.54 seconds," I said after looking at the watch.

"No way," said Coach Johnson. "Let's try that again." And he marched Jason back to the starting line and said, "Start here." Then he walked up to the 40 yard mark – exactly where I had been – and yelled, "On your marks, set, go!" Coach Johnson stopped the watch when Jason flew past, and stared at it for a few seconds. All he said was, "Wow" and then turned around and handed the phone back to me. It read 4.53 seconds.

"Son," said Coach Johnson, "do you live around here?" Jason explained that he had just moved into the school district a few weeks ago. Coach asked if he had played football.

"I've played before," without offering any more details. Coach started talking *blah blah blah with your speed we could really use you blah blah blah* . . . but Jason interrupted him and said "Coach, I don't mean to be rude, but I plan on joining the military, and will look at attending one of the military academies or participate in ROTC. I'm not going to try and play ball while in college."

"You could play ball at Army, Navy or Air Force," Coach said. "In fact . . ," but Jason cut him off again.

"Coach, if I did go to one of the Academies, I'd want to concentrate on my studies. Football is a big commitment, and to be honest with you, the Academies run an option offense with not a lot of passing. I'm a receiver. I mean, I was a receiver, and I like throwing offenses. Playing football in college is just not an option for me for a lot of reasons. Besides, I may want to try some other sport. Like lacrosse." He tilted his head so he could see around the eclipsing earth, and gave me a little smile. *Nice answer.*

"Son," said Coach Johnson, "I'm not saying you should play ball in college. Let me ask you a question: have you played some defense before or only offense?"

"I played both sides of the ball," said Jason. "Strong safety."

"We run a 43 defense with the strong safety cheating up a lot," said Coach Johnson.

"I played in a 52 defense and sometimes moved up to the monster position," said Jason. *Okay, what language were these guys speaking? And what's with Jason playing the "monster" position?*

"Look, let me lay it out for you, son. We're a smaller school than most of our opponents. We could adopt the Service Academy approach and run the wishbone offense. But we don't. We run a pro-style offense with a heavy passing attack. We throw the ball 70 percent of the time, and we have a quarterback who can sling it. I've got sixteen starters returning from last year and we're going to make a run at the conference championship – something we've never won before. But, I lost my starting slot receiver and my strong safety to graduation, and I need to fill those holes.

"Come out for the team. If you don't like it, you can quit. But you'll like the guys. I guarantee it. And you can still play lacrosse since it's a spring sport and football is in the fall. Heck, lots of our football players play lacrosse too – even in the fall. They have football games on Friday nights, and then they play fall lacrosse league games on Saturdays. What do you say?"

And just like that, I lost him. It's not like I can blame Coach. He felt truly blessed to have Jason fall onto his field to fill his starting receiver void. A gift from above and a gifted athlete all rolled into one. Smart, quick to learn, the desire to excel, and on and on and on. Who could resist recruiting him, on the spot, and for that matter, who could resist him, period? Certainly not me. Especially all the way home in the car when he couldn't stop trying to convince me how fun it was to be on a team. But, like I said, who could resist him? Again. Certainly not me.

It turned out he'd played *a lot* of football before, and for many years. "So Jason," I said with a melodramatic look on my face, "What's with the *Dr. Jekyll and Mr. Hyde* monster thing?"

"What?" he asked, not quite following. He realized I was teasing and figured it out. "A monster position is usually a defensive back that comes up closer to the line of scrimmage. It's . . . well, never mind, I won't bore you with the details. You just have to come and see for yourself, unless of course, you're too afraid of monsters."

I didn't answer. *You have no idea what scares me.*

He would start football practice in a few days, but for the next three nights he came over to our house to chat about lacrosse. He knew Jon was going back to school soon, and Jason wanted to learn all he could in that short time. Jon had given him some old CDs of lacrosse films, and Jason asked him a ton of questions about the game and proper defensive techniques.

We played in the backyard those three glorious nights, me at Attack or Midfield and Jason defending. This meant that I had to wear all the protective gear the guys play with: helmet, mouth guard, shoulder pads, elbow pads and gloves. Guy's lacrosse is a contact sport, and I was the guinea pig for Jason. He was lightning fast and very strong, but I'd also played this way with Jon for several years, so I didn't try and out-muscle him – I played a finesse game – underhand shots, behind the back shots, no-look shots, letting him push me back so that it created space between him and me so I could get a quick wrist shot off, etc. After a while Jon said, "You know sis, you're not a bad player. All those years of utterly humiliating you have paid off." Turning to Jason, he said, "She's pretty lax-savvy. Most guys will not avoid contact as much as she does."

Well, I might not mind *a little* contact. "*Quit thinking like that,*" I said to myself, which worked *for about two seconds*.

Jon tried to cram years worth of expertise into Jason's brain in just three days. They talked about zone and man-to-man defenses; slides; passing the ball and shooting the ball and the different techniques for both; clearing the ball; stick checks and poke checks; man-ball concepts; full-field and mid-field zone traps — how to run them and how to beat them. Jon explained that playing defense didn't mean that you never gave up a shot — it meant you gave up the shot that you wanted to give up. "I prefer to give up an eight yard low-angle off-hand shot instead of a twelve yard power hand shot in front of the goal," and then he would explain why.

Jon talked about penalties and said that some teams had "enforcers" who would take a penalty to intimidate the other team. "I don't do that," said Jon, "and I don't like those that do. The only time I take a penalty is when a player has an unobstructed path to the goal and he's going to be able to walk right up to the net and shoot from five yards. In that case, I'll take him down before he gets to the net. I'll do it as cleanly as possible with no intent to cause injury, but I will take him down, and if I get a penalty in doing so, then so be it . . . but that shouldn't happen very often."

Jon explained the ability to substitute "on the fly," meaning you didn't have to wait for a whistle or dead ball before substituting. "Four of your players must remain on the defensive side of the field when your team has the ball on the offensive side of the field," said Jon. "Normally those four players are the goalie and three Poles. Sometimes though, an athletic Pole might get a loose ball and decide to bring it into the offensive side of the field."

"Middie back!" exclaimed Jason.

"Correct!" I replied. "A midfielder must now stay back on the defensive side of the field since a Pole crossed over into the offensive zone. You learned a lot while watching Jon's game last week, didn't you?" Jason shrugged his shoulders. He was picking up the finer elements of lacrosse very quickly.

Jon was one of the smartest players I'd seen, and he started talking to Jason about the cerebral aspects of the game. "I watch players before a game – particularly the Attack guys. I look at their shots during warm ups. Are they comfortable using both hands? Are their left-handed shots noticeably weaker than their right-handed shots, or vice-versa? Do they have certain moves they like to repeat? A lot of lax bros will run at a defensive player and then stutter for a few steps before making a quick move to their left or right. Most guys do about a five step stutter before accelerating, so I often wait until they are about three steps into their stutter before jamming my Pole into their gut. It makes it harder for them to switch their stick to their other hand, not to mention make a move with a Pole stuck in their gut," Jon said with a wicked little grin.

Jason soaked up everything Jon taught him and we practiced some of these techniques. Even though Jason would be playing football this fall, I could tell he really liked lacrosse and would go for it in the spring. Finally Jon's last night came, and Jason thanked us for our help.

"No problem," said Jon, "but you need to practice throwing, catching and running with the ball starting right now all the way up to lax season. Play football, but grab some Power Geek and make them run and pass with you every chance you get. Oh look, here's one right here." And he nodded to me. I ignored his insult, and he added, "Actually, she's a pretty good practice partner, and a lot quicker than you think. You should grab her . . . *(sweet setup, again)* and practice as often as you can."

We said our good byes for the night, and although Jason would now be focusing on his upcoming season, I knew I wouldn't lose my lax bro to the dreaded sport of football after all. Cheerleaders, on the other hand, were much more dangerous adversaries.

❂

It wasn't that bad at first. The football team would lift early in the morning so Jason could come home, crash for a bit, and then hang out. He made friends with a guy named Sam, a solid athlete but not one of the jerks, and he was able to catch rides to and from weight training. They shared the same warped sense of humor, and enjoyed playing nasty tricks on each other. In the morning, I would do the pre-season running workout downloaded from the cross country website page and grumble about being talked in to going out.

Then, we would get together to play tennis *(poorly)* or grab ice cream *(cautiously)* and he'd fill me in on the prank play of the day duel between him and Sam. And we would practice lacrosse; passing on the run, making up scenarios, challenging each other with less-than-perfect passes. Eventually, July came to an end. Best month of my teen life. Which made it even harder to accept the dreadful approach of August, the new football practice schedule and the knowledge that soon I would be returning to haunt the halls of high school.

Two-a-day football practices had become my nemesis. Two whole weeks, the last two weeks of summer, wasted. Jason was exhausted, but sounded happy in our text world, too tired to hang out except on the weekends, but then he had his regular chores and family obligations to deal with which meant little spare time. He'd ask me to stop by practice if I could, and check out his new team.

> **(unknown number)**
> **This is Jason on Sam's phone**
> **Stop by end of practice today?**
>
> **(me)**
> **Hi Jason on Sam's phone**
> **Maybe**

I had said maybe, but I knew I would go. I automatically added Sam's number to my very short list as *sfb (Sam football)*. It joined the lonely party of *dad, jon* and *jason gb*. I worked around the yard and then got cleaned up. I decided to go to practice and try to catch his eye *(and hopefully no one else's)* and take him out for ice cream after.

Wearing my ball cap and shades I felt concealed. But when I drove up and parked on the hill overlooking the stadium field I looked past the players and saw the future.

Down on the field, to deliver ice to their warrior knights were the lady cheerleaders impatiently-in-waiting. So, now Jason was truly going to be knighted, no doubt, by some fair maiden. I didn't even bother to turn off the engine. I was gone. *Like the wind. Like a ghost. Invisible once again.*

8

"Amazing Grace"

It was the last day of summer vacation filled me with dread. The countdown was over, and soon, so too would be this too-good-to-be-true relationship. The world would right itself. We would return to the different hemispheres we belonged in, him in the bright sunshine, and me in some dark, forgotten wasteland.

We hadn't talked in days, thanks to my enemy, football. At three in the afternoon when I got a text from Jason, which was really odd since he should be at the second of his annoying practices.

(jason gb)
Stuck at practice, Sophia 2
Parents working late
U hang with Gracie 4 a few?

Without thinking I responded.

(me)
Sure

He immediately texted back.

(jason gb)
Thanks a bil. She won't be a bother
GTG

What had I done? I'm not babysitter material. In the midst of a showdown between the forces of good and evil in Michael J. Sullivan's *Riyria Revelations Series*; the fate of mankind, wizards, elves, knights, heirs, dwarves, empires and kingdoms hung in the balance. Now I have to hang out with a twelve year old I haven't talked to since our embarrassing introduction the day after I met her big brother?

But I went over and rang the doorbell because *"I meant what I said and I said what I meant, an elephant's faithful one hundred percent."* She opened the door.

"Hi Gracie, I'm Joan Next Door remember? Jason asked if I could hang out with you. I guess practice is running late."

"Hi. He called me." Stepping aside to let me in, she seemed different than before. Sad. Withdrawn. No witty banter.

"Help yourself to anything, the television is in there, kitchen is that way," she said as she pointed this way and that, "I'm finishing up a book so I'll be in here . . . ." She curled up in a big chair.

"Sure, that's great, I brought a book with me so I'll just sit here," I said, settling down in the matching chair, relieved. Too good to be true! Soon, I was lost in a duel for the good of all humankind and other creatures of Upper Earth. The long lost heir was about to be revealed, when . . .

Gracie took a deep breath, set her book aside, and released a soft, almost musical, mournful sigh. Reluctantly, very reluctantly, but purposefully and politely, I set my book down.

"What's the matter?" I asked her.

She sighed again, and shrugged, looking over at her book.

"Didn't you like the ending?" I asked, trying to figure out her twelve year old brain.

"Yes, that's the problem. I loved it. The beginning, the middle and now the end. But it ended. They always do. I get lost in them, become one of the characters, and the others are my friends, and I'm carried away off on their adventure, and then I finish the book. And they leave. And I'm alone, again. Just like when we move someplace new, and I meet kids, and we start getting to know each other, and then they have to move, or I have to, and I never get to see them again. So I never have a chance to keep a friend. I'm

sorry. I am so boring. This must be torture for you, having to hang
out with your friend's little sister." She sighed again.

And it hit me. I was looking at myself five years ago. The time
I was reading a book in the car when my mom and I pulled into
the grocery store parking lot. I asked if I could finish the book
and meet her inside. She smiled, knowing that even though I was
sitting next to her, I was really far, far away. She put the windows
down a bit, locked the doors and told me to be careful walking
across the lane and then left me to my fictional world.

I was the young Indian guide, helping some explorers find their
way across a vast frontier. And when it ended, I was still the Indian
girl. Slipping out of the car, looking both ways for the best place
to cross the river, making sure no wild beasts were lurking in the
forest beyond ...

"I used to know someone like you. I think you are interesting.
You must be, a song named after you."

"What song do you mean?"

"Amazing Grace."

"You're crazy," she said, shaking her head, but she smiled a
little smile. Ooh I recognized that uneven smile. Sweet genes.

"I try to be. What can we do now that you finished that chapter
of your life?" I asked.

"Do you want to go outside and shoot some baskets?"

"Sure, I challenge you to a game of HORSE."

"We can play PIG if you'd rather, it's shorter. Sofi does because
it's a hassle playing with me and it goes quicker," Gracie said, in
a matter-a-fact tone.

"She's probably just afraid to play you once you've warmed
up," I answered, attempting to make her feel better. Sister Sofi
sounded like a piece of work. We took turns shooting, losing, and
winning, for an hour or so. Then went back inside. She poured us
each a glass of water.

"Have you lived here all of your life?" Gracie asked.

"Pretty much, as long as I can remember," I replied.

"Do you have the same friends that you had in middle school?"

"No, not really, my eighth grade class split into two high schools, and most of the kids I had known for years went to the other one. Then we kind of lost touch ..." I shrugged. *And I became a ghost.*

She looked at me, expecting more. "I'm kind of nervous about going into a middle school. I don't know how to make friends."

"Well, let me think," I said. After I planned what to say and how to say it I continued, "How about this. On the first day of school, when you get your food and go into the lunchroom, look around for someone sitting alone and go sit by them. Maybe even a boy. Boys have less drama. Not as manipulative and petty as girls can be. Introduce yourself, ask them their name. Then if they tell you and stop talking, ask them which teacher they have and if they like him or her.

"Briefly tell them who yours is, and your opinion of the classroom. Lots of books, good. Not enough books, bad. Mention some of the titles and ask if they have read them. If they say they don't like to read, you could tell them that maybe they just haven't found the right book. If they then say that it's boring or dumb or a waste of time, that's when you look around the room for a new friend contestant. But wait until the next day; give them a chance to redeem themselves in some other area, like a sport, or musical interest, or hobby. If nothing comes of it, chalk it up to experience and move on. *Fortune favors the brave."*

She took it all in, carefully contemplated, and nodded. "I'll try it. Thanks. What should we do now?" she asked, looking up to me.

I tried to remember how Jon entertained me when I was younger. "Do you have any decks of cards?"

"Yes, I think so," she said, and darted off to the family room to search. She returned with three decks and handed them to me.

"Okay, now how about some rubber bands?" I asked, and once again she disappeared, then returned quickly with a huge handful.

Handing her a deck of cards and half the rubber bands, I pointed to the other side of the room, "That is your kingdom; you have ten minutes to build a card-house empire. I will do the same over here. When the time is up, we take turns shooting rubber bands at each other's castles until the winner knocks down the loser's. Understand?"

She giggled and scampled off to make her card fortress. From across the room I offered suggestions, how to start with a few cards leaning on a chair leg, overlapping edges to fortify and adding layers to strenthen the walls, but for the most part we each dove into our fantasy realms, and concentrated on defending both our subjects and our honor.

Ten minutes flew by, and it was time to battle. I let her go first. She stood tall, placed the rubber band on her shooting finger, and let it fly. Zap. It approached my front wall, but fell short.

"Your turn," Gracie announced.

I stood and took aim. Just as I was about to release, Jason walked in behind his little sister, who from his angle, was in my direct line of fire.

"What's going on?" he asked, looking at me then her.

"SSSShhhhhhhhhh! Joan is about to shoot down my castle!" Gracie admonished in a whisper.

"Cool!" Jason whispered back. "Can I have a shot?"

"Get behind the builder and wait your turn," I said, still aiming, then released and took out her tower, which in turn, collapsed part of her castle.

"Yes, get thee behind me, peasant," Gracie mimicked. His mouth dropped open, then turned up in a smile, *and it got suddenly brighter in the room, and the choir started up again . . .*

Gracie looked at me, and back at him, then rolled her eyes like only a sixth grade girl can do. "Thanks, Joan. You win this round, but I will learn to strengthen my kingdom before our next battle and then victory shall be mine!" She bowed, and left.

After recovering from the latest choir concert I called out to her, "See you later, Squirt, you are a worthy opponent."

Then I turned to Jason and pointed, "Pick up a rubber band and shoot, peasant." He was way ahead of me, instead of one; he fired five in rapid succession, decimating my castle. I shrugged, laughed and gathered up my cards while he picked up the remnants of Gracie's village.

Jason walked me home, and thanked me. "I appreciate you hung out with her, she's having a hard time meeting kids. Hopefully, it will be better tomorrow when she gets on the bus ..."

Tomorrow. The bus. Tonight is the last day of summer. Six weeks of summer, smiling, laughing, tennis, running, music, riding "topless" in the Jeep, playing lacrosse in the back yard . . . getting ice cream ... over. "So ... (*back to reality*), do you think I can catch a ride tomorrow? I don't want to be 'that guy,' you know, the only senior on the Big Cheese," Jason was saying. *Okay, this is it. The moment I had been dreading since I first met him.*

"Jason, there is something I need to tell you." *Wait a minute; did I say that out loud? I think so! Yikes!*

"What Jett, you dropping out? Joining the Peace Corps?"

"Well nooooo," I said. *How do I explain it?*

"Spit it out then. What's the problem?" He laughed. "Are you afraid to be seen with the 'new kid'? You could drop me a block away and I could walk the last block, friendless, car-less, it'll be a great way to make friends and influence teachers," he said and *actually looked a little nervous.* Which was kind of cute, of course, because that's just the way he rolled. High cute factor. A perfect 10 on the Cuteness Scale. *Focus.*

"All right, here goes. I'm *different*, at school; I'm not the person you live next to there. I'm invisible, I mean. You won't want to be seen with me. Nobody knows me, I'm just ... different." *There, I said it.* It was out in the open for all to see. That would make sense to him, after all, we'd only been hanging out pretty much daily for half the summer except for the dreaded football double practice days, and now I lay this on him. Crystal clear, right? I braced myself for his *goodbye, see ya later, it's been real. Have a nice life ...*

"Whoa! You? *Different?* Really? News Flash at Ten! Joan Jett is *different!* I didn't see that coming! Seriously, you make being *different* an art form, you are like the Renaissance of *different*. If being *different* were an Olympic sport, you'd be the gold medal winner champion! If *different* were a dinosaur, you'd be Joanasaurus Differous! If ..."

"Enough, I get it, I am really good at not being normal. Now, if you don't want to be 'the senior guy most likely not to survive his first day of senior year' you had better knock it off. Good night." I said, reaching for the door handle.

"No worries, Jett, normal is highly overrated in my opinion. Don't forget, we have to go early to get our I.D. cards! That reminds me, I have to go practice making *Calvin and Hobbes* faces in the mirror. I'll tell you about it tomorrow morning. I need your help with something. See you at seven sharp!" he said. I watched him saunter back to his house, whistling like he didn't have a care in the world. Must be nice to live there, in his world. Back in mine, *I'd just been granted a stay of execution.*

9

Liars and tyrants and stares, oh my. Walking down the hallway with Jason was like that dream when you forgot to put clothes on, and give a report in front of a crowd and look down . . .

And here I tried to make it just another normal day of school. As a ghost. Invisible. Like I had been for the past three years. Black tee shirt, black jeans, black tennis shoes. You know, my invisibility cloak. The problem is it didn't fit anymore.

Or maybe it just didn't work with my dazzling new accessory.

He was so happy jumping into my car this morning. Rambling on all the way to school. Greeting every kid in the parking lot. Holding the door open for me to walk into school while everyone watched. Gasped. Whispered. Who is that? Where did he come from? Who is she? What is he doing with *her*?

As we walked down the main hall everyone stepped aside. Jason smiled and guided me like Theseus through the labyrinth. I was numb. In shock. Not a ghost anymore. No longer invisible. And then when it could not possibly get worse, it did.

Chelsea, Commander of the Mean Team, stood in front of her fan club as the kingpin, or in this case, the *queenpin*. A pyramid of pins behind her stood at attention, like in a bowling alley lane. Gorgeous teeth *(oooooooh that smile must have cost a few bucks)* shimmered between her glossy, pink, cheerleader lips.

"Hello Stranger," she purred as we walked by.

"Oh, hey, how's it going?" He glanced at her briefly and kept walking, still talking about his plan *as he turned back to me*. Her eyes narrowed, and she licked her lips and mouthed "fresh meat" as Jason walked by, only loud enough for me to hear. I now had a *new* enemy, and she was *blonde*.

I felt her eyes burning into my back as Jason carried on about getting his I.D. card. His plan was to make a goofy *Calvin and Hobbes* face right when photographer snapped the picture and then escape so they had to use it. He enlisted me to create a diversion, which totally went against my nature. Me. Bring attention to myself? On purpose? You have got to be joking. But how do I say no to such a harmless request? Especially when he smiled and asked so adorably?

Still reeling from the *Close Encounters of the Mean Kind* and he acted like nothing weird had happened. What was I thinking? Why didn't I create an escape plan?

I.D. scheme went off without a hitch. Unbelievable. But since it was his plan, I shouldn't have been too surprised. The photographer told me to go sit down on a stool. I stared into camera lens. Expressionless. Void of emotion. My mask. Until, Jason danced around behind the photographer. All *Footloose* and fancy-free.

I broke. Laughed. Smiled. Click. Busted. Move on.

His turn. He handed me his books with a secretive smile and sat on the stool like he owned it. His throne. I slipped back behind the photographer. Jason smiled. That glorious smile. And time froze. Sound evaporated. Everyone gazed upon him.

He winked at me and I woke up just in time to drop all the books. BAM! And in that second he put the goofiest look. At the exact moment the camera clicked. Then he dashed away. Leaving me to face the wrath of the photographer who had too many other students and no time to chase down my golden friend for a redo.

Bending down to pick up the books, I hid behind a wall of black curls and tried to disappear. But realized, I was no longer invisible.

❂

My first two classes went okay. I found my favorite seat, first row, and last desk. It was the perfect place to avoid attention and blend into the background. No one could sneak up on you, but you were still close to the door for a quick exit. I watched and listened. The "new kid" buzz was everywhere. And I was once again nowhere. But for some reason, it no longer felt like home. Instead, it was like I stood with my nose pressed up to a window looking in. Dark curly curtains blocked my view. And nobody bothered to look out.

The plan was to meet Jason in the cafeteria for lunch. Seemed simple enough, but walking into the cafeteria the ground shifted, or maybe my stomach lurched. Chelsea's groupies surrounded him, circling his table in the center of the room. The next ring around him was the football players. I rotated slowly around the outermost orbit and split off into the food court area.

I grabbed a carton of Greek yogurt, granola, apple and a bottle of water, paid, and escaped outside through the side door. By myself. Alone again. In space. I was not hungry. But of course I had to eat, because today was the first day of cross country practice.

And since I didn't want to call attention to myself it would be better to not pass out on my first team run. I ate without tasting. My thoughts were behind me. Inside. In the middle of the room. I could still feel his gravitational pull. The object of everyone's attention. Feeling light-headed, I took a bite of the apple, looked at it, then rolled it down a small hill to a squirrel. "Here you go, Newton, welcome to my world." The squirrel stared, then bit the apple and scurried away with its prize.

I waited until the bell was about to ring to slip unnoticed back into school and made my way to third period. It was uneventful, meaning I was able to get my favorite seat and blend. Unfortunately, fourth period was a nightmare. Psychology. I had taken a pretty heavy load, so I needed a class that didn't give a ton of homework, and this one fit that bill.

Apparently I wasn't the only one who had checked into it, because when I finally got to the classroom on the other side of school, it was packed. Only one empty desk left. Front row. Center. In front of my new adversary, dazzling Chelsea The Maneater. She looked almost as pleased to see me as I felt seeing her.

She *definitely* could see me. Nowhere to hide. I looked down just to make sure I wasn't naked. I now understand how nightmares were created.

Sliding into the seat, I tried to focus. Breathe. Tighten. Relax. Misty. A run in the woods. Diving into a pool. All of the usual techniques to regain composure. None of them worked. I searched my consciousness to determine what was blocking inner peace. Oh, I found it, that made total sense. It was the two laser beams of raging blue icicles stabbing through the back of my head. Perfect.

I was out of my seat and the classroom even before the bell stopped ringing. I then made it through the crowded halls, down the stairs to the athletic area, into the locker room and dressed out for practice. I needed to escape into a run. Luckily the coach was really cool. I could tell she was a runner herself, so she didn't make us sit around getting lectured forever. She told the returning runners to take us on an easy warm up and then meet out on the closest track. The one that revolved around the turf football field. Of course it did.

I merged into the back of the pack as we took off. Gradually I relaxed, hit my groove, and as the group thinned out, started to move up until I was behind the leaders. I settled in and started to coast. Surprised. It wasn't bad. Everyone seemed chill. A lot of the kids were in my more demanding classes, and they kidded around as we ran in a friendly way.

We went through some woods that I had never noticed and looped back in and spread out on the track to stretch. Only then did I allow myself a peek at the football guys. *Wham.* There he was. Pads, helmet, cleats and all. Tricked out like the cover of a sports magazine or the top of a trophy. Jason Golden Boy. *And day turned into knight.*

After we ran some intervals and did a cool down, Coach told us to go on in. The football team was on a water break. I was dehydrated too, but visually rather than physically, so I looked over to see if I could quench my thirst. I was rewarded to find Jason looking at me. His eyebrows rose up, asking a question. How was it? I smirked a response, and shrugged my shoulders. Not heinous. He smiled even bigger, relieved, pointed at his wrist like a watch and shook his head. I knew he meant football practice would be late. After rolling and stretching out in the gym, I changed, put my gear in my newly issued athletic locker *(!)*, and checked my phone.

(jason gb)
Think fb will run later than xc
I'll catch a ride with Sam
Where were u at lunch?

How do I explain my absence? All I could come up with was I was allergic. Not to nuts, dairy or gluten, but rather jocks, cheerleaders and crowds. My life had gotten a lot more complicated, but always, honesty is the best policy. Followed by a quick change of subject.

(me)
Grabbed a quick bite
You looked busy
Good first day?

I drove home alone. Made dinner for Dad and me. I was hungry after practice. I showered. Threw on comfy sweats. Checked my schedule for the next day, mostly talked to Misty. I knew that I was waiting. Waiting for Jason to get home from practice. Eat. Shower. Talk with his family . . . call me. About eight thirty my phone rang. I jumped a foot off the couch.

"Hey Runner Chick, how about a milkshake?"

"Okay Football Dude, as long as you buy."

"Surprise, I can drive, in fact, I'm in your driveway."

"Oh, okay. What's the hurry?" I teased.

"I just got home, and I'm starving, and they close at nine."

"All right then, I'll be right out." He skipped dinner! Can't keep that kind of awesome waiting. I shouted to my dad I was going for ice cream, and I'd be home by ten and was out the door in less than a minute. It must have struck him as being pretty funny because I could hear him chuckling as the door shut behind me. Although I was the source of his amusement it was a lovely sound.

"What's with you driving? Afraid to mess up your hair in the Jeep?" I asked as I got into his mom's cool sky blue Mini Cooper with black stripes racing up the hood. Way too much fun. It was a visual party in a can. As always, I digress. But it was a sweet, sweet ride. And it was doubly nice to be able to sneak a quick look or two *(million)* over at Jason while he drove.

"After being hit, tackled and smacked around for four hours I felt I had risked my life enough for one day," he rebutted.

"Oh I see, a wise guy. I'll remember that the next time you need to sponge a ride. By the way, shouldn't you be treating Sam to a milkshake now instead of me?"

"No, we're good, I filled his car up with gas on the way home from practice, and bought his lunch today." He glanced over.

"It's good to know you settle your debts," and to detour around the lunch route I added, "Other than being beat up, how did the rest of your practice go? Has Coach found his starting receiver?"

"Looks that way. Didn't think I'd get up to speed quick enough to play here in the States senior year, but my old coach knew his stuff, and pick up games with my dad's squadron on the beach paid off as well. Our first home game is this Friday. Are you going to come watch?"

"Not big on crowds as you know, any chance it'll be on *ESPN*?"

"Not this week, maybe later in the season," he countered. I thought about it for a minute. There had to be a compromise.

"How about if I park the Jeep in the front row of the parking lot overlooking the stadium and watch from there?"

His face lit up. "That should work since I'll be spending most of the game in the end zone! Every time I score a touchdown at your end I'll hold the ball out to you."

"Okay, Mr. Heisman. And I'll flash my lights and honk the horn." Secretly relieved and more than slightly flattered.

With that worked out, we went in to get our special order milkshakes complete with a sidecar scoop, chocolate syrup, whip cream, cherries, peanuts, and of course, a spoon and a straw. Eyelash Lady didn't flirt with Jason like she did when we first came in together, but it was close to closing so she probably wanted to get everyone out. We ordered ours *To Go* and went and sat out in the car.

"I like your mom's car," I said, when we got in.

"I thought you might. It reminds me of you."

"Really, how's that?"

"Well, it's quiet, has lots of cool surprises, and it likes to run," he said casually. Spooning in a mouthful of ice cream, cautiously. *Wow. Wow. Wow.* I crushed.

"So it gets a lot of style points, but how is it on reliability?" I wondered. Also dipping in and taking a spoonful, carefully.

"That remains to be seen, but it gets good gas mileage so it is economical. Has an upgraded stereo so it can blast if the tune demands, but, unfortunately, unlike the Jeep, it only has a sunroof so you can only go partially topless," he said, trying to keep a straight face. Failed. Snickered. Choked back a full-blown guffaw.

"You are a jerk. It's a good thing we are in your mom's car or you'd be wearing that shake," I threatened. How long had that comment been waiting to come back to bite me? Brat. I admitted *(to myself)* a charming, attractive brat.

"In that case, we better head home before I get in any more trouble," then he added, "How did your practice go? You look like you fit right in and held your own."

"It wasn't terrible, the other runners are nice. I'd stereotyped high school athletes in the jerk category, my mistake. I thought you and Sam were anomalies. It was a good reality check. You know, *'don't judge a book by its cover'* or for that matter, where it was published, or who wrote it, that sort of thing. I have classes with some of them, so that will help if we need to work together on assignments, another first for me," I said, pondering it out loud.

"Look who's talking," he said as he pointed to my sweats. "You are one of those high school athletes. And it looks good on you. Not that there is anything wrong with your usual black bad-ittude' look," he said quickly, looking to see if I were offended? "And it will be good that you have some *compadres* in your classes, especially when you have to leave school early for meets. It's too bad we didn't get any classes together. That would have been nice, but at least we have some of the same classes, if not the same teachers. We can work together some of the time," he mentioned.

I liked the sound of it. *Together.* He pulled into my driveway, turned off the car and apparently got out and walked around to my side. To open the door for me I figured out, too late. Awkward as I had opened it and was getting out. We both laughed.

"Well then, thanks for the milkshake, and ride, and thank your mom too please," I said, as I nodded toward the car. The moment felt a little formal, strange, but nice just the same.

"Okay, I'm riding in with Sam because we lift before school, but I'll see you around between classes or practices. And I need to grab my books from you eventually. Thanks again for being my accomplice with the I.D. stunt."

"You're welcome, and responsible for any future therapy I require. Go eat something besides ice cream so you can get in some good practices. If I am forced to attend your football game, you better make it worth my while," I added, looking over my shoulder as I walked up to my front door.

"Ha! Prepare to be dazzled and amazed!" He shouted as he went around to the driver's side.

Already have, already am.

10

"Fire and Rain"

Friday. First home football game. Dressed in black, but clothed in dread, parked in the dark parking lot at top of the hill overlooking the stadium. Invisible. I sat on the outer rim of the hazy glow; the field below bathed in lights focused on the turf stage. Everyone who is anyone is down there. Up here I heard the pep band playing some popular movie tune as the rowdy crowd milled around. The sound traveled but was distorted by the distance. Like a secret code I couldn't break.

Suddenly a cheer exploded from the stands as the cheerleaders tumbled out across the field in front of the marching band. The dance squad followed behind the band, holding a giant banner that read "TONIGHT'S THE KNIGHTS!" in blue and silver paint. The band then blasted what I assumed to be the school's fight song as the football team assaulted the field. The cheerleaders and dancers grabbed their shining silver pom poms and jumped around the team as they huddled around the coach. The fans all stood, clapped and cheered. Sensory overload! Welcome to my new *knightmare*. The band then marched off the field and joined the crowd in the stands. The dancers went to the far end of the track to practice their halftime routine. And the cheerleaders took center stage between the fans and the players by their bench.

I squinted and scanned down the team shuffling around on the sidelines getting ready for the playing of the National Anthem. It did not take me long to find him. He stood at attention. Helmet off. Hand over heart. Focused on the flag. #7. Lucky number 7. 7th Heaven. Oh thank heaven. My new favorite number. When the band finished, the Knights lined up against their opponents on opposite ends of the field of battle. The snare drums started the drum roll. The kicker moved slowly forward with the tide of his team in his wake as his foot connected with the ball; it launched up into the cool night air and arched back down to the opposition. Game on.

After trading possessions back and forth a few times, it was near the end of the first quarter. I saw Jason line up behind the quarterback. I think this was the play they had worked on the past week in practice.

"Honk the horn and flash your lights when I score," he'd said. "I'll hold the ball out to you." So of course he did, and as he stood in the end zone and offered up the ball to the sea of darkness, I broke through the wall of silence and dark invisibility, honked twice and flashed the lights seven times. And I grinned. I could see a flash of white under the helmet as he smiled back, and then he quickly turned and prepared for the giant wave that was rolling in to congratulate him and return him to the bench. Wow. Despite my earlier and most-likely forever apprehension, this turned out to be a good knight after all.

❂

The next couple of weeks were a blur. Between schoolwork, homework, housework and running there was precious little time to eat, sleep or spend time with Jason. Not necessarily in order of importance. I had done a pretty good job maintaining my new slightly visible wallflower status that had replaced the old invisible ghost in the hallway mode. Or so I thought.

At school, as far as I knew, the only person who connected the dots between Jason and me was Sam. Jason had introduced him to me in the training room after practice one day a while back. After that he'd say hi or wave or make a funny face in the hall when we'd pass each other, and I would return the greeting, wave or slight grin as inconspicuously as possible. What I didn't realize was that this was like tossing a gauntlet to Sam. The quieter, smaller, barely noticeable response I gave him, the louder, larger, more outrageous he was the next time. It was pretty funny, being sucked into their wonderful world of pranks. Or so I thought.

It was a Friday. Away football game that night and the first home cross country meet early in the morning. I just had to make it through the day. Practice would be easy. Up to this point I had managed to avoid the lunchroom theatrical scene by escaping outside, but fall had arrived and with it the changing weather. The day came when it was more unpleasant to be out in the elements than be inside, out of my element.

Thus, I made a tactical error. I bought my food and retreated to the farthest table, next to the exit, back to the door, and prepared to watch the lunchtime show. Or so I thought.

Next thing I knew I was being lifted up by my elbows and carried to the dreaded center table. Where I found myself wedged between Sam and Jason. My food was delivered by some new accomplice with all of the flair of a Broadway actor slash waiter. And there I was. On stage. In the center of the universe. Burned by my proximity. I tried to laugh a bit, to cover the fact that I was off the charts mortified and to deflect the attention. A valuable illusion I had learned from Jon.

Gradually the focus left me as the entertainment value shifted to the next unsuspecting victim. After giving Sam a sarcastic *"oh you are so clever"* look I turned and gave Jason the *"dirty look to end all dirty looks"* look, which honestly could probably burn through steel. Then I kept my gaze down and tried to swallow my food. And it seemed to work. Or so I thought.

My burning blush subsided, my breathing was back under control, and then it seemed to be getting cooler. Down right chilly in fact. Strange. And that's when I looked up. Straight into the seething eyes of Chelsea. Realizing too late that I had unintentionally violated the territory of a hunting lioness. I was doomed. Or so I thought? No. I *knew*. No fact check required.

Third class block was uneventful. Fourth was typical. The new Psych teacher wrote the notes on the board straight out of the book for us to copy down.

I had flown under the radar *(since eighth grade, but even more so now)* since the first day of school. The day Jason had given Chelsea the glorious quick glance blow off and had miraculously turned back to me. I thought she had gotten over it. Apparently that was not the case. I could *feel* her fuming.

My backpack hung on the back of my seat so I could grab it and make a quick escape. Just before the end of class I heard a zipping sound behind me, and when I turned to investigate, the bell rang as Chelsea's pen slid my backpack strap off the back of the chair, dumping all its contents. Into the aisle. Right into everyone's way. So they had to detour around us.

"Oops," she said.

I looked at her.

She stared, slouched back in her seat like she owned it. And pretty much everything else in the school, or the world for that matter. After fast forwarding through some pretty graphic scenarios of actions I could have taken, I opted for the "bigger man" option and bent down to pick up my calculator, binders, mechanical pencils, cell phone, etc. Shielding myself from her obvious wrath with an armor of long dark wavy curls.

"So *Joan*, apparently you are Jason's *unworthy* neighbor," I heard. I ignored her, or I fantasized about ways to rearrange her expensive dental work.

You pick.

Still committed to taking the high road I asked, "Excuse me?"

"No. I don't. And won't. Who do you think you are? This whole 'dark and mysterious' thing that you are working is lame. *I* could see it from a mile away, the way you play cute little games with Sam in the hallways to get him on your side because he's Jason's friend. It's not going to work. By now you should have figured out that Jason is way out of your league and just *feels sorry for you* because you are *so odd.* So congrats, you were the first person he met when he moved here. He must have been pretty desperate to hang out with you. *We* all know he's a nice guy.

"Ironically he tried to help you fit in, but now after that fiasco at lunch I think even he has realized you are hopeless. You don't fit in. And you never will. Thank goodness he found Sam and the football team; otherwise he would have been labeled a loser and ostracized like you. Why don't you do the right thing and let him go? *With us.* Where he belongs."

Ouch. She had nailed it all in one fell swoop. All my insecurities about him rolled into one bag of too-good-to-be-true. Thanks for the reality check. I think I'll cash it and bounce.

And with that, after collecting my spilled stuff with the exception of my pride, which was still scattered across the floor, I was gone like Donkey Kong.

And in a really, really bad mood. To make matters worse, as if that were possible, after changing and heading out to the track, I walked by the football team's bus heading to their away game.

I could not help but look for Jason, despite the last twenty minutes of torture Chelsea had put me through. Oh wait, matters did get worse, silly me. I could see tall, tan, and golden locks shimmering #7 with his back to me, which was an awesome sight, but the worse part came in the form of sweet, bubbly, smiling and "all good luck – you'll be awesome– just like me," Chelsea. She saw me too. And she grabbed his arm and pulled him into the bus. I kept walking. Walk. Do. Not. Think.

There was nothing like internal ranting to motivate me when I ran. At practice we were supposed to take it easy since we had a meet in the morning, but I felt the need for speed. I threw myself into the training run. I wasn't paying attention, just focused on the run and dissecting every sentence, word, syllable and letter Chelsea had venomously spit out. One of the guys, Trent I thought was his name, dropped back from the lead group of veteran runners and fell into pace with me.

"Hi, Joan is it?" I looked at him, startled back to reality. I nodded.

"I'm Trent, so what's the hurry? Are you trying to make the top five for the meet tomorrow? Because I think the roster is set, but keep up this pace and you'll be in the top five for the next one for sure," he continued. "I can't believe the condition you are in for a first year runner. Have you trained a lot?"

"Ha, thanks but no, neither. Just running away," I surprised myself by saying. Okay, that was weird, and a little dramatic, but I'm not used to talking when I run, so I'm not in conversation mode, except with myself. And at that moment *myself* was in deep discussion with *itself* weighing the truths or lies contained in Chelsea's verbal beat down. "I mean running away *through* the woods, I don't want to lose the head group since this is a different route than the one we normally do."

"Oh, this is the one we take the day before a race because it simulates a lot of the courses we will run this season. It's got hills, a creek, curves, turns, and then circles back to school, or the finish line. It's a 5K, or 3.1 miles," Trent explained.

"Thanks," I said to be polite. And thankfully he stopped talking. But he stayed with me so I couldn't zone out and go to Joan's World of I Wonder What Jason Really Thinks of Me. We circled back to school and stretched out on the turf field because the football team was gone. I tried not to think of the buses filled with all the psyched up players, coaches, managers, and of course, the cheerleader and dance squads. And Chelsea with Jason. Let's try to forget that visual. *Please.*

❂

I woke up the next morning to gloom and doom, and outside it was pretty nasty too. That meant that the forecast for my first ever school sporting event was miserable, cold, rainy, with a definite chance of soaked shoes running through a freezing creek bed.

That prediction was spot on. My dad took me to the school to catch the bus, the whole way going over different strategies for every possible situation. I, on the other hand, was wondering just why I was out of my warm, dry bed on this awful wet day, preparing to go run hard enough to puke my guts out at the end. In public. Awesome.

He promised to be at the start, the halfway point, and then the finish line. Apparently that's what the spectators do at meets; they run back and forth across the course so they can cheer at key points in the run. I contemplated asking why he didn't just run the race for me, and I would wait on the bus until we drove back to school, but I didn't want to bust up his supportive dad pep talk.

His running conversation *(pun unintended, on any other day I would be congratulating myself on my cleverness)* was helpful, in a way, as it made it impossible to dwell in the horrible town of Chelseaville, Population: One Really Mean Girl and her Fan Club. That unpleasant train of thought got interrupted as we arrived at the school. I thanked Dad for his advice, grabbed my stuff and stepped out into a puddle. Fantastic.

After grabbing all of our gear and getting on the bus, we were on our less-than-merry way. Coach went over strategy as we drove through the downpour to the district park. I paid attention so I wouldn't get lost on the course, and go off on my own tangent down a well-traveled road to Nothing Good Can Come of This Trek. But the informational talk ended and I was left to look out the window and wander on my mental way.

I went over every detail of yesterday's lunchroom prank. In retrospect, it had been a little enjoyable until Chelsea's version has poisoned it. I hadn't talked to Jason since then, or heard from him. But thinking back, did he seem weird? I didn't think so, but then why didn't he comment about it? Or about his away football game? Or about my first cross country meet? Especially since he had encouraged me to participate? Granted, I hadn't mentioned it either. I was torn between wanting him there and not wanting him there. *(To see me mess up, fall down, and of course, throw up.)*

I shook myself out of it when we arrived at the park. It was an invitational, so they were a lot of teams from our area. We set up camp under a tent, and waited until it was time to go for a warm up jog before our event. It was going to take all day. When our turn finally came, we shed our warm, dry, school issued gray warm ups and revealed the blue and white school uniform that consisted of a tank top and short running shorts.

It had a silver lighting bolt that went across the chest and down across the shorts. Flashy. I wanted to crawl under a rock. But instead I went into auto pilot mode and switched out of my wet running shoes into my soon-to-be wet racing spikes, braided my hair back into a ponytail, and jumped out to go jog with my team to get ready to race. This was it.

At the worst part, two miles in, when all I wanted to do is fall down, roll off the trail and disappear, I heard music. Coming from around the curve. Not the usual contemporary, synthesized, heavy pump up drum, psych-up for competition song, no, I heard a corny, old-fashioned, show tune blasting . . . I think it was, no it couldn't be . . . Gene Kelly from the musical, "Singing in the Rain . . . ."

And there he stood. Soaking wet. Adorable. Gloriously adorable. Smiling. Holding out mini speakers. He was going to get it for this, but I couldn't help but finish the race with a silly grin on my face. What would Chelsea's spin be on this? Was there even a glimmer of truth to her rant? Or was Mr. Too Good To Be True all of that and more?

Since my race was the last one, and it was pouring down rain, as soon as we crossed the finish line Coach hustled us back to break camp. We quickly took down the tent. I grabbed all my wet gear and helped clean up the snack trash and then headed to the bus for the return trip to school. All the while trying to catch a glimpse of the mischievous music maker.

Just as I was in the line to get on the bus I spotted him. Talking with my dad. I tried to break out and go over to them, but I got a gentle push from behind and was swept up onto the bus. I walked down and dumped my stuff on the first empty seat on their side of the bus, and quickly wiped away the fog on the window glass from the humidity of thirty sweaty, soggy runners.

Jason stood, drenched, with his backpack hugged to his chest, probably protecting the speakers, chatting it up with my dad like it was a sunny afternoon in our backyard. I took a deep breath and sighed on to the glass, clouding up the clarity I was seeking once again. I was brought back inside the bus by a question.

"Is this seat taken?" Trent asked, as he stopped next to me.

"No, help yourself," I answered, moving my stuff to the floor. "Sorry, I shouldn't have put my gear on the seat, it's all wet," I said, trying to wipe it off.

"News flash, everything is soaked. I can't wait to get home and get dry. I saw you run today, you looked strong. The weather didn't seem to bother you. You looked oblivious. How did you feel?" he asked, stowing his gear and sitting down.

"Cold, annoyed, wet, miserable, exhausted," I blurted out, clearly not thinking how it would sound to a stranger. It was how I would talk to Jon, Jason or myself.

"Whoa, don't sugar coat it, how did you really feel?" he laughed and continued. "I guess that pretty much sums it up though. Cross country is not for the worthless or weak. Remember our motto: Our Sport is Your Sport's Punishment."

"Clever, hadn't heard that," I said. My personal motto was more like, "Running, it's Cheaper than Therapy," and even though I wanted to return to the window to catch another glimpse of Jason with my dad, I felt I should make some effort at conversation now that I had rejoined society.

"We have Psychology together. I saw when you got stuck front row center. Worst seat ever. No chance to catch a nap," he laughed. Couldn't agree more I thought, but for a much blonder reason.

"Unless you have trained yourself to sleep with your eyes open, which I have," I joked. Yes, me. Joked out loud. With a virtual stranger. Weird. I talked to him, or at least listened to him, all the way back to school.

When the bus got back to the athletic parking lot we were dismissed quickly so we could get home and dry out. Dad was waiting for me in the parking lot. He was excited to relive his cross country career and look forward to mine. Well, mine was not going to be a career, more like a short term internship that requires an enormous amount of dedication and work and in return doesn't pay anything. He, on the other hand, had studied both training and racing strategies.

Up to this point my running had been a form of escape. Now I needed to revise my thinking to be a competitive athlete. It was fun to see him so excited and engaged. Our conversation about the meet ran its course *(arh arh arh)*. I tried to steer it toward *after* the race. Because although I was open to improving my running technique, I also really wanted to know what he had talked about with Jason. But before I could find out I got a text notification. I apologized to Dad for taking it, but he told me to go ahead. I had a sneaking suspicion he had been expecting the interruption.

(jason gb)
Beautiful day for a run
U did gr8

(me)
Thanks Mr. DJ
Who made you tunes chairman?

Kris Abel-Helwig

(jason gb)
Hahahahahaha
Thought u might need
a little inspiration

(me)
U were correct
It was a mess
I was a mess

(jason gb)
Not from where I was standing
but then, it was raining pretty hard

(me)
So I heard. Literally
Jokes on u. I like running in the rain

(jason gb)
But do you like singing in
the rain?

(me)
Very funny
We'll see who gets
the last laugh

(jason gb)
Is that a promise
or a threat?

(me)
Both. How did your game go?

(jason gb)
Awesome. We won

(me)
Did you dominate?

(jason gb)
I did ok

(me)
Modesty becomes you.
How many TDs?

(jason gb)
Three. We won 21–7

(me)
Ummmm.
No expert here
But you got ALL the touchdowns?
What did Sam do?

(jason gb)
What can I say?
I inspire him to try harder

(me)
Can't wait to hear his version
Seriously, thanks for braving
the elements to watch my misery

(jason gb)
My pleasure.
Felt I owed it to you, after all, I did talk you
into it. R U mad?

(me)
I don't get mad
I get even
Goodnight Even

(jason gb)
Can't wait.
See you later Jett

I looked up and out the window. Dad was humming a song as he drove into our neighborhood. I gazed out the window. The day long dark, ominous gray clouds had melted into twilight. The first star winked down at me. Without thinking I made a wish. *Star light, star bright, first star I see tonight, I wish I may, I wish I might, have the wish I wish tonight.* Crazy. I shook my head. How could I dare make a wish? You only get one per first star. And mine had come true even before I could make it. *Cosmic.* Which fit because once again, I was trying to make sense of chaos, and once again, I was totally star-struck.

11

"Mean"

Participating in a sport required a lot more time management skills than being a hermit. The cycle of school, practice, dinner, homework and sleep, pretty much summed up my life. Throw an away meet early dismissal into my carefully planned schedule, and I had to do make-up work on much less sleep. Healthy food was a major requirement, so Dad and I took turns launching grocery store raids and talked over meal preparation at least three dinners a week. The Sunday after running in the rain found me playing catch-up. Which was okay because I hadn't heard what he and Jason talked about at the meet.

"How about leftovers for dinner tonight?" Dad asked.

"Sounds good, we have take-out from after the meet yesterday. I'll put something in the crock pot before school tomorrow to get us going for this week," I set the plates on the island. We heated up the food, cut up some fruit and took our seats.

After chatting about school and work, I finally asked, "What was with Jason and you at the meet yesterday?"

"I was wondering when that was going to come up," he laughed. I just looked at him. He returned my stare and finally said, "I've told you. I think Jason is an exceptional young man. He got up after a late night of football and drove all the way out to the middle of nowhere to cheer you on in awful weather. That speaks volumes of his character. He felt a little responsible for encouraging you to go out for the team, and wanted to support you. The song choice was a little old school, but it was clever and different, just like you. I'm glad you have such a nice . . . friend," he finished.

"Yes, he is nice," I responded. Almost too nice. Responsible, too. Maybe Chelsea is on to something. Or maybe not. I was used to going over every single thought of my own from every angle. It was much harder to decipher the thoughts behind the actions of others. And I was woefully out of practice.

Monday flew by at school. All of the teachers were trying to cram in reviews for midterms. I looked for Jason between classes but he was nowhere to be found. Fortunately I didn't have to endure the wrath of Chelsea as it was an off day for that class.

I had thrown soup ingredients in the crock pot as promised before school, so when I got home from practice I started to make some corn bread muffins to go with it. Dad had texted that he'd be late, so I put on some music and was working in the kitchen when the doorbell rang. Which was weird, because no one ever comes over unexpectedly. Imagine my surprise when I opened my door and saw Jason's sister Sophia standing on my doorstep.

"Hi, I'm Sophie, Jason's sister," she blurted out. "I left my phone at school and we don't have a land line so may I borrow yours to call my mom?" she added nervously, biting her pretty, pink, lip-glossed lip.

"Sure, I'm Joan. Come on in."

"Um, I could just stay out here."

"Well you could, if you have really long arms. My phone is in the kitchen," I explained.

"Oh, okay then." She stepped in.

I led her down the hall to the kitchen, picked up my phone and handed it to her.

"Ummmm, may I use your restroom? I didn't get a chance to when I got home," she asked, her eyes darting around.

"Sure, it's down the hall on the right," I pointed for her, and then turned to finish putting the muffins together. It was a little weird, and she was acting really awkward. *Oh well, who am I to talk?* At least I was the calm one for a change compared to the mess I was meeting other members of her family. A few minutes later she returned and handed me my phone.

"Here you go, thanks," she said, sounding relieved.

"No worries. Anytime. Nice to meet you, Sophia," I said, trying to be casual and not pry.

"It's Sofi, not Sophia," she said, tossing her long, blond hair over her shoulder. *Hmmmmmm, who did that remind me of?* She seemed stiff, almost like she was trying a new move on for size. She turned and walked quickly down the hall to let herself out. Strange thing was, when she took her hand out of her jacket to open the door, it looked like a cell phone in her pocket. It was probably a wallet, I thought to myself. Why else would she need my phone?

I put the muffins in the oven and spread my books out on the island to start on homework for tomorrow. Tuesday I had class with Chelsea. As much as I dreaded revisiting my embarrassing ordeal with her, it nevertheless marched uninvited into my thoughts. I quickly fast-forwarded through the scattered backpack, and her grabbing Jason and getting on the player bus. Ouch. Let's skip to the next day at the meet. The cold run, the goofy tune, the hot spectator . . . I couldn't help myself, without thinking I grabbed my phone and texted.

(me)
Mr. Kelly, thanks
for the inspiration

I hit send and regretted it. *Instant Text Remorse.* I put it down and tried to get back on task. After looking at it twelve times, I took it back into my room and plugged it in to charge so I wouldn't keep checking for a response. He probably wasn't home from practice yet, either that, or he was sick of being nice and responsible, tired of our friendship, wanted to sever all ties and never see me again. *Whoa*, who is going *all drama* now?

❂

But that was just the start of the death drop from the top of the roller coaster I apparently was living on now. Tuesday rolled into Wednesday into Thursday. Still. No. Response. By then a billion scenarios of why he hadn't texted back had gone through my brain. The only time I was completely not dwelling in text-less despair was when I was running. Needless to say, I was getting some really good practices in. Without realizing it, I had also acquired a new running partner. Trent.

He waved to me during the pre-workout pep talks and we'd walk out to do warm-ups. I guess he noticed I was pushing hard. He kept a running *(unintentional pun)* conversation about how I had increased my pace. He assumed I was working my way up the roster. Truth be told; I was running away from my inner thoughts and trying to find a way off the roller coaster. We cooled down after Thursday's practice then headed to the parking lot.

"Are you going to the football game tomorrow night?" Trent asked, just as my phone swooshed an incoming text alert.

"Um. Yes. No. Maybe," I stuttered. I frantically wanted to check my phone, which had finally broken its code of silence, but I didn't want to be that typical teenager techno addict.

"Can't make up your mind or are you trying to be mysterious?" Trent laughed.

"Both? Neither?" I answered. And it came to me then and there. I cannot and should not let a text message rule my life. I stopped reaching into my bag for the dictator, and mentally banished it into the depth of my backpack.

"I sometimes go to the games, but I sit in my car in the upper lot, not the stands," I explained, or so I thought.

"Can I ask why, or is it part of your mystique?"

"No, I can assure you that I'm nowhere near that interesting. I guess I haven't been bitten by the school spirit bug."

"Well, a bunch of the cross country team go and all sit together and we have a lot of fun. We watch the game now and then, but it's more of a hang-out session," he said, and then added, "How about venturing into uncharted territory for a change? Or, if that doesn't sound good, I'd be willing to join you in the great beyond if you'd prefer?"

"RETREAT!" the voice in my head shouted. Fortunately, I have a pretty good poker face. I looked away for a second as if contemplating my options for his sake. There was no way I'd have him sit up in my car with me. What if Jason scored and held the ball out to me? Then again, what would it mean if he didn't? I chose the lesser of not necessarily two evils, but high on the scale of "Top Ten Uncomfortable Situations in a Teenage Girl's Life."

"Let's see what the weather throws at us. If it isn't freezing, I may consider making the trek into the unknown wilderness," I compromised.

"Great! See you later," he said as he went to his car.

I quickly unlocked the Jeep and jumped in. Sanctuary. And then I tried. Really. But couldn't not stop myself as I dug into my backpack to grab my exiled phone.

(jason gb)
Coming to our game tmo night?

(me)
I think so

I wrote back. And then waited. Waited. Waited.

(jason gb)
What's that supposed to mean?

(me)
I may actually be in the stands for a change

I wrote back. And then waited. Waited. Waited. This was strange.

It didn't usually take this long for one of his quick one-liners. It was like a forced commercial break during a football game on TV.

> (jason gb)
> Kk, I guess I won't hold out the ball.
> Since I won't know where you are

> (me)
> I'll be the one yelling the
> loudest in the stands

I wrote back quickly. Too quickly maybe? And then waited. Regretted. Possibly even fretted.

> (jason gb)
> Kk, I'll see you around then

What was that about? I said I would be there. Just not in my car. What difference did that make to him? I said I would be cheering for him. Isn't that what he wants? Another cheerleader? And with that bitter thought, a chill crept up my back. It had nothing to do with the *weather.* It had everything to do with *whether or not.*

✿

We were sitting on the back porch swing looking out at her garden. I had just run home from the bus stop and had burst through the house and into tears when I found her in the backyard. She knew she couldn't ask me what was wrong immediately as it would just make the faucet flow more. So we had gently swung back and forth, listening to her waterfall gurgling while I gushed. Finally, I had calmed down enough to tell her how I had been betrayed by a classmate, Janie, who I had thought was my friend. She had told a very special secret to a group of kids at recess because she was mad at me. She said she had just pretended to be my friend, so I would tell her, so she could reveal it and show everyone how silly I was. I was in fourth grade. (What did that make me? Nine?)

"*I trusted her,*" *I whispered.* "*I will never do that again.*"

"*Never is a really long time,*" *she gently responded, and waited.*

"*Janie stood there, holding everyone's attention in her hands, and then spilled it out, for everyone to see, and then pointed and laughed at me,*" *I whispered, almost in a trance, unclenching my fists that had been holding my eyes in my head and looking down at my open, extended, moist palms.*

"*What did you do?*" *Mom asked softly.*

"*I laughed right back at her, like Jon taught me. I shook my head and looked at the crowd like she was nuts. I made a funny face and shrugged my hands like this.*" *I showed her, then quietly added, staring out through seeking eyes,* "*And that made her mad. She said she hated me, and she never would ever talk to me again.*"

"*Like I said, never is a very long time,*" *Mom whispered.*

"*Why did she have to be so mean?*" *I asked the age-old question.*

She thought for a long moment, and then said, "*There are so many explanations, some right on the surface and some deep. Maybe she is hurt, or scared, or insecure, or neglected, or maybe, just maybe, she is just plain mean. What is important is what it taught you.*"

"*It taught me to never ever share my secrets,*" *I whimpered.*

"*Safe. I suppose. Locking your thoughts away. But rather, instead of never sharing, be a little more careful about what you share and with whom you share it? You, my sweet, sensitive love, are a compassionate, honest, creative soul. Eventually, there will be special people you will learn to trust, that will be there for you no matter what. And even some that love you, like your pesky brother, who will still tease you without end. But they will also always support you when things get tough. Life is not easy. Sharing it with those you can cry to or laugh with makes all the difference. And for the ones who can't be trusted? They have missed out on a wonderful friend. I feel sorry for them.*"

My Friday morning wake up. I closed my eyes, willing my mind to return to the warmth of her arms. Swaying on the swing. Being nine years old again. Seeking insight. Her insight. Momentary silence. Then, the sound of my alarm ripped her away. I was left to figure it out alone. Again. The warmth evaporated as the chill of last night returned to haunt me. I jumped up to escape the thoughts that sleep had protected me from, now that I had to wake up and face the day.

"Meow!" Misty voiced her displeasure at being kicked from her comfy spot at the foot of my bed.

"Sorry kiddo, that makes two of us. I will probably be a mess again tonight." I cradled her.

"Meow."

"Confusing boy trouble. Mean girl trouble. The usual teenage angst." I scrunched her belly.

"Meow."

"Seriously. Tell me about it. Why all the drama? Is it necessary?" I returned her to the bed and got dressed.

"Meow."

"All right, thanks. Be prepared for a therapy session tonight."

"Meow." I heard as I went down the hall to breakfast.

"Good morning Sunshine! How is my true source of light and inspiration on this otherwise cloudy, dismal day?" Dad greeted me enthusiastically.

"Ugh," I grunted.

"Woke up on the wrong side of the bed, did you?"

"What does that cliché mean?" I grumbled. "Is there a correct side to wake up on to ensure a bright, cheery outlook on the wonderful day ahead? Because if that's the case I think you bought me a defective bed."

"Well, aren't you just Miss Merry Sunshine Smarty Pants?" he asked. "To what or to whom do I owe this charming, darling, downcast mood you are experiencing and sharing so delightfully?"

"Oh, you know. Typical Teen Drama," I mumbled.

"Care to share?" he asked, more seriously.

"Nope. I think I'll just keep it bottled up inside and let it fester into a swirling vomitus mass that I can unleash in the cafeteria at lunchtime, or perhaps even better, in the stands at the pep assembly today," I added and visualized with artistic up-chucking flair.

"Hmmm. At least you're being mature about it and not bowing to Peer Drama Pressure. Your act of defiance will, no doubt, be spectacular," he snickered. "Would you like to add eggs, toast and jelly to the swirl?"

"Why yes, thank you, why not?" I accepted graciously and gratefully. I even managed to eek out a little smile.

He brought over a plate, set it down in front of me and kissed the top of my head. "You know, you can tell me anything. It may cause serious irreversible damage to my so-called adult – and I use that term lightly – psyche, but I will always be her, I mean here, for you," he accidentally slipped up.

I quickly covered it. "I know Dad. You are awesome. And it does put what seems to be desperately important into perspective. I'm trying to fit in the game, figure out who's on my team, get scouting reports on my adversaries, and determine how to best influence the referees to make their calls go my way," I smiled up at him. I had to protect him. Still. Always.

"That's my girl," he grinned, and left to go instill knowledge into the brains of the much more mature and focused college kids.

12

"Impossible"

At school the next day, I searched for Jason to clarify the confusing text exchange and the prior lack thereof, to no avail. I had forgotten Trent asking about the football game until he caught my arm on the way into the gym for the pep assembly. He guided me to sit with the other cross country seniors to watch the three-ring circus.

The pep band sounded great, and the tumbling cheerleaders had serious skills. Jason's sister, Sofi, was a crazy good gymnast. She did back handsprings across the gym floor ending with a high back-twisting flip thing. She really could fly. Another girl, Shelley, I think, from my history class, an outgoing brunette with giant brown eyes, nearly jumped out of the gym. They were both very talented and looked sincerely happy. Genuine. I had to admit I was impressed. Good for them.

Then the student council president called the football team out on the microphone and reminded the crowd that Homecoming was in two weeks. I wasn't paying attention as I spotted Jason and Sam as they strutted out in their team jerseys and blue jeans. It was obvious they were well-liked, not just because they were voted captains, but because they fed off each other's natural charm, and the crowd ate it up. It was like a stand-up comedian's show as they threw one-liners back and forth over the microphones. The crowd loved them. It was infectious. I smiled. My guys.

Then Chelsea ran over and jumped in between the two of them, grabbing the microphone from Sam with one hand and Jason's arm with the other. She gazed up at him and turned to the crowd.

"Don't forget guys, the Homecoming dance is only two weeks away, and we girls need to get our dresses. Don't wait until the last minute to ask us, or you just might miss your chance!" I stopped smiling. The herd cheered and then we were dismissed.

I coasted through practice in the fog, literally and figuratively. Trent wanted to talk but wisely read my mood and kept silent for a change while we ran. It started to drizzle as we jogged our cool down.

"So how about the game tonight? Have you decided to join us? You aren't afraid of a little rain are you?" he asked, sounding hopeful.

I looked up at the ominous clouds and said, "Sure why not? It looks like it will be such a lovely evening. No point in staying warm and dry at home when I could be freezing, sitting on frigid metal bleachers with a crowd of frenzied fans." *(After all, I had texted Jason I would be in the stands, right?)*

"Great! Dress warm! We'll all be standing next to the pep band. I'll see you there for kickoff at seven!" Trent said, relieved as he walked away, seemingly oblivious to my sarcasm.

I sighed deeply. A puff of vapor hung in front of my frozen face. Perfect. Then I walked to my car to go home to change. *Like that was ever going to happen.*

I told Dad about the game. He wisely sensed it wasn't a night for witty banter and let me slide. I dressed in black layers, fitting my mood, style and signature. Promised Misty I'd be home early. Drove to school. Parked in my usual spot up on the hill next to the locker room. Took a deep, icy breath, and then ventured into the lion's or was it the lioness' den?

✪

Trent saw me first and called my name, really, really loud. "Joan! Joan! Over here!" He stood waving frantically so I quickly motioned to let him know that I saw him, relieved that no one else noticed me. Then for some bizarre reason, my eyes ventured down to the track. Where someone did. You guessed it. Chelsea. The lioness.

She looked from me to Trent, back to me. And. Then. Slowly. Smiled. I'm not going to lie; she looked just like The Grinch. *(Before his heart grew three sizes.)* And then she looked over to the group of football players.

I couldn't help but follow her gaze to Jason. Standing in the middle of the pack. Psyching his team up for the game. Oblivious to me. Thankfully. Mercifully. Ironically. For the first time NOT wanting him to see me, being seen by Trent, being seen by Chelsea, being seen by me. *(I should seriously think about taking Drama next semester.)*

In the meantime, I made it over to "my team." The cross country squad. They enveloped and insulated me. It was a new experience. Acceptance. Inclusion. Who would have thought that this was something I was missing? Me. That's who.

The game played out. Jason scored two touchdowns at our end of the field. Each time he neglected to hold the ball out to the dark parking lot above. I felt a haunting sense of loss, sadness, and emptiness each time. I yelled, as loud as I could, not sure what, but just yelled, because I had texted I would. After the game, we all stood around as the crowd trickled out. It was fun being with the cross country team.

Jason had been right. I would tell him that now I understood being a part of something and smiled thinking about how he would look, all proud that he was right. He might even throw out an "I told you so."

It had been a pretty good night after all, or so I foolishly thought.

Trent volunteered to walk me up to my car, away from the brightly lit field, to the dark parking lot next to the player's locker room and I absentmindedly agreed.

"So did you have a good time with us tonight?" Trent asked.

"Believe it or not, it wasn't a total Titanic experience, except for the ice, of course. It was crazy cold."

"Can I take that as a yes?" he smiled and shook his head.

"Yes, the team was nice. Fun. Thank you for inviting me."

He paused. Thinking. Took a deep breath. Then deployed a bomb. "I was wondering. Like they said at the assembly today, the Homecoming dance is in two weeks and I was thinking it would be fun if we went together," he said as he loudly exhaled.

Boom.

I believe the correct term is "blindsided."

"What?" I questioned, awakened from my team-bonding reverie.

"The Homecoming dance, in two weeks, will you go with me?"

I turned to look up at him as we stood next to my car, trying to figure out where we were and what he was talking about. Then, as if it could have possibly gotten more embarrassing or awkward, even more catastrophic, I happened to look over his shoulder and saw Jason. Standing there. With Sam. Outside the locker room.

I'd parked next to the players' locker room! They stood beside Sam's car, looking at us. I froze. Thawed. Attempted a small wave. They got in the car and drove away. Leaving us alone, together. Trent followed my gaze and watched them drive away.

"Well?" he asked, sounding more than a little annoyed. I could not breathe, or did not choose to breathe, you pick. Focus. Homecoming. Dance. Date. Escape.

"Sorry, what day is that?" I asked.

"Saturday, two weeks from tomorrow," he answered, waiting. Waiting. Waiting.

"Um, oh, I am so sorry. But I am away that weekend. I had no idea it was Homecoming. I have to go to my brother's lacrosse tournament, out of town. I promised. It's a big deal. His senior year and all," I fumbled. "But thank you for asking. It was very nice of you." And with that, I punted him into the "friend-zone." He took it pretty well, but I think he figured it out. After all, he was a smart guy.

✸

I sat up in bed, choking on phlegm. After coughing up a gross mess from my throat to my mouth I got up and spit it out into a tissue. My head felt like it was full of snot. Congested. Freaking miserable. Great. I went out to the kitchen to raid our medicine cabinet and realized we needed to stop calling it that because we were basically out of medicine. Another coughing fit. I opened my mouth to call to Dad and nothing came out but a raspy squeak. That's when I saw the note on the island.

Ran to the gym to workout.
I'll be home around ten.

I opened the refrigerator. No orange juice. Went to make tea. Gone. Hot chocolate? None. *Are you kidding me?* It was the last straw. I went back to my room and threw on sweats, a scarf, hat, and grabbed my car keys. I backed out of the garage and into the garbage can. Really? "*AHHHHHHHHH,*" I silently screamed and pounded on the steering wheel. I got out and lifted the can back up and then started picking up the spewed trash.

"Need some help?" I heard and almost burst into tears. I shut my eyes and counted to five exhaling. Lifted my face to the sky, then turned to the son.

"Hey." Which came out more like a choked "eh."

"You sound awful. No offense, but you sort of look like you sound," Jason stated. Fact. I put both hands on my throat and shook my head. "Where are you going? You should go back to bed. Is your dad gone? Do you need me to go get you something?

I pantomimed. Pointing out. I shook my head up and down. Yes. Inhaled. Exhaled. I shook my head up and down. Yes. I shook my head up and down. Yes.

"What do you need?" he asked. You. *Forever and ever, amen.* Instead, I pointed to my throat and pretended to cough. Then didn't have to pretend.

"Cough drops?" he asked. I shook my head up and down. Yes. And then I pretended to drink a cup of tea, with my pinkie finger raised.

"Tea?" Seriously, the guy should go pro. I shook my head up and down. Yes.

"Anything else?" he asked.

How do you act out an orange? A banana is easy you jump around like a monkey. But an orange? Letters V *(vitamin)* C? I shook my head and looked around at the scattered trash and finally grabbed a magazine, pointing to the color on a picture of a sunset over water.

"You want me to go get you a sunset? Be back before sunset?" he questioned, confused.

I covered my face. And started to laugh behind my hands. He mistook it for crying which escalated into a more serious game of charades on steroids.

"A boat ride? A bottle of water? I'm sorry Joan; can you give me a better clue? What else can I get for you?" he asked, exasperated.

I looked up at him. And smiled to show him I was laughing. *Just show me your smile, and everything will be sooooo much better.*

He smiled. "Alright, I'll be back in a little bit. Put the Jeep back in the garage and go in and get warm. I'll get you cough drops and tea. And maybe some oranges, I think you need some vitamin C."

✺

I pulled the Jeep back in and went inside. Ran into the bathroom to survey the condition of my face and hair. Pathetic. I brushed my teeth, hair and washed my face. Pale. Normal. I then went back to the kitchen and grabbed a pad of paper and a pen and wrote.

Thanks a billion. Good game last night.
You played well, as always.

And then I waited impatiently for him to return. After an eternity, or twenty minutes, the doorbell rang. I went and opened it and let him in.

He went into the kitchen and opened the grocery bag. He handed me the cough drops and went to the cabinet, pulled out a coffee cup, filled it with water and opened the tea box to add a tea bag to the mug. Placing it in the microwave, he hit two minutes, and got out a knife to quarter an orange.

All the while I sat on a stool and watched. Inhaling, exhaling, sighing, or coughing. While the tea heated up he looked over at me and I pointed to the pad of paper on the island. He read it.

"You're welcome. Thanks. It was cold but the team played well," he said. Paused. And then said, "I was surprised to see you there. I thought you texted you weren't going."

I looked at him and raised my eyebrows as if questioning, threw up my hands and shook my head. I looked around for my phone to show him my text but it was back in my room charging so I wrote on the pad.

I texted you that I was going to sit in the stands. I sat with the cross country team. They invited me.

"They?" he asked, frowning.
I sighed. And then wrote.

Yes, well, one of the captains – Trent asked me,
as a team-building get together. It was fun.
The kids are nice.

"Oh, well, I'm glad you had a good time with your new friends. I'm sorry you got so sick though, let me know if you need anything else," he added. *If only I could!*

And just then Dad showed up from his workout. Since I couldn't talk Jason explained that he had seen me in the driveway looking "really tired" *(he didn't mention the trash can incident)* and had offered to go to the store for me. Dad just looked back and forth between us, nodded and smiled. The tea timer went off and Jason got it out and brought it over to me and excused himself.

I tapped on the top line on the paper again, thanking him, and he waved it off. Dad walked him to the door and thanked him too. When he came back into the kitchen and looked at me with a sparkle in his eye and smiled. I pointed that I was going to my room, collected my tea, cough drops and orange, and resisted the urge to wipe the silly grin off of my dad's face.

❂

The cold hiked down from my head and set up camp in my throat so I had laryngitis for a week and a half. It didn't make a whole lot of difference in my classes because I rarely spoke. My ears were working fine though, too fine as I got to hear all of the hype about Homecoming all day long.

I hadn't told anyone that I had turned down being Trent's date, and apparently he hadn't either, as the team carried on business as usual. Chelsea was a whole different story. And since she sat in between us in Psychology, Monday was a whole new level of torture.

"Well, if it isn't the cross country lovebirds!" Chelsea turned around and asked Trent in a very loud, purposeful whisper. "I'm SO sorry to keep you apart, would you like to switch seats so you can whisper sweet nothings into each other's ears?"

"No, that's all right," Trent whispered back.

"I'm sorry, I couldn't hear you. You mean you don't want to be closer to her? I can't say that I blame you. Looks like we have another sympathy friendship," Chelsea said, her voice gradually getting softer so she could add extra venom to the last insult and only be heard by her prey, "Sorry Joan, or what is it Sam calls you? Jet? Is that because you are fast, at running of course, or because people can't wait for you to take off?"

I didn't answer, out loud. But there was a whole lot of something going on between me, myself and I. Before the end of class I moved my backpack to my feet so we didn't have another dumping accident. Not looking forward to the class Wednesday and Friday, or the next week either as it would escalate the closer it got to the Big Dance.

Unfortunately, I was right. Wednesday was still aimed at us, which was especially unfair for Trent. He not only suffered collateral damage because of me, but also friendly fire as I had shot down his offer. He was nice at practice, but no longer ran with me. It was just as well because coughing every step got old fast so I had to stop. This increased my anxiety, as my need for escape was rapidly building.

I hadn't had a chance to talk to Jason. Or at least play charades. We hadn't cleared up the text miscommunication, and I had an awful feeling that Chelsea was planting rumors that Trent and I were together. Not to mention greasing the wheels for her obvious goal of captivating *(or at least capturing)* Jason.

I decided after her last verbal beat down that I'd try to clear some of it up and sent a text before practice.

(me)
Thanks again for the house call doc

I waited. And waited. Then sighed, switched my phone to vibrate and put it in my backpack. I changed out for practice but Coach told me to stay inside and stretch and do a weight workout if I felt up to it. I rode the exercise bike, but even it caused a hacking fit, so I wandered back to wait for team to come back. A group of runners returned, Jill and Erin, the top girls, came in with Trent, Scott and Jeff, the lead guys. They left the guys and came over to where I was sitting and started to stretch out.

"Hey Joan, feeling any better?" Jill asked.

I hand signed "a little" with my thumb and index finger, but rolled my eyes, pointed to my throat and shook my head meaning "still no voice."

"I hope you are better in time for the Homecoming dance! You are planning on going, right? We are going to get dresses this weekend, do you want to go with us?" Erin asked with excitement.

They both looked at me. I shook my head "no," and ran fingers across my hand and pointed away, meaning *(hopefully)* that I was going out of town.

"That's too bad! It should be great, especially since we are seniors! Erin is going with Scott, and I'm going with Jeff, and Trent asked Rachel, so we are all going in a group with other runners. We were planning on you being with us!" Jill exclaimed. I was touched. Really. So much that I was almost tempted to stay home and join in, now that Trent had asked someone else, but I knew it would be wrong. He would know. He had suffered Chelsea's rants in silence. Hopefully she would see him with Rachel at the dance and get off his back. Not that it would let up for me. For whatever reason she seemed bent on my destruction, or at least total humiliation. We finished up and went into the locker room. I immediately checked my phone, no message.

✵

No text response Thursday. Or Friday at school. I turned my phone off and stopped checking it. Something was going on; I hadn't seen Sam or Jason all week. I dreaded my last class, Psychology, and waited until the bell was about to ring to avoid Chelsea. But she was primed and ready for me. As soon as I sat down she turned to one of her fan club and announced, "I can't wait until Jason sees my dress! It is this stunning, shimmering blue that totally matches my eyes!"

Her adoring fan whispered the correct response, and it almost sounded like it hadn't been rehearsed a hundred times. It didn't matter. It achieved the desired effect. I stopped breathing. It's done. She's won. I'm lost. Fading. Forgotten. First he moved in and now he's moved on.

An announcement was made releasing all varsity football players and cheerleaders for early dismissal for the away game. Chelsea made a big production of packing up to leave.

"Bye kids have a fun run today," she said, with a little laugh as she left to no doubt hunt down Jason. For all I knew, he was a willing victim. I switched to autopilot and copied down the rest of the class notes without registering or digesting them. When the bell rang I took out my phone. I turned it back on while everyone was filing out. No messages. I decided to make one more attempt. Pathetic? Maybe. Desperate? Sort of. Naïve? Definitely.

(me)
Good luck tonight.
Let me know how it goes.

Practice was easy. We had an away meet far away this weekend. Although I wasn't running because of my cough, I planned on going. Mostly because it would get me out of town and away from the recent disappointing turn of events. It was also an opportunity to hang out with my team. My team. What a concept. I went home to talk with Misty and hopefully get some much-needed rest.

Dad made dinner and we ate and talked about running. Well, he talked and I listened, but he didn't need to give me a pep talk since I wouldn't be competing. He asked about the Homecoming game next Friday and then wanted to know if I were going to the dance Saturday night. I said no. Then in the spirit of full disclosure I told him about turning Trent down.

"Trent is a nice guy, I honestly didn't see it coming. We've been talking and running some, but I thought it was a teammate thing," I acknowledged in a weak, raspy voice.

"Well I'm not surprised about you getting asked, just about who actually did the asking," he said.

I knew where he was going with that so I quickly said, "I didn't know what to do so I told him I was going out of town to Jon's lacrosse tournament. And although he asked someone else it wouldn't be right even to go stag with the group."

"I see your point. Okay, we will be gone all day and not get home until ten or so. Honestly, I am a little disappointed that you'll be missing your senior dance," and slyly added, "and I bet someone else will be too, and I don't mean Trent."

"I wouldn't put a lot of money on it if I were you," I softly croaked, and then went to bed to try and not think about Chelsea and Jason on the return trip of the player's bus.

❂

The weekend flew by. Monday morning I dragged myself out of bed. At least I would only have Psychology two days this week. Since I still hadn't heard from Jason, I figured in reality maybe I was hearing him loud and clear. Maybe. He was pulling away. But that didn't seem like him. So maybe he's not. But if not, why wouldn't he text back? I was in limbo wanting to know, and afraid of finding out.

Decorations and posters were everywhere in the hallways. The school was Homecoming buzzing. It was spirit week and everyone was in pajamas for the Monday theme. I wore black sweats.

Tuesday was dress in your favorite color day. You guessed it. My teammates were getting a kick out of my interpretations of the daily spirit week themes. It became a contest on the cross country team as they tried to guess what I'd be wearing the next day. It was a pleasant distraction.

I braced myself for Psychology and went in. Trent was in on the contest, and since he had moved on, *(Hmmmm, should I be detecting a pattern here?)* he greeted me with a big smile when I walked in and sat down. Chelsea of course took it all in, interpreted it to mean something else entirely and made some smart comment about our "on-going running relationship." Trent laughed and winked at me.

I was relieved that we had gotten past the awkward part, but on the other hand, it was uncomfortable how soon he had. What did I expect? After all, he was a runner. Dark humor inserted.

Mercifully, Chelsea didn't gush about Jason. I was thankful for that too. She must have gotten past my past with him. Obviously I wasn't a threat anymore, as if she considered me one in the first place. She was wearing pink. Shirt, jeans, lipstick, and chewing bubble gum to complete the look for her favorite color day theme.

Wednesday was dress as your favorite movie character. I was torn between Professor Snape and Wednesday, the cryptic daughter from The Addams Family. But since it fell on Wednesday, of course Wednesday won out. Pun intended.

I finally felt better *(physically anyway, mentally the jury was still out, most likely heading toward a mistrial)* so Coach told me to run a couple miles and then go to the trainer. My shins were a little sore, so I grabbed two paper cups of ice, peeled back the paper and hopped up on a table to ice them. The trainer left to go check on an athlete in the weight room and told me she would be back in five minutes if anyone needed her.

In walked Sam. We looked at each other. *Awkward.*

"Hey stranger," I whispered to break the silence, since I hardly had a voice.

"Whoa, sexy voice Jett, are you going into radio voice overs?" he said, recovering quickly.

"Ha ha," I croaked, and had to ask, "So where have you been hiding?" *And why have you deserted me?*

"Nowhere, I've just been busy with football you know," he said, somewhat sheepishly.

"Oh, right. Football." I gave him a look. He squirmed.

"So, how is the cross country team treating you? I heard you are fitting in REALLY well . . ." he threw it back at me. *Hmmmm. Confrontational? Protective? All of the above and before?*

"Meaning?" I choked.

"Easy for you to say, or not," he responded, and then added, "What's with you and Captain Trent?" he challenged.

"Teammates, nothing more," I countered.

"Word in the halls is that you guys are all hot and heavy in Psych," he blurted out. "And we saw you up in the parking lot after the game!" I stared. Seethed. Inhaled. *(No doubt flaring nostrils, the whole nine yards.)* Exhaled. Inhaled.

"Nope. You've been fed bad intel," I whispered.

"But Chelsea said . . . ," he murmured.

"Chelsea doesn't know my life," I whispered, rolling my eyes. Probably even better than a sixth grade girl. No. At this point, definitely better than a sixth grade girl. After all, I'd been tutored by the best.

"She smoked us?" he asked. I shook my head up and down.

"Sorry Jett. My bad," he apologized. I shrugged.

Just then the trainer returned and Sam chatted her. I jumped off the bench, threw away the cups and went home to sulk. *I can't believe that they believed her!* Who am I kidding? There's no doubt she can be *very persuasive.*

Dad came home, and seeing I hadn't made anything for dinner and sensing my mood, correctly, again, decided to take me out. We small talked through it, confirming our plans to go see Jon this weekend. The restaurant was busy, so we got home late for a school night. I had left my phone plugged in to charge. I checked it as soon as we got in. Nothing. I hoped Sam had talked to Jason and that it made a difference. Apparently it did not.

Thursday was Class Color Clash Day. Freshman – Pink *(like babies)*. Sophomores – Blue *(sad they are still underclassmen)*. Juniors – Green *(with envy of course)*. Seniors – Black *(mourning their last year in high school)*. Oh, the irony. We had an away meet so we had early dismissal. I ran okay, not awesome, but it was fun to compete again. It was nice to run away.

Friday was Spirit Day. School colors – Blue & Silver. I compromised and wore gray sweats. A dull version of silver. Which is remarkably close to how I felt. We had shorter periods all day so we could once again be herded into the gym for our Homecoming pep assembly.

I found the cross country team seniors by myself this time and sat next to Jill and Erin. The Student Council had some class competition games that were entertaining. Then they called out all of the fall sports' captains to introduce themselves and tell us how their seasons were going.

I pushed Jill and Erin off the bench so they could go join Trent and Jeff for Cross Country. I clapped for them with the rest of the cross country team. When all the team captains had talked about their seasons, they sent them all back to the bleachers. Except for football. Then they called out the rest of the football team, cheerleaders and dance squads to lead the school fight song. As always I was watching Jason and Sam. They were laughing and pretending to sing. I smiled. My guys. At the end of the song Jason looked right up at me in the stands and our eyes locked. Frozen. I could feel the corners of my mouth start to curve up into a . . .

when Chelsea jumped in front of him, severing our connection, threw her arms around his neck and practically knocked him down with a violent hug. Jill was laughing next to me and turned to yell at me, but when she saw my stare she followed it to them. Back to me. Back to them.

"Oh girl. That explains a lot. Let me get you out of here." She grabbed my arm and pulled me up the bleachers to the upper exit. We went to the locker room to change out for practice. I sat down on the bench and stared at my locker. *What an idiot I am! Why did I let myself get set up so bad? Was I that pathetic? How could I ever think we could ever be more than neighbors? Friends? Work out buddies? When he could date girls like Chelsea. Hadn't I predicted this?*

"Hey kiddo, let's go. We need to get to practice," Jill softly said.

"Yeah, you're right. Thanks. Go ahead. I'll catch up," I whispered. She agreed and left. I closed my eyes. Inhaled. Exhaled. I opened my eyes first and then my locker. Quickly changed into my running gear. Grabbed my shoes. Slammed my locker shut and hit the exit door. BAM! Right into someone, who was standing on the other side.

"Ouch!" Jason yelled. Surprised. Surprising me. I looked at him. "Hey, hi!" he said, rubbing his shoulder. "We could use you on the line of scrimmage."

"Hey," was all I could manage to choke out.

"Um. Are you going to make it to the game tonight?" he asked, somewhat hopefully. Innocently. Incredibly. *What was wrong with this picture? I asked myself. One cheerleader not enough for you?* But it's him. *Golden Boy Jason.* So I answered, or at least tried to.

"I don't know. Maybe. If I do I'll be back up in my Jeep. In the lot. Alone." It just spilled out, like a confession. "I'm late for practice. Good luck tonight," I croaked out. And then I walked away, rounded the corner and bumped into Jill.

"You okay?" she asked, her eyes filled with concern. "I didn't know what to do. He was hanging outside the locker room like he was waiting for you. I don't get it. What game is he playing besides football? He seems so sincere. But why does he let Chelsea hang all over him if he is really into you?"

I looked at her and shook my head. *Welcome to my world.*

❋

I went home, showered and changed, or more appropriately, *changed back,* into black. I made dinner for us and waited until Dad got home to eat. We were both pretty tired. It had been a long week of grading midterms for him so he was quiet and ready for a calm night at home. He told me to go ahead, he'd get the dishes.

So I found myself driving to the Homecoming game. I pulled into the parking lot and went to my dark spot, next to the locker room, overlooking the field bathed in light. I turned off the radio, the car. And sat. Thinking about the last few months. Mad. At what? Jason? What had he done? He wanted to fit in. Try, convict, and lock him up. Seriously?

He's a gorgeous, smart, talented, nice, funny, considerate guy. He'd befriended an antisocial loner, encouraged her and made her feel special. He offered a ray of light into an otherwise dark existence. An existence that had been an escape from the deep, dense pain. Remorse. Regret. But sitting up here in my black Jeep in the dark by myself didn't feel safe, secure or like a sanctuary anymore. It felt claustrophobic.

The game started. Tumbling cheerleaders. Now I recognized Sofi and Shelley lead the tumbling charge. Next the pep band with that drummer who was in my math class. He always had his sticks with him and practiced rhythms on his notebook. Then the dance team. I thought Jill's sister Lisa might be holding up one side of the banner. And then came the football team. Jason and Sam out in front.

The students stood, clapped, yelled, and jumped up and down. People I now knew. Trent, Rachel, Jill, Jeff, Scott and Erin. Together. And I sit out here. Cold. Alone. *I am SO over it.*

The kickoff. First, second, third downs. Fourth and goal. Fumble. Pass. Catch. Run. Touchdown! Extra point. Stop. Press play. Repeat. First quarter, second quarter. Halftime. Cheerleaders cheer. Dance squad dance. Third quarter, fourth quarter. Tied score. Ten seconds to play.

The ball was hiked to the quarterback. He faked a handoff and then fell back to throw. Jason exploded from the line of scrimmage and hauled down the field towards me. The quarterback pitched it to Sam who had looped back behind him, but then faked like he was passing.

Sam faded back and slowed down, seemingly out of the play. He didn't even look for Jason. He knew where he was and where he was heading. Sam launched a rocket. Jason looked back over his shoulder; saw it airborne and burst away from his defender.

He made the catch and the winning touchdown, and jogged to a stop, and looked up. The crowd went crazy, trying to storm the field; the cheerleading and dance squads invaded his team. But he stood there in the end zone. Waiting. And I sat here in a war zone. Wondering. *What if she were telling the truth? Why else did he cut me off? What if he only felt sorry for me? What could he possibly see in me? Look at him; he's a football hero. And I'm nothing but a ghost once again. Except that now I've had a taste for living. Great. I've turned into a zombie. How trendy of me.*

But, instead of doing something, I did nothing. No horn blasts. No flashing lights. As I looked down, he looked up and seemed to see right through me. But to my surprise, curiously, miraculously, he shrugged, and held the ball out to darkness. Heroically. Ironically. But sadly, I drove away.

✵

We got up and on the road early to head to the tournament. Dad drove without talking. Listening to classic rock on the radio. I watched the landscape float by and tried not to think. We rolled onto campus in time to park the car and find the field.

Jon saw us immediately and waved. It was great to see him play again. Poetry in motion, stick check, knocking the ball out of the opponent's stick, scooping it up. Weaving back and forth down the field clearing the ball and passing it off to an Attack. Setting up the shot. Assist. Goal. Jogging back to defensive end with confidence. Dad and I cheered for him. In between games Jon came up, threw a stick to me and motioned me out to an empty net.

"Let's see if you still have a shot," he challenged.

"Okay, but I've been running more than shooting," I replied.

"No excuses. Sling it," he ordered. And we played, taunted, shot goals, and laughed, all the time. Pretty soon some of his teammates found us and he introduced me. After finding an extra helmet, pads *(Dad's request)* and gloves we even played a little pick-up game. We had a couple of hours so we went to grab something to eat before Jon's last game. Dad dropped us off to get a table and went to park the car in the restaurant parking lot.

"Hear you are breaking so many hearts you had to leave town," Jon teased.

"Ha, you are grossly misinformed as usual."

"What's up with Jason? He seems like a great guy," he said, nothing like cutting to the chase.

"Sure. But surprise, surprise, we aren't the only ones who figured that out."

"So what? You have competition. Deal with it."

"Easy for you to say. Look at me. Not a whole lot to work with."

"Give me a break. Take a long look in the mirror Joan. You've been dealt a good hand. You also have a brain, thanks to Mom and Dad. And a warped sense of humor and a wicked shot, thanks to me. What else could any guy worth anything ask for? Quit making excuses and get back in the game," he admonished.

"Thanks Coach," I grumbled. My voice was coming back, but ironically I had little to say.

We drove home in the dark and got in around 10:30 pm. I fed Misty and then started cleaning up around the house. I was antsy and not ready to go to bed. Jon's lecture was still fresh in my head. Finally, I couldn't stand it anymore; I threw on sweats and told Dad I was going for a run.

"Do you want me to go with you?" he asked.

"No thanks, I'll be fine. I just need to stretch out my legs from sitting in the car. I have my phone with me."

"Okay, but be careful. Don't go through the woods. Stay on the neighborhood streets that are well lit," he said.

It felt good to run. I started out easy, and then built up to a sprint for a hundred yards and then slowed back down. Around the block. Island hopping between the pools of light provided by the street lamps. In and out of darkness.

I saw some car headlights make the turn onto my street and for some bizarre reason I dodged over and hid behind a tree. Who am I? A spy? I watched a light blue Mini Cooper with black racing stripes drive by slowly. His mom's car. *Of course, it would have matched her shimmering blue mermaid dress and her eyes.* I melted into the tree.

I watched as the car went into the garage and waited for the door to go down before I dared move. But instead of going into the house, Jason came back out and walked to the end of their driveway. *Did he see me?* I shrunk even further into my shield.

He walked up to the big empty trash container with something in his hand. The street lamp caused a glint off some plastic container. He looked down at it for a moment, then lifted the lid of the can and dropped it in. He grabbed the can handle and wheeled it back into the garage. The light went out. The door went down. I waited for a minute or so. And then slowly walked home. Alone.

13

"Eye Of The Tiger"

Sunday after the dance I was just hanging out. The teachers had realized that not much would be accomplished so they hadn't bothered to assign homework over the weekend. I was out back shooting on goal.

Dad called from the kitchen, "Joan! How about a grocery store run and then hit the ice cream shop on the way home?"

"Sounds like a plan to me. I'll get the Jeep," I yelled back.

As we pulled out of the driveway I checked the mirror for cars *(and garbage cans)* and caught a glimpse of myself. Black ball cap and shades, hair back in a ponytail. I looked like the poster child for Witness Protection. Oh well. Who did I need to impress?

We finished shopping and headed to get ice cream. Dad was driving now so he dropped me off and waited in the car. I ran in to pick up our order to go so we could get the groceries home. As usual, the Eyelash Lady was working. She recognized me and smiled, asking what she could make for me today. When I ordered two different items she looked around me.

"Where's that handsome guy of yours?"

"Um, you must mean Jason, he's not with me. I mean, he's not here, now. And is definitely not 'mine,'" I fumbled.

"What are you talking about girl? The way he looks at you, and you alone, it's like you make the sun shine, the moon glow and paint every color in the rainbow," she teased.

"Ahhhh, you must be mistaken," I stuttered.

"I may not know a lot about a lot of things, but when it comes to the matters of sweetness honey, the bees come to me for my recipes!" She laughed, and left to make my orders, still chuckling. *In that case, would you mind jotting down one of those recipes and placing it on my tab?*

I was still shaking my head and smiling a little when I returned to the car. We sat for a minute so Dad could wolf down his cone before he drove home. He had not mastered the artful technique of slow ice cream eating.

"What's so funny?" he asked, in between licks.

"Just something she said, about Jason and me," I thought a minute and added, "The two of us used to come here, so she thought we were, you know, *together*."

"Well, I'm not so sure about what *together* entails, but I *am* sure that you *are* friends. I'm also confident that you will find your way back here, *together*. Some things just take time," he said.

Jon? Eyelash Lady? Dad? *What do they see that I don't?*

The entire school seemed asleep on Monday. Homecoming week had worn everyone out. I caught snippets of drama in the hallways, but otherwise it seemed to be in the past now. That is until Psychology class.

Chelsea was seething. By the end of class I think she had single-handedly raised the temperature in the room by ten degrees. The good news was that she completely ignored Trent and me. We stole a glance at each other when she was going through her backpack. I raised my eyebrows pantomiming a question. He just shrugged and shook his head, relieved.

The bad news is that Chelsea's full-blown wrath did eventually rain down on someone. I didn't see for whom the bomb exploded, but Jill and I heard the explosion when we walked past cheer practice in the small gym on the way out to the track.

"What was that about?" I asked Jill.

"If it's what I think, it's more about who than what," she answered, and then asked. "Have you heard about the dance?"

"No, after Friday's assembly I avoided the topic like the plague."

"Well, I don't think you'll mind this too much, except for the middle part that is. Just stay with me. Despite Chelsea dropping hints the size of Volkswagens, Jason did not ask her to the dance.

She thought he would, right up to the last minute, when he drove his sister, Sofi to the dance. Sofi is also a cheerleader. You know the really good blonde tumbler. Well, Chelsea blew up Sofi's phone, told her to get Jason over to pick her up or else.

But Jason refused. He said he had planned on asking someone, but when that fell through he was going to fly solo. Period. By the time they got to the dance, Sofi was a wreck. And I bet Chelsea almost caused a few more as she drove herself.

I saw her arrive and toss knives at Sofi, Jason and anyone else within throwing distance of her blazing blue eyes. She calmed down though, and walked around asking every single guy, with the exception of Jason, and even a few that were on dates, to dance.

At ten thirty they announced this year's Homecoming Court. And this is the bad part so I'll make it quick; Chelsea was named Queen, and Jason, King. So they had to do the royal slow dance. She was all smiles and gushing thank you to her royal subjects. Jason did his part the best he could, but it was obvious his heart wasn't in it.

So as soon as the song ended he excused himself and left. Apparently, the Queen had not dismissed him. I bet *that* was the *what* we just heard, and Sofi was the *who* on the receiving end. I sure wouldn't want to be in Chelsea's spiked heels when Jason hears about what she did to his little sister."

✲

Now that I knew Chelsea had been faking that they were dating,

I didn't dread seeing her. But it did make me wonder who the mystery person was that Jason wanted to go with, and why hadn't it worked out? I hadn't seen or heard that he was hanging out with anyone else. That must be why he had stopped calling and didn't answer my texts. Whoever it was must be blind not to see what she could have had.

It was comical to find myself in the same boat as Chelsea as far as he was concerned. I felt at least that I still had a paddle. I'm sure she had tossed hers overboard when she went off on Sofi. I couldn't imagine what Jason would do if he heard about her rant last night at practice. From personal experience I knew that as bad as Jon teased me, nobody else would have dared mess with me when he was around.

I had an early dismissal for a meet and had to talk to the teacher about an assignment after the announcement so I was late getting to the locker room. I flew in, changed into my uniform and started to run for the bus, not paying attention to anything or anyone.

"JETT!" I heard. And skidded to a stop and turned around to see Jason trailing behind me. Just then Coach came out of her office. She looked at Jason down the hall. Then back to me.

"Let's move it Joan, bus is leaving," she said as she walked towards me. I couldn't help notice the wink as she passed.

"Ah, well. Go. Good luck. Text me!" he said. *Are you kidding me?* I threw my hands up in the air and stared at him.

"All right. But text me back then, will you, *please*?" I said. He looked confused as I turned to ran out the door.

Jill and Erin were waiting for me on the bus.

"Where were you? Coach said you had some last minute business to take care of," Erin said. I looked at Jill and shook my head.

"Don't ask. I can't even begin to tell you," I answered.

"That pretty much explains it then. Guys," Jill said, grinning.

"What about guys?" Trent asked from the next seat.

"Nothing, Joan is just having guy problems," Jill said. I blushed;

I still hadn't told anyone about turning down Trent. I was pretty sure he hadn't either, especially since he was sitting with Rachel. But to my surprise he chimed into the conversation.

"Joan doesn't have problems with guys, she has problems with girls who like guys that like her. So her problem is with girls," he laughed, and winked at me. *Good grief!* What's with everyone acting like they are in on some joke? And how did I go from invisible to the center of attention in sixty seconds? Can't there be a happy medium?

After that everyone settled in for the ride and started thinking about their upcoming race. Jill whispered, "You want to tell me about it, quietly I mean?"

"After. Let me use it for the race," I whispered back.

"Deal. Nothing like using frustration for fuel," she answered as she put on her headphones and started her pre-race playlist.

I mentally tied myself to Jill and Erin and matched their killer pace. When I felt like letting up his face appeared, saying, "Text me!" like it was a new freaking concept. Huge hill, two times through the creek, shoving through the tight spots. I held on.

Even though Dad couldn't make it today his voice yelled splits in my head. Painful last hill, into the stadium and up to the finish. Personal best time. Tenth overall, number three for our team behind Jill and Erin. A good run. And I didn't puke in pubic. Who could ask for anything more? We broke camp and went to the bus.

"Spill it," Jill whispered.

"Okay, it's nothing. As I was going out the door Jason suddenly appears and yells for me to text him and let him know how it goes. That's what Coach meant; she came out of her office and heard him call down the hall to me. The thing is, he hasn't texted me or answered mine or called *in three weeks*. Not to mention he LIVES NEXT DOOR. How hard is it to stop by, well except he did, when I went out to get medicine for my cold, and he saw me knock over the trash can so he went to the store for me . . . ," I rambled.

"What? You lost me there," she interrupted.

"Suffice it to say, it's just weird about the phone stuff that's all."

"Are you sure your phone is working? Have you upgraded your system lately?" she asked. "Send me a text."

I did, and it went through fine. "It was worth a try. Now text him. See what happens."

(me)
Went well. Personal best time

Waiting. Waiting. Waiting. Nothing.

"You better talk to him tomorrow before you explode," Jill said.

"Aye aye Captain," I said as we settled down for the ride back.

In the morning I gave Dad a quick play by play of the race then left for school. I felt pretty good about the run. I felt pretty confused about the rest. Sam still picked up Jason early so they could lift before school. Either that or he had found an alternate ride. Hoping to catch him before class, I didn't see him. Now who was invisible? I gave up and went to my first period and was surprised to see Jason standing outside of my classroom.

"Hey Jett," he said, like it was the most ordinary thing.

"Hey, where did you come from?" *Seriously,* I asked.

"I came up from the weight room to catch you. Have to head over to the other side of school in a second," he said, then added, "I just wanted to see how your race went yesterday."

"Didn't you get my text?" I asked, trying not to burst.

"No. I thought you forgot," he said, kind of confused.

"Are you joking? Look, here, I'll show you," I said, then dove into my backpack for my cell and pulled it up on the screen.

He took his out and checked. Nothing.

"What's going on with our phones?" he asked, just as his sister

Sofi came around the corner. She looked back and forth between us and at our phones, didn't say a word, looked away and blew by.

I remembered what Jill and I heard as we walked by cheer practice last night and wondered if Jason knew about it. I didn't know for sure what had happened so I went fishing and said, "Sofi just walked by, and she looked stressed out."

"Cheer drama. She told me there was a misunderstanding but she had worked it out," he answered, still checking his phone. "Let me send you one and see if it goes through," he said, typing.

Nothing.

The bell rang.

"Oh, got to go, I'll *talk* to you later," he said as he took off down the hall. I *physically* went into my classroom and sat down in my normal seat. I *mentally* ran down the hall and tried to catch up with my abnormal friend. The rest of the day I had difficulty concentrating, walking, or talking, and especially running, but I didn't mind at all.

"Did you get a chance to talk to Jason?" Jill asked as we stretched out in the gym after our run.

"Kind of, he was in a hurry," I told her. "It turns out something is messed up between our phones. Can you believe it?"

"I guess, but I don't get it. Our texts went through okay. I wonder why your phones don't? Different providers maybe?" she asked.

"Well it explains some of the weirdness between us lately, but not everything. He said we'd talk later," I told her.

"Good. But try to get mad at him before our last meet on Friday. It worked well yesterday!" She laughed as she got up.

"No worries, I'm sure I'll manage to mess up by then." I drove home and took my time pulling into the garage, hoping to catch a glimpse. Nope. Dad came home and we ate. I did my homework. Got ready for bed. Nothing.

Stupid smart phone. I plugged it in to charge and went to bed.

❁

Thursday morning I hoped to talk to Jason before school. No such luck. He was late yesterday after our hallway chat so he probably didn't want a repeat performance. My visual drought continued through the day. After weeks in the desert of No Jason, the quick exchanges must have only been an oasis. And the glimmer of hope it rekindled must have been a mirage. *Drama.* Again.

Fortunately *(sarcasm)* I had Psych class today. Maybe I could do a little self-diagnosis. At least Chelsea had stopped harassing Trent. She must realize he was with Rachel now. Hopefully she was through with me too now that Homecoming was over. No such luck.

"Hmm *'gb,'*" Chelsea whispered to her cohort, loud enough for me to hear and added, "What does it stand for, I wonder?" It took me a second to tune into what she said. "Great bod?" she fished. "So good at being bad?" she added. "Getting bored?"

She never saw my phone. How did she know that's how I had identified him? Why had I added that in the first place? *It had come back to bite me.* The lioness still had teeth after all. Apparently I had left the desert and entered the savanna.

After class I escaped to the locker room, changed for practice and tried to figure it out. I don't check my phone during class so she couldn't have seen it over my shoulder. We had never hung out anywhere that she could have had access.

During school it was in the bottom of my backpack. *(Unlike almost any other high school girl, I no longer put it in my back jeans pocket. Bad experience with a toilet. Twice. Not good for phones. The "rice in baggie trick" had worked, even though I used brown rice, as it was the only kind we had on hand. My iPhone probably preferred it.)* I digress. Again.

During practice it was in my athletic team locker. Had I left it unlocked by mistake one day? How would she know it was mine?

What were the chances she could track it down on that specific day? Not likely. Then how did she know? Bam. I ran the locker room door into someone.

"Ouch!" I heard from my unsuspecting victim. I looked around the door and there *he* was.

"What's with you hanging outside locker room doors?" I said, a little louder and angrier than I had meant. Still reeling from Chelsea's assault.

"Sorry, I just wanted to catch you before practice," Jason said.

"Oh no, I'm sorry. I was just thinking about someone else and was worried about being late," I mumbled. *Awkward.* Stupid. "I mean I was thinking about something a girl said, and I need to get to practice because it's the last one before our final meet . . . ."

"Oh, okay," he said, trying to figure out my runaway train of thought. "I just wanted to tell you I lost my phone, not like it matters now that ours don't communicate. Which is dumb. They used to be fine, and now they aren't. You know what I mean? But you better get to practice. Have a good one," he said, and jumped on board his own out-of-control train, that carried him down the hall to the door on the tracks leading to the student parking lot.

I watched and tried to figure out what had just happened. Two words. Train wreck.

Practice consisted of a pre-race pep talk and an easy run. I was numb. When I drove home and into our driveway I couldn't help but look over to Jason's house. How did everything get so screwed up? Again?

Friday morning brought little relief and even less explanation. The cross country team was released early during lunch. As I was going through the cafeteria on the way to the locker room I heard "Joan, wait up." *Of course I did.* Jason continued, "Hey – good luck today."

"Thanks," I managed. Just then my phone swooshed a text alert from my backpack. I did not even attempt to check. Why would I?

He was right here in front of me.

"I wish I could make it to the meet! You came to my football games and now basketball has started so I have practice."

"It's okay. I don't think even your super motivational tunes can help today," I said, trying to lighten it up and keep us talking!

"What's wrong? You need to get up your last race!"

"I doubt that's going to happen, but thanks. I'll try. I've got to run, literally. We'll talk later?" I questioned. *Implored.*

"Yes." He smiled. Just then Jill and Erin walked up.

"Let's go Joan, show time!" Jill said as she walked by with wide eyes and arched eyebrows.

"On my way, behind you, my usual place and pace," I added.

"See you," Jason said. I think maybe, just maybe, he could.

"Okay. See you." I turned to follow Jill and Erin. Closer than I would during the race to be sure. I changed into my uniform and sweats and jumped on the bus. Jill and Erin had saved a seat.

"Spill it Jett," Jill said.

"Not much to spill, he wished me good luck today," I answered. Just then I'd remembered the text notification. I dug through my backpack for my phone and checked.

(jason gb)
Good luck today

"That's weird," I said, checking at the time of the text.

"What is?" Jill asked.

"I got this text while I was talking to Jason, but didn't check it until just now, and it's from him, and his phone is lost." I wondered.

"That is strange, but your phones have been out of whack right? He probably found it and forgot to mention it. And coverage is bad in the cafeteria hall. *The Dead Zone.* The message probably got delayed until you got outside," she said.

"Well at least they work again," I said, and wrote him back.

(me)
Thanks! You found your phone?!

Nothing.
Of course. Oh well. At least we are talking again!

✪

The race was a wet, messy, gray blur. The start went okay, and we took the first hill and looped around through the woods twice, but as we crossed the creek at the two-mile mark all the runners seem to converge at the narrow pass. The bottleneck created havoc. I tripped and went face first into the mud, rolled out of the way and pushed my way up to get back in the race.

Despite what had seemed like forever had only been a moment. Fortunately I hadn't lost too much distance. Focusing on my breathing and not the runners, I weaved my way through.

The leaders were going at a killer pace, but I gained on them. A final hill loomed ahead. Legs numb, I pushed through the exhaustion. The last straightaway took us into the stadium and the lead pack dug down deep for the final push. Crossing the finish line was a blur, and bile rose up my throat. Channeled into a single-file line to get our placement, I was twelfth. I staggered forward and found Jill and Erin, who had place 2nd and 4th, respectively. They were going to go to state. I was going to go throw up. Relieved. Happy? Tired. Satisfied? Strange. Especially when I was about to puke in public.

(sfb)
Jason here. How did it go?

(me)
Okay, took a dive into a creek
Why are you on Sam's phone?
Thought you found yours

(sfb-jason)
Nope. Still MIA
(that's missing in action)
You ok?

(me)
Lovely, covered in mud
Fortunately brown is
the new black

(sfb-jason)
Did you get hurt?

(me)
Just my pride

(sfb-jason)
I'll let you school me in lax
That will fix it

(me)
You'll LET me?

(sfb-jason)
Touched a nerve?
Meet me on the field tmo morn @9
before I leave for bball scrimmage
Bring your stick

(me)
Bring your stick. And balls,
if you have any

(sfb-jason)
lols
It's good to catch grief
from you again

(me)
We'll see what you can
catch tmo

(sfb-jason)
Deal

Well that was pretty crazy. And fun. It made me wonder though. If it were fun to catch grief from me again, why hadn't we been doing this all along? What had messed up our communications besides our phones? Was there someone else? Did it end with the mystery person he wanted to take to Homecoming? All I knew was it was good to hear from him again. I couldn't help but smile at the thought of throwing the lax ball around with him. *Tomorrow.*

I put up with Dad's teasing about being covered with mud. After a long shower I threw on sweats and returned to the kitchen to go through the race. He was sorry he had missed it, and pleased with my finishing so well my first year. Afterward a late dinner, I went to bed to tell the rest of the story to Misty.

I woke up in a good mood for a major change. Did some cleaning around the house to kill time; grabbed my lax stuff, threw it into the Jeep, and took off for school. Jason and Sam were already at the field throwing, so I parked next to Sam's car and watched them mess around on the field. They looked good.

Well, duh. But I mean, Jason was much more confident with the stick and ball. Using both hands. Shooting on Sam in goal. Wow. When did that happen? And why didn't I know about it? He turned, smiled and waved. *Wow.* After observing the return of the sonshine I shook my head and went out to get warmed up. As if?

It was just like last summer. Except now the student was torching the teacher. I could not keep up with his juking back and forth. I was in running shape, but not stick shape, and his skills had caught up and passed me.

"Where did that come from?" I asked after he first faked me out and shot upper left corner past Sam.

"Sam and I worked on moves after football practice during the season, and now we pass it around after lifting some mornings.

What do you think?" Jason asked.

How's that for a loaded question? What did I think of his new lax skills? His adorable smile? Why we hadn't talked for a month and now it's like nothing had happened? Before I could think of a witty comeback Sam bailed me out as he passed the ball to me and said, "Okay Jett, cross country is over, it's time for you to shake the dust off your stick and show me what you can do."

And so we played and laughed for an incredible hour. Just the guys and me. My guys. Too soon it was time for them to get ready to catch the player's bus. We walked up to the cars. Jason just chatted it up as always, even as he was rummaging through Sam's car to grab his gear.

"Sweet! Check it out!" he exclaimed and pulled something out from under the passenger seat. His phone. *His phone.* "Wow! I haven't seen this for three days! It must have slid out of my backpack."

It did not make sense. How did I get a message from him when his phone was under the car seat? "Interesting! Haven't heard from it for so long, I can't even remember your phone number, what was it again?" I wondered. *I wondered.* How can that be? "Here, write it on my palm pilot," I said, handing him a pen as I reached out my hand.

"Ha, funny, here you go. He took my hand in his *(!)* and wrote his number on it. Program it into your phone before you wash your hand and call me sometime!" He shut the door and turned around to look at me. "Okay?" he asked, the smile looking a little less confident.

"Ah, sure. And seriously Jason, you aren't a lax newb anymore. Looks like you'll be a three sports stud and will have to use your stick to push away your adoring fans," I said. It came out more serious than it had sounded in my head.

"Not likely, but thanks Coach, talk to you later?" he smiled, with a tilt of his head. *Definitely.*

Sam waved over his shoulder and the two of them walked towards the bus. I watched them go then slowly took out my phone. I went to my contacts list. Pulled up his contact info, *jason gb*, and looked at his number. Then at the one he'd written on my hand. *They didn't match.*

Who have I been texting and for how long? I sat there. Frozen. I don't know how long I zoned out, but when I thawed back out the bus had left. I pulled on my seat belt, started the car and backed up, physically and mentally.

Traveling over my phone history for the past month. Starting with Jason finding his phone today, Saturday, which had apparently been missing since Wednesday night. I know that because we had checked them that morning before school to see if our texts were going through. They were not.

Next I went over him texting me from Sam's phone after the meet on my way home on Friday night. I had assumed he'd found his so I asked why he was using Sam's. He said his was still MIA.

Before that we hadn't talked until he caught me leaving early to go to my meet on Friday afternoon. And I got a text from him, his phone? *That was under Sam's car seat?* While we were talking? I hadn't checked it right then. I wish now that I would have! I didn't see it until I was on the bus. Jill thought it was bad cell coverage. It was definitely bad, but with who?

I backed up next to Thursday's train wreck in the hallway, when I slammed into him again coming out of the locker room. I had been upset, so our conversation had been weird. Why was I mad again? Oh, that's right. *gb.* Chelsea had dumped on me in Psych. She had been wondering out loud what *gb* stood for. *How did she know that was his contact info?* How had Chelsea seen my phone? That was where I ended driving up to my house. Just as Sofi was waved to someone after getting dropped off. She went into their house next door.

A light switch flipped on in my head. *Sofi.* Next door. On the cheer squad. With *Chelsea*. Then I remembered the first time I talked to her. She'd come over to borrow *my phone*. And was nervous. She'd flipped her hair back over her shoulder like she was rehearsing something. Playing a part. *Like an understudy.*

I drove into my garage, turned off the car and pushed the remote to close the door. *Sitting in the dark suddenly it was very clear.* Using my phone flashlight I stowed my lax gear away. I went in my house and out the front door. To Jason's.

I pulled out my cell, made sure it was on silent, and turned off vibrate. Hitting phone contacts, I scrolled to *jason gb* and rang the doorbell. Then waited. Someone come down the hall. The door unlocked. I pressed call and put my hand in my pocket as the door opened.

Sofi answered. Her smile vanished. She frowned as her phone vibrated in her back pocket.

"Go ahead and get that. I don't mind. It may be important." I stared into her startled blue eyes. She still hadn't said anything to me, but she couldn't resist answering her phone. She pulled it out and looked at it. She saw the caller I.D. Then looked at me.

I pulled my phone out of my pocket and held it so she could read see it. And I could see her, seeing it.

"Busted," I said. It started to ring.

To my surprise her face went from panic to obstinate. "Well, what are you going to do about it?" Sofi challenged. That was it. No denial. Defiance was more like it. Ouch.

"Care to tell me why?" I managed to ask.

"I did it for him. To keep him away from you," she answered, bluntly. Again. Ouch.

"Why?" I asked, my turn to be surprised.

"After we moved here it was 'Joan this' or 'Joan that' all day, every day. Then when we started school people warned me about you and your creepy past. So I did it to protect him." Ouch. Again.

Just then I heard the voicemail answer on my phone. Still

looking at her I lifted it up and said, "Hey Jason, Joan here, Sofi's got something to tell you. Or I will." I hit *End*, turned and walked away. Stunned.

Back in my house I went straight to my room. And Misty. I sat down on my bed and pulled her up to my chest, hugging her tight. She softly meowed, and then started to purr. I buried my face in her fur. And then cried. And remembered.

"Not everyone is going to like you Joan," she said, tucking the renegade copper curl behind my ear for the zillionth time. "That's just the way it is. And very few will try to understand you. People can get caught up in their own world and not want to expand into yours." We sat on a bench in the park. I was in junior high and trying to navigate the new social scene. She told me about when she and my dad got married and both started teaching at the university. They were at a faculty dinner, and a woman got mad at her husband and my parents because they had been talking too much about work and she felt left out.

"She didn't have anything to contribute to the conversation. She also did not appreciate that I did and that both your dad and her husband were obviously amused. I apologized for talking shop and tried to engage her in the conversation, but she was bound and determined to be miserable and not like me. I was upset. Some women are intimidated if you get along with men. I think that may have made it worse for her.

"Your dad and I share the same warped sense of humor, and I encourage you and Jon to make sure to have that in common with your future partners. It makes life together so much more fun. I talked about it with your dad on the way home. After we had discussed it we came to the shocking conclusion that not everyone was going to like us, no matter how hard we tried. The best we could do was to treat people with respect and only use our warped sarcasm with each other and for the greater good, like nurturing it into our children.

"You need to be careful with it though, and not hurt people's feelings who aren't used to it or don't understand it. Does that make sense? What I'm trying to say is you can't make people like you. So you need to like yourself. You will find others who want to get to know you, and eventually I am sure they will like you too."

I had dozed off. I opened my eyes and looked around. Misty stretched next to me and nudged me with her nose to get scratched under her chin. The garage door open. Dad was home from his Saturday morning workout. I picked up Misty and took her down the hall to feed her and find something for Dad and me.

"Good morning Sunshine! Did you just get out of bed?"

"No, I went to throw with Jason and Sam believe it or not, then came home and fell asleep again with Misty," I answered.

"Really. That sounds interesting. How did that come about?"

"Oh I just laid down and the next thing I knew I woke up," I said, sarcastically.

"Funny, I mean with Jason. Thought you weren't *together*?"

"We are not *together*, but Jason texted me on my way home from the meet last night. Apparently he and Sam have been practicing lacrosse after football practice all season. He smack talked me so I wanted to see if he *could walk the walk*. Or more appropriately, catch the throw, throw the pass and shoot the shot. And wouldn't you know, Jason has improved. I think he'll be ready to start in the spring on the high school team," I answered.

"That's awesome, I'm sure Jon will be thrilled to hear about his protégé."

"Yeah, even Jon will be impressed, unless Jason torches his records for assists and goals," I added.

"That good, eh? Or are you just a little biased perhaps?"

"You can see for yourself if you go to some games," I deflected. Throwing up the shields in anticipation.

"I will at that, and you can sit right next to your dear old dad. I promise to do my best to embarrass you."

"No doubt," I laughed. "Not to change the subject, but should we plan our colleges road trip or are we just going to wing it?"

"Okay, we'll put Jason on the back burner until you are trapped in the car. This is the itinerary I have set up. We pack up and take off tomorrow morning around nine. A full day's drive will get us into Boulder. We'll check into our rental cottage at Chautauqua and then go grab some dinner on Pearl Street. You need to register for your Buffalo Visitation Day at eight the next morning, and you are on your own until I meet you for lunch at the Union.

"We'll take an abbreviated tour of residence halls, rec center, stadium, and then hike up the trails behind our rental. Tuesday morning we get up, check out and grab breakfast then head into the mountains and out to Aspen. We'll continue around through Independence Pass and head south to Twin Lakes. Then down the Arkansas River to Highway 24 and head east to Colorado Springs.

"We'll stay overnight in Colorado Springs, and get up and go to Garden of the Gods for a hike. And then east to the University of Illinois to spend Thanksgiving with Jon. We are staying in Champaign to hang out with him since he only has off through the weekend. We'll find someplace nice for a Thanksgiving dinner and then tour around campus.

"Friday he has another tourney, and then on Saturday, November 30, we will have a special eighteenth birthday dinner celebration for you, and then head back home Sunday morning. How does that sound?" he asked.

"Sounds like you have it all set," I said.

"Well, some of it I remember from a family trip we all went on when you were little, but you probably don't remember. I don't think Jon does either," he said, and then zoned out. Thinking back, no doubt. I was thinking too, but not about Colorado, because he was right; I had no memories of my own there. Or about the University of Illinois campus either. Despite Jon's being there for almost four years, I never wanted to stick around and investigate it for my own sake. There were always too many stories about Mom, and I felt her ghost everywhere on campus.

It has always been too raw, and the wound too deep and not healing. Hopefully things would be different now. I don't know why, but I felt it was time to confront my loss and fears. I hoped it was time at least. We would see.

I went for a run before dinner. It was the first chance since my surprise confrontation with Sofi that I could focus, dwell and analyze it. I also knew I owed Gracie an apology. She definitely was not Jason's "Most Annoying Sister." What had Sofi heard? I had a pretty good idea about who she heard it from, but I doubt Chelsea knew I existed before that fateful first day of school this year when I walked in with Jason. What was my "creepy history?" Not that I thought for a minute Chelsea was above creating a history story based loosely on anything resembling the truth.

Jason had said he would be home late so I assumed I wouldn't see him until after break. I forgot to tell him we were leaving. I had been so thrilled to be talking again that it slipped my mind. And even though I had his real number, I didn't want to use it until I was sure Sofi had confessed.

That brought back the ugly scenario that had played out with her this morning. My "fight or flight" or in my case "flight very fast" response had kicked in. At least it hadn't triggered a migraine. Come to think of it, I hadn't had a migraine since the day I had met Jason five months ago! That was weird.

My cycle used to trigger them, so I thought they were hormone-related. Since I had been running so much, I was skipping my period some months. Maybe the increase in consistent running had helped prevent migraines too. Wouldn't that be sweet?

Now all I had to do was to run twenty miles a week until menopause. So eighty miles a month times twelve months times forty-some years. Awesome. On the other hand, stress or panic attacks relating to flashbacks about Mom had also caused them.

But even becoming visible again at school, thanks to Jason, and being harassed by Chelsea, *(and now apparently her sidekick Sofi, wait a minute, do bad guys have sidekicks or are they just considered henchmen?)* also thanks to Jason, had triggered my flight response, but not a migraine. Interesting. And I have had a few flashbacks about Mom that have not shattered me lately. Was I, maybe, getting better? Accepting her . . . death? Inhale. Sharp. Stabbing. Pain. In my heart. Close eyes. Exhale. Slowly. Maybe not. Entirely. Yet.

❂

Sunday morning Dad had me pull his car out on the driveway so we could pack it up to take off. As I loaded up the trunk I heard the neighbor's door open.

"You guys heading out for break?" Jason asked.

"Yep, doing the 'ole college visit thing," I answered, shutting the hatchback.

"Really, are you still thinking humidity and mosquito-free Colorado? He asked. *And remembered.*

"Yep again. Heading west to visit CU, do a little nostalgia tour, and then heading east to U of I to spend Thanksgiving with Jon."

"Sounds fun. Say hi. I hoped he'd be back over break to give me some pointers."

"I'll let him know, but I think you are good to go after yesterday. You put me to shame," I said.

"Not hardly. You'll be smoking me again in no time. What are you doing with Misty? Do you need me to take care of her?" he offered. *Seriously.* Dude.

"No thanks, she's going with us. She would never let me hear the end of it. It will be bad enough when I go away to school. Next fall. I am putting off thinking about it."

"Well okay. Have fun. I'll see you in a week or so," Jason said with a little smile. Just as I returned it with one of my own, I saw something move in a top floor window of his house. I was pretty sure who was spying on us.

"Sounds good. Have a great time with your family." *Especially Sofi.*

"Will do. You too," he said as he walked back to his house. I went in to find Misty and convince her that she wanted to get into her prison, I mean carrier. Which made me think about Sofi. I wondered when she planned to tell him. After all, she said that she did it to protect him. From me. Thanksgiving might be a little tense this year at the Halsted residence.

❀

We were good together on the road. Music on, mostly classic rock. Misty freed from her carrier, purred on my lap. We would stop every couple of hours to stretch our legs. And then hit the road again. Looking out the window as the flat Midwest gradually changed to foothills and eventually, the Rocky Mountains. A giant walled fortress-standing guard to the West.

As we neared Boulder I looked up at the awesome Flatirons. Giant, red, jagged slabs of stone slanting up to touch the dark blue sky. Reaching for heaven. We took Baseline up the entrance to Chautauqua, got the keys to our rental cottage, deposited Misty with her food and travel litter box, and headed down to Pearl Street at sunset. Pink to orange clouds converged in the darkening sky over the mountains.

As the stars came out above, twilight gave way to the twinkle of thousands of lights up and down the walkway. Every imaginable type of food was available. It was tough to decide what to try! And the shops. An artistic energy empowered the city. If art is life, then this was the cradle of creativity. I felt at peace. And I loved it.

The next morning I woke up and looked straight up the Flatirons from my bedroom window in the little cottage. "I could get used to this," I said to Misty. She meowed and went back to sleep. I seriously doubt I would get a view like this from a dorm, but one could hope. By the time I got up and dressed, Dad had made breakfast. I gulped it down and we left to go check in for my campus visitation day.

He left me at the registration table and went to explore. I walked into the auditorium and sat down for a welcome speech and fun video showing why one should pick CU Boulder. Worked for me! After that, we were introduced to a panel of super stoked students and then went to some sample lectures by way-too-cool professors. Everyone seemed thrilled to be there. Walking around the campus I could see, hear, smell, and taste why. It just felt right.

❂

Dad checked us out of our cottage; I collected Misty and our stuff. We headed up through the mountains to Aspen. The golden leaves had fallen in the wind, leaving beautiful eyes of black peering out from the stark, slender white tree trunks. The designer shops had all sorts of expensive cars lined up in front of them. To my surprise, I saw a gorgeous horse tethered to a parking meter in a parking space next to a sports car! The horse's tack probably cost as much as my dad's Subaru. We left town and wound around the mountain filled with tall aspens that reached up to capture a glimpse of sunlight. We continued our ascent up to Independence Pass which appeared to be the top of the world. Coming down the other side was probably the scariest thing I have ever experienced. Up in the sky, above the tree line, without any guardrails. Oh my goodness.

Why didn't they have the guardrails to stop us from falling into the abyss? Maybe, just maybe, it was meant as a warning. And a lesson. About life. *It's not always going to be safe.* Or protected.

Driving along on the edge. It seemed like we could be blown off to oblivion by a strong blast of wind. I did not breathe normally until we were safely down to the town of Twin Lakes.

We continued south following the Arkansas River on the beautiful Colorado day. Stopping once, pulling over to walk to the river for a rock-skipping contest. We sat down next to the gentle rapids and Dad commented on how the water washing over the rocks reminded him of Mom's waterfall back home. He was quiet then for a while. So was I.

"Well kiddo, what did you think of CU?"

I thought a bit and responded, "I love the campus, and the town is ridiculously cool."

"Yeah, your mom loved it here too. I wish we could have made it out again."

I tried to fill in the silence. "I know. She got me into the photography she loved. I can see why it meant so much to her. Clean, fresh, nature at its best. Inhaling is a joy. I can almost taste the sky."

"You are strange," he said, then continued as he glanced over at me, "I love that about you."

"Takes one to know one," I responded. And with that we got up and went back to the car. The fact that my heart didn't feel like it was being stabbed wasn't lost on me. Crazy. Hopefully Dad was okay too. Maybe. Just maybe. We could do this. Move on I mean. No doubt he hoped the trip would help to heal us. At least a little.

We hit Highway 24 and took it east through Woodland Park, past the Dinosaur Resource Center and weaved down into Colorado Springs. We saw some signs for the Cheyenne Mountain Zoo and Dad started laughing. He told me about the trip we made when we were little. Apparently Jon was not as enamored with the western landscape as Mom was. They had gone down to the Grand Canyon first. We were on the north side, without handrails, and Mom made Dad promise not to let go of Jon's hand and stayed in the car with me until they returned. Then she left for her turn after we were all safely locked in the car. Dad said she took her camera and went off to "capture incredible." From there we eventually drove north into Colorado.

Dad seemed to be lost in time. Although he looked out at the highway, I think he was mentally traveling down a different road. He went on to tell me Mom couldn't wait to see the Rocky Mountains. When she finally did she had *oohed* and *ahhed*, mesmerized. Dad said she kept pointing them out to Jon until finally he said, "I don't see what the big deal is with mountains. They don't do anything. They just sit there!"

So when she asked if he wanted to see the Cheyenne Mountain Zoo, he only heard *mountain* and not *zoo* so he asked why he would want to go see yet another mountain. She told him that it had the largest herd of giraffes. "Giraffes? In Colorado? Roaming wild in the mountains?" And Dad laughed and teased him about the giant herd of giraffes wreaking havoc on the Front Range. I remember seeing pictures of Jon feeding the giraffes over the railing on the elevated walkway.

There were some of Mom too. Smiling. Laughing. As a giraffe tried to pull her ball cap off of her ginger ponytail. Dad still had those pictures next to his computer in his office. There was a picture of me too. I had a giraffe ball cap on top of a head of shiny orange poodle curls. I was grinning from ear to ear, thrilled with life as I knew it. At that moment in time.

Back to the present. We headed north on I-25 and exited to drive through the Garden of the Gods Park. A "must see" for sure. Giant red rocks again, like the Flatirons in Boulder, but this time ridges of them, forcing their way up. *Challenging gravity.* They seemed more successful at that endeavor than I was. We drove into the park and wove around, taking in the splendor from different angles. Kissing Camels. Balanced Rock. We parked and hiked in, away from the tourists, all waiting for their turn at pretending to hold up the rock as they had their picture taken. We worked our way back and sat on a giant flat rock looking out over and up to Pikes Peak.

It was frosted with snow. I'd read it had snow on top ten months of the year. What was amazing was with the incredible warmth of the sunshine *(300 days a year)*. Although it was only sixteen degrees it felt like forty. I leaned back and closed my eyes. I inhaled, filling my lungs with the crisp, delicious air. Yep. I could get used to this. Although I had applied to Stanford as my "reach school" I think I'd found what I was reaching for: Colorado. Memories of Mom visiting, but not living here. And not dying here. It appeared I was ready to move on from nowhere, and I think I had found my somewhere.

We hit the road again heading north on I-25, passed the Air Force Academy and on toward Denver. I waved so long farewell *(for now)* to the Rocky Mountains as we turned east back to poison ivy, mosquitoes, humidity, wet cold and hot Jason. Weird. I had been so caught up in the trip he almost slipped my mind. *Almost.*

14

"You Give Love A Bad Name"

Thanksgiving Day, we rolled into the University of Illinois around lunchtime. We dropped Misty off at Jon's rental house. He lived with three other pigs, I mean guys, so I left her in her carrier after she used her travel litter box *(no doubt confusing in this rat hole apartment with litter everywhere)* and we went in search of turkey, mashed potatoes, gravy, green bean casserole, cranberry sauce, crescent rolls and blueberry pie. After sufficiently stuffing ourselves, we grabbed Starbucks and did our own campus tour Bennett-style. This was the part I had dreaded. Up until now it had been Jon's school, so we had dropped, dined and dashed at the beginning of the semester or packed up, picked up and got the heck out of Dodge at year's end. This time I had to look around, absorb the atmosphere and see if I felt at home here like Jon. Dad. And Mom.

Her ghost was everywhere, never a wallflower, she bloomed and thrived wherever she was planted. She had run track and been a cheerleader in high school so when she came here she tried out and made the cheerleading squad the spring of her freshman year. She was relieved because she had told herself if she didn't, she would have to try out for the track team, and knew that track practices would be a lot of work and nowhere near as fun as cheering!

She was asked to join different sororities, but declined, lived in the dorms for two years and then in a rental house with a variety of girls. Dad took me by her dorm, Van Doren, and showed me her window on the ground floor. He had been placed in Taft, the dorm that was connected to her dorm by a lounge in between. The first time he saw her he was tossing a football with a buddy. She came around the corner into the sun – her hair on fire – and almost blinded him. He missed the ball. She bent down and picked it up; rotated it to place her fingers on the laces and threw him a perfect spiral. Which he caught. And held tight.

He said he had jogged over and asked if she wanted to play but she was on her way to a lab. However, she told him to organize a game, and she would play after the football game on Saturday. So he, of course, worked hard on getting it together the next morning and then went off to the game.

He said he was sitting in Block I, the super fan section, and looked down and there she was. Flying through the air with a flash of golden orange fire. A cheerleader. He waited around until after the game and caught up to her as she left the stadium and walked her back to her dorm.

She went in to change and was out in five minutes. Hair pulled back in a ponytail so she could see to catch the ball. Ready to play. How can you not fall in love with that? Dad was smiling. Jon too. He had heard the stories before, and would jump in with "remember whens?" and Dad would nod and launch into the different good times of the past. I watched them together, reminiscing. Wonderful, warm memories. Not painful cold nightmares filled with . . . with . . . what?

"Look the gate is open, let's go in!" Dad said. We had walked over to the stadium. We went in, hit the track and started walking around. "This is where I ran, Joan. I walked on freshman year and made the team. It was the big leagues. I did the steeplechase, which is one of the most miserable methods of torture ever invented. Running, jumping over a barrier and landing in a slippery water pit on an incline that you had to run up back onto the track. Can't say I enjoyed the event, but I loved running here." His run down Memory Lane intersected my coming up Melancholy Drive.

"Well Dad, I'll be leaving all of the collegiate glory days for you. Don't even think you are going to talk me into going out for track or cross country in college," I answered.

"No need to, there are so many different intramural teams and games that even an inept slacker like you can do," Jon chimed in.

"Thanks for your support bro. Takes one to know one."

"Ahhhh, feel the love. Let's head back and take a look at the State Farm Center, back in my day it was called the Assembly Hall, and then the Recreation Center," Dad said.

"I thought Jon was going to show us his honorary desk at the library, and then take us to the orphanage where he volunteers every Friday night," I teased.

"Maybe tomorrow, after our Alumni Lacrosse Turkey Tournament," Jon laughed.

We left the stadium and got back in the car. After a drive around the athletic facilities on the south side of campus, Dad drove us down Third Street and then turned on Daniels to go toward The Quad at the center of campus. We drove by a bar named Kams and Dad pointed to it and said, "The cheerleading squad had to earn gas money for the away games by bartending there on Tuesday nights. A brilliant marketing strategy thought up by the manager. Your mom was surprised people would go out during the week, but I assured her they did their homework before they would go. It was a Greek bar then, meaning most the fraternity and sorority kids hung out there. Like your mother, I didn't go Greek either, but you can bet that I would go with my roommates to keep an eye on her! The guys she cheered with were good about it too. Not that it made me feel any better. But after all, five of them came to our wedding, with two of the girls."

❉

We parked the car to walk across Wright Street to cut through to the Quad. Grass surrounded by red brick buildings with sidewalks cutting across it. Jon said this is where a lot of kids ate lunch on nice days. Students would throw Frisbees and lounge around before heading back to class. Every once in awhile, someone would bring a dog, which got a lot of attention. He said it was weird to see a little kid or an elderly person since it was its own city of people with ages ranging from eighteen to fifty, the latter being the professors.

I looked around, imagining what the now bare trees would look like in the fall adorned with the glorious oranges and reds. It was nice, what I expected Ivy League schools looked like, with ivy hugging the buildings, and tall, aged trees. I could almost see her there. Coming out from one of the surrounding buildings as the bell rang. Laughing. Talking with friends. She would have fit in here. I pictured her showing me all of these sites. Excited to share them with me.

But that was not the case. The feeling of loss was still there, hiding in the shadows, following me as I searched for her ghost. Desperate to – yet afraid of – finding it. I shook my head to leave my daydream, or "dayscare." *Maybe that's what you should call a nightmare that you have when you are awake?* Why was it so different for Jon than it was for me? He embraced her memory here, felt closer to her, whereas I pulled away. Not wanting to remember. Not wanting to feel the pain of loss her absence amplified, here where she had walked, laughed and loved. Why? Once again I was brought back to reality.

"You guys had enough?" Dad asked. I looked over to see both of them looking concerned.

"Oh sure, I'm good. It's nice," I said, forcing a smile.

"How about we get you checked into your hotel, and then go for a run?" Jon offered.

"Sounds good, but let's swing by and grab Misty. I don't want to leave her in your filth," I said, with less conviction than usual.

"Ha, she will be crying to stay with me," he countered, still accessing my mood.

"Keep dreaming. The only reason she would stay at your place would be to catch all the mice that probably breed in your walls. Watching you through the vents as you sleep. Waiting to launch an attack," I added.

"We'll see about that," Jon said, looking less worried.

We drove to Jon's place. After we had collected Misty, we went and got her settled in our hotel. Then Jon and I took off for a run. I needed to. Being surrounded by Mom's history was opening doors I forgot existed. I needed to run away. Dad stayed behind and went to use the elliptical in the hotel gym. He said his knee had been talking to him. I also think he needed to process his memories of Mom after reliving their college days. And I think he wanted me to have some time to decompress with my brother.

Jon took me on a lovely route out to south campus. We ran past a grove of aspen that reminded me of the tree trunks with the quiet, dark eyes that stared out at me in Aspen, Colorado. Come to think of it, I'd seen a picture of these trees, with Mom's college memorabilia. We continued on through the agriculture area and looped back in toward campus. When we got a couple of blocks from the hotel he slowed to a walk for a cool down.

"Well, your lax skills may be rusty, but you have become quite the runner. I think the cross country team was good for you, in a lot of ways," Jon said.

"Such as?" I asked.

"You seem happier, no, actually, happy. More confident. More content, except when you space out like you did at the Quad. What was that about . . . Mom?" he wondered, sounding serious again.

"I guess." I thought for a few moments. He let me. Gave me time. He was good at that. Patient. Like Dad. Giving me space. "You embrace her memories. I reject them." I sighed.

"Why is that, do you think?" he asked.

What could I say? How could I answer that? The question I'd been asking myself for three and a half years? And then I receded into my head. Thinking. Searching. Sifting back through the stories I had heard.

She was diagnosed at thirty-one. Dad had been in his early thirties. Jon had just turned four years old. She had told me she had tried to plan it so he would be born on Valentine's Day. Her funny Valentine she called him, because he was strong-willed from the get go and wouldn't leave her safe, warm, expanding, exploding abdomen. He ended up being eleven days late to throw off her plan. Just as well, she had said; he would have been mad if he had to deal with all of the valentine birthday card combos.

And then there was me. I had just begun. Conceived at the same time as her cancer. My evil twin. Or. Or. What? *Was it me?* Was I the cancer? *That ultimately killed her?* And survived, but refused to thrive? *Because of the guilt?* My guilt? Is that why I went into hiding? And disguised *(and despised)* myself for it? I had hoped it would help for me to change my hair color so I wouldn't be a constant visual reminder of her natural glow. For Dad, Jon and myself. But in reality, I had just managed to dye out her last spark.

Busted.

"Earth to Joan," I heard Jon say.

"What?" I said, blinking back tears.

"Hey, what's up? Head hurt? Take a deep breath," Jon said, as he steered me through the lobby to our room. *Just like old times.*

"N – no," I stammered as my dad came out of the bathroom into our suite, where Jon had sat me down on the couch.

"I'm going to find oranges for Joan," he told Dad. And hurried out the door. Leaving me with Dad. Who sat down and put his arm around me. Waiting. I exhaled. Inhaled. Exhaled, slowly. Calming myself. Reviewing my revelation in my head. Then spoke.

"I'm sorry," I whispered.

"For what?" Dad whispered back.

"For Mom," I choked out.

"What do you mean, for Mom?" he softly asked.

"For ... killing ... her," I murmured, trance-like.

He didn't even wait a second as he pulled me into a hug, which pulled me out of myself. "Don't ever, for a moment, think you had anything to do with Mom's death," he softly cried.

"But if it weren't for me, she could have been treated sooner. And beat it. Instead, she wasted time growing me as it grew. And she lost. And you lost. Jon too," I whispered.

"Joan you can't look at it that way, and I'm kicking myself that I've let you blame yourself. I'm the one who should apologize," Dad said as he choked back tears. "I should have explained it to you more as you got older. I am so sorry," he took a breath.

"When we found out she was pregnant with you we were thrilled. She'd had a couple of miscarriages after Jon and was very cautious to take care of herself so she could take care of you. She was so young she hadn't started mammograms yet. She found a lump, but it was a cyst, it turned out that the cancer was hidden behind it under her arm in the lymph nodes.

"She refused all anesthesia except for a topical one when they did a needle biopsy so you wouldn't be affected. The tumor had been growing a couple years undetected. It was an aggressive type, and was multiplying rapidly, but she refused to have surgery until you were completely developed and safely born.

"She wanted you so much Joan. Don't ever think for a moment that she hesitated about the course of treatment she chose. WE chose," he took a breath. Exhaled. "Life is a series of choices. She tried to teach you that and so have I. When faced with a dilemma, you need to think about it, analyze it, and act on it. We made a conscious decision. To not have surgery until you were safely out, and then hit it hard with everything we could. And we did. It was just not enough," he sighed, and was quiet for a while.

"Conversely, you can also put off doing something like I regretfully have done. I should have discussed it with you more often. Asked if you understood. Made sure you understood. Procrastinating and not doing anything can be a choice in itself. To do nothing," he added. He was crushed.

"Dad. Don't blame yourself. You have been amazing. Supportive. Unconditionally. I have never doubted your love for me. Honestly, I've only questioned it. I've never felt worthy of her sacrifice. How could I? Mom was so incredible. How can I ever live up to that?" I asked.

"That's another thing Joan. I'm afraid I have made a martyr out of her. Believe me, she was human like the rest of us. She made mistakes. But you were not one of them. She would over think everything and dwell on scenarios until she drove me crazy. And if she made a mistake she would go to any extreme to rectify it.

"If she accidentally hurt someone's feelings with her wacky sense of humor she would do back flips to try to patch things up. She had a strong sense of right and wrong, and would not put up with anyone making fun of someone who could not defend him or her self. She loved and lived the meaning behind the song 'Point Of Light.'"

Slam. There it was. The elusive, nagging point I'd missed. Lost. Denied. When I had first dyed my hair black. The promise I had made her, but in my descent into darkness had dismissed. I was supposed to be enlightened, to be a point of light, not hide in the dark, not wallow in the dark void of my loss.

My mom had lived her life that way, and had raised me to do the same. I thought back on times when I had done nothing. Like at the Homecoming game, when Jason held out the ball to me and I froze and didn't honk the horn or flash the lights. When I got mad at him for not returning my texts instead of asking about it. Why hadn't I just texted Sam's phone instead of pouting? And when Chelsea teased Trent and he took it, why didn't I tell her to leave him out of it? And that was only in the last month or so. What about the last three years? What else had I failed to do?

Jon knocked on the door and Dad let him in. He had a platter of oranges quartered and brought it over to hand to me. "Hopefully this will help ward off a migraine," he said in a concerned voice.

"Thanks. But it's not a migraine," I said to assure him.

"Oh, good. Oops. I pretty much cleaned out the stock of oranges in the hotel kitchen," he said sounding relieved.

"Well then you have to help me eat them," I replied.

"That's not much of a dinner," Dad said.

"Right. I better go get cleaned up," said Jon.

"Okay, we'll pick you up in an hour. Joan, it's your turn to jump in the shower. I'm going to check out dinner options at the front desk. It's going to be tough to find something open for a late supper on Thanksgiving," Dad added as he opened the door and left with Jon. I stood up and went to get my stuff out of my suitcase before going into the bathroom. It didn't take much of a genius to figure out Dad was going to fill Jon in on my meltdown. They were so close. It gave me some time to dwell, just like my mom used to do.

After the shower I stepped out into the steamy bathroom. The mirror was completely fogged over. I dried off and wrapped a towel around me. Then I took another towel, wrapped my head in a turban and looked at my foggy shape in the mirror. I leaned forward and wiped off two ovals about an inch apart. I looked into the green eyes looking back at me. "Hello Mom," I said, softly, to myself, and to her ghost. No longer dreading it. I stood there as the fan cleared the steam and watched her fade away. I felt the usual sense of loss, but not the stab of pain. At last. It was time to leave the dark side and once again enter the blazing world of light and color.

We grabbed a late dinner and then called it a night. Jon had to be at the field early, and we were worn out from our campus tours, physically and emotionally. The next morning we ate a quick breakfast and stopped at Starbucks on Green Street on the way to the tournament. All the while Dad was whining about how much the campus had changed, he missed his old hangouts. I vowed that I would try to embrace change from now on. Look back fondly but not regretfully. Time would tell.

After Jon finished playing on Friday, we all got cleaned up and had an early dinner. We hung out after playing cards and watching corny holiday movies and called it a night as the tournament continued tomorrow.

Saturday, November 30. My eighteenth birthday. I woke up and decided to go on a solo run through campus since Jon had the tourney to play today and Dad's knees were still bothering him. I put the earbud in one ear so I could still hear sounds around me, loaded up my running playlist and hit the path that went from our hotel to campus. It was a partly cloudy day. Which fit my mindset as I thought back over the last couple of days.

It was weird; I hadn't thought about Jason much over the past week. And by much I meant constantly, without ceasing. I had gotten used to not hearing from him because of the whole Sofi thing. I wondered if she had told him yet? I doubted it. I think he would have texted me after he changed his hijacked phone back. At least we were talking again, which begged the obvious revelation that if we had just tried to call each other instead of texting we might have figured it out a little sooner.

Technology hadn't done us any favors in that department. The jacked phone thing made sense out of the text communication breakdown, but the other question, the identity of the person that

Jason had wanted to take to the Homecoming dance, came back and slammed into my running inner conversation. I had been so caught up in the Sofi dilemma I had forgotten about that.

And why was Chelsea so bent on my character destruction if he were interested in someone else? She must not have known about her. Maybe she went to a different school?

But that didn't make sense because Sofi would have figured it out and, therefore, not bothered messing with our phones. Our phones. *His and my phones.* Lightening bolt. I skidded to a stop. Stared straight down the path without focusing on anything in front of me. *Duh.* Could I be that dense? Clueless? Insecure? Stupid? Apparently. Maybe?

"You need to pick the restaurant. I'm going back to my place and shower," Jon said after playing in the championship game. I decided on deep-dish stuffed pizza for dinner, so Jon took us to a place known for its "Chicago-style" specials. After we finished eating, the waitstaff brought me a cake with eighteen candles ablaze. To draw even more unwelcome attention, they sang "Happy Birthday" to me and encouraged all the other diners to join in. Looking over at Jon and Dad laughing while they sang, I couldn't be too mad at them. Incredibly embarrassed? Yes. Contemplating revenge? Certainly. Wishing I were anywhere else? Not at all. It was so fun to see them happy.

After all of the congratulations and salutations we were left alone and they gave me my birthday gifts to open. A matching citrine necklace and earrings. My birthstone. The fiery gemstone was thought to provide hope, energy and warmth. Holding them up to the lamp over our table made them look like they were flames captured in glass. Tiny phoenix. Reborn. Maybe it was the start of my new beginning too.

15

"Point Of Light"

Once again it was a quiet but comfortable ride home. Dad and I were both in reflective moods. I was trying to figure out my latest revelation about whether or not I may or may not be the person Jason had wanted to take to Homecoming. Could it be any more confusing? After we had returned home, I had to run out to pick up some groceries from the store. Leaving the store, I saw a group of guys huddled up in a corner on the side of the building.

I wouldn't have thought anything of it until I saw a flash of blonde hair in the middle behind the biggest guy. I read his last name on the back of his letter jacket. His first name was Hank, and he played on the football team. We had gone to elementary school together.

He was talking to a girl, blocking her exit, backing her up to a wall. I looked around. Nobody else was there. Just me. Her. And three guys. *Fight or flight?* Analyze and act? Do nothing and turn away? Before my brain figured it out, my feet had decided. I took a breath and let it out slowly as I walked toward them instead of away.

As I got closer I could hear it sounded more like bragging and teasing, not flat out harassment, but I didn't like the thought of where it might go. As he turned to look at one of his buddies, I saw the smug look on his face. And I saw her. *Sofi.* I also recognized the defiant gaze I had not so delightfully discovered at her doorstep, but there was also concern as she quickly glanced around, looking for an escape route.

"Hey Hank!" I said louder than planned.

He turned to look at me and squinted, trying to figure out who I was and why I was butting in on his game. I could see the same question in her eyes as they grew wide. I stopped about ten feet away and said, "Why don't you come over here and talk with me for a minute?" in a surprisingly calm, somewhat flirty voice. *(Where did that come from?)*

He looked at the guys, and back at Sofi and then smiled. "I'll be right back, looks like someone else wants my attention." And then he sauntered over to me with what I assume he considered swagger. I leaned back into a doorway, so his back was to them while he faced me.

"What can I do for you?" he asked in a cocky, clumsy way as he put his hand on the wall over my shoulder and leaned in close and winked at me with a dark brown eye and a silly smirk.

"How about a walk down Memory Lane?" I said, staring him in the eyes. He smiled even bigger, turned around and gave a thumbs-up to his buddies, then looked back at me.

"Well sure honey, anywhere you want, but do I know you?" he said, trying to be suave.

"You probably don't remember me, but do you remember back in third grade? A little boy getting picked on by some older guys after school in an empty hallway? One was holding his arms behind him, and the other two were tickling him, saying how cute he sounded when he giggled like a little girl. He pleaded with them to stop but it was too late. They exploded in laughter and then left him there," I said quietly.

Hank's eyes opened wide. I let it sink in, and then continued. "He was crying so hard that he ran into the girls' restroom by mistake. Obviously soaked, he'd wet himself. To make it worse, if that were possible, when he wiped his eyes he saw a little girl standing in front of him. He looked at her, mortified, trembling. She looked back at his face, not down. Silent. Then quietly said, "Go into the first stall and lock it. I will run to the office and get you a change of clothes; they have them, for times like this, I'll be back, don't worry; I'll be back in less than five minutes. You can count. Count to sixty, five times, and I'll be back before you finish. I promise. And I won't tell anyone in the office. I promise. You understand?" he nodded.

"And with that she disappeared and ran, and returned, in less than five minutes, with a clean pair of underpants and sweatpants in a plastic bag. She handed them under the door and said, "You can put your old things in the bag to take home. I'll be in the hall." He came out from the restroom a minute later without the bag. She asked if he needed a ride home. He shook his head side to side and told her he lived close to school. She said she'd go out to the curb first; her mom was picking her up, but he should stay inside until she made sure the bullies she had heard in the hall had left.

"He nodded. She went outside and looked all around. Seeing no one lurking around, she turned back and gave him a thumbs-up. He stepped outside. Looked into her eyes one last time then dropped his gaze and ran ... and that was the last time you actually looked at me," I said. His eyes popped even wider as he figured it out, his mouth dropped open wide.

"You," was all he said.

"Yes, me. I heard the jerks tease you about your dad leaving. The sorry thing is how it tore apart your family. It's too late for your brother – he made his bad choices. But it's not too late for you. You can change. Your mom needs you to. Think about it. It's time you did something for her," I whispered. "And if I ever see you harassing a girl again I will spill it all to your linebackers back there," I added. "I made you a promise back then. I'm making you a promise right now. I will humiliate you if that's what it takes to stop you from bullying." I stepped around him and walked back to Sofi.

"Hey neighbor, how about a ride home?" I reached out, took her arm and gently pulled her away towards the parking lot. I looked back over my shoulder and saw Hank standing where I had left him. Mouth still dropped open, looking stunned.

"Thanks," she managed to spit out as we walked to my car.

❁

"That. Was. Awesome!" Sofi exclaimed once we were safely locked in the Jeep.

"It was, wasn't it?" I said, exhaling loudly.

"Did it feel as good as it looked?"

"Better," I said as a smile spread across my face.

"What did you say? It looked like you dropped a ton of bricks on him!"

"Nothing, just a little reminder of days gone by," I said, vaguely. She was quiet for a moment.

"Why?" Sofi asked.

"Because he needed to remember something," I answered.

"No, I mean why did you come help me, after what I did to you. You could have walked away."

"Where's the fun in that?" I asked trying to lighten it up.

"Great. That makes it even worse. What I did. I'm such an idiot." She shook her head, wavy blonde shimmered in the sun.

"What?" I asked her.

"What I did, with the phones. I should have believed Jason and not her," Sofi sighed.

"*Who?*" As if I had to ask.

"Chelsea," and then she spilled it. After finding out whose sister she was and whose neighbor I was, apparently Chelsea had launched a very effective smear campaign throughout the hallways. I squeezed the steering wheel and slowly inhaled. Exhaled. Then I let go with one hand and picked up my phone and handed it to Sofi. She looked at me, questioning.

"Remember this? Throw it in the glove box for me will you?

Unless you need to 'use' it again."

"Ouch. I deserve that. How long is this going to burn me?"

"For a very long time, and then some."

She winced as she took it and opened up the glove box. As she put the phone in a photo fell out. She picked it up off of the floor and studied it.

"Is this your mom?" Sofi asked. It caught me off guard, and it was hard to switch gears, mentally and physically, as my body froze. She looked over at me. "I'm sorry. Is it hard to talk about her? Jason told us. She was beautiful. Is that you with her? Is this your natural hair color?" She gasped, pointing at the copper penny curls. Changing the subject. Smart girl.

"Yep," I answered. Driving out of the parking lot.

"No offense. Your black look is cool. But honestly, this color is smoking hot." *Hmm where had I heard that expression before?*

"Yay, I've been thinking of going back to it someday."

Sofi looked out the front window, "Quick, pull in there!" She pointed to a drugstore. I pulled into the parking lot and looked over at my animated passenger. She added, "How about if *someday* is *today*?" She took the photo in with us to match it. She was like the proverbial kid in a candy store looking at all the boxes and comparing them to the picture. It was kind of weird.

No, not *kind of* weird. *Completely.* Chelsea's co-conspirator turned double agent was now my confidant. She found a match and brought it to me for my approval. When I looked at the box Mom smiled up at me. I bought it. As we left the drugstore we passed a discount shoe store. Sofi stopped and grabbed my arm.

"Look! Orange Converse! Perfect! They will totally match! What's your size?" She opened the door and waved me in.

"This girl can switch gears faster than my car!" I said to myself. Or maybe out loud. It wouldn't have mattered as she was already out of hearing range and heading down the aisle to ask the clerk.

✡

By the time we were back in the car I'd had a chance to filter thoughts about my mom so I had gotten up the nerve to ask, "What did Chelsea say about her?" I nodded to the photo, prepared for the worst.

"Nothing. I honestly don't think she knows. The only thing she said about your family was that you had a super hot older jock brother who was normal. Sorry. Again. It was part of her rant about how weird it was that you turned out so different," Sofi said.

I exhaled slowly. Well, that was somewhat of a relief. No lies spinning out of control about Mom. Just me. I can take that.

"I shouldn't have listened. I know Jason didn't. He ignored her when she trashed you. He would just look at her without saying a word. Then excuse himself and walk away. It made her crazy. He told me that you were indeed different, but in a good way. Clever. Funny. Quiet. Confident. That's what he likes about you," she said softly.

"I was jealous. We were both so excited to get back to the States and meet new people. Then he stumbles on to you next door the day we moved in. Really? Next door? The first day? Typical Jason. And you were so cool. And crazy athletic. He would tell us about what you said, or did. And then you watched Gracie that one time and she jumped on the 'Joan is awesome' wagon, and I was left behind," she finished as she looked out the window. Suddenly, I no longer cared what Chelsea thought or what she said. Because Jason didn't either.

"Don't beat yourself up. You have made a lot of friends and found a good fit," I said to let her off the hook.

"Except for the obvious exception," she sighed.

"Of course," I agreed.

"Your tumbling is impressive, as are your techno skills." I glanced over at her. She flinched but could tell I was joking. "Did you come up with the phone hijack or did Chelsea?" I asked. Maybe I still cared a little.

"She suggested it, but I had to figure it out. She had the motive and I had the opportunity. The perfect crime. Or so we thought! Then you and my bro started texting in some bizarre code that only you two understand. What's up with that? It was like living outside of an inside joke!" she exclaimed.

"I only tried to mess you guys up once – with a football game. I could tell Jason was bummed then and that was hard. After that I just deleted them, but then Jason tried calling you, again and again! And left voicemail messages. Seriously, what kid still leaves *voicemail* messages? Or answers them for that matter? Don't worry. I didn't listen to them. I draw the line at espionage."

That earned a raised eyebrow look from me. She continued, "Then I saw you guys comparing phones in the hallway and freaked out!"

"I remember that day. You looked upset, I thought it might be because of the scream fest I heard the day before when I passed by cheer practice," I said, fishing, I admit.

"Oh joy, wasn't *that* a blast? No. I was way over that mess. I told Chelsea to forget about our little escapade. She threatened to tell Jason. I told her to go ahead because I knew she wouldn't dare. I still felt I was doing the right thing, in the wrong way I admit, but I wasn't cool with you because of Trent. I thought you were two-timing Jason and stringing them both along. Then I saw him at the Homecoming dance with someone else?

"BTW, what was that about? I started to figure out that if Chelsea had been lying about that maybe she was just full of it. I waited a day or so after I saw you with the phones, when I knew you had a cross country meet, and texted you a simple 'good luck' message to throw you guys off. And wouldn't you know it? My dufus brother had lost his phone! You texted 'Jason' back asking if 'he' had found it and I knew it was game over. I tried to figure out how to switch them back and then you busted me. That was painful. Even more so now. Through all of this my ego has taken a major hit. I thought I was protecting him and ended up screwing up big time. Again. Sorry. A billion times. Forever and always."

"Forgiven. That being said I'm not above torturing you about it for, I don't know, a decade or so."

"Good. I deserve it. Jason won't be as forgiving I'm afraid. I think I may have burned down that bridge forever," Sofi softly sighed, suddenly serious.

"I doubt it. Your brother is dedicated to you and the rest of your family. I'm sure he'll get over it quickly."

"I hope so. He is a great guy. The real deal. Do you know about his community service project he created for his ROTC application?"

I shook my head 'no' and she continued, "He calls it Checkmate Cancer. He has been going down to the Children's Cancer Center in town for the last couple of months after practices. He goes in on weekends too. He teaches the little patients going through therapy how to play chess to keep their mind off of the chemo infusions. Sometimes Gracie goes with him. She is so easy-going with the kids. Relaxed. Not freaked out at all. I think Gracie is more like him than I am."

"She is quite a character, but so are you. Don't sell yourself short. Cheer up. Ha! Get it? Cheer up? Me, telling you, cheerleader, to cheer up! Now that's funny," I laughed, trying to lighten her mood. She looked over at me, incredulous.

"Ugh. Puns? That's the way you roll? You are weird," Sofi said, hiding a smile, and then added, "So what do you think? Do you need some help with the coloring tonight or do you want to stay in character and go solo?"

"No, I think I've got this. Thanks for the pep talk. Ha ha! Again! Pep talk!" I laughed, as we pulled into her driveway.

"Groan. Joan. Oh, that rhymes. Ha ha. Right back at ya. Now

I'm a poet, gee, look at my feet, they're Longfellows!" Sofi rolled her eyes *(Gracie-like)* and jumped out of the Jeep. She waved, turned and walked up their driveway. Wow. Their driveway. Talk about weird. What parallel universe did I just enter?

❂

I thought about Sofi's offer to help. I'd said I needed to do it on my own. She looked a bummed, but not surprised, especially after what she had put me through over the past months. Probably assumed I didn't trust her, but that wasn't it. I wouldn't be alone. A ghost would keep me company.

I took my new products to my room then started dinner. Dad would be home from the gym soon. We ate in silence; it had been an eventful week. Spending time with his oldest in his last year of college and his youngest in her last year of high school probably gave Dad abundant food for thought, as we ate. *Pun intended.*

❂

Afterwards we cleaned the dishes, did laundry and watched Sunday Night Football. I excused myself for the night and went back to my room to unpack my purchases. The shoes were totally fun. Not exactly ruby red slippers. No telling where they would take me tomorrow if I tapped the heels together to escape. I studied the other packages. One box to strip away the darkness. One box to bring back the light. I inhaled. Exhaled. Picked up both and went into my bathroom.

The years of solitude and guilt, after the grief and pain suffered, washed down the drain in swirls of black dye. I watched and let it go. With no desire to follow this time. After adding the copper penny color, I wrapped my head in a plastic bag to wait for it to sink in. I did not look in the mirror.

Back in my room I picked up a book but after reading the same page five times I tossed it aside. I looked at the new shoes by my closet and thought about how excited Sophie was when she saw them. Boy, had I read her wrong. I think we both could learn a lesson. A series of clichés ran through my head. *What goes around comes around. You have to break a few eggs to make an omelet. You can't judge someone until you've walked a mile in his or her shoes.* The drift is, I had been jumping to a lot of conclusions based on emotions rather than facts. *All jocks are ... All cheerleaders are ... All teenagers are ...* and one by one my generalizations had been shot down. A hard lesson to swallow, even with a spoon full of sugar. Oh well. *A journey of a thousand miles begins with the first step.*

Might as well plan tomorrow as I waited. Heaven forbid I fly by the seat of my pants. Even after I turned on the light in my closet; it was still dark inside. Filled with black. Shirts, jeans, a stack of tee shirts and shoes. My invisibility wardrobe. I did have a pair of faded blue jeans, and a white tee shirt. It would work.

I checked the timer then went back into the bathroom and dimmed the lights. Pulling off the plastic bag, I leaned over the sink, shampooed and rinsed three times then grabbed a dark towel to rub it dry.

The wet curls were still dark. I added conditioner, bent over and started to blow dry. Lighter and lighter, the curls came alive, spring back and take flight as the warm air blasted through them.

Finally, I stood up. Turned up the lights. And looked into the mirror. The color was dazzling. An explosion. But that wasn't the surprise. A stranger looking back at me that I wasn't expecting. Not a younger Mom, or an older me. Someone new. I stared into her green eyes. She stared back into mine.

"Hello. I'm Joan. Jett. Bennett. Welcome back." We exhaled at the same time, and then together, we smiled.

❂

My alarm woke me up. I shook my head. *Wow.* That seemed so real. I stumbled out of bed and walked into the bathroom, turned on the lights and jumped looking into the mirror. *"This is going to take awhile to get used to!"* I said to the red head staring at me. I put on a white tee, jeans, white footies and my new orange Converse, and went to give my dad a heart attack.

"Morning." I walked into the kitchen. Dad's back was to me.

"Good morning Sunshi ... ," he stuttered as he turned around and saw me. He stopped, stunned. Stared. Shocked.

"Sunshine," he finished. Smiled. "You look great, as always," he said and then looked down to divert the attention, "Are those new shoes?"

"Thanks Dad. Sorry for the shock treatment. It feels both right and weird," I said honestly, tugging at a curl from the shiny mop on my head.

"It looks amazing, just a second," he said as he left the room and returned with a photo album. We looked through it and laughed at old pictures over breakfast. He had turned back to some of my mom before they met, when she was in high school. He pointed to a cool old school green jacket that she was wearing and said, "I think we still have that. Finish eating and I'll be right back."

He returned with the jacket and held it out for me to try. I slipped it on. It felt good. Right. Strong. Safe. Like armor. Armed and ready to face the day. He gave me a quick hug then held me at arms length. "Go get 'em tiger," he said. Then he turned to go refill his coffee cup and blink back tears.

16

"Roar"

I drove to school and parked in the back lot. As I walked up I caught a glimpse of myself in the front window. Yikes! It looked like my head was glowing. This was it. I took a deep breath, opened the door and walked down the middle of the hallway looking straight ahead; I could feel the stares and hear the whispers.

"Who is *that*?"

"Is she new?"

"Check out her hair!"

"Where did she get those hot orange kicks?"

I could hear the talk around me, about me; kids in the halls and teachers who didn't recognize me at first, even though I sat in my usual seat.

Second period we had a substitute teacher, the one who had seemed to see me even when I was invisible. In the halls, she would always wave to me and smile. And talk to me in the classroom when no one else was there. Today she looked up when she called my name for roll and smiled. After that, she asked me to take the attendance slip to the office and then pick up a TV/DVD cart from the library that she had on reserve. She quietly commented that she liked my new look. I said thanks, took the slip and a classroom pass and escaped the whispers behind me as I walked into the hallway.

After dropping off the attendance, I went to the library and approached the check-out counter for technology. I looked over at the adjacent computer lab and saw him. Jason. He was sitting next to Sam, and they were talking with their backs to me. I gave my pass to the librarian and impatiently waited for her to get the cart for me so I could duck behind it before they could see me. No longer invisible but barely recognizable. *Who am I? What was I thinking? Where can I hide? When should I talk to him? Why did I do this? How do I sign up for a Journalism class?*

❂

Back in class I tried to pay attention to the movie we were watching but it was tough to concentrate on the cosmos when thinking about lunch next period. I would see Jason, or more importantly, he would see me. What would he think of it?

I remembered his compliments on my "cool looks" that matched my black car. What if he were allergic to ginger? *But wait.* This wasn't about him. *For a change.* This was about me, and my mom. *I had made it through the fire.*

I tried to psych myself up for a grand entrance then entered the cafeteria.

"Joan!" I heard an excited voice. Looked around and up bounded Sofi. "*Wow,* seriously, *dude,* you're spectacular! Amazing. Truly. I'm glad I found you. Just wanted you to know. I told Jason about the phones. After we got back from the store. He was seriously furious. I told him we were cool though. I hope that was okay?

"You know self-preservation and all. And I told him about the thing with Hank too. How you stood up for me and got me out of there. But I waited until late last night so he couldn't call or anything. I thought he was going to explode he wanted to talk to you so bad! I told him to wait to talk to you today at school. That's the upside.

"The down side is he is very ticked at me. Won't even look at me. But I think he'll get over it. He called Sam and made him go in early but they missed you. Were you running late or planning to surprise him?

"Don't worry. I didn't tell him about your hair! He is going to freak. And look, there he is with Sam. Quick! Come over with Shelley and me so you can surprise him. This is going to be great!" Sofi gushed.

Seriously. I needed a double espresso to listen as fast as she could talk! I wanted to evaporate. Disappear. Escape. *Or did I?* Yep. Definitely. But too late. *Show time.* We went through the line as Sofi rattled on about my hair. She waved to Shelley, who caught up with us.

"Shelley, this is Joan, I don't think you've actually met. She's my neighbor and Jason's friend. The one I've been messing with," confessed Sofi.

"Hey! Love the new color. I liked the black before, but this is crazy fun. Nice to meet you. Glad you didn't go nuts on Sofi for the phone thing. She told me about it, but after what Chelsea told her, us, whoa, don't look now, but guess who is inbound and seething. Stand by for some fireworks. She just caught sight of us and *does not* look happy," Shelley gasped and giggled. Both. At the same time. It was exhausting trying to keep up with these two. Nothing to do but jump on for the ride.

"Hi Shelley. Thanks. Nice to meet you too. I've seen you tumble or whatever you guys call it when you flip all over the place. It looks amazing and must take a lot of work," I said knowing full well they didn't hear a word as they watched her approach.

"Quick! They aren't looking! Sit over here, with us, with your back to the guys," Sofi whispered. She shielded and steered me to their usual table. At this point in time, believe it or not, I was not thinking about the table where Jason sat behind me as I watched the charge of Chelsea in front of me. She did not look pleased that I was invading her territory or table.

Sofi sat next to me so she also saw her approach. Even though Shelley was across the table from us, I could tell by her enormous brown eyes she could sense it. She bit her lip, raised up her eyebrows, smiled a truly wicked smile and winked at Sofi.

"Hey Chelsea! You know Joan. I invited her to sit with us today," Sofi threw out, with a lot more confidence than I expected. Feisty. Reminded me a bit of Gracie. Good for her. Good for me. I looked up at Chelsea as she stood next to Shelley and fumed. I dipped my chin once in a nod. She glanced at me and then glared at Sofi.

"What – ever," she shrugged, looked behind me, and then sat down next to Shelley. That wasn't as bad as I expected . . . and then she studied my hair, my face, back to my hair.

"Poor Joan. So, the 'dark and mysterious look' failed to get you noticed. This obnoxious orange practically screams desperation," Chelsea sighed under her breath. *Fight or flight?* Or fight fire with fire? I looked straight into her icy blue eyes.

"Just keeping it real for a change, or changing it back to real." I took a spoonful of yogurt. Without breaking our stare. I heard both Shelley and Sofi suck in air.

In the wild, when one animal breaks the stare the other attacks. I held it. Without blinking. She noticed. Blinked. "What – ever," she said again, with the accompanying eye roll. Then to exclude me, "Shel and Sof, don't forget practice is going to run an hour later tonight to prep for our first home game." And with that I was dismissed as she refused to look my way and rambled on about everything and anything that didn't relate in any way to me.

Which was fine by me. I had already gotten enough attention for a lifetime and was looking forward to being ignored. Which, as my usual luck would have it, would not be the case. Shelley's eyes practically popped out of her head as she looked over my shoulder just as I heard . . .

"So, what's your name?" I turned and looked up to see the shock in Sam's eyes as I heard an explosion behind him.

"You know my name Sam. What's with the noise at your table? Someone steal your Twinkie?" I asked, sounding much smoother than I felt.

"J-Jett? What the? What happened to? What's up with *your hair*?" Sam stammered.

"It was time for a change. No big deal," I said. More like an ENORMOUS deal.

"Well, it looks nice, doesn't it ... Jason?" Sam smiled, as he turned to look at Jason, who was turned in his seat, gaping at me.

Jason. Just. Stared. Then turned back around to clean up the mess from an apparent food fight that covered their table and floor. The other guys laughed at Sam and Jason, not me, but I felt my face glowing hot. I had turned a bright shade of red to clash with my new copper penny hair. I turned back around so my back was to the guys. That did not go well. Despite my obvious embarrassment, Chelsea still didn't look happy. I thought she would be thrilled to witness my epic fail debut.

Shelley and Sofi were still laughing at the guys. "Did you see the look on his face? I think he went into shock!" Sofi cracked up.

"Well of course, the circus is in town, and Joan and Sam are the clowns – Joan certainly looked the part, and Sam performed in it," Chelsea said, as she rolled her eyes. Again.

"No, I meant Jason. He was drop mouth speechless! Believe me that is a first. No witty remark or anything," Sofi laughed.

"Totally! And Sam was trying to be so cool. What a goofball!" Shelley said. Chelsea just fumed.

Having had enough of the spotlight, I threw away my food and exited the circus tent.

17

"Name Of The Game"

As soon as the last bell rang I rushed to my locker, grabbed my mom's green jacket *(armor)* and put it on. Though washed out and well worn, it still gave me the strength I had lacked. Reinforced, I walked quickly down the hallway and out of school.

Jill and Erin stopped me in the parking lot and went nuts about my hair. I thanked them but explained it was overwhelming and I needed to run, literally. Of course they got that, and sent me on my way with a promise to fill them in later.

I needed air, space, speed and solitude. At home, I threw on sweats and took off; my hair flamed out behind me like an orange banner in the wind. After a mile my breathing regulated and pace relaxed. Listening to the rhythm of my footsteps I settled into the zone. Where I could think. Consider. Comprehend.

It was not about him. It was about *me*. And *Mom*. How she had wanted me to live, after she no longer could be here for me. She had wanted me to be strong. Self-reliant, not self-absorbed. Enjoy life. Live life. Not fade away. See what's wrong. Make it right. Analyze and act. Be a point of light.

Redirected, I was on my way back. Lost, but newly found. For *her*. For Dad. For Jon. For *me*. Stronger in the knowledge that I didn't have to make it on my own. Jill, Erin, Trent, Rachel, Sofi, Sam. Jason. All pieces of the new puzzle that is my new life. The one I choose to live *out loud and in color*.

That being said, I do not and will not ever desire to be the center of attention. I know, I know. Good luck with that. Be careful what you wish for, or don't wish for, for that matter.

✹

After an introspective run through the woods I cooled down. Almost home but a million miles away, I was brought back to reality walking up my driveway.

"Hey." Jason sat on my front step. Spinning a lacrosse stick.

"Hey," I said, making eye contact. Wow. He looked serious. Seriously wow. Clouds were covering the son. Storm brewing?

"Good run?" he asked.

"Yep," I answered.

"I looked for you after school but you disappeared."

If you only knew. *That's what I do best!*

"Crazy day. I just needed to bolt."

"Must have been a lightning bolt."

"Pretty much." I sat down on the sidewalk in front of him to stretch. Breaking eye contact, I leaned forward nose to knees to stretch. An eruption of lava spilled from my head and covered my face, legs and surrounding sidewalk.

"It looks good. On you. Great really. It was a surprise. At lunch today," Jason said quietly.

"Kind of surprised me too. It was time. Well, I had help with the timing." I peeked through renewed copper penny curls.

"About that. Thanks for rescuing my back-stabbing, brat of a sister," he said a little louder.

"No big deal. She can take care of herself. I just gave her an out from the conversation and a lift home." Wow. A shift. Defending? Protecting? Excusing?

"Good for her. For a change. Helping someone else that is. But wait, come to think of it, she has been helping someone, Chelsea, for quite awhile. And it was definitely not good. For you, or me. It messed us up. All of the lies, the phones, the deception. And for what? To be popular? How lame is that?" he said, sounding angry.

"I don't think that's why she did it," I said slowly.

"Why then?"

"To protect you."

"Protecting me? From what? Making friends? Having fun?"

"From me. From becoming a social outcast. A pariah," I said quietly.

"What?" he asked, still angry and now confused.

"I tried to tell you, remember? The night before school started. I warned you I was different. I hadn't met her, but she heard about how strange I was. Reclusive. A nobody. I tried to warn you. That you would fit right in and find better people to hang out with than me. I was expecting you to," I said, looking away. I couldn't bear to witness his realization.

"And I told you that I liked different, REMEMBER?" he shouted. Yikes, I had never heard or seen him angry. A new perspective. Still very attractive in a strong, self-righteous, go out and save the world sort of way to be sure. I looked back at him.

"Well, yes, you did say that. But you hadn't met anyone else. I just assumed once you had found more interesting things ... people ... girls ... to hang with ..." I said, trailing off at the end.

"You *assumed?* That I was shallow and superficial like Chelsea? That I wanted to be popular like Sofi? What did I do in those six weeks that made you assume that?"

"Well. Nothing," I admitted. *Ouch.* Tough to swallow. Sudden epiphany. I don't like to be proved wrong. Or admit it. Even to myself. Say nothing about putting it out there in the universe.

"Is that why you started hanging out with Trent so much? Because the cross country kids are above all this high school *drama?*" he asked. *Whoa.* Slow down. Where did that come from?

"Wait a minute. Why bring Trent into this? He was being a good guy. Making me feel welcome on the team *(mostly, really, maybe?)* I explained that to Sam. In the training room. A while ago. Didn't he tell you? And speaking of *hanging* out with new friends, what about Chelsea? You didn't appear to mind her *superficially* hanging all over you on numerous occasions," I challenged. For no other reason than pure, everyday, unmitigated jealousy.

"That was all show on her part. It would have been cruel to push her off in front of the whole school. I told her in private I was not interested. It just made her more determined," he said.

And that's when things got quiet. I looked down, shut my eyes, and thought back. Reflected. Refocused. Vanilla and chocolate ice cream runs. Fireworks in the black sky above the canoe. Football games as he held the ball out from the bright field below to the shadows above. Inviting me in from the dark. Again and again.

"Thanks," I said softly.

"For what?" he asked, calming down quite a bit.

"Bringing me back."

"From?"

"The dark, despair, pity, self doubt, guilt, you name it, I've been there."

"You're welcome," he replied. And waited. Patiently.

I shifted, bit my lip and looked away. Inhaled. Exhaled. Time to attempt an explanation.

"Okay. You see my mom loved this song. Lived this song. It's called "Point of Light," and it says if you see something wrong you need to fix it. Then you will light the way. But when she died I was in such pain I colored my world black to escape. And it worked for a while. Blocked out the light. Avoided the overwhelming loss, but in doing so, I rejected her memories. Her ideals.

"She wanted me to be a candle, but I blew it out. And became invisible. *That's* what I tried to warn you about. *Me.* I'm the one who hid in the shadows, buried with her convictions, and made the choice to do nothing rather than stand up for anything." I sighed.

"You, on the other hand. Do the right thing. *The light thing.* Even when people let you down," I explained. We sat there for a while. Thinking. Contemplating. Silently. Dwelling.

"That may be how you see yourself. But that's not how I see

you. Others just think you have your own agenda and stay out of your way. You are different. It's not the norm for a teenager to care less what their peers think of them. It scares some, and attracts others. *Just like a flame.* You may think you covered it up, or blew it out, but believe me, you burn like the Olympic Torch. Just ask Gracie. Or Sam. Or Sofi. Even Chelsea. She doesn't understand you, or want to, but she sees it. Anyone who takes the time to look can. Ask Hoss," he offered with a sly look.

"Hoss?" I asked.

"You know him as Hank. We called him Hoss in football. Why do you think I didn't find you right after school? I tracked down a mouthy linebacker. Got him back in line. I knew you could take care of yourself, and you did of course, and Sofi too. But nobody messes with my sisters, or friends. Guys talk a big game, but it's not cool to play it out that way," he said. *Wow.* And I thought *I* was different. We sat there looking at each other for a moment. Then I looked down at the lax stick he was spun in his hands.

"Speaking of talking trash. You ready to be schooled?" I said, pointing to the lacrosse stick.

"Girl please; I was born ready," he said with a slow smile. And the son broke through the clouds.

❂

"You know, the first basketball game is tonight. Are you going to come? If so, you can't sit in the Jeep anymore, you have to come into the gym," Jason said as we passed the lacrosse ball in my backyard.

"Ha ha. I might take you up on that. It's not as bad as I had thought, sitting in the stands, kind of fun really. The one time I did was when I texted you I was going to be in the stadium. I enjoyed it. Being included in a group. It was nice. But, that's also when Sofi changed the message I think. Which wasn't so nice," I said.

"That was when Sam and I saw you with Trent and thought you were going out," Jason said, taking a shot on goal.

"Yes. He walked me up to my car," I explained, leaving out the part about rejecting Trent. "He went to the Homecoming dance with Rachel," I added quickly.

"I know. I saw them together. I pointed it out to Chelsea when we were dancing. She told me you and Trent were all over each other in Psych. I didn't believe that, didn't seem your style, but things had been so messed up between us and then we saw you guys in the parking lot I thought there might be something to it.

"But then Sam talked to you, and he told me Chelsea was full of it. I kept trying to talk to you but something always got in the way. Sofi really messed things up with her stupid phone jacking. We could have been hanging out that whole time. And the dance would have been a lot more fun if *someone* had been there," he added. *Wow.*

"By the way, I hear congratulations are in order Your Highness," I said quickly, filling in the awkward silence and added, "I wish I could have seen you crowned!"

"So do I," he said, scooping up the ball to pass. "It would have been a lot more fun dancing with you."

"Oh no. I don't dance." I cradled the ball and dodged, literally.

"What do you mean? You seem comfortable enough dancing across a lax field," he laughed.

"That's different. It has a purpose. To run, cut, juke, pass or shoot makes sense. What reason could I possibly have to shake and jiggle around with people watching? Judging? No thanks! I'll pass," and I did, to his left, and he caught it and put it in the net.

"Okay for now. We'll keep our dancing on the field. Which begs the question, why haven't you ever played lacrosse on a team? You would totally dominate. And now that you've tried to go out for a sport, why don't you consider playing another?" he asked.

"Well for one, our high school doesn't have a girls' lacrosse team. They picked up gymnastics when the guys added lacrosse.

"What about a club team then? Aren't there any around here?"

"Well, that brings us to the second and more important reason. In girls' lacrosse you get penalized for trying."

"You what?" he asked, as he stopped to look at me.

"In all of the girls' games Jon and I have seen they get penalized for trying, really. It must be frustrating as some Amazon races down the field, and you can't do one darn thing to stop her from scoring without the referee throwing a flag for obstruction or interference." I scooped up the ball and put it in the net.

"I wonder ..." He stood, leaning on his D Pole.

"About?"

"It's a shame to waste a player with your lax skills, how about going out for the guys' team with Sam and me?" He challenged, with a taunting smile.

"Are you crazy? As if people don't think I'm whacked enough! Can you imagine the field day Chelsea would have with that?"

"Since when do you care about what she thinks? Or anyone else for that matter?" he laughed. *If you only knew!*

"I know the coach, and he loved having Jon play for him but I'm sure he would flip if I showed up to tryouts! No way."

"Well at least talk to Jon and see what he thinks."

"Sure, because I know he'll shoot the idea down in a heartbeat."

"All right then! I better head home, grab some chow and get over to the school for warm ups. See you tonight then?" he asked, tilting his head.

"Okay, if I must. I'll give some cross country kids a call," I said, as if he were asking for the world.

"Some, as in Trent?" he teased.

"Maybe, but more likely Jill since I have *her* number."

"Great, I'll be the one hanging on the rim." He smack talked.

"Fabulous. I'll be the one sweating in the stands."

He paused when he lifted the latch on the gate and looked over his shoulder at me. *Whoa. Flashback.*

"So are we cool again?" he asked, implored.

"All cool," I responded. Frozen by his look. *Looks.*

"Good," he said as he smiled and walked out the gate. After what seemed like forever I exhaled. And stepped back up onto the merry-go-round. Again.

18

"Larger Than Life"

I wandered into the house. Misty brought me back to reality demanding dinner. I fed her and then looked into the refrigerator to see what to make for Dad and me. After grabbing some ground turkey and putting it on the stove to brown, I put a pot of water on the stove to boil for pasta. I was locked into autopilot, going through the motions of our quick "go to" entree. I found some frozen veggies to steam and put them in the microwave, and then cut up some fruit. After everything was in the works I called Jill.

"Hey Joan, what's up?" she answered.

"Not much, just wondering if you were going to the game tonight," I asked, trying to be casual.

"I was thinking about it, are you? We could get some peeps and sit in the Spirit Block if we wear white," she asked and answered.

"Oh that's right, it's a White Out Night," I responded.

"Well, look who's going all crazy school spirit mode! Are you going to watch anyone in particular or just supporting your team?" she teased.

"I could give you the run-a-round but we know you'd smoke me, so yes, busted. Jason asked me to go."

"Tell. Me. Everything."

"No biggie. He stopped by after my run. Do you think Erin would go?" I dodged.

"Probably. And don't even think you can divert me that easily. How about I swing by and pick up both you and Erin? Then you'll be trapped until you fill us in on everything, and I do mean everything," Jill offered and threatened.

"Great. Sounds painful," I sighed.

"Only for you. See you at six-thirty," Jill said as she signed off.

❂

The gym was an oven. Hundreds of half-baked humans milling around trying to find their friends. All walking, texting, eventually looking up to get a visual. Jill, Erin and I found some other cross country kids. In the Spirit Block. All in white. No longer a knightmare. On the contrary, the excitement was contagious. All of us laughing, talking, having too much fun just being together.

And then the lights went out. The noise level went up. We stood in total darkness. Electric. It felt nothing like before. Back when I tried to feel nothing. Rather than being totally void, the black was now a combination of all of the colors. And sounds. And smells. Perfumes and colognes, to attract and appeal, as well as a variety of deodorants and antiperspirants, to cover and repel. All in a sensory competition before the actual game began.

A spotlight materialized, cutting through the dark, beaming down to the players exiting the locker room. As the darkness evaporated the noise level intensified, only to halt suddenly as a student stepped out onto the gym floor with a microphone. She sang "The Star Spangled Banner" a cappella. Quietly at first. Her voice quivered a bit. Her eyes were closed. Gradually the notes and words strengthened. Her eyes opened, and she looked up to the flag. And from there she nailed it. Didn't go off on an ego trip. Sang it the way it was meant to be sung. Her voice was so clear and pure no one dared to pollute it with his or her own. And when she hit the last phrase, all of us fortunate enough to be living here in the land of the free and the home of the brave erupted in appreciation.

Of course my eyes had radar-locked on Jason the moment he entered the madness. I watched as he again stood at attention.

Different sport, same #7. Hand over heart. Focused on the flag. After the anthem he turned to prep for the game. I noticed his curly hair was getting long. *(Sigh. Again.)* He kept running his hand back through it to get it out of his eyes. *(Jealous. Again.)* The shining lights lit up the remaining golden highlights left over from the summer sun.

The announcer introduced the non-starters and then the starting five from the opponent's team. Then our non-starters. No Jason. I shouldn't have been surprised that Jason was our starting point guard. It was crazy that he could land into two starting slots in two different sports as a new senior. Make that three in the spring with lacrosse. Amazing. Even more so that he wanted to spend time throwing with me. Hanging out with me. Being. With. Me?

As they announced our starters, Sofi and Shelley took turns tumbling back and forth across the gym. The Spirit Block fans counted their back handsprings out very loud and went crazy as they finished and staggered back to the squad. Slightly dizzy and definitely happy.

The game began and the block of students remained standing. Cheering. Only to sit and quiet down when a player was injured. Then we were reduced to a simmer. A murmur. When the player was escorted from the floor we erupted back to a full boil, springing to our feet again with increased volume as well.

Jason got a fast break and took it down the court. At the last moment he dished it back to Sam who was right on his heels. Sam took it up and dunked it. He hung on the rim for a split second, then dropped down to go back and jump, hip bump with Jason. The crowd went nuts.

I looked over to the cheerleaders and caught Sofi's eye. She waved. My gaze fell on Chelsea. She didn't. Her eyes narrowed, cat-like. She spun. Twirling her skirt. Then started a new chant. Smiling up at everyone. Almost. I looked back at Sofi. Even though their motions were identical, their actions spoke volumes.

To me, it seemed Sofi adored what she was doing. In contrast, Chelsea appeared to be doing it to be adored. Not my concern. My attention left the sideline and got back into the game.

Halftime came, and the players left the court and headed for the locker rooms. And the crowd started chanting over and over.

"NAY – KEDS! NAY – KEDS! NAY – KEDS!"

And that's when they showed up. Ahh yes, The Nakeds. Jill tried to explain them to me. Two juniors everybody called "Naked 1" and "Naked 2." Born two years ago as two freshmen that went to the first home football game, which happened to be unseasonably warm. So, being silly freshmen, they took their shirts off and went shirtless for the entire game. Everybody got a big kick out of it, except for the school administrator, so their shirts went back on.

However, the next game they showed up in tight tan athletic shirts, shorts and tennis shoes. They never did get naked, but their attire was close enough that they earned the name. They were drummers in the school band who were too junior to play in Pep Band, so about the fourth or fifth home game, they grabbed a couple of giant plastic garbage cans, emptied the trash, and then snuck them into the student section of the stands. They turned the trash cans upside down and began banging on them with some drumsticks. The noise echoing from those garbage cans on the aluminum bleachers was deafening, and they had invented some catchy little refrain that was a mixture of Lady Gaga's "Poker Face" and what the witch's guards sang in *The Wizard of Oz*.

The students loved it, and The Nakeds were now an integral part of most football games. How had I missed out on them as I sat up in my car? They must not have been at the game I had sat in the stands, because believe me, I would have remembered!

The Nakeds decided to take their show not only to football games, but to all the minor sports as well. By now, they were skilled at finding plastic garbage cans at home sporting events, and, in fact, if there were any garbage in the garbage can, they would empty the garbage into plastic bags and then dispose of it after the game. And after every game, they would scour the stands for garbage on the ground, collect it, and put it in bags.

This endeared them to the school janitors and administrators, who could find no fault in The Nakeds – after they put shirts back on. Attendance was increasing at all sporting events partly because of them, and The Nakeds were helping with post-game clean up.

Their brief life almost came to an end at the first minor sport at which they made an appearance. They decided to start with a girls' home volleyball game, and brought in two large garbage cans and about ten of their friends. They had invented a cheer that went something like "Schuck chuck . . . BOOM!"

The intent was to time the BOOM part of the cheer with the exact moment that one of our girls was hitting the ball on a serve. The Nakeds tried this approach by first yelling very long and loud for Jenny Myers as she was preparing to serve. Coach Smith – the girls' volleyball coach – was okay with fans yelling for Jenny prior to the serve, but she went insane with rage when somebody – ANYBODY – dared yell during the actual serve.

Jenny Myers, however, a notorious weak serving sophomore *was thrilled* that somebody – ANYBODY – was cheering for her, and when the BOOM part of the cheer went off, she launched a sidewinder missile of a serve that totally aced the Woodland High team. And then she did it again. And again. After two more wicked serves, Jenny's sixth serve went out of bounds, but by then Coach Smith's attitude had changed to one of, "Well I guess it's okay if you come to our games and cheer and as a matter of fact we would appreciate it if you could bring more friends and would you do that BOOM thing for all our girls every time they serve?"

Apparently the Woodland High coach went back to her school and told all of their students how much support our school had provided at the volleyball game and how embarrassed she was at the lack of fans from Woodland High. We had a lot in common with Woodland High. Many of the students at both schools knew each other and played on club teams together, so there was already a friendly rivalry. But now the rivalry got a little serious. Fans started showing up for games between Woodland High and us in large numbers, for all sports.

But what really got the rivalry going was the graduation speech two years ago at Woodland. Two years ago – the same year The Nakeds were born – the Principal at Woodland High stood up at graduation and announced that Woodland High had smoked us because they won 12 of the 23 head-to-head sporting contests.

The crowd went wild, and from then on, it was a major battle in all sports. Football, of course, was still the main attraction, but now other sports like swimming, soccer and lacrosse were crucial when it came to Woodland versus us. The athletic directors at both schools tried to schedule all of the spring head-to-head events in two or three days, meaning that everybody went crazy trying to keep track of what school was winning in what event and what the overall score was between the two schools.

Somebody coined the term "Judgment Day" for those days in the spring when we played Woodland in every sport. When our team was losing in one sport, the students from our high school liked to point out that our test scores were higher. So when Woodland was winning and their fans yelled a chant something like,

Scoreboard!
Scoreboard!

Our fans would respond,

Test scores!
Test scores!

Or worse,

That's all right!
That's ok!
You'll all work for us some day!

Unfortunately we had lost five of seven contests in the last days
the previous year, and had lost the overall contest as well, so we
had to endure,

That's all right!
That's ok!
We smoked you on Judgment Day!

Woodland even made t-shirts with "Judgment Day Champs"
and other insulting slogans plastered all over them. We wanted to
beat Woodland High, and they wanted to beat us.

The Nakeds knew it and fueled the rivalry. Halftime flew by as
both teams tried to shout each other down. It continued through the
entire second half as the score went back and forth. Exchanging
baskets. Staying within two or three points.

The crowd was in a frenzy. Boiling over. We were down by
one. They took a shot and it bounced off the rim. Sam got the
rebound and dribbled down the court. Dodging players. Looking
for another dramatic dunk no doubt. Suddenly he tripped and as he
fell he desperately dumped it out to Jason who was slightly ahead
to his right. Calling out to him. Jason turned and looked. But did
not see. His hair had whipped into his eyes. He missed the pass
and it flew out of bounds. The buzzer went off. Over.

Our opponents cheered. Winners congratulated each other.
Losers lined up for handshakes. I watched Jason shake his head.
Sam punched his shoulder. After going through the handshake
line, they grabbed their warm ups and went to the locker room

without looking back. Oh well. I thought it had been a good game. But I doubted they felt the same.

We were done. The oven turned off. We emerged to cool in the chilly night air. Hurting and hungry from our loss, we realized the cure could and would only be found in hot, salty french fries.

❁

Tuesday at school was the same old thing. I kept looking for Jason but didn't see him all day. I knew he would busy after school with practice. I went home and ran before it got dark, ate dinner with Dad and then worked on homework. I received a text swoosh notification *(!)* around nine asking if I could go out on a quick ice cream run. I answered yes as fast as my fingers could fly across the keys and went to tell Dad. *(And escape before he could tease me.)*

Jason's mom's car was in the driveway, but some college kid in a sweatshirt with short hair was holding the passenger door open for me. Confused, I stopped. And stared. No. He. Didn't.

"Hey Jett. You're not the only one who decided it was time for a change," Jason grinned. *Noooo!* Gone. Golden sun-kissed curls. *Gone.*

"Ah. Ah. Wow. You sure did. You look older. *(And hotter?)* Good, *(meaning great)* but seriously dude, I thought you were some college kid, or some military dude visiting your dad in my driveway by mistake," I stuttered.

"No worries, I asked the lady to leave some boyish charm," he laughed. "Are you going to get in?" he asked.

"I don't know," I said, recovering slowly, "I'm not allowed to get in cars with strange men."

"What do you mean? It's still little 'ole me."

"True, you're strange, but you look like an elder creature now," I countered to cover that fact that I was once again in super hard crush mode. Which was exhausting! *Nauseating!* And so much more than slightly infuriating. *HE'D CUT HIS HAIR!*

I got in and buckled up. Reverting to a familiar action to calm my inner screaming. Jason got in, buckled up and turned the key. Just as he turned to back up the car he flashed me this quick look with his lopsided grin.

I just about fainted. And I had thought he couldn't possibly get better looking. Still, I had to mope, mourn, be miserable and therefore retaliate for the dear, departed curls.

"So where did you go to get beheaded?" I asked.

"A new place in town called Delilah's," he answered as he drove.

I burst out laughing. "You're kidding me, right?"

"No. Why?" he asked, innocently. "It's over by the mall."

"Never mind," I answered, then added, "I think that's our turn Samson. Need help turning the wheel?"

"Oh right. I get it. Samson and Delilah. Very funny."

"Just saying, if I were a guy I would've thought twice before I let someone named Delilah talk me into losing my curly locks . . ." I teased.

"Well she didn't see me choke away the game last night. A lot of good my curly locks did then. Besides, I've got some scholarship interviews coming up. It was time to lose the surfer dude look," he said, sounding a little more serious than I expected.

"I guess. As if I have any room to talk. It looks great, really. *(Really, really.)* I'll get over eventually." *(Maybe.)*

"That's good to know Ginger, let's go get some ice cream," he said. The crazy thing was short hair made his eyes look even bigger. Justice? Anywhere? Hardly.

Eye Lash Lady did a double take as we entered.

"Look what the cat dragged in! Where have you two been? *(As she winked at me.)* Did Hollywood steal away our two favorite celebrities? Figures. Did you all come back to rub our noses in it?" she teased.

"No ma'am, if Hollywood came knocking they would beeline to

your door first," Jason said with a straight face.

"Look who's turned into a fresh comedian. Just for that I'm going to get your lovely lady friend her treat first! What's it going to be sugar, your usual? Take your time, you're worth the wait," she said, pretending to shun him. I looked back and forth between them and wondered when the world had turned upside down.

After getting our ice cream creations we sat down and negotiated a treaty, *(Get it? Treat-ee?)* so we could eat in peace. I asked him about Checkmate Cancer, and his face lit up as he launched into his small act of goodwill that had blossomed into an all-out success. He loved teaching the kids chess and they no doubt loved learning from him, being around him, looking up to him. Of course, he didn't tell me that, but Sofi had and I believed it. After all, I was an authority on all of the above.

The next three weeks between Thanksgiving Break and Winter Break were a crazy blur. One week of a ton of material crammed into us. One week for review. Then a week of final exams and projects. Not to mention every senior who planned on going to college next fall had to get in last minute early decision applications for schools and scholarships. Deadlines galore. On top of the college prep and schoolwork Jason had his basketball practices and games. Needless to say it didn't leave us much time to hang out.

I made it to most of the home games and couldn't help but notice Chelsea's attention had shifted from Jason to a guy named Will. He was a captain on the hockey team. At the pep assembly right before the break she was all over Will. Can't say that he minded. Can't say that I did either. Jason was also thrilled to have her off his back. *Win, win, win.*

She still was not a big fan of me, and she made that clear anytime that she could. I couldn't figure out why, but I didn't dwell on it.

Jon was supposed to be home for a week and I was psyched. I thought the three of us could grab Sam and play some lacrosse after he shot down Jason's idea about me trying out for the guy's team. It didn't work out how I had planned. *(When does it ever?)*

It turns out Jon was going on a senior vacation trip to an exotic beach somewhere. Figures. I did get around to asking him about going out for the guy's team. He got a huge kick out of the idea. Wished he could see the look on Coach Hutchins' face. And was totally on board with it. *Surprise, surprise.* And then of course, he gave me my "serious training program" to get me ready. Intervals, wall ball, burpees, intervals, wall ball, burpees, intervals, wall ball, burpees.

19

"I'll Make A Man Out Of You"

As basketball progressed and then wrapped up, Jason, Sam and I conditioned for lacrosse season whenever we could. We had to figure out how to pitch my going out for the guys' lax team to the Athletic Director. We were talking about it at lunch one day after winter break, oblivious to anyone else, when someone behind me joined our conversation.

"I'm in. I'll go in with you. To see AD Williams," Hank/Hoss simply said. I hadn't noticed him sitting near us, and I hadn't talked to him since the Sofi incident. But I knew Jason had. "I'm a returning Pole. I haven't seen you play Joan, but if they believe in you, it's good enough for me."

I looked at Jason, and then Sam, who shrugged his shoulders. Both said it couldn't hurt to have more back up, especially a returning senior. We decided we would go in on Friday after school. I'd be lying if I said I weren't a nervous wreck, and I made it a policy to never lie.

Thursday night I could not get to sleep. Running through different scenarios and anticipating the AD's reaction to each. I was exhausted when my alarm went off. I fought the urge to return to my invisibility wardrobe and dressed in a Knights hoodie Jason had given me for Christmas, and blue jeans and gray Converse. *(My gift to him was getting his lacrosse stick restrung. How is that for romantic? Pathetic, I know.)* I had not only reintroduced color back into my clothing but my kicks as well. To date I had four pair of low top Converse, black *(of course)*, orange *(thanks to Sofi)*, navy blue and gray, and a sweet pair of old school cream canvas high tops. I almost wore one blue and one gray for Friday Spirit Day, but that would be too crazy for the mood I was sporting.

The school day went well enough. The beginning of a new semester was normally chill. Everyone tried to get back into school mode after three weeks of holiday eating, staying up and therefore sleeping in late, and purging data from the first semester in order to clear the brain and make room for new material. Classes covered mostly administrative stuff.

Finally, the last bell rang and I met up with Jason, Sam and Hank in the main office. We asked the secretary if we could see AD Williams and she called back to make sure he was available. I almost hoped that he was gone. No such luck. It was time to act.

The AD's secretary ushered us into his office. The three guys and I stood in front of his desk. He looked up, smiling at us, and invited us to sit down. We all looked back and forth at each other, obviously ill at ease, and declined.

"What can I do for you today?" AD Williams asked politely.

"Sir. I would like to, I mean, I am planning on, trying out for the boys' lacrosse team. I felt I should make you aware of the fact," I said, exhaling.

AD Williams drummed his fingers on his desk, cleared his throat and asked, "Why don't you play on a girls' team? I don't suppose I need to tell you how physical boys' lacrosse is do I?"

"No sir. I've been playing with my brother and his friends for years. And to be honest the girls' lacrosse version isn't anything like the guys. Nowhere near as fun. And we don't have a team at our high school. So technically, as you know, I am allowed to play, or at least try out to see if I am good enough," I answered.

"I see," he said looking from me to Jason, to Sam and then Hank. "And are you boys trying out for some girls' team?" he asked.

"No sir," Jason quickly said as Sam and Hank shook their heads side to side. "We're going out for lacrosse, just here to support Jett. Joan. Her." They all three shook their heads up and down.

AD Williams ran his hand over his baldhead as he looked at his desk. "It doesn't look like I can talk you out of it, so I had better go to the first day of tryouts. Coach Hutchins and Coach Slamovich are going to have kittens . . . and *that* I've got to see," he said as his usual sweet expression broke into a mischievous grin.

❂

So we were going to try out for the boys' high school lacrosse team. Well, I would be trying out. Jason was sure to make it. Tryouts were over a three-day period, after which players would be assigned to the Varsity team or the Junior Varsity team. Coach Hutchins would be evaluating players along with Coach Slamovich, who was the JV coach. Everybody called Coach Slamovich "Slammer," but in reality he was widely respected as a fantastic coach. So was Coach Hutchins, for that matter.

The boys' lacrosse team had been in existence for ten years, and were in an eight-team conference. We were one of the smaller schools in the conference, and although we had good teams and winning records over the years, we had never made state playoffs.

Only the top two teams in the conference made playoffs, and we were cursed to have both the Metro East and Rockledge High in our conference. Both schools were much larger than ours with well-established lacrosse programs, and they had finished first and second in the conference for the past ten years.

There weren't enough lacrosse programs in the state to form several classes – your school either had less than 1,000 students – which meant you played in the "A" division, or your school had more than 1,000 students – meaning you played in the "AA" division. We had 1,200 students, so we had to play schools that typically had more than double our number of students.

I still remember Jon's senior year when it looked like we would make playoffs for the first time. We'd beaten Rockledge High –

the only time ever – and all we needed was a win over archrival Woodland High to finish second in the conference and make state playoffs. But Woodland played the game of a lifetime, took us to overtime, and eventually won.

I can still see Jon sitting on the bench after the game was over, head in his hands. He was a three-time all-conference Pole, honorable mention all-state his junior year and second team all-state his senior year, but all he wanted was to make state playoffs, win a few games and have the chance to play in the University's stadium where the state semi-finals and finals were held. He never got that chance. The current group of lax bros was hoping this year would be their year to finally make playoffs.

About 50 guys *(plus me)* showed up for tryouts. Most of the guys knew each other and knew each other's lacrosse capabilities. No one knew me except for Jason, Sam and Hank. I had put the strip of white athletic tape with my last name written in all caps on the front of my helmet like everyone else. My hair was braided and tucked up and under. I felt like a spy. "*Man up,*" I told myself.

Coach Hutchins did not like to carry a large varsity roster, and he advised us right off that only about 22 players would make the varsity squad. I couldn't help but compare myself to the other Middies trying out.

It looked to me like maybe there were seven or so Middies that would be considered better than me – they were either faster or stronger and had decent stick skills. Coach would probably be keeping eight or nine Middies on varsity, so if my assessment were accurate, I had a decent shot to make the varsity team. *If of course, he was willing to waste a spot on me.*

I might be overlooking a couple of newbs or overestimating my own skills. And Coach might put me on the JV team so I could actually play. *And I would then be Coach Slamovich's problem.* If I made varsity, I'd never see the field. Only the top five or six Middies played any significant amount – the rest sat on the bench.

Well, not exactly. In lacrosse, you never sat on the bench unless you were injured. Everybody stood in a line on the side of the field, but I wouldn't get to play much at all. That would be fine with me. Just practicing with the team would be fun, and watching Jason play in the games would be frosting on the cake. With vanilla ice cream and sprinkles.

Tryouts started with a mile run, and then we broke up into groups of Middies, Attack and D Poles. We Middies did some ball drills with Coach Hutchins encouraging us to go faster and faster. He had us all simultaneously chase loose balls. It was a mess, and I wondered what purpose this drill could ever serve.

I was pleasantly surprised, though, to see that I was faster than most of the Middies. There were several that I would never be able to outrun, but for the most part I could hold my own. He then had us line up in two lines and run up and down the field passing to a partner from the other line. He told us to switch lines and do it again. Duh. What difference does it make what line we were in?

Throughout these drills, he would sometimes say something to Shelley, Sofi's friend from cheerleading, who was trying out to be the lacrosse manager. She was nervously holding a clipboard and would write whatever Coach said down very quickly, rarely looking up or making eye contact with anyone. Which was good. For me. I didn't need her to recognize me and make a big deal about it.

Coach picked up a stick and had us stand in a single line as he threw the ball to us. "Give me a good hard throw," he would say each time. After the throw he would say to some Middie, "Water," and that was the key for that Middie to go take a water break. Other times he would run up and down the field with the Middie, throwing the ball several times before telling them to get a water break. After each Middie was complete, he would tell Shelley to write something down. We'd all have given a million dollars to see what was on that clipboard.

After a while though, I began to see a pattern. Coach Hutchins did not waste time with several of the Middies we all knew would make the varsity, but sent them for water immediately. Those newbs who were obvious JV players were sent for water as well. But for many of us who were "maybe" varsity players, he was testing us.

When he told us to give him a good, hard throw, he was identifying our power hand – the one we favored and felt most comfortable using. Then, he would make most of his passes to the player's weak side, to see if the Middie felt comfortable using the off hand. "Get it back to me quickly," he would say after passing to a right handed player's left side, and then he would watch and see if the player threw it back left-handed, or wasted time switching to his right hand. Clever. Jon frequently told me that he identified opponent's weaknesses by doing just what coach was doing – observing their comfort and skill level passing with either hand.

When my turn came, I was tested with several passes to my left side. I guess that was good news, meaning that coach was giving me a chance to compete for the varsity team. I handled all of his passes to my left side easily. Years of playing catch with Jon made it very natural to catch and pass from the left hand. Coach then started throwing to my right side, just to ensure I was not left-handed, and again there were no problems. Then it happened. He threw a quick low ball to my right and without thinking or looking at it, I did a one-handed right snag, switched back to my left and threw it to him. He caught it and squinted to read the name on my helmet. Realization hit him.

"Are you Jon Bennett's little brother?" he asked.

"No sir Coach!" I shouted back.

"Wow, I would have sworn you were. You looked just like a mini-version him; he played here a few years ago," he said, shaking his head.

I took a deep breath. Exhaled. And trotted over. When I got to where he was I looked up and stared straight into his eyes.

"I'm not Jon's little brother Coach. I'm his younger sister." I held my gaze.

His jaw dropped, and then his mouth closed and tightened.

"What should I call you?"

"First name is Joan, but the guys call me Jett, it's my middle name," I answered, still not blinking. Chin up.

"All right Jett, go get some water."

I grabbed water while Coach finished up with the other Middies. The break gave me a chance to look down at the other end of the field where the Poles were. Slammer was explaining basic defensive concepts including slides, man-to-man and zone defenses. He was using three Poles to demonstrate the concepts, and I could tell they were the three defenders everybody said would start varsity this year. Jason was not one of them. Hank was.

The rest of the day was spent doing more Middie-only drills, including 3-on-2 drills and 2-on-1 drills with multiple variations. Same stuff I'd seen many times before when I came to Jon's practices.

Afterwards, I asked Jason how tryouts went for him. "Okay," he said, but added that most of the day was focused on explaining concepts and not a lot of actual game-like situations. As we walked off the field, I noticed Coach Hutchins talking to Coach Slamovich. He nodded my way. I had my helmet on so they couldn't see me watching them. Coach Hutchins then looked over at the bleachers where AD Williams was sitting. He walked over to him and shook the AD's hand, then shook his head. As we walked, they talked. And we went home, wondering.

Day two we were again split into groups, but this time things had changed. Ten of us were in one Middie group, and I instantly saw that this group contained only potential varsity players, while the other group was JV only caliber. Wow. In a single day, the coaches had determined what Middies had varsity potential.

Gone were the Middies who had lagged behind in the speed drills, or who couldn't catch and throw with either hand, or weren't quick enough playing defense. The Attack players were also narrowed down to about five or six players, but the Poles were still in one large group working at the other end of the field. Tomorrow would be the last day of tryouts.

Day three was an intense day of scrimmaging full field. The coaches would frequently stop the scrimmage to explain some concept or to correct some mistakes, but overall it was frustrating. With so many people rotating in and out, it was hard to stand out. There were so many Poles trying out that Jason didn't play too much, but when he did he didn't allow his man to score.

The next morning we all hurried down to the gym, where the Varsity and JV rosters would be posted. I got there early, but there were already a dozen guys ahead of me, crowding around the rosters, congratulating or consoling each other.

Jason arrived at the same time as I, and we wormed our way up to the bulletin board that had two sheets of paper posted. One sheet of paper was entitled *Varsity Roster* and my eyes sped up and down the sheet. There, under *Midfielders* was my name. I looked at the other Middies that made it – a total of eight of us. These were the guys that deserved to make the team, and I made a note to myself that Jon was correct – Coach Hutchins knew what he was doing.

I glanced up at Jason with a little smile, but he was staring at the varsity roster. I mentally kicked myself for being selfish and not congratulating him, and scanned the roster for his name.

It wasn't there.

I looked again, this time slowly.

I eventually found it. On the *Junior Varsity Roster*.

I was stunned that Jason didn't make varsity, but was sure it was an oversight on the coaches' part. That afternoon before practice, I stopped by Coach Hutchins' office to talk. He invited me in and

I started to explain that there was a mistake and that Jason should be on varsity. He interrupted me.

"Bennett," he said. "There was no mistake. Jason's an exceptional athlete, but he's never even seen lacrosse played. We don't have time to develop a player starting his senior year, especially since we have a ton of Poles with many years of experience."

I explained that he didn't need any development, that he was G2G already. I wanted to tell him that Jason had studied lacrosse CDs, that Jon had data-dumped all of his lax experience into Jason's head, that Jason had built a wall in the backyard, that we had practiced together a lot, that I WOULD BE MISERABLE IF HE WERE NOT ON VARSITY WITH ME, and that the universe would certainly cease to exist if he didn't move him to the varsity squad right now. But Coach cut me off before I could explain these ramifications and utterly humiliate both Jason and myself.

"Bennett," Coach said. "There are ten starting lacrosse players on a team. All of the rest fight for playing time. Do you know which ten players should start?"

Jason and whomever else you want, I thought, "No."

"I'll tell you who should start, according to every parent. The nine best players on the team – plus their own kid – that's who should start. I've got every parent of every kid who doesn't start telling me their kid needs more playing time. I've got every buddy or pal of some bench warmer 'helping' me by telling me that Little Jimmy is better than Little Johnny and should be playing more. I've got every girlfriend of a guy telling me that their Bobby is better than Billy, and if I just gave him a chance, I'd see."

By this time, I had a glimpse of some of the not-so-pleasant aspects of being a high school coach. I vaguely remembered some of Jon's lacrosse games and afterwards seeing Coach Hutchins talking with parents who were no doubt expressing concern over their son's lack of playing time.

I said, "Coach I'm not telling you how to run your team."

"Yes you are," he said, and laughed. "I appreciate your concern, but we just don't have time to spend developing a player when we have other players who have much more experience. We'll see how he handles a few game situations at the JV level and reassess after that. Let's move on.

As for you young lady, we wouldn't be having this conversation if I weren't impressed with your obvious skills. I had the pleasure of coaching your older brother for four years, and it is apparent you've been trained well. That being said; you will not receive any preferential treatment. Do I make myself clear?" he said, looking me straight in the eyes.

I nodded silently. "Great. See you at practice," he finished and turned back to his paperwork. I was dismissed. And that was that. Epic failure on my part.

20

"My Guy"

So the season began. We had 22 varsity players, and had made it a team goal to make the state playoffs. The same goal the team had every year but had never achieved. Sam was goalie, and was a good one. Everyone called him "Wall" because in theory anything shot at him would not penetrate for a score. At least that's what the team hoped.

We had three starting Attack players who were basically clones of each other. They were all about five feet ten inches tall, slender, quick, and could ride well. Blake, Steve and Curt were their names, but we referred to them as *The Three Stooges*, and called them Larry, Moe and Curly. They were maddening to defend against because they were so similar. One game Larry would get hot and score three or four goals, and the opposing team would focus on stopping him, so Moe would score a bunch the next game, and Curly would lead scoring the game after that. None of them would make First Team All-Conference, but all three of them would make Second Team All-Conference or Honorable Mention. They were solid.

Our three Poles were okay most of the time. Hank, "Hoss" held down the middle of the defense. They called him Hoss because he was huge. As I had mentioned, he played football in the fall and weighed 235 pounds if he weighed an ounce. He had decent speed for his size, but like all of our Poles, he was uncomfortable clearing the ball when pressured. Paul Jacobsen, "Jake," played the right side of our defense and was competent, as was Chaz Fletcher, "Fletch," on the left side. The problem was that our

Poles were good players, but they weren't great. They were fine for almost every game except when we played powerhouse teams like Metro East and Rockledge – teams that somehow found a way to exploit little weaknesses in our defense.

The first four or five Middies on our team were very good. Coach Hutchins kept a depth chart posted on the locker room bulletin board, so we all knew where we stood and what number Middie we were. This was especially important for us Middies, since we ran the entire field and frequently had to come off the field to catch our breath. Since there were three Middies on the field at a time, we knew the number four Middie would go in for the first Middie substitution, and the number five Middie would go in for the second substitution. By the time another Middie substitution was required, the number one Middie had often recovered and was ready to go back in again. So, using timeouts wisely, substituting smartly, and occasionally having an Attack player play Middie, we could get by with five Middies playing most of the game.

Our number one Middie was Brian MacDonald, "Mack." He had blazing speed and was an all-around good guy that everybody liked. Number two was Freddie Ziffle, "Zif," who was a Mini Me of Mack. Not quite as athletic, but a superb player. Number three Middie was Scott Raymond, "Scotty," who did the dirty work of guarding the other team's best Middie. Scotty could score, clear, pass, play defense – whatever was needed. Our top three Middies could play with anybody. Will Brooks, was the number four Middie. Will, captain of the school hockey team.

Hockey players were used to playing with sticks, moving fast and going behind the goals, like in lacrosse. It can often be an easy transition between the two sports because of these similarities. Which is good. But, *(you knew there had to be a but)* he was also the new flavor of the month in Chelsea's World. I was hoping that wouldn't be a big deal.

Tom Sapper, "Sap" was the number five Middie. He and Will

were roughly equivalent in talent. Both were top-notch Middies. Number six Middie was Rich Carlson. He was the only Middie I didn't particularly like. He liked to cheap shot other players by hitting them late or from behind. He also liked to shoot a lot, and didn't like playing defense and was lazy in practice. He had the latest and greatest in lax fashion and gear and thought that alone should make him a starter.

I was listed as the number seven Middie ahead of Grunt. Grunt was an anomaly. He was about five feet five inches tall, and built like a bowling ball. He was purely a face-off Middie, also called a FOGO for Face-Off Get Off. After a team scores in most sports, the other team gets the ball. Not so in lacrosse – a face-off ensues. It's possible for a team to score and then immediately regain possession of the ball, which is critical in lacrosse. Winning 60% of face-offs, for example, is considered a huge advantage, and having a FOGO capable of that is very important.

Grunt loved to get down and dirty on face-offs, grinding away in the mud and dirt as he wrestled with his opponent trying to win the ball. I didn't even know his real name, and most other players probably didn't either. Grunt was the world's fastest human in a ten-yard dash and the world's slowest human in anything over forty yards. He was lightning quick during face-offs, and lived and breathed for them. They were his only contribution to the team, and he would immediately come off the field right after the face-off, whether he won it or not. If we won it, he would come prancing off the field with his knees bouncing high, and then would sit on the bench rocking back and forth talking to himself saying, "Tuktuktuktuk" over and over again. A "Tuktuk" Grunt meant a happy Grunt.

If we lost the face-off, he would sit muttering something unintelligible. In fact, most of the time Grunt's words were unintelligible, but Scotty was able to interpret what he was saying, and convey Grunt's thoughts if required. And every once in a while, Grunt would surprise everybody by speaking in perfectly clear English, which always cracked us up.

We had a 14 game schedule, with the first seven games against non-conference teams, and the last seven against conference opponents. Coach liked to schedule the first couple of games against easier teams, and then make the next five games prior to conference against tough teams to get us ready for conference play. We always had a couple of non-conference state powerhouse teams scheduled, and this year was no different.

True to his word, Coach didn't take it easy on me. He made a brief statement that my being on the team would not create any unnecessary distractions. Period. The three weeks of practices before the season started were okay, but not a blast. The first reason was Will. He went out of his way to shove, poke my ribs or point out any mistake I made when we went one-on-one practicing defense. It was annoying, but not worth dwelling on.

The second reason was Jason. Practicing with the JV team players on an old grassy field next to the stadium, while the varsity team practiced in the stadium on the artificial turf. So, I never got to yell at him, tease him or watch him practice. Occasionally we'd have a water break or there would be a lull in practice when I could look over at the JV team, and I could see that the starting Poles for the JV team were a freshman and a sophomore that they were trying to develop and finally Jason. He hardly got a chance to play in game-like situations because they were teaching the younger players the basics.

The last reason frustrated me the most and was also related to Jason. His attitude. He didn't complain. Ever. In fact, there were several nights during the first weeks of practice when everybody had left the field except for Jason, Sam and Coach Slammer. I asked Jason what he was doing, and he said working with Coach on some of the finer techniques of playing Pole and he left it at that. Sam would stay after to help. He had been a pretty good

Middie before he switched to goalie so he would run through drills with them, and then give Jason a ride home. And then at night – every night in fact – I would hear the faint thump-thump . . . pause, thump-thump . . . pause, of Jason practicing on the wall in his backyard.

❂

Our first game was away, and we were going up to Rolling Hills High School in our brand new jerseys, looking sharp and excited about the season. Well, varsity players had new jerseys—the JV players had hand-me-down old varsity jerseys that looked like rags. We had to wear our jerseys to school on game day, and I felt terrible that Jason was wearing a tattered jersey with a faded #20, while I was wearing a brand new one, #7 *(his number, in hopes of returning it to him when he moved up to varsity)*, but he never complained about anything, including his uniform.

Chelsea found out that I had made the guys' team. Yes, a poor choice of words, which hadn't escaped her nasty mind either. She didn't wait long to tell me how pathetic I was. When she saw me in my jersey she smugly pointed out that since I couldn't get a guy to notice me off the field, apparently I had to go out for their team to get some attention. Fortunately, her opinion was not one I valued, so I shrugged it off. As I was dismissed early, I heard her snicker, "Break a leg, or an arm, or a nose . . . ."

I went down to change in the girls' athlete team locker room, but it was locked so I had to get the key from my cross country coach, who was teaching a P.E. class. She wished me luck with a big thumbs-up and sent her TA to unlock the door for me. I was still the first to get to the bus, and as I stepped up, the driver said, "Excuse me Miss, this is the boys' lacrosse bus."

"Yes sir," I said as I continued up the stairs and walked to a few rows in. I chose a seat, braided my hair, and tucked it into the back of my jersey. The JV team had already left on their bus, so I didn't need to save a place for Jason. And Sam and Hoss would probably be in the front. As luck wouldn't have it, Will came on next. He walked up and pointed to the back of the bus.

"Don't you think you should move that way Bennett? No need for you to be in a hurry to get off since you won't see the field." No longer invisible. What had I gotten myself into? I closed my eyes, inhaled. And then slowing let it out . . . and remembered, *"And for the ones who don't choose to like you? Who won't get to share your insight? What a loss for them."* *We were back sitting on a park bench. And she was still trying to comfort me and explain the unexplainable. Relationships. Friendships. A worthy, if not futile endeavor. She continued, ". . . because they will be missing out on one of the most dazzling secrets of the universe. My shining star. My miracle. You."* Thanks for the mental pep talk Mom, but in this case I don't think Will cares diddly squat about your shining star or her dazzling secrets. I came out of my reverie as Noise, and its constant companion, Smell, filled up the player's bus. Lacrosse players never clean their pads. Gross. Then we were off. Here goes nothing.

We showed up at Rolling Hills High at the halftime of the JV game. I could see Jason was suited up on the JV sideline. The rest of the varsity went inside and got dressed; I already had my gear on so I didn't need to go into the locker room. Since we were keeping me on the down low, we didn't ask the opposing team to open a different locker room for me.

I hit the port a potty to avoid the obvious questionable looks of going in and out of the ladies' restroom, and then went to watch the JV game. Jason didn't play any of the second half. It was so frustrating to watch the JV Poles try and catch and defend, when I knew how much better, faster, quicker – everything – Jason was. He never appeared mad or upset; I don't know how he kept it in.

It was interesting to watch Slammer coach the JV team. Anybody who knew anything about our lacrosse team knew Slammer was an awesome coach. He was a two-time D-III All-American Pole from a small college out east, and was a perfect match for Coach Hutchins.

Slammer could have won 10 or 12 JV games every year, but he never did. As soon as a player was good enough for varsity, he would inform Coach Hutchins, and the player would move up, leaving Slammer's team weaker. Slammer also insisted on focusing on fundamentals at all times.

We would lose a few JV games each year because some newb would try to clear the ball by *(correctly)* putting his stick in his left hand away from the defender when clearing. Inevitably he would lose the ball because he wasn't coordinated enough to use his left hand, but Slammer said trying to do the right thing as a JV player led to good habits as a varsity player.

Slammer-trained lax bros were fundamentally sound, and were a major reason we were so competitive on the varsity team. Coach Hutchins liked his assistant for many reasons, but he appreciated Slammer's honesty most of all. Slammer never offered suggestions to Coach Hutchins unless asked, and always said something like, "You might consider this . . ." instead of being pushy.

The JV team won 10-6, and varsity went out to get warmed up. I was nervous as we ran out onto the field. I couldn't help but look over at the JV team who had just finished shaking hands with their opponents. Jason was at the end of the line and went over to gather up his gear. When he saw us come out he scanned the team until he found me. And even though he hadn't even gotten to play much, and he was a senior on JV, he still managed to pull off his gloves for a double thumbs-up and a glorious good luck smile. *What a guy.*

On the other hand, Will slammed his stick down on mine during ground balls warm ups and Yard Sale'd me, that's when the ball and stick get knocked out of your hands and are lying out on the lawn, for anyone to see, and purchase in theory. Yep. He did that, to me. His teammate. Before the game. *What a jerk.*

"You better pick up your doll, the game's about to start. Not like that matters to you. But you need to leave the field. Have fun cheering from the sidelines Joanie," he whispered as he ran past. Ironically, rather than upsetting me it got me up for the game. *Channel it Jett.*

At game time we huddled together. "Let's go!" shouted Mack.

"Come on team!" yelled Wall.

"Scwitzelburf!" yelled Grunt. The game was on.

Grunt won the face-off, trotted off the field, and sat on the bench rocking back and forth, "Tuktuktuk!"

I heard someone call me and looked over to see Shelley frantically waving to me from the manager's table. I moved over and stood next to her, still looking at the field.

"Joan, can you help me?" she asked quietly.

"Sure, what's up?" I asked, still watching the field.

"I'm not sure about some of the stats. I hate to bother you, but I'm paranoid I'll do it wrong, and mess everything up," she whispered.

"No worries, it's not like I'll be creating any stats of my own. What don't you get?" I asked.

"Assists mainly. But ground ball pick-ups too," she answered.

"Okay, did you get that Grunt just won the face-off?" I asked.

"Yes," she replied.

"Good. We can go from there," I responded. And I double-checked with her the rest of the game.

We ended up winning 12-6, which was the expected result. On the way home both buses stopped at a burger joint, and Jason and I were next to each other in line.

"Twemnostexuntofgorn," Grunt placed his order.

"Excuse me?" the cashier asked.

Scotty jumped in and said, "Give him a number 6 with fries and a coke to drink please." And everybody was happy.

I asked Jason if he were okay, and he said, "Yep, I'm good." It had to be killing him to be watching from the sideline, but he took it well.

"Did you get in the game?" he asked.

"No," I replied.

"Next time just jump in there when a Middie comes off the field," he advised. Here he was encouraging me when it should have been the other way around. I didn't know what to say. And that night about eleven after I'd finished some homework and turned the volume of my tunes down, and I could hear the thump-thump . . . pause, thump-thump . . . pause, of Jason practicing on the wall in his backyard. Again.

The next day the coaches were a little hard on us. Although we won the first game, they had seen some things they didn't like. Poles were too slow to slide, we had trouble clearing the ball, and we threw the ball away too much. Practice focused on some fundamentals and we knew the schedule was going to get tougher in a few weeks. But we were also super excited about our first home game against Springs High in two days. My dad would be there, and we'd have a good crowd, including The Nakeds.

We won our first home game against Springs High 13-7. We were expected to win, and we did, so no big deal. No real surprises or issues, except occasionally we'd show a little hint of weakness. Defensive slides were late in coming a few too many times, or we'd have trouble clearing the ball against a pretty soft midfield defensive trap. These were the same issues we'd seen our first game. The coaches were concerned, and kept harping on the Poles to react quicker, for the Middies to execute clears better, and for Attack players to force their shots less.

During our first home game, Zif had come off the field and Sap was a little late substituting for him, so I ran onto the field and played a few seconds before being called back to the sidelines. "We'll let you know when you need to go in," Coach said to Carlson and me.

Will translated it for us, "Just in case you newbs didn't understand Coach, he meant NEVER," and turned back to the game.

"This is so lame," Carlson said in response, but only loud enough for me to hear. In fact, that was all Carlson ever said in practice and during games when he and I were standing together.

Finally I asked him, "What's so lame?"

"Me, not getting into play at all," was his reply. Evidently Carlson believed attending every lacrosse camp qualified him to start at midfield. His attitude was annoying, and it wasn't just me. He bothered others as well.

I didn't have any other issues with teammates or coaches except for Will. All of the other players treated me okay, and why not? I wasn't a threat to take anybody's playing time, and I worked hard and encouraged everybody, so the rest accepted me. Except Will, and I had a pretty good idea why. Or more importantly, who. I'm not sure he even knew why. But during drills he would intentionally throw low passes that were difficult to catch, or give me an extra unnecessary shove during scrimmages.

We worked our way through the first half of the season, and had a 5-2 record. We lost to two private schools, and beat the others we were supposed to beat, but none of that mattered – only conference play counted if we wanted to make playoffs. Dad was supportive and encouraged me when I didn't get in. "Maybe next time. Just be prepared." And then sometimes he would rant and rave a little bit about us public schools having to compete against private schools, ". . . with their eight coaches while we only have two . . ." and so on. Just as we were gearing up for conference play, Carlson quit the team. It was a relief for all of us, as he didn't contribute in any positive way. So, I was the number six Middie and Jason was "playing" Pole on the JV team. Which meant nothing because only the top five Middies were seeing the field, and the coaches weren't letting Jason play much either because they were getting the younger guys some game experience.

But every night after practice when Jason wasn't working with Slammer we'd run up and down the field throwing the ball. Sometimes we'd pretend I was clearing the ball and was being pressured, so I'd throw it to him and he'd clear it. My passing was pretty good, but occasionally I'd throw a not-so-perfect pass just to keep him on his toes and he would catch it every time. His ability to grab anything thrown near him was incredible. And every night I'd hear him in his backyard, thump-thump ... pause ... thump-thump ... pause ...

Our first conference game was against Lighthouse High, and was a home game. Lighthouse was really a weak team, and the only team in the conference that wouldn't be somewhat of a challenge for us. We always laughed at the name "Lighthouse" because lighthouses were usually near the ocean or a major lake, and we weren't within a thousand miles of the ocean. An odd name. Everybody looked forward to the Lighthouse game, because we were going to win by a lot, and that meant that benchwarmers like me would get to play. I was hoping Jason would play a ton in the JV game, but Slammer used two freshmen as Pole substitutes when the JV team started winning by a big margin. Jason didn't get to play any of the second half. Again.

I didn't get in very much either since we didn't get a decent lead until midway into the fourth quarter. I was pleasantly surprised to see I could compete with Lighthouse's Middies. Maybe they were tired or weren't that good, but it was clear to me that the hours I'd spent in practice trying to guard Mack, Zif and Scotty had paid off. Jon had always told me the biggest difference between the various levels of lacrosse *(like between JV and Varsity, or between high school and college)* was the speed of the game.

"It takes a little while to get used to," he would always say. "And then, after a little while, you realize you're good enough to play at the next level, and the game slows down for you, or you realize you are not good enough, and you need to be moving on to something else." The game had slowed down for me, compared to the first week of practice. So, against Lighthouse, I ran up and down the field enough to start working up a sweat, took a turn sitting out a Middie shift, and went back in for the last few minutes. I never touched the ball, but that was okay, as I didn't let the guy I was guarding score.

We played Fairview High next, and conference play was now starting to get serious. Fairview was a decent team that always gave us trouble. We couldn't afford to lose to Fairview, with Rockledge, Metro East and Woodland on the schedule. In fact, we could only afford to lose one conference game if we were to make state, and we'd never done that before. So, we rolled into Fairview needing – and expecting – a win.

Things started poorly for us. Fairview had improved a lot, and they had a devastating midfield trap that we had a hard time defeating. Even if Sam were able to stop a shot, he had trouble getting the ball to the Middies for a clear.

Fairview dropped off our Poles and double-teamed our Middies, making it near impossible for a Middie to take the ball across midfield. That meant we'd have to have a Pole try to clear, or throw a desperate pass to our Attack players and hope they'd win the ball. Sometimes they would win the ball, but often they wouldn't.

Our Poles just didn't have the skill or confidence to clear the ball themselves. It was a nightmare, and just kept getting worse. We were down 6 to 2 at halftime, and hurting. Coach Hutchins tried to encourage us, and emphasized the need to transition from defense to offense quicker, but Fairview's trapping defense was smothering. "Exposed," Jon used to say. Meaning that when you played the good teams, your weaknesses – which might not be so apparent against average teams – would suddenly, painfully, become obvious. Fairview had become a really good team, and we got exposed.

We ended up losing 12 to 6. Fairview got a few lucky breaks, and we got some bad bounces, but the fact is they beat us fair and square. The bus ride home was silent. Fairview! We lost to Fairview! Forget state playoffs; forget beating Rockledge and Metro East and Woodland High Schools. We just got spanked by Fairview!

Word spread quickly in the conference about losing to Fairview. A couple of guys on our team said their friends from other schools told them that Fairview had become a top-notch team, and not to get down about the loss. Others, including several from Woodland, lit up their Facebook pages with jokes about our loss, promising a double-digit win against us on Judgment Day. Ugh. I'm glad I hadn't bothered to create a FB page.

We didn't have time to dwell on the Fairview loss too much since two days later we had a home game against Metro East and two days after that we had another away game against Oak Park – a team Fairview had lost to already. Coach Hutchins tried to keep our spirits up at practice the next day, but he wasn't particularly successful.

It was a short practice since we had a game the next day, and everybody cleared out quickly, except for Jason and Sam who were going to work with Slammer after he met with Coach Hutchins for a few minutes up in their office. In the meantime, Hoss *(I finally was used to calling him that)* and I went over to talk to the guys and we started playing a bit. Sam was in goal and Hoss was defending against Jason and me.

Out of the corner of my eye I saw Will talking with Chelsea, who'd come out to watch the end of practice. I didn't think much of it. Why should I? I was having a blast goofing around with my guys.

I ran hard at Hoss, dodged, and when he came to me I gave a beautiful assist pass to Jason but he choked it away wide. Sam heckled us both. "Some Knight you are, you shoot more like a Storm Trooper," Sam laughed.

We all thought it was pretty clever, until we heard, "Does that make you Princess Leia?" Will asked me, as he apparently had caught Sam's Jedi reference. He and Chelsea had walked up. She looked over at me, and squeezed his arm.

"So, let me see, we've got Han Solo, Chewbacca and Lando too," he laughed as he looked to Jason, Hoss and Sam, and then back to Chelsea for approval.

Wow. He must have a Death Star wish. Thinking quickly, *(before "Chewy" could rip his head off)* I challenged Will to best two out of three face-offs. He scoffed and quickly agreed.

"And when I win, you have to wear my jock like a hat to school," he added smugly.

I shrugged, disgusted but with my best poker face added, "And when I win you have to get off my back, play nice and start treating me like a teammate," he shrugged. Like that *would ever* happen.

Hoss said, or more appropriately growled, that he'd officiate. I was surprised how oblivious Will was to the danger looming over him; clearly he only had Chelsea on his mind. Hoss stood over me menacing and protective at the same time, as Sam, Jason and Chelsea looked on. I quickly ran through all of the nasty tricks in my head that Jon had taught me. Some legal. Some . . . not so much.

First try. We crouched down and Will went a millisecond before the command and didn't even go for the ball, just knocked me back hard. I was expecting that. Hoss held out a hand and helped me up. I could see Jason clinch his fists but I gave him a look, and shook my head as if to say "I've got this," and he stepped back.

Second try. I flipped it back to my foot, kicked it behind, turned left and scooped it up and continued. Will looked surprised, and then determined. Chelsea frowned. Clearly she had enjoyed the first try more.

Third time I didn't even try for the ball. I waited for him to clamp down on it and then with all my weight I slammed my stick down on both of his wrists, which caused the ball to pop out from his stick, I turned, scooped it up and went to my right. His offside.

"You cheated!" Will yelled.

"What is it you are so fond of saying? If you ain't cheat'n, you ain't try'n?" I asked as I walked away. With Hoss whooping it up, and Sam and Jason grinning from ear to ear. Chelsea, on the other hand, was not amused.

21

"U Can't Touch This"

The Metro East game was a disaster. They won 14 to 6. Since I didn't get to go in, I tried extra hard to analyze the game while it was being played. Why were we losing? Were their Attack players better than ours? Not really. And Wall was as good of a goalie as any in the conference. I watched their Middies closely. Good. Very good. But no better overall than ours. Poles. Ours were okay. But they couldn't clear. I watched Metro East's top Pole scoop up a loose ground ball, and confidently weave through several players before he crossed midfield and passed it off to one of his Middies.

None of our Poles could do that. Poles that weren't a threat to clear allowed a trapping defense to double-team our Middies, which in turn led to turnovers, which led to scoring chances for them, and not for us. Pretty simple. Exposed. Again.

So we started off with a conference record of one win and two losses. Season essentially over.

Another short practice on Thursday, since we were traveling on Friday to play Oak Park. Leaving the parking lot after Thursday's practice I noticed Will was walking out of the lot onto the road. This was strange, since he had a car. I almost drove by but then for some reason stopped and asked if he needed a ride.

"No," he said when he saw who I was. I asked why he was walking, and he replied rather tersely that he had locked his keys and cell phone in his car, and needed to walk home to get the spare set of keys.

"Jump in," I said, "I'll give you a ride."

"I'm fine," he replied.

"I don't mind," I said.

"I'm good," he said.

I don't know why, but I started honking my horn.

"Stop it!" he shouted, looking around, but I continued to blast my horn. Finally, grudgingly, he got in and directed me to his house, which was only a mile or two away. We rode in silence except for the directions he gave me. When we got there I told him to go get the spare and I'd give him a ride back. The ride back to school was just as quiet. When I pulled up to his car he got out of my Jeep, shut the door, and started to walk away. Then he stopped, came back, opened the door and said, "Thanks." He then slammed it shut and walked away.

The following day we got on the bus and off we went. The team captains tried to get everybody pumped up during the bus ride to Oak Park, and I thought we had a decent attitude at game time.

As usual, we warmed up on the sidelines while the JV team was playing, went into the locker room for a quick talk, and then came back out to start warming up on the field. But the JV game wasn't quite over yet, so we hung around on the track behind the bench for the last few minutes of the JV game.

All of a sudden there was a big commotion along the sidelines. We all stopped and looked, but couldn't see anything because of all the JV players blocking our view. Somebody was screaming loudly. I took a look at the scoreboard: Oak Park was winning 13 to 8, and there were 52 seconds left in the game. What could anybody be upset about? The outcome of the game was not in doubt. But the yelling continued, and got louder and louder. Somebody was upset, and the screaming was coming from the Oak Park bench. I double-checked the scoreboard. Yep, Oak Park was going to win. What's up?

The JV game eventually ended, and after the post-game handshakes, we started to take the field. I grabbed Greg Johnston, who was one of the sophomores on the JV team that I knew, and asked what had happened.

"Their coach just went crazy," Greg said.

"Why?" I asked.

"He accused us of using Varsity players in a JV game."

"What?" I said. "All our varsity players were in the locker room."

"I know," said Greg. "Everything was going along fine until about four minutes left in the game. Then Smitty got hurt and had to come off the field." Smitty was Eric Smith, one of the freshman Poles on the JV team. But it still wasn't clear what had happened.

"So Smitty came off the field," I said. "What's the big deal?"

"There were only a few minutes left in the game and we were going to lose, so Slammer yelled out 'I need a Pole' when Smitty came off the field. That's when The Hammer sprinted out on the field."

The Hammer? "And who is The Hammer?" I asked.

"Jason."

Interesting.

"What happened?" I asked. Giving him my undivided attention.

"They had these two hot-dogging Attacks. Every time they scored they did some obnoxious dance together right in front of us and were talking smack the whole game."

Hmmm . . . Oak Park was not known for being the most sportsman-like team in the conference. I believed Greg.

"Okay, so what happened?" I asked.

"Hammer went into the game and when Mister Attack started doing his fancy moves, Hammer wrecked him. Laid him out. Totally clean hit. Scooped up the ball, ran through one of their Middies, and cleared it to our Attack. They had to help their Attack dude off the field. Two minutes later, he did it to the other Attack, who had been talking trash all game. Their coach went crazy after those two hits, but they were both clean."

"Ok," I said. "But why do you call him 'The Hammer'?"

"Because he is one, and so we gave him the name right after he came off the field," said Greg.

"Jett," he said, pulling me to the side a little bit and dropping his voice, "I've never seen anything like that. He absolutely wrecked those two Attackers. He hit so hard and so fast. It was amazing. Their Middie tried to stop him, but Hammer ran over him. Wrecked him too." Apparently "wrecked" was the word of the day for Greg Johnston.

"For some reason Slammer didn't start or play him tonight, so that's why their coach thought that #20 was a varsity player when he saw Jason play in the second half."

"Got it. Thanks," I said, and trotted onto the turf to warm up for a game in which I would not be playing. But I ran into Jason just before making my way onto the field.

"Oh, so you're The Hammer now?" I teased.

"Apparently," he said and added, "At least Coach finally let me play hard in a good game. Jon was right; it was a blast! Now it's your turn. Light 'em up Jett!"

Our game got underway, but it didn't go well. Oak Park had evidently scouted us when we played Fairview, and they set up a pressure trap defense similar to Fairview's. While we did better in clearing than the previous game, we still turned the ball over too much. Our offense was decent when we were able to set it up, but you can't set up an offense if you can't get the ball across midfield. Our Poles just weren't comfortable clearing the ball, and the Middies needed some help. Exposed. Again.

Oak Park scored with under a minute to go in the first half to make it 7 to 3, and just when we thought we'd get into the locker room trailing by four, they scored again with five seconds left in the half for an 8 to 3 lead. Sap tried to make a play on a loose ball, rolled his ankle and was laying on the field, obviously in pain. When he got up, he couldn't put any weight on his foot, so he was carried off the field. Our first half ended.

Unbelievable.

We trotted off the field to the locker room. I hung back a bit to help Shelley, who was trying to get some ice for Sap's ankle and at the same time get the stats sheet to Coach Hutchins. But we didn't need to see any statistics to know what was going on. We weren't a great transition team, and the midfield trap was killing us.

As I ran to the locker room, I could see Slammer had caught up to Coach Hutchins and was talking to him. Coach Hutchins looked over at Slammer after Slammer addressed him, and I saw something in Coach Hutchins' eyes. Hurt. I instantly felt horrible for him. This was going to be the year. We had the talent and the skill. Except maybe we didn't. We were just a little too vulnerable with our Poles. What was Coach going to say to us at halftime?

"Hey guys, would you try a little harder?"

"Hey guys, could you not stink it up so much?"

"Hey guys, do we all realize our season is ruined, even though we are pretending it's not?"

As I ran past the coaches, I heard Slammer say, "Halsted is ready to play varsity. Now. Right now." As miserable as Coach Hutchins was, he knew what Slammer was saying. Slammer hardly ever provided unsolicited advice, and when he did, it was always in the form of a gentle suggestion. To say such a thing at this moment, when Coach Hutchins didn't want to talk to anybody, meant something.

"Fine," said Coach Hutchins, "Bring him in the locker room with the rest of the varsity."

Slammer turned around and nodded to Jason, who had obviously been instructed to wait nearby while he talked to Coach Hutchins. Jason and I ended up being among the last players into the locker room, and sat down next to each other. The last player into the locker room was Grunt, who walked up, sighed, and sat down between Jason and me.

As previously mentioned, lax players are notorious for not

washing their gear, ever, and Grunt was as ripe as they come. I had to breathe through my mouth. Coach walked in and closed the door. Down 8 to 3 at half. Playoff hopes gone. It couldn't get any worse.

But it did.

There came a tapping sound on the locker room door, and when coach opened it, a middle age man met him. They talked a bit, and then coach closed the door. "Sap's ankle is bad," Coach said, "That was his Dad. They're taking him to the hospital."

And then coach sat down, lowered his head, and rubbed his hands through his hair. What could he say? We all felt horrible. There was silence for about a minute.

Suddenly, out of the blue, in perfect English, Grunt said, "We need to stop sucking." A few heads perked up.

Jason, who was sitting next to Grunt, spoke up, "We need to stop sucking. I promise I'll do my best to help the team even if I never play." Several of the lax bros who had played football with Jason murmured approval.

Mack, looked at Jason and said, "We need to stop sucking. I promise to clear the ball, and get it to the Attack."

Will, who was sat across from Mack, looked directly at me and said, "We need to stop sucking. I promise to treat all of the players on this team with respect." He almost sounded like he meant it.

Jim Crawford was next. He was a Pole who would not see the field this year and whose greatest contribution to the team was stinking up the bus after games. He said, "We need to stop sucking. I promise not to fart so much in the bus on the way home." Everybody laughed.

I could see where this was going. We were working our way around the room with our promises, but what could I say when it was my turn? I had nothing to contribute, not even something funny like Crawford. I looked at Jason, who had the guts to address a team that he wasn't even part of five minutes ago.

I slipped away without being noticed and followed Slammer to the equipment room. Jason would need a varsity uniform. Clearing my throat, "Coach, can I exchange my jersey for #6? Since I'm number six middie now that Carlson he quit?"

He squinted one eye to study me.

"I'll give Halsted #7, it was his football number, I think." I stuttered, then shrugged.

He rubbed his chin. "Sure." He tossed me the #6 jersey and grabbed a pair of shorts. "You can swap in here." He shut the door behind him. Blushing, I was pretty sure he'd figured out my ulterior motive, but I didn't care. Too much.

After switching jerseys, I snuck back in unnoticed. Except for Jason. His eyebrows furrowed reading my new number, then rose when I handed him #7.

The players had worked their way around the room to Coach Hutchins with their promises. It got quiet; everyone looked toward Coach, who looked like he was about to explode, but then said, "We need to stop sucking. Guys, I don't know where we're going with this, but I promise to stick with you if you'll work together." There were several loud shouts of support for Coach.

Finally it was my turn. I wasn't sure what to say, but I was the last person in the room to speak, so at least we'd be done with this experiment soon. I said, "We need to stop sucking. I don't play much. But if I get in, I promise not to be completely inept."

I sat down. Silence. *Nice speech Bennett,* I thought. Way to blow it. *Oh to be invisible again.*

More silence. Then I saw movement to my right.

Grunt stood up, turned around, and positioned himself in front of Jason and me. He looked at both of us, back and forth several times. Then he stared down at his own filthy uniform, then at our clean ones. His. Ours. His. The entire locker room was frozen, quiet, watching this scene play out.

Suddenly, Grunt shouted, "Yip!" and ran for the locker room

door. He grabbed the handle, shouted, "Thremprocuzzlwig!" and dashed out, only to return seconds later with mud covered hands. Grunt walked over to Jason, grabbed him by the shoulders, and wiped mud down the previously clean sleeves. Satisfied that his uniform was now ready to play, Grunt sat back down on the bench. "Tuktuktuktuktuk."

A knock came on the locker room door. It was the head referee. "Two minutes, Coach," he said.

Coach Hutchins said "We've got two minutes before the second half. Shelley! Get new roster up to the press box. Now!" She grinned at me and took off.

"Now, we shake up the batting order a little bit. Halsted, why don't you give it a go for me down low on close D," Coach Hutchins said. "Fletch move to LSM. Let's go!"

Jason was going to start the second half!

We didn't even have time to warm up, but took the field directly from the locker room. The Fairy Tale version would be that we walked onto the field and immediately scored. Reality was that Grunt did a decent job on the face-off, but Fletch was little slow coming in and Oak Park got the ball. They worked it around for a while, and then one of their Attacks got a half step ahead of Jake and threw in some lucky prayer of a shot that scored. It was just one of those things that happened now and then. Score was 9 to 3. The jeers started coming from the stands again, and their goal took all the air out of us.

As we got ready for the next face-off, I heard Jason yell at Fletch, "Hey Fletch, how about I take this?" Jason was going to take the face-off on one wing, with Mack on the other. Of course, I thought. Jason and Mack were our two fastest guys. It only made sense they should be on the face-off. The referee blew the whistle; Grunt fought for the ball and flipped it out to the side where Jason was. Their Middie fought for the ball with Jason, but it wasn't even a contest. Jason was faster and had the long Pole, so he scooped the ball up, and tossed it over to Mack, who started to set up the offense. It was so easy, so simple. How a face-off should be.

I watched Jason after his pass to Mack. Instead of coming off the field as a true LSM, he went back to play defense while Fletch came off the field. Jason and Hoss were talking some while on the other end of the field our offense tried to score. We were patient and worked the ball around for a good shot, but the shot went wide. Their goalie made a miraculous save on our next shot, and they started to clear the ball.

Karma. It just didn't seem right. They had scored on some sloppy shot, and we couldn't score on a good one. As they transitioned across midfield, I noticed something different in our defense. Jason was playing in the middle, with Hoss and Jake on the wings. Yes, I thought. That way Jason can provide slide help for either Pole if they need it. And they would need it.

One of their Attacks starting doing his thing – operating back and forth, spinning, dodging, working his way closer to the goal. We'd been a victim to this move several times in the first half. A hard spin to the outside and here comes the reverse with a shot to follow. There was a streak of blue. As their Attack turned for the shot, that streak turned out to be 6' 180 lb. 4.53 second 40 yard speed Jason impacting their Attack player head on. 6' 180 lb. 4.53 second 40 yards hit him so hard, that he . . . well . . . *wrecked* him. Johnston was right. I had never seen anything quite like it.

As their Attack player was lying on the ground trying to recalibrate his brain, Jason scooped up the loose ball and flipped it to one of our Middies for the clear. Down the field went the Middies to set up our offense. Again, they were very patient, but couldn't score. Totally frustrating. We were taking good shots, but it wasn't going our way.

Oak Park cleared into our defensive end, and began working the ball. It was obvious that one of their Attacks wanted to score – not the one that had been laid out the last time, but another Attack.

With an attitude like, "You knocked one of our guys down, so I'm going to show you." A screen by one of their Middies caused Jason to be matched up against him one on one. Jason could have switched back, but everybody could tell this Attack player was determined to shoot, so Jason stayed on him. As he started his moves, Jason, instead of staying back, jumped up right next to him and began aggressively pushing him and going for his stick.

Attack started running to his left, but Jason moved his body in front of him and continued shoving him back towards the sideline. Attack rolled back to his right and was met by Jason's stick impacting his ribs as well as his own stick. Faced with that unpleasantness, Attack rolled back to his left, and got shoved and pounded some more, eventually dropping the ball, which Jason scooped up and flipped to a Middie.

We went nuts on the sideline. We were used to seeing our defenders play, well, defensive – trying to stop the other team. Jason was playing *offensive* defense – attacking the other team. A beautiful thing to behold. *(!)*

Once again we pressed into the offensive zone and worked the ball around. True to their word at halftime, our players were not selfish and looked for a good shot. Once again, we came up short.

Our defense was playing well, we were getting good shots, and yet Oak Park had only increased their lead since halftime. Mack was tired and needed a break. He came off the field and several players yelled, "Middie!" which was the clue for Will to go in for Mack. Will had been watching and was ready to go in. He sprinted onto the field.

Zif needed a break too, and came running off the field. "Middie!" Two or three players yelled.

Nobody moved. "Middie!" they yelled again as Zif approached the sideline. Somebody shoved me in the back. "Get'em, Bennett!" he said, and I was shoved out onto the field.

Wait a minute, what's going on? Oh, that's right! With Sap hurt,

I was the number five Middie!

I ran onto the field and marked up #22, who was eyeballing me, sizing me up. "How am I going to school this chump?" he was probably thinking. "I might be able to get past him, but there's this problem with that Pole behind him . . ."

Jon's words came to mind.

"Joan, there isn't a player on the planet who can stop another player from scoring all of the time. It's going to happen occasionally. What you have to do is play good, smart defense, and trust your goalie. Shove them outside, and down low. Outside and down low. If they shoot, make sure it's a low angle shot, taken from outside and down low."

I could tell #22 favored his right hand, and that was fine with me. He was on my left side, and started to make a run at me. I accelerated into him and shoved him to his right, and I did it again. I wasn't knocking him backwards, but he was moving to his right. I continued to shove him right, and I guess he got tired of it, because he finally did take a shot.

Oh no, I thought. *My man is going to score.* But it was a low angle shot and Sam had no problem getting a leg in front of it. The ball bounced around in front of the goal a bit, and then somebody kicked it. It ended up rolling toward me.

Instinctively I scooped it up and started to run. Out of the corner of my left eye I could see #22, about three or four yards away, and moving quickly towards me. On my right was another one of their Middies, closing in on me. I accelerated to top speed, but could tell it would be just a few seconds more before I was going to become the inside of an Oak Park sandwich.

I had nowhere to go, and I panicked.

I turned and threw the ball backwards, toward my own goal. To Jason. I could hear the Oak Park sidelines laugh, *"He's shooting at his own goal!"*

Please, Jason, be there. I thought. It was a high pass, like the many I'd thrown to him before – too high for a Middie to reach comfortably, but one he could catch with the long Pole. He looked surprised for a second, and then reached up into the air, snagged the ball, and started up the field. The Attack player he had been marking was trailing him, and the two Middies that had been closing in on me had circled back to Jason, like a wolf pack moving in for the kill.

"Run!" yelled Jason. Well, okay, I guess I could do that. I turned and ran up the field ahead of him. Just like a thousand times before that we'd done in the winter, or on weekends, messing around.

The two Oak Park Middies had almost reached Jason, when he wound up and threw a rocket pass. To me. Like a thousand times before. I stuck my stick up and felt the ball land in the mesh. I turned and began to sprint. Since the two Oak Park Middies had turned around to cover Jason, I now had a fifteen yard lead on them. They were fast, but they weren't going to beat me in a 50 yard dash when I had that big of a lead. I looked ahead. Waiting for me were their three Poles, our three Attacks, and their Goalie.

"The thing about fast breaks," Jon said, "is that everybody knows what's supposed to happen. The two lower Poles are going to play a zone defense. Top Pole's job is to stop the ball and force a pass. If the Poles can force a few extra passes, then their Middies have time to get back from the offensive end of the field and play defense. Attack's job is to get a good shot within a couple of passes before Middie help can arrive. So it goes down like this, top Pole will jab step at you, pretend to give you a shot and do anything he can to confuse you and make you hesitate. But ultimately, he MUST stop ball and make you pass. He simply can't allow you to walk in and take an uncontested shot. What he wants to do is force you to pass too early, so that he has time to slide. Don't pass too early. Be prepared to take a shot if he gives it to you. You MUST be a threat to score."

Jon's words echoed in my head as I approached their Pole. He was big and tall, and pointing the Pole at me, daring me to try and score. He shifted a few inches to his left, giving me a little room to my left. I switched the stick to my left hand. He hesitated. Began jab stepping at me. Trying to make me pass early, or to slow down. I didn't. At fifteen yards out from the goal, I began bringing the stick back, winding up.

He was going to let me shoot! No, he wasn't! At the last second, he ran at me, not allowing the shot, forcing the pass, just as he should. He was very fast and surprised me a bit. But I had played with and against Jon Bennett too many times. I got the pass off to Larry just before their Pole knocked me into next week with a clean, hard hit.

It knocked my breath away, and I lay on the ground for a few seconds trying to breathe.

Suddenly the Three Stooges hands were grabbing my hands and my jersey, pulling me to my feet.

"Great pass Bennett!" yelled Larry.

"Woo Hoo!" shouted Moe.

"What happened?" I asked as I staggered to my feet.

"Pass from you to Larry to Moe to me," said Curly. "Goal. Nice job!"

I trotted off the field *(slowly)* as we prepared for the face-off. "Good clear, Jett!" Jason yelled at me.

"Frimexerban," said Grunt as he ran by and high-fived me. Several of the players on the team congratulated me on the sidelines. Slammer smiled and nodded his head – the ultimate compliment, coming from him.

Grunt won the face-off; Jason scooped it up and kicked it over to Mack. Simple. Easy. We ran up and down the field a couple of more times, and the offense was starting to click. Mack scored to make it 9 to 5. I went in again on defense to give him a break. Oak Park had now resorted to taking longer shots – none of them wanted to go inside and risk facing Jason.

On my second shift, Jason knocked the ball out of somebody's stick, and again it was rolling on the ground near me, but this time there were other players nearby. I could see a big Attack player from Oak Park moving quickly for the ball, and could tell we would get there about the same time. He was eyeballing me, and looking to knock me down.

"Man Ball!" yelled Will to me. I looked to my left and saw Will closing in on the ball too. Will could probably get to the ball a split-second before I could, but his "man ball" call signified something else. Oak Park's attacker was looking to light me up, and as I scooped up the ball, he veered away from any attempt at getting the ball and ran directly at a defenseless me.

There was a sound of thunder.

I was still standing, rather, running up the field. I looked behind me quickly, and saw what had made all of the noise – Will had destroyed their Attack. He was lying on the ground, with his stick about five yards away. I guess Will had meant what he said at halftime! Finally!

I ran quickly up the field, but a Middie had angles on me, and moved to cut me off. Just before he reached me, I casually rolled the ball on the ground to my left.

"WHAT?" I hear somebody from the Oak Park stands shout. The ball was rolling towards the sidelines, and it looked like I had intentionally thrown it away.

Suddenly Jason appeared from nowhere, and moving at Mach speed, scooped up the ball and was gone. Just like a thousand times before, when I'd rolled the ball out in front of him. Jason exploded through the trap that two Oak Park players tried to initiate, and took the ball down the field. Their Pole prepared to meet our Pole. Jason pumped-fake a pass at twenty yards out, which moved their Pole just enough so Jason was able to wind up and shoot at about fifteen yards out. Even from where I was, it was terrifying to see him twist his body around to get more torque on his shot – as if he needed it. He came over the top, releasing the ball from about 11 feet in the air.

Their goalie stood like a champ, waiting to make a move on the ball. But he never saw it. The ball flew past him and into the net. Score was 9 to 6. Our sideline went insane. We hadn't had D Poles that could clear the ball, much less be an offensive threat. But now it appeared we had both. All in one.

Things just started to run smoothly for us after that. Grunt would win the face-off. Mack or Jason would scoop it up. We'd go on offense and work it around for a good shot. If we didn't score, our defense played tough. Jason held down the middle, and helped whenever somebody got beat. It turned out that Hoss and Jake were really good playing close defense on the wings – especially when they knew Jason was in the middle and could slide to provide help if required.

We didn't fear the trap anymore. The rest of our Middies watched me feed Jason, and did the same. If they double-teamed one of us Middies, we'd get the ball over to Jason, and he'd bring it across. If they didn't double-team a Middie, the Middie could clear. Even I was comfortable doing that. I'd spent years dodging Jon's attempt to dislodge the ball from my stick, and could hold my own against any single Middie.

We did have a couple of times when we were offside. Jason would bring the ball across midfield, and all three Middies would come across as well. But after a while, it was unspoken what Middie would remain behind – the one who was most out of position, or who needed a rest the most.

Oak Park was winning 9 to 8 when the third quarter ended, but you wouldn't know it from the sidelines. They were all yelling at each other, complaining, trying to figure out how to stop us.

We were yelling too, "Hey Halsted, stop sucking!" and having a blast. Until that is, the Oak Park Attacker that Will had laid out for me decided to retaliate cheap and dirty. Mack was clearing the ball and sent a high pass towards Will. Big mistake, as he had to jump and stretch while twisting his body. He caught it of course – Will had skills – but as he turned and landed he got lit up like the Fourth of July. And believe me, as he flew backwards and landed hard, he no doubt saw fireworks. The crowd even "oooohed and oooouched."

But not me. I saw the whole scene play out like a horror flick from down field. And I took off. Back towards the midline. Building my speed like a steam engine until I was going full tilt. So when my 132 pounds of righteous fury hit the cocky Attack, who had lazily scooped up the ball and turned towards me without looking – yep – you guessed it – "I ran train" on him – legally. Justifiably. Gloriously.

"For every action, there is an equal and opposite reaction." Of course with all that momentum I went flying after the impact too. Straight into my sideline team who caught me, made sure I was okay, and then pounded on me. In the meantime Jason got the ground ball pick up, and took it down and passed it to Mack who put it in, and quickly ran back to check on and apologize to – Will. Who had gotten up, painfully, and was back sitting on the bench trying to figure just how many ice bags he needed to put Humpty Dumpty back together again.

We scored early in the fourth quarter, and kept rolling. Oak Park tried slowing the game down, speeding the game up, calling time outs, switching players, zone defense, man-to-man defense – it didn't matter. We won 15 to 10. Jason scored two goals and was a clearing freak.

The guys had learned from me, and saw that if Jason wasn't open for a pass, it didn't mean you didn't throw it at him. Several times he was covered, so I just threw it to open space. *If your guy can outrun Jason, then you are welcome to have the ball* was my philosophy. But they couldn't outrun him.

The ride home was quieter than expected. I sat near the back of the bus next to Jason because he was definitely, totally, justifiably on varsity now. I could see Coach Hutchins and Slammer engaged in deep discussions about the team. Now and then a player or two would turn around and look at Jason, and then whisper something to the guy they were sitting next to.

I knew what everyone was thinking. *How are we going to use this awesome, terrifying new weapon that we just discovered?*

When we got back home, Coach Hutchins called a team meeting. Uh-oh. Usually Coach let us go straight home. The last time we had a team meeting after an away game was a few years ago, I was told. A couple of guys were goofing off in the restroom of the restaurant where we stopped for dinner. They were splashing water on each other, and made a mess by getting water all over the floor. The team had to run sprints as a result of that little episode. One of the culprits was rumored to be a Mr. Jon Bennett, but it was never confirmed. Or denied.

Instead of running sprints, though, Coach had us sit in the locker room. A cell phone rang. Not good. Coach had us turn off our cell phones whenever we had a team meeting, and violating this rule was not funny to him. But it was his cell phone that rang. We all gave him grief for this egregious transgression, but he motioned us to be quiet and answered the phone.

"Hello . . . yes . . . yes . . . great. Tell him to get better soon," he said into the phone.

"I left my phone on for a reason," said Coach with a smile. "That was Sap's Dad. Sap has a pretty good ankle sprain, but it's not broken." *Good news for us.*

"Folks," he said. "I made some mistakes this year. I think it's pretty obvious from the second half of this game what kind of team we can be. I just didn't see it, and that's on me. But it's not too late to change," he continued. "I want to switch up the composure – the attitude – of this team starting right now," he said. "We are no longer a slower paced, deliberate team. *Effective immediately,* we are a high-octane, fast-paced team. We are going to win loose balls and face-offs, and set up a deliberate, passing offense. But on defense, we are going to punish teams for missing shots and we're going to do it by becoming a quick transition team."

He looked at Sam and said "Wall, I want the ball out of your stick within two seconds of making a save. Hit the open Middie. If a Middie is not open, throw it to Halsted. If Halsted is not open, throw it to space near Halsted, and let him run after it."

Sam nodded.

"Middies clear the ball quickly and look for 5 on 4 or 4 on 3 opportunities. Wall is going to get you the ball so quickly the other team will not have time to fully set up their trap. If you do get double teamed, kick it over to Halsted. I want you to run like crazy when you are on the field. Come off when you need a break." We all nodded.

"Halsted, you are authorized to clear the ball yourself, at every opportunity. Look for chances to score off an unsettled situation."

"Attack. Keep working the ball like we did in the second half. I expect each of you to give me a shift or two in the defensive end of the field each quarter. We'll need to rest our Middies, so we'll rotate a Middie down low and an Attack up high for many of our offensive shifts. High Attack will drop back and play D, giving the Middie a break. We're going to be thin at Middie for a while, with Brooks and Bennett being the number four and five Middies, and no other subs available."

"Yay Coach!" the Three Stooges yelled together. They could all play good defense, and a fast break, running offense meant that they would get opportunities to score more goals.

"Another thing. Crucial in fact. I don't see a need to share any of this with anybody, do you? No need to tell anybody about our new offense, our new plans, and new players we've discovered. No talking with anybody. Nothing on Book Face or Tweeters. Or whatever else you guys live on. Got it?"

We all nodded.

"Ok. Go home. See you tomorrow."

I walked out of the locker room with Jason. The Hammer and me. The Hammer and Middie number five. As we walked to the Jeep we saw Sam, Hoss, and then Shelley a few cars away. Sam pointed towards her and shrugged his shoulders. I rolled my eyes and yelled over to her. "Hey Shelley, we're going to go grab some burgers, shakes and fries to celebrate. Do you want to come? You can jump in with us."

"Heck yes!" she said in a heartbeat.

After eating we hit the grocery store for candy. Sam offered to drive Shelley back to her car, which was *(ahem)* in the opposite direction of Hoss' home, so we offered to take Hoss so he could get home faster. Not to mention help Sam out. It had been so nice that we had dropped the roof of the Jeep. Hoss stretched out in the back and made himself comfortable. Jason challenged me to an orange bubble gum bubble-blowing contest. Which I totally dominated thank you very much, until a bug flew into it. Crunch. *Yuck,* but still funny.

When we pulled into Hoss' driveway I saw the lights were still on. As he jumped out of the back the front door opened and a woman walked out. I assumed correctly that she was his mom. She came right to my car door and looked at me. *Studied me.*

"Thank you," she said and gently rested her hand on my arm.

"You're welcome, he was no problem," I said, politely. She seemed so earnest it contrasted our celebratory mood and threw me off balance.

"Yes, he most definitely was, but that's in the past now, thanks to you," she said, with a heavy dose of double meaning as she slid her left arm around his back and looked up at him, then back to me. "I knew your mom, you're a lot like her," she said.

"Hair?" I questioned, holding up a messy curl.

"No, here," she said, moving her hand from my arm and resting over her heart. "She'd be very proud of you."

Ouch. But it was a bittersweet pain.

We said goodnight and headed home. I silently filed her comments away to dwell on later as Jason and I reverted to our previous, victorious, magical mood. Teammates. *Together.* Alone. *At last.*

22

That's right. There I sat in his driveway babbling on about the game. I could not get over how awesome it felt, "and then he did this, which made me do that, and Will came out of nowhere and cleaned that guy's clock, and then I rolled the ball out to my left and it was like sweet music seeing you scoop it up, switch hands, and pass it to Mack ... what a game! Could anything ever possibly get better than that?" I asked, looking up at the stars as they celebrated above us in the dark moonless sky. And with that I looked over at Jason. Staring in. To me. Not at me or through me. Not dazed and confused or bored, or what in the world is she babbling about? No, it was a deep, incredibly intense gaze like nobody else existed in this galaxy gaze.

"And?" he asked, not breaking said glorious gaze.

"And?" I asked, stunned, speechless. *(Almost.)*

"You were saying?" he smiled.

"I was?"

"Yes, you were. You were giving an exact play by play action sequence that is probably the coolest slash hottest thing I have ever heard slash seen," he said.

"Oh." Oh. Again. Sorry Jane Austen.

And with that he reached over and tucked a wayward curl gently home behind my ear. *First kiss.*

"Jett, may I kiss you?" he asked. Just like that. Seriously. Killer.

"You just did," I murmured. *(Yep, a murmur, sorry that was the extent of it, but considering the situation, could you blame me? Give this girl some slack.)*

"I did what?" he asked, a little confused at this point, but I admit sometimes it was difficult to follow my train of thought, or see the engine, dining car or the caboose anywhere in sight for that matter.

"You just kissed me our first kiss," I whispered. *(Slightly more audible than a murmur.)*

"How's that?" he asked, still wondering but still watching.

"It was awesome," I sighed. *(Forgive me, but one must exhale.)*

"I mean, when did I kiss you? I'm pretty sure I would know it after all this time when I finally got up the nerve to ask if I could."

"Well, it wasn't a traditional kiss, as kisses go, would you like me to explain?" I asked. Really? Really? I'm prepared to go all lecture-mode? *Now?*

"Please do." He grinned. *(Not helping with the concentration.)*

"Okay, you kissed what is known as the Tuck Random Curl Behind The Ear Kiss," I said. Which amazed me, since I doubt that I had taken a breath for like two, maybe three minutes.

"Never heard of it, can you demonstrate?" Not breaking eye contact but the corners of his eyes crinkled up in a smile. Yes. Haven't we already established the fact the guy can smile with his eyes? Shoot me.

"Okay, but it will have to be modified Samson, since you chopped all of your lovely locks off," I muttered.

"Are you ever going to get over that?" he laughed.

(Visible, exaggerated sigh.) "Probably, but not until you suffer awhile longer. But back to the demo," he was resting his hand on my shoulder but I forced my way through the distraction *(!)* and reached up to his ear, then traced the question mark from the top curving down with my index finger, and gently pinched the lobe between my finger and thumb, making the dot.

"Wow," he said softly. "But you must be mistaken. That wasn't a modification. That was a whole new ballgame. Our *second kiss*."

Stunned. Recovered. Slightly. Shrugged. "That is a technicality that could be argued," I conceded, as I rested my hand on his shoulder. And with that he leaned in, still looking into my eyes. I could go on and on at length about the color of his deep blue eyes and the beauty of his soul opening within the incredible depth of them, *(oops, I just did)* but I was interrupted by our third kiss. But not until we had an up close and personal conversation about three inches away from each other that had me extremely thankful for, and singing the praises of, sweet, sweet, orange bubble gum.

"Aren't you going to close your eyes?" he questioned.

"Nope."

"Care to elaborate?" he laughed. Which was a puff of warm, citrus sunshine traveling from his mouth to my nose.

"Well . . . I want to be able to see who I am kissing, and I want them to see me. Because if they close their eyes, then they can imagine they are kissing someone else, and so they are not really kissing me," I explained, from three inches away. He thought for a moment.

"It's difficult to fathom why anyone fortunate enough to be kissing you would ever want to imagine that they were kissing someone else," he said, which sounded way better coming from him, let me tell you. I thought for a moment.

"And that it is precisely why, we are sharing our *third kiss*," I whispered, leaning into him, and softly, dryly, pressed my lips on one side of his slightly curved lips.

He smiled wider. "And what do you call that?" he asked.

"Hugh," I answered his smile.

"Hugh?" he questioned. "Just Hugh?"

"Well the technical term is Soft, Dry Kiss To The Corner Of A Lopsided Grin, but I call it Hugh for short," I told him.

"Oh, I see. That makes perfect sense." He shook his head. After one last long amazing look he said, "You were right, it was an awesome game of lacrosse tonight, but for arguments sake, *it did possibly get better,* even though you couldn't imagine how, *after all.* But I better let you go now, so Sofi and Gracie can get some sleep."

He broke the world's most glorious gaze to date, and tilted his head to glance up to a window on the second floor.

I followed his eyes just in time to see two shadows melt away from the sheer curtains. He moved his hand from my shoulder up to my ear, silently traced the newly invented Question Mark Kiss *(fourth kiss)* and got out the car. He waved up to the window, then turned, kissed his fist, double pumped over his heart and tossed it to me with a two fingered "Peace Out" sign. *(Fifth kiss.)*

23

"Hit Me With Your Best Shot"

That was amazing. *What a dream.* I didn't want to wake up or ever open my eyes again if I could just watch it over and over on the inside of my eyelids. I stretched out my legs, which brought an annoyed *"meow"* from Misty as I disturbed her catnap. I heard a text swoosh and picked it up to check.

(sofi)
Can we catch a ride?

(me)
Sure, what's up with Sam?

(sofi)
Nada. He took J

(me)
Who's we then?

(sofi)
Shelley and me!

(me)
Kk, why didn't you go with Sam?

(sofi)
Lol! R U kidding me?

(me)
No . . . what?

(sofi)
We want details

(me)
About?

(sofi)
Hahaha

(me)
What?

(sofi)
Jason and Joanie
Sitting in a jeep. . .

"Ouch!" I cried out as the corner of my phone bounced off my bare foot. It served the purpose of "pinch me to see if I am dreaming" while I hopped on the other foot. Fortunately the screen was okay, my foot on the other hand . . . *it was not a dream!* Whoa! Awesome! Until I picked up my phone and read.

(sofi)
Driveway in ten
xoxoxox lols

Dream over. I grabbed a granola bar and an apple and pulled out the Jeep. True to her text, they were waiting for me in my driveway. Oh joy. This is going to be a riot.

"Helllloooo Joan!" they sang together.

"Morning."

"Well?" Sofi asked.

"Well what?"

"Details!" Shelley demanded.

"About?"

"Last night! In the driveway! True Love's First Kiss!" Shelley exclaimed as she climbed in.

"What?" I tried again.

"You heard us, spill it!" Shelley demanded again.

"Sounds like you overdosed on *Princesses* last night."

"Not me, I think you roll more like Mulan – you know – kick butt, take names, rescue the emperor, get the guy." Sofi laughed.

"No comment," I said. "Now unless those boots are made for walking, no more questions. I mean it."

"Anybody want a peanut?" Shelley giggled from the back seat.

How could something so great turn into something so embarrassing? Awkward? And I hadn't even seen Jason yet. For the first time I was glad we didn't see each other during the school day, and we didn't have lunch together today.

So potentially, the first time we will see each other will be at practice . . . then I remembered! Jason is on the varsity squad! We get to practice together! Uh ooooh. We get to practice. Together. *With everyone else.*

This calls for a plan. *Compartmentalization.* That's it. I can do this! After all, two men – boys – apes raised me – so it was time for this monkey to do what Bennett's do best – *compartmentalize.*

We had all been doing it for years – four years – actually. But now it was no longer essential due to a tragedy. My newly visible life, a comedy, made it a necessity. I needed to think. And since I was currently in my composition class – make an outline.

Compartmentalization Skill Development

I. Caveman
    A. Hunter
        1. see it
        2. track it
        3. get it

B. Hygiene
   1. sweat
   2. smell
   3. wear dead animal skins

II. Cavewoman
  A. Gatherer
    1. find it
    2. gather it
    3. eat it
  B. Low standards
    1. give birth without painkillers
    2. ignore smells and lice
    3. forgive lack of communication skills

III. Choosing a Pet Dinosaur
  A. Herbivore
    1. eats a lot
    2. grows a lot
    3. poops a lot
  B. Carnivore
    1. sharp fangs
    2. sharp claw
    3. may very well eat you while you sleep

It helped to pass the hours until it was time to dress for practice. I ran into my cross country coach on the way into the locker room, and she asked how the season was going. Super supportive. I got ready and ran out to the field where Coach Hutchins was already picking teams for a scrimmage. We were going to try his freshly revised game plan out with our charming new "stop sucking" attitude. I kept my eyes on him, and him only, like he was giving instructions on evacuating from an airplane or ship or pterosaur and my life depended on it. He called out my squad and told us to turn our pinnies to blue. He called off the other squad and told them to turn theirs to Golden Boy. I mean gold. Boy. Was I a mess.

We were placed on opposing teams, and as I cleared the ball and approached the opposing goal Jason appeared out of nowhere and checked me crisp and clean, knocking me off my feet. Onto my butt. "Don't bring that weakness in here little girl," he said as he reached his gloved hand down to help me up. With an adorable Jason the Golden Hammer Boy smile.

I grabbed his glove, looked up at him, lifted myself and spit out my mouth guard, "You better be wearing a cup." Just then Sam looked around him and laughed at me.

"That goes double for you 'Wall,'" I threatened.

"Why Jett? Is your aim off today?" Sam heckled.

"Nope. Dead on," I answered without a smile and walked away.

"Jett. Jett. Joan! I'M NOT!" Sam yelled. I had to laugh. My guys. Maybe this won't be that bad after all.

I went back to the blue pinnie huddle so we could strategize. Will said, "Jett, you take it in fast and dodge but let Jason push you right; I'll set a screen, and then cut and scream for the pass so Hoss slides to me giving you a clean shot."

"Sounds good, let's burn 'em." I shoved in my mouth guard.

"And Princess Leia," Will said. I looked over at him, confused that he had reverted to his previous jerk-mode.

"Use the Force," he smiled.

I laughed as I spit out my mouth guard and turned to face the goal, and then swept my stick across in front of my body saying, "These aren't the droids you're looking for." And then back to Will, "Help me, Obi-Wan Kenobi; you're my only hope."

Worked like a charm. I took it in, dodged left, back right, faking like I wanted to go back left just as Jason expected. As promised Will set the screen and then took off yelling for the ball. I faked the pass to him and then wound up and cranked off a top left corner shot. As soon as I released I dove across the crease and rolled away from it.

"Well done! What was that last move?" Coach Hutchins asked.

"That was something Jon taught me to avoid a crease violation and another "late kiss" by the close D." I said with a straight face.

"Ha! 'Late kiss.' That's a good one!" Coach chuckled as he walked away right past Jason. My eyes followed him.

"Yep, it was," I said, sneaking a glance at Jason. His eyebrows rose. *Compartmentalize that!*

❂

Three days later we played Pine Forest High at home. Normally at games like this we might expect to see a few players or fans from Woodland at the game scouting us, but since we had pathetically lost to Fairview, nobody considered us a threat anymore.

We focused on some of the basics Coach had talked about after the Oak Park game – rotating Attacks up top to buy rest time for the Middies, clearing the ball quickly, and things like that. With Jason The Hammer directing the defense and serving as a clearing alternative, we started to gel. Middies started taking advantage of his ability to clear; Attack now understood how to take advantage of our fast breaks.

By halftime we had a 10 to 1 lead, and Coach started mixing in JV players for the rest of the game, until the entire last quarter when our entire team was JV players or varsity benchwarmers. We eventually won 14 to 8; it felt good to yell for some of the dudes that didn't get to play a lot.

Jon called the next night. He usually called once or twice a week to try and cheer me up since I wasn't playing much, but now that I was playing a lot and Jason was too, he was ridiculously excited. The same night we beat Oak Park, Woodland had beaten Rockledge. "A major upset," I told Jon.

"No, not at all," replied Jon and added, "Woodland is a strong team this year." And then he found some high school lacrosse website with an article from a month or so ago and sent me the link. The article predicted that Woodland would finish second in the conference over Rockledge. And us.

"When did they get so good?" I asked.

"It's been coming for a while," Jon said, "They have a solid youth program, good coaches, and a good senior class. Obnoxious, but good."

"Wow. To think Woodland will be going to state in lacrosse," I said. I didn't like the sound of it.

Silence.

"Unless you go," said Jon.

"What? We can't make it," I said, "Too many losses."

"Unless you win out," said Jon. "Your conference record is three wins and two losses. If you beat both Rockledge and Woodland, you and Woodland will both have a five and two conference record, you will win the tiebreaker because you beat them head-to-head. Rockledge would have three losses – Metro East, Woodland and you. You'd go to state."

He was right. I couldn't even begin to fathom it, however. We'd only beaten Rockledge once in our existence, and Woodland was tough this year – projected to go to state.

"You can do it," said Jon. "Look, you racked up 11 goals in one half against Oak Park once you figured out how to play. Oak Park is a decent team – they played Woodland and Rockledge tough. You have to believe."

❂

Three days later, Rockledge rolled into town. The great Rockledge High School. Twice as big as our school. Only beaten by us once in our history. There wasn't much of a crowd, although Dad was there, and I knew he would be yelling for me. The first day of the three day stretch of "Judgment Day" was beginning today, and one of the head-to-head contests with Woodland was the girls' soccer game at Woodland, so The Nakeds were supporting them and weren't at our game.

Rockledge hit us with their midfield trap, but we were ready. We'd worked hard on clears the last week, in anticipation of this big game. Sometimes during clears all three Middies would cross midfield as well as Jason, which normally would be an offsides call, but one of our Attack would have stepped across the midfield line into the defensive zone, allowing the play to continue.

Rockledge had seen several Poles who were big and fast and could clear and shoot, but they hadn't seen a Pole who was this fast and could dodge, like Jason. We were up on them 8 to 6 at half, and Coach Hutchins was giving it to us at halftime.

"We can beat this team, and you know it," he said. "Don't let up. Keep attacking. Keep the pressure on them." We had turned into a running team when we had the opportunity, and I was getting a lot of playing time. It was funny – we were a "push, push, push, run, run, run" team when we were clearing the ball and during face-offs, but were a deliberate, passing team during settled offensive situations. We knew when to push the pace and when to slow things down.

Nobody scored for the first three minutes of the third quarter, and everybody knew the next goal would be huge. If we could score first, we'd be ahead 9 to 6 with some serious momentum. If they scored, it would be 8 to 7 and they'd feel like they had us. Zif needed a break and came off the field, and I went in. There were a couple of transitions up and down the field with nobody scoring, although their #6 Middie who I guarded tried. He was fast, but I played him straight up and forced low percentage shots. I wouldn't win any awards for Defensive Middie Of the Year, but weeks of playing against Mack and Zif in practice paid off.

Sam made a save on a shot, and cleared to Jason, who began running up the field. #6 correctly perceived that Jason was more of a threat than me, so he left me to double team Jason, and I waited until he turned his back on me, then cut across the field. Jason saw the cut but waited until #6 was almost on top of him before passing to me, and I caught the ball, turned and ran. Our Middies had stayed back, and I wasn't sure why, but I had a clear thirty five yards in front of me, and a potential 4 on 3 break.

Accelerating, I saw out of the corner of my eye that Jason was now ten yards behind on my left, and hitting top speed. We were going to have a 5 on 3 break for a second or two.

"The thing about a Pole," Jon had said, "is that he sees only what he sees, and not what you see. But he reacts to what he thinks you see. So if you look over the Pole's right shoulder and wind up like you are going to pass, then Pole thinks there is somebody behind him on his right side. You, however, don't want to give away a teammate's position by looking at your teammate. A Pole may see your teammate that is behind you, but if you haven't looked at your teammate, the Pole doesn't think you see him and doesn't think you'll pass to him. That is your opportunity . . ."

I ran directly at the top Pole, and didn't look behind me at Jason. Instead, I slowly started drifting to my right like a newb who only had a right hand and didn't want to challenge the Pole. The Pole moved with me, opening up the middle of the defense, and at about twenty yards out, the Pole committed to me.

I couldn't throw a right-handed pass across the front of my body because the Pole was trying to separate my arms from my torso with his stick, so I threw a behind the head no-look pass to . . . to . . . to a space in front of the net. Like a thousand times before when practicing over the summer, or after practice, or on weekends . . . .

As soon as I let go I knew it wasn't a perfect pass. It was high and I was praying Jason had moved up the field with me.

He had.

Jason had to jump for the ball, but top Pole was out of position and Jason caught it, wound up and threw a cruise missile that goalie had no chance to stop. 9 to 6, and the momentum was ours.

"BTW your pass sucked," said Jason, when I went over to congratulate him.

"Sorry, Sloth," I said. "Got tired of waiting for you to catch up. Could you please try a little harder to keep up next time?"

This conversation was within earshot of Rockledge's Pole, who looked at both of us like we were crazy. Laughing, we both jogged back – me to the bench, Jason for the face-off.

Jason's goal broke Rockledge's back. They continued to fight for the rest of the game, but we were better, and they knew it. We won 15 to 10, and it wasn't even that close. Our conference record was 4-2, and we were going to play Woodland High for the right to make state playoffs.

24

"When We Stand Together"

Two days later, on Friday, the school announcements began with "Judgment Day is upon us," just like it had Wednesday and Thursday before. Except this was the last day of the Three-Day Judgment Day Contest, and today we were going to play Woodland in four, count them, four sports, including lacrosse.

We were losing to Woodland 12 to 9 in the overall head-to-head matchups, so it looked like they would be overall Judgment Day champs again. Of the four remaining sports, we were only favored in the boys' baseball game. But a win against their lacrosse team would be huge. Whatever team won the game would be go to state for the first time. Local radio and TV stations were talking it up.

Jon called on Tuesday night, excited that we had beaten Rockledge. "I'm taking final exams early, so I can get home and watch your game!" Then he hesitated, "I might bring somebody."

"Somebody?" I knew what that meant. Jon had a girlfriend.

We wore our jerseys to school on Friday, just like we had for every game. At lunchtime, I saw Sofi and a few others standing behind a table, promoting our lacrosse game. "Travel on the fan bus to the lax game!" she and the others were shouting. I asked if any fans were signing up to ride the bus to the game and she replied with a twinkle in her eye, "One or two, Joan. One or two."

Our game time was seven, but Coach wanted us at the school at five thirty. A thirty minute bus ride would give us thirty minutes of time by ourselves before team warm ups began. During the thirty minutes prior to warm ups, some of us like to listen to music, be alone, talk with each other, whatever. The coaches used this time to talk one-on-one with a player about a particular aspect of the game, or remind them about the tendencies of our opponents.

We met at the school at five thirty, but instead of the normal single bus, there were three buses parked in a row. Confusing. Players were getting on the first bus, and I saw Sofi and her friends directing people into the other two buses. Sofi had a clipboard in her hand, and was checking names off when they got on the buses.

"What's up, Sofi?" I asked.

"Just getting these fans on the buses," she said.

"Buses?" I replied. As in more than one.

"Wow, looks like a bunch of people," I said.

"Yeah, about 100 or so," she said.

"A hundred?" I replied. "You told me at lunch 'One or two.'"

"One or two buses, Joan. One or two buses."

"I don't think we've ever had a hundred fans at a lax game," I said, and added, "Thanks for organizing this."

"Oh, we're not going to only have a hundred fans. These are just the freshmen that don't have a driver's license or a ride. The entire school will be there." She laughed.

"Entire school" was optimistic, but I appreciated her help. We rode to the game and got onto the field before anybody else. Empty stadium one hour before the opening face-off.

At fifty five minutes before face-off, Jon came walking across the field. He made it to the game!

Walking next to him was "somebody." I hugged Jon, and he said, "This is Linda."

She was a little taller than me, with straight dark hair and a great smile that made me like her right away. Time to see what Linda was made of . . . .

"Is this the best you can do?" I asked her, tilting my head to Jon.

"No," she replied instantaneously. "Total sympathy date. You know how it is."

Nice. I liked her. Jon laughed, and said that Dad was in the stands. I looked over, and he waved to me. "We'll talk after the game. Joan, try and do something, anything, for a change," added Jon. *Touché*.

At fifty minutes before face-off, The Nakeds and twenty of their friends showed up. The friends immediately claimed the best seats right in the middle of the Visitor's section. A few minutes later, The Nakeds were busy towing plastic garbage cans behind them.

I smiled, knowing what was about to happen. As soon as The Nakeds got close to their group of friends, a gap in the crowd of twenty opened up for just a second or two, and the two plastic garbage cans simply disappeared. I knew in less than an hour, The Nakeds would be pounding on those garbage cans with clubs, and the stadium would be shaking. But then The Nakeds left for a minute, and came back with two more garbage cans. They disappeared into the crowd of twenty as well. Four plastic garbage cans. There was going to be some serious percussion coming from the stands tonight.

Forty-five minutes before face-off, it seemed like every person on the planet began pouring into Woodland's fan section. Tons of kids, the high school band, parents, everybody and everything.

Forty minutes before face-off, the Channel 2 News Team arrived with two cameras – one at each end of the field – and began setting up their equipment.

Thirty-two minutes before face-off, our fan buses arrived, and our side of the stadium filled up too. Upperclassmen who could drive came early to get good seats.

Twenty-five minutes before face-off, our pep band arrived. We had no idea they were going to show up. Mrs. Johnson, all five feet one inch of her, was our school faculty representative in charge of the band. A huge man from Woodland intercepted Mrs. Johnson and informed her that our band would not be allowed in the stadium and that they must leave. Mrs. Johnson replied that she would be happy to remove our band from the stadium, as soon as the Woodland High band left. Both bands stayed.

Twenty minutes before face-off, Channel 8 and Channel 13 mobile news teams, informed by alert listeners that they were about to get scooped by Channel 2, rushed into the stadium and set up their cameras, jockeying for position along the sidelines.

At eighteen minutes before face-off, three police cruisers pulled up and six uniformed officers got out. They established themselves along the stadium steps separating our fans from Woodland fans. They were polite and smiling, but made it clear there would be no physical interaction between the fans. The entire main side of the stadium was now filled with people, standing room only.

Fifteen minutes before face-off, the Fire Marshall arrived, and indicated there was an unsafe condition in the stadium due to overcrowding. He directed Woodland personnel to open up the other side of the stadium. Most of the adults groaned a sigh of relief. Since all of the students would be standing the entire game, the adults would have to stand as well if they wanted to see.

Opening up the other side of the stadium meant the adults could move, sit for the game, and still see it. As the adults filled up the other side of the stadium, the students in both sections who had packed together with the density of plutonium expanded. The result was that the main side of the stadium was now "only" filled to capacity while the other side of the stadium was approaching capacity as well.

Ten minutes before opening face-off, we heard a huge roar from our side of the stadium. It turned out that our boys baseball team had indeed beaten Woodland at home as expected, and rather quickly. Instead of hanging around and celebrating, they ran over to the girls' field hockey game.

Our girls, suddenly inspired by the arrival of two dozen athletic boys wearing tight baseball pants managed to score a late goal and win the game 2 to 1. Both teams immediately jumped into vehicles and drove like Formula 1 racecar drivers to Woodland

High, where they started cheering like mad for our girls' softball team.

The softball team, equally inspired by two dozen boys in tight pants—and not to be outdone by a bunch of field hockey chicks wearing skirts—somehow managed to score three runs in the top of the seventh inning and withstood a furious comeback from Woodland to win 4 to 3.

All three teams then sprinted over to the main stadium where the lacrosse game was to inform our student body that the Judgment Day score was now 12 to 12. Winner of the lacrosse game was going to state for the first time, and would be the Judgment Day champion. Players from all three of our teams were somehow absorbed into the student section.

Five minutes before opening face-off, somebody sang "The Star Spangled Banner." I stood next to Jason. All the players were nervous and fidgety, but managed to endure it.

Three minutes before opening face-off came the mandatory "sportsmanship" reading from the press box area: "Fans, we ask your help in ensuring the highest degree of sportsmanship . . ."

"Please refrain from making any adverse comments about officials or players . . ."

"This game will not remembered for the score, but for how we behaved . . ." Yeah yeah yeah.

"We're asking your support in demonstrating proper behavior . . ."

And furthermore, and so on and so on. It seemed like the announcer would never stop talking. Finally, one of the students yelled "AWWWWW LET 'EM PLAY!" and turned and threw a half bag of popcorn up at the press box, which was above the concession stand.

Suddenly the skies were filled with paper products being launched at the poor parents in the concession stand. Nothing was thrown that was heavy or could hurt anybody, but the parents who were selling concessions had to duck down behind the counter for a bit until all of the paper products were exhausted. Everybody laughed at the situation including the police, but it was clear that the fans weren't in the mood for a lengthy sportsmanship lecture.

Starting lineups were announced, handshakes among the captains, the opening whistle blew, and Grunt was on the ground battling for his life against Woodland's FOGO. Game on.

One of the most noticeable things about this game was how loud it was. Right after the it started, The Nakeds pounded on garbage cans, the band followed, and the stadium started shaking. Both teams were a little nervous at first, but then the game settled down.

We'd watched film of Woodland, and it was hard to find any weaknesses with their team. They had a decent defensive trap, and when we broke it, they were very quick getting back to recover. On the other hand, our defense was playing well too. It went back and forth, and was relatively low scoring – tied 4 to 4 at halftime.

I hadn't done anything noteworthy in the first half, which was probably good. *"Don't try and be a hero,"* Jon had said, *"just do your job."* I played straight up defense on the Middies, and had forced several low percentage shots. "Good job Bennett," Coach Hutchins said several times in the first half as I came off the field.

The second half was like the first, except that Jason managed to break away a few times. He scored a goal and got an assist, and Woodland wisely started respecting his offensive and defensive capabilities. We were tied at 6 to 6 in the last minute, when Hoss slipped trying to stay with one of their players, leaving their Attack with a wide-open shot, which he converted. Their side of the stadium went nuts, and ours went silent. We lost the face-off, and Woodland tried to kill the last forty seconds of the game.

Scotty was on the sidelines and I was in the game for him. He was exhausted, but rested now and we looked for a way to get him back into the game but didn't have an opportunity. Their Middie had the ball out top and was trying to keep the ball in the box. Mack got on one side of him and got their Middie turned so his back was towards me, and I saw a chance.

I moved over for the double team and started hammering on him. Mack stepped back and let the Middie go between us – violating the cardinal rule of letting an offensive player split the defense. Their Middie took advantage, but had his back turned towards our goal as he split us.

Suddenly I saw why Mack had let him go. The Hammer had moved up quickly from down low and as their Middie turned to face our goal, he was freight-trained by Jason. The ball and stick flew out of his hands, and Mack scooped it up. Their Middie "accidentally" tripped Jason as he went to pick up his stick, but Mack and I yelled at each other, "Go, go, go!"

We had fifteen yards on the Woodland Middies when we reached their defensive zone. I started yelling "Ball, ball, ball!" as we got closer to their goal. Mack and I both knew that I was the last option for his pass, but I hoped to draw a defender to me by yelling.

Their defense was tough and Mack had no alternative but to throw it to me, and I immediately threw it right back to him, which surprised top Pole. Mack blew by top Pole but #38 – a lightning quick Pole almost as good as Jason – slid quickly and Mack barely got a pass off to Larry, who slammed it home. We were going to overtime and sudden victory.

The huddle before the start of overtime was insane. We had to move out to the center of the field to hear Coach Hutchins because the crowd was so loud. "Listen up!" he said. "We are going to win this game right now! Grunt, their FOGO doesn't flip the ball or rake it between his legs. He likes to rake it to his left side. So if he gets the clamp, expect a left-side rake, okay?" Grunt nodded.

"Halsted, line up on their FOGO's left side. Expect the ball and get it. We'll call time out as soon as we have possession. Mack, keep the LSM off Halsted. Be ready for the ball – things may not go as planned," Coach instructed.

The face-off whistle blew, and Grunt was grunting and fighting for what seemed forever. Eventually, the ball did pop out to their FOGO's left side, but their short stick Middie had been instructed to not let Jason get the ball at all costs, and was hammering away on Jason's stick. Mack and their LSM had overcommitted, running past the two FOGOs for the loose ball. Jason's stick was tied up, but he reached out with his foot and kicked the ball past the FOGOs. Everybody hesitated for a millisecond, and then chaos broke out. The ball seemed to roll in slow motion as Grunt's short little legs started churning.

I don't know why, but my mind went back to when I was eight or nine years old, and we were visiting some friends of my parents who had a little terrier dog as a pet. That dog loved to chase a tennis ball, and I threw it for her several times. One time I threw it too far. It went under a chair in the kitchen, and the dog was so focused on the ball that she ran right into a crosspiece of the chair, hitting her head and falling down. I felt terrible, but the dog got up and still went after the ball. That dog's sole purpose in life was to get that ball, and Grunt was now that dog. His essence – *his very reason for existence* – was to get the ball. He cut off their FOGO with surprising speed, scooped up the ball and pulled the stick in close to his chest, knowing we would call time out right away.

"TukTuk," he grunted as Coach screamed for a time out. Instructions in the huddle were simple. Be aggressive. Take a good shot. Let's go.

We worked the ball around for what seemed like forever, but as I looked at the clock, I saw that only thirty seconds had elapsed. While a couple of our guys could probably operate one on one, their #38 Pole was so quick to provide help they didn't get the chance. Mack had the ball up top when Larry set a good screen for

Moe down low. Not a big deal, except Woodland Poles called a switch and #38 was suddenly a little farther away from the center of the crease than he probably should have been.

Did Mack see it?

He did. He immediately put a hard move on his defender followed by a nasty double move that snapped his defender's ankles. He moved in quickly and slide defensive help responded, but a little late. Our All-Conference Midfielder got a shot off from only eight yards away. Mack didn't miss many shots from eight yards, and he didn't miss this one. We stormed the field, unaware that ten billion of our fans were behind us.

Jason and I were trying to get to Mack to congratulate him, when a tsunami of our fans pushed us to the ground and piled on top of us. We were pinned down on the ground, unable to move, and barely able to breathe because we were laughing and yelling, and because people were piling on top of us.

"Hey Halsted!" I yelled.

"Hey Bennett!" he yelled back.

"We're going to state!"

All season Coach had wanted to keep the fact that a girl was on the team on the DL to avoid both unwanted attention and distraction and keep us focused. After each game when we'd go down the line and shake hands with the other team, it had always been, "Helmets On, Gloves off." Except this time. He looked right at me and said, "Helmets Off, Gloves Off."

I scrambled to be second to last in line, Hoss in front of me, very effectively blocking me from view. I took off my helmet and my gloves and dropped them as my braided rope of hair fell down my back. Jason said, "Let it fly."

I pulled out the braid with one hand as I shook each opposing

player's hand with my other saying "good game ... good game ..."
and watched as each pair of eyes scanned my face and every mouth
dropped open. By the time I got to the end of the line my hair was
blowing everywhere and I was face-to-face with their coach. He
stopped, looked down at my face then my jersey number with his
jaw set tighter than a vice.

"We just got beat by A GIRL?" he growled.

That's when I felt Coach at my elbow, and heard him say, "Yep,
you just got beat by MY GIRL."

Their coach turned red, looked me in the eye and snarled, "Well
done Missy ... now get off MY field."

Lifting my chin, I met his gaze. "Gladly, it smells like all of the
jocks we faked your defense out of ."

His eyes squinted to narrow slits; he started shaking and then
burst out laughing. When he had recovered he looked at Coach
and asked, "She doesn't have any little sisters does she?"

"Unfortunately, no," Coach Hutchins replied returning his
smile, and then he told me to go get to the bus. *Now.*

❂

Jon and Linda found us, as we were about to get on the players'
bus. "You two were awful," declared Jon.

"Dad always liked me better," I replied.

"Your boy here is a has-been," Jason said to Linda.

"You guys are nuts," she replied.

We all laughed. Dad took a bunch of pictures, and then they
got the car and followed the bus to a pizza place to celebrate
along with what seemed to be the entire town. Later on I saw Jon
introducing Linda to Coach Hutchins. "Wow," I said to myself,
"this is a big deal if he's introducing her to Coach!"

Later when I got off the bus back at school I was surprised to see
Jon's car in the spot where I had parked the Jeep. I said goodbye

to the guys, walked over, saw Jon sitting in it and got in. "I sent Linda home in the Jeep to unpack," Jon said.

"Jon's got a girlfriend!"

"Brat."

"Takes one to know one. How did she get stuck with you?"

"This is my party. I get to ask the questions."

"Well okay party-starter, let's get this party started."

Jon was quiet for a moment. Then he got all serious and looked over at me and nodded to my hair, "You were on fire tonight. On and off the field."

"Thought it was time to lighten up a bit."

"Good for you. Dad told me but I wanted to see for myself. I'm happy for you. Seems like things are working out. What's going on with Jason?"

"Teammates. Finally."

"Nothing more?"

"Nothing less."

"What about after the season ends?"

"I haven't a clue. Just living game to game. My turn, how did you and Linda meet?"

"Intramural volleyball team. The Slammer Jammers."

"You guys serious?"

"Rarely. If ever." He laughed. "Glad we had this little chat," he said as we pulled into our driveway.

"Me too." Smiling, I got out of the car.

❂

The next week was a blur. State playoffs consisted of 16 teams, and because we finished second in conference, we were seeded below all the conference champs. The first playoff game was against Ridge Heights, a conference champion from up north. They played in a weaker conference than we did, and although it was an away game for us, we expected to win. We were better, and I think they suspected it too.

By now, our team was hitting on all cylinders. Sap's ankle had healed, and he was going to be able to play some of the first playoff game. We rolled into Ridge Heights, and had a 10 to 2 lead by halftime. Even with Sap back, I played almost as much as I did before. Coach Hutchins was stressing the high-tempo offense, meaning we Middies were running a lot.

Near the end of the third quarter, we were winning 13 to 3, and I threw a nice little pass to Moe right in front of the net. Normally he would have shot and scored, but instead, he threw it back to me.

I was surprised a little bit, but we worked it around some more, and eventually Larry had an opportunity for a shot that he normally took. Instead, he tossed it to me and said "Shot!" I didn't feel comfortable shooting, so we worked it around some more. At the end of the third quarter, Coach Hutchins told me to take a shot when I had it. Odd. He always appreciated me passing rather than shooting the ball.

"Yo Jett," said Jason fourth quarter as he headed out onto the field, "Pull the trigger on the shot when you get a chance."

Et tu Brute? Jason never told me when to shoot . . . Ah ha!

The guys were trying to get me a goal. They knew that I did a lot of the dirty work clearing the ball and that I had taken a lot of hits after passing the ball. Passes that led to them scoring, while I was getting creamed. Many times I'd come off the field after having been knocked down, and Coach Hutchins would ask "Bennett, you all right?"

"I'm good." Even though I had tears in my eyes from getting pounded. Some of those Poles *hit hard.*

With a minute left in the four quarter Coach sent me in as a wing on the face-off. The ref was taking his sweet time so the opposing player next to me decided to chat. He looked me up and down a couple of times and squatted to inconspicuously *(ha)* check out my legs, which were pretty much covered by my leggings and mid calf socks. I heard, "So, what's your name?"

"Jett."

"Hmmm." *Pause.* "Is that your first name or your last?"

"Middle name." *Long pause, sigh.* "First name's Joan."

"Hmmm." *Pause.* "Is that a guy's name or a girl's name?"

"It's a girl's name I suppose. I'm a girl. With girl parts. Playing on a guys' team with a guy's skills." *Significant pause.* Head nod.

"I respect that." *Another long pause.* "Why haven't I heard about you?"

"I'm no big deal. I don't play that much."

"But, you're on a face-off."

"Dude, we're up by eleven with a minute left."

"Don't be too hasty! Yo. It's comeback time."

"Bring it."

"I won't take it easy on you."

"I respect that."

The whistle blew and the game was back on.

I finally did score in the last few seconds. My dad stood up in the stands as I came off the field and smiled as he pumped his arms in the air. *So proud.* The problem with my goal was that my normal shot was not particularly fast by guys' standards, and though the goal was well placed, it was a slower speed than my average shot. So I had to endure the insults and good-natured teasing that came at the hamburger joint on the way home.

"Bennett, that was a great shot. What third grader taught you to shoot that fast?"

"Bennett, that shot had deceptive speed. It was much slower than it looked."

And from Jason, "I saw Bennett take the shot and ran off the field to get a drink of water. I was back in time to see the ball hit the back of the net."

It was fun to be part of the endless insults, french fry stealing, and name calling that went on after winning a game. Jason and I sat across from each other, crammed in a booth with Sam and Hank, with others spilling over from both sides. We were just teammates celebrating a victory. I made it a point to avoid eye contact with Jason, lest I fall into the aforementioned beautiful blue pools and forget to climb out. Believe me, it was not easy. Especially when he trapped one of my feet with both of his in a hidden hug under the table. *Compartmentalize. Compartmentalize.*

And then there were eight. The Elite Eight. The eight teams left in state playoffs, and there would be no easy games from here on out. We played Central Valley next, the number three-ranked team in the state. The game was almost the opposite of the Woodland game, in that it was high scoring. It was tied at 10 to 10 at half, and the reckless pace continued into the second half.

It was 14 to 14 after three quarters, and it was 17 to 17 with less than a minute remaining, and still both teams pushed the ball. Something had to give. Somebody was going to blink, and it was Central Valley that blinked first. Maybe the pressure got to them – I don't know – but they threw the ball away. Coach Hutchins had talked about playing under pressure before this game, "Most teams have played a single playoff game. This will be our fourth. A playoff game means win or the season is over, and we had games like that against Rockledge, Woodland, Ridge Heights and now Central Valley. So relax."

Scotty *relaxed* to the tune of scoring the game winning goal with twelve seconds left as he made a nice cut twenty five yards out and Curly hit him with a great pass. Final Four here we come.

Nobody was more thrilled than Jon that we made the Final Four as that had been an unfulfilled goal of his in high school. It was a huge deal, and participating was much more fun than even the State Championship game, for several reasons. While Final Four is a common term for the semifinals of sporting contests – especially basketball – in high school lacrosse a much more common term was Jacket Day. It takes a bit of explanation . . .

Fans of lacrosse decided to promote the sport by making a big deal out of the best teams each year. They hold the Final Four contest at the University stadium, bring in lacrosse equipment vendors, and display banners congratulating the Final Four teams. They invite coaches from college and university levels to come watch the games, and they put on a huge feast after every game.

All players from the previous game would wear their jerseys and meet at the food court and be treated to a barbeque meal. Players who were trying to kill each other thirty minutes before would laugh and swap stories, and it worked out well with no hard feelings. The Final Four for the class A teams was held on Friday, while our games – class AA – were on Saturday. There would be two boys' AA games on Saturday and two girls' AA games as well.

One of the favorite parts of the Final Four was the college recruiting aspect. If you were a college lacrosse coach and didn't have time to travel from state to state and watch a bunch of different games, you would come to the Final Four and watch the games over a two day period, and would see most of the higher level lacrosse talent.

College recruiting rules didn't allow a coach to offer a scholarship at the Final Four, and in fact, it was an unwritten rule that you didn't say what college or university you were representing. But if you wore a sweatshirt or jacket with your college's name on it, then the player you were talking to would know just what school you represented. Hence the name Jacket Day. It worked out well since the players could figure out what colleges might be looking at them, and the coaches could find out fairly quickly if a player were interested in their school. It was Jon's dream to attend Jacket Day, and he would do so as a fan, yelling for us.

We showed up at Jacket Day fairly early, and sat in the stands for some time while the girls' playoff game was being played before ours. I'd never watched an entire girls' lax game before because of my previously mentioned rant. The girls didn't wear helmets, they wore goggles instead. Contact was minimal, and the sticks with their shallower pocket made holding onto the ball more difficult, and throwing the ball with much speed was evidently more challenging too. Defenses appeared governed by specific rules, and the whistle blew too often.

I sat with a few of the guys watching the game, and we saw players do something that would never occur in the boys game: keeping a right-handed grip no matter which way a player was passing, running or shooting, and spinning blindly back into the heart of the defense were common examples.

I shuddered to think what would happen to me if I reversed course without looking when other defenders were nearby. I'd get knocked into next week. It appeared to me that any form of aggressive play was met with a whistle. I wondered out loud why the girls didn't stick check, because there seemed plenty of opportunities to do so.

"You can only check by moving your stick away from the player's head," came the reply. I turned and looked behind me and saw who had answered my question. She was an athletic-looking woman in aviators, maybe an older sister of one of the players.

"Thanks," I said.

A little later, one of the girls made an aggressive move, and was whistled for it. "What was wrong with that?" I asked nobody in particular.

"You can't do that," Jason said.

"Do what?" I asked.

"Try," said Jason. "Remember what you told me? She got penalized for trying."

"Since when do you listen to me?" I said. We all laughed. It seemed to me that the game was "dumbed down" for the girls and that they couldn't showcase their athleticism because of the equipment and rules.

Then came #19. A loose ball appeared on the turf, and #19 moved in to get it. She hardly slowed down when she scooped it up, and started to fly down the field. A couple of defenders tried to catch her, but #19 switched gears and torched them. Whew, I thought, #19 can flat out burn. She took the ball down the field, roll-dodged and switched hands while doing so, pump-faked a pass to her left, *(How did she pump-fake with that shallow pocket?)* then threw back to her right to a player she must have seen out of the corner of her eye. Goal. Impressive.

It was time to get ready for our game so we stood up and moved off of the bleachers. When the guys left to get dressed I watched the girls for a bit longer, and then I gathered up my gear to go change. As I walked past the bleachers the woman who had answered my question earlier approached me and asked, "What do you know about girls' lacrosse?"

"I don't know that much about it," I answered.

"Then maybe you shouldn't be criticizing it. Are you a manager or just here to watch the guys?" she asked.

Uh-oh. Serious hostility. Angry Chick was evidently not too pleased that we had made fun of the girls' game. She was fairly tall, looked like she could run all day, and it was apparent she spent some serious time in the gym. "I play on a guys' team."

"I see. Maybe I'll stay and watch your game. Are you playing on this field?" she asked as she looked down at the jersey that I had draped over all of my equipment on my stick.

"Yes."

"Good luck. I look forward to seeing how the game is *supposed* to be played." She returned to the bleachers.

Great. Angry Chick was going to watch me while I competed against some of the best players in the state. She'd get a chance to point out my flaws after the game. Awesome. Open mouth, insert cleat. Size 8.5. Yummy.

❄

We had some fairly extravagant introductions before the game, but it finally got underway. Our opponent, Hillsdale High, came in ranked number two. A perennial powerhouse, the stands were full of coaches who were interested in multiple players from Hillsdale. Hillsdale had several players who were exceptional, but they had an Attack player who was all world – #13. We'd watched film of Hillsdale, and #13 was just plain scary. Even Jason, who normally joked while watching film, was quiet. Usually we played a zone defense, which allowed Jason to provide slide help, but we were going to go with a man-to-man defense today. Jason's job was to guard #13.

Hillsdale won the face-off, and worked the ball around. They were very patient, and #13 was unselfish. After a minute or two, he made a nice hard cut and a quick pass made its way to him. Jason was ready, but #13 was slimy and got off a quick shot just before Jason hit him. Goal. Jason stood there, fuming. He knew his job was to stop #13, and he didn't do it that time.

Grunt won the next face-off, and it looked like neither FOGO would dominate the other. That was good. We didn't score and Hillsdale got the ball. They didn't score either, and the game settled down. The next time #13 got the ball, it looked like he wanted to operate on Jason – a little one-on-one action. Their players cleared away to let their superstar go to work. Instead of sitting back and reacting to #13, though, Jason crowded him. Both players started pushing on each other, and after a bit, #13 had to take a step back.

Then he had to take another step back. He realized he wouldn't be able to out-muscle Jason, so he tried moving to his right. But Jason was quicker and moved his body in front of him, and when #13 moved back to his left, he was greeted by a 6 foot Pole slamming into him, blocking his way. For a second #13 looked confused. *Don't you know who I am? You can't do that to me.* But Jason kept doing it, and backing #13 farther and farther out until he was about to be shoved out of bounds. Realizing he was going to lose the ball, #13 jumped up and tried to throw the ball to a teammate, but Jason was too quick. He blocked the pass, scooped up the ball and was gone. Ten seconds later, Jason scored.

My first shift was a disaster. Sam made a nice pass to me, and I started to clear. But a Middie closed in on me faster than anticipated, and knocked the stick out of my hand. Yard sale. Turnover. I'll bet Angry Chick was laughing in the stands right now. *Compartmentalize.*

I settled down after that, and Hillsdale began to look confused as they tried to set up a decent midfield trap. I think part of the reason was we didn't have any set plays for breaking a trap. Sometimes Mack or Scotty or Zif would clear the ball; other times it would be Jason. Even Hoss and Jake felt comfortable clearing, although they would give the ball up as soon as possible after crossing midfield. My job was to continue to cut back and forth across the field, presenting our players with a passing option. Since I could catch pretty much anything thrown at me, I was a decent alternative if they got in trouble.

Jason and I were clicking, even more than usual. I'd throw the ball back to him, or roll it to the side where he'd outrun Hillsdale players. One time Sam threw the ball to me on a clear and I immediately laid it on the ground near a Hillsdale player. Hillsdale dude went to pick it up, but didn't see Jason come screaming in from behind him, scooping the ball up and accelerating to warp 8.

We ran up the field together and had four passes back and forth before the Middie between us eventually tripped trying to stop us. Top Pole took Jason who passed to me. I drove in, and when the slide came, dumped it to Larry just before I got creamed. Ouch. But we scored.

At half we were down 6 to 5, but we knew we could win. #13 hadn't scored since the opening two minutes, and we had confidence. Things went back and forth in the third quarter, but we could never take the lead. It was 9 to 8 at the end of the third, and 12 to 11 with a few minutes left in the game. Jason was playing great D on #13, and Sam made a huge save and cleared to Jason who hit Mack.

We moved up the field, but didn't have a fast break opportunity. Sometimes in a settled situation like this, I'd come off the field and we'd get Mack or Zif or Scotty in the game if they had been on the sidelines, and that was the case now. I turned and started sprinting for the sidelines. The Middie, who was guarding me, knew that we'd essentially be man down for about ten seconds while I ran to the sidelines and Zif came on the field, so he turned away from me and ran to double team the ball. I immediately stopped, turned and ran back towards the goal.

Mack saw I was open and looked away, not giving away my position. A few seconds later he threw a laser beam pass to me that I caught on the fly. I was moving from the goalie's left to right in front of the goal, so the best option was a left-handed shot. I switched to my left hand, and put the ball in the four-hole for a goal. Score was 12 to 12.

Grunt won the face-off and we got a few good looks at goal, but nothing went in. Hillsdale countered, worked the ball around, and made a great pass to a cutting Attacker who scored with fifteen seconds left in the game. We fought like mad the last fifteen seconds, but couldn't score. Hillsdale won 13 to 12.

It's horrible to stand in the handshake line after losing. You can hear the whoops and hollers of the winning team, and see their mocking looks. *We're Hillsdale and you're a podunk school from nowhere.* But we didn't see that. We saw respect from Hillsdale. And relief. Hillsdale was fortunate to beat us, and they knew it. They congratulated us, and said we'd talk in the food court after the game.

It was quiet in the locker room. The coaches were making their way around to each player, and talking to them briefly. I saw Coach Hutchins say something to Jake, who was standing next to me. Jake's lip started to tremble, and he looked down to the ground. When Coach got to me, he said, "Bennett, this season has been the most fun I've had in my life. Thank you." I nodded and bit my lip and started to cry. But it felt okay.

Coach Slammer was next, "Bennett, I am so proud of you." He had tears in his eyes too, and he moved on.

Coach Slammer was now talking to Jason, who was next to me, and I heard Jason say, "Thanks for believing in me Coach."

After a minute, Coach addressed the team, "Listen up. I want to thank you all for this season. Now get out there and have some fun. Eat some food. Don't worry about this game, but celebrate our season. It was fantastic. Besides . . ." he said with a little smile, "I think there are some college coaches out there just itching to talk."

Coach was right. We'd played hard, and some close games had gone our way this year. I had a decent game after the yard sale, with a goal and two assists, and my man never scored in the game. Jason The Hammer held #13 to two goals and had scored two goals himself. And it was a blast getting to play in the stadium, even though we lost.

We went outside and grabbed some hot dogs. "You evil hag," somebody said behind me. I turned and looked – it was #11 Middie from Hillsdale. Jason turned too, and took a step closer to me.

"What?" I said.

"I was guarding you when I thought you ran off the field," he said, "I went to double team the ball, and next thing I know, you schooled me and took it in and scored." And then he laughed and did an exaggerated bow to show he was kidding.

Jason smiled and relaxed next to me, "Welcome to my world bro, she taught me everything I know." Several other Hillsdale players joined a bunch of us as we re-lived the game. They were decent guys. I told them that I hoped they won the state championship.

We walked out of the food court, and into an open area. College coaches and boosters were all over several Hillsdale players, including #13. As soon as we entered I could see some coaches notice Jason and excused myself to go use the restroom to give him a chance to mingle. I saw Mack and Zif and Scotty all being approached at different times by coaches.

The Three Stooges were talking to several Division III coaches, and even Hoss and Jake were talking to lacrosse club teams' coaches. I was happy for all of them. Not all would play in college, but the fact they were being approached was nice. After awhile I slid over next to Jason, and heard him say, "Thank you sir, but I'm looking at attending a school with an engineering program." Several coaches left after they heard Jason say that, but a few coaches from schools that had an engineering major stuck around.

From behind me I heard a voice say, "Bennett." I turned and saw Angry Chick. Oh no. I was not in the mood to be lectured. "Nice game," she said.

Well, that was surprising.

"Do you have any plans after high school?" she asked. Just then we were interrupted. A girl walked up and said "Hey Coach."

Coach? I looked at the girl; she wore a jersey. #19. No way.

"I am Coach Cori. This is my new recruit, Maddie," said Angry Chick/Coach. "Your first name is ?"

"It's Joan," I said, "Joan Bennett," I reached out to shake hands with Maddie #19.

"Joan's been playing with the big boys and thinks some of the girls' lacrosse rules are stupid," said Coach Cori. Maddie laughed.

"Joan," said Coach Cori, "the girls' rules could use an update. But you have to play the game now by the current ones. We'll start moving more towards the guys' lacrosse game eventually. Allow a little more contact, start wearing helmets, deeper pockets on sticks, and fewer restrictions on defense. But the guys' game isn't perfect either."

She was right.

"In the meantime, you need to be true to the game now."

Coach Hutchins often said the same thing. "Be true to the game." I had seen him pull players back to the sideline after they went onto the field too early on a substitution or took some late cheap shot. Must be a lacrosse thing.

Maddie #19 said, "Coach thinks we should have a shot clock. And that we should have a brick wall behind goal so that shots bounce back into play instead of going out of bounds." I figured out that Maddie #19 was probably kidding about the brick wall.

"Ohhhh, I like that," I said. "But players might run into the brick wall and get hurt. So you'd need a moat in front of the wall so players wouldn't be tempted to slam into it."

Maddie #19 didn't miss a beat. "But that's still boring. The field needs to have Sharknados swirling out of the moat. And there should be trap doors that could be released randomly during the game with tigers coming out of them. Like the Roman Coliseum."

"Okay gladiators, that's enough," said Coach Cori.

Evidently Maddie #19 had seen one of Russell Crowe's finest.

"So," said Coach Cori, "do you have any plans after high school?" She took her sunglasses off, only then could I tell by the laugh lines near her eyes that she was older than twenty five.

"Yes, as a matter of fact I do have plans after high school," I said to myself, "See Golden Boy over there? Surrounded by all those coaches? After high school he's going to ride up to my house on a white stallion with a wicked fast black mare for me, and we are going to race off into the sunset. We'll trade our lacrosse sticks

in for light sabers and battle Evil and Mean Girls all day. We're going to live in a castle in the sky and raise pet dinosaurs and . . ."

"Joan," Coach Cori said, bringing me back to reality. "Do you have any plans after high school?"

"I'm going to college. Not sure where yet."

"Good," said Coach Cori. "I'll be in touch."

"Nice to meet you Joan, we'll leave you to your gladiators." Maddie #19 looked over at the guys, "and watch out for tigers."

"I will, thanks, you too," I laughed. Before they turned away, I glance down at the front of Coach Cori's jacket and read:

Cori James : Head Coach
University of Colorado
Women's Lacrosse

25

"Something To Talk About" "

Lacrosse was over. Or was it? I kept thinking about what CU's coach had said, "Good. I'll be in touch." How did she know I was a senior? I hadn't told her. Who had? But as always in high school, there was the next big thing to deal with, angst over, dwell about, and look forward to or dread. Prom. Yep. The four letter word that strikes fear in the heart of many a senior girl. Guys too maybe? I honestly didn't know.

Jon had rarely stressed about anything school related. As for the female of the species, it's like when the terrorist chick is finally brought to justice in an apocalyptic movie, and it all gets summed up neatly in the statement, ". . . if only she'd been asked to her Senior Prom, none of this would have happened." *Ugh.*

I'd been oblivious to the build up of Prom tension due to the much more interesting and exciting Lacrosse Playoff Season. Although I had been spared somewhat, the inevitable came crashing down when Sofi, now a permanent passenger to school, jumped in the Jeep Monday morning and announced, "I want to go to Prom with Trent, can you talk to him and see if he wants to?"

Sofi was out for track and knew Trent from practices. He and Rachel remained friends but had not dated after Homecoming.

Sofi was having a blast competing in a sport other than cheer. She ran hurdles and a sprint as the last leg in the 400-meter relay. Trent ran the 1600 and 800 meters. Sofi liked his dry sense of humor and the way he could laugh at himself. He also had been teasing her a lot lately, so she thought he might like her too. But since patience was not her one of her virtues she wondered if I would facilitate. I asked her if I could borrow her phone.

"Ha ha, no thanks," she laughed, "just use the old-fashioned speaking in person thing you do so well."

"Is that your weak attempt at buttering me up?" I asked.

"Call it what you will, but will you?" she implored.

"You're in luck. I have Psych with him today." I answered. The thing was, she seemed oblivious to the elephant in the car. The invisible one named Jason. Her brother.

Now that lacrosse was over, and we didn't have practice or games and wouldn't be spending time as lax bros, pretending like we didn't *like-like* each other, would we get to, you know, *date-date*? Maybe?

Did he even want to? Or had I officially compartmentalized myself back into the friend zone after padding up and playing with the guys? Did he now think of me as one of them? You would think that Sofi would be all over this topic, studying us like the famous anthropologist Jane Goodall. But no, she rambled on about track and Trent simultaneously and interchangeably. Annoyingly.

I got to Psych before Chelsea, so I sat in her seat and turned to chat with Trent. "Dude, I'm not good at this sort of thing so I'm going to throw this out. How about asking Sofi Halsted to Prom?"

"You're right, you aren't very good at the subtle nuances of setting someone up. However, in your defense, you were quite eloquent at shooting someone down." Trent laughed.

"Ouch. Thanks for reminding me."

"I mean it, you were caught off guard and let me down gently, and were cool keeping it on the DL. I could ask Rachel without any stigma of her being second choice."

"I'm glad for that, but I'm sorry I didn't stop Chelsea's verbal rants in here. I regret letting you take the heat on that for so long," I apologized.

"No worries. That's on her, not you. As for Sofi, I assume you have inside intelligence and you're not setting me up for another shut down?" he slyly asked.

"Affirmative. But as I alluded, she's not only a goofball she's impatient, so be creative and quick about it, after all, she is a sprinter."

"Okay, thanks. You better get back to your seat, you know who is inbound," he added as he looked over to the classroom door.

"Well, look who is all cozy," Chelsea commented. "Are you two going to give it a go again? Oh, that's right, you didn't end up going anywhere after all. So are you just lobbying for Queen again Joan?"

"Why do you ask?" I questioned. A subtle way of saying, "It's none of your business."

"So you are trying for Queen again!" Chelsea exclaimed. I turned around and looked incredulously past her to Trent, who snickered and shrugged his shoulders.

"No thanks. Ever. Really. Once a commoner, always a commoner," I muttered.

"Actions speak louder than words, especially when you whisper," Chelsea said.

"Word." I whispered, to her and myself as I shook my head. When class was over Trent walked out with me.

"So who are you going to Prom with, as if I need to ask?"

"Ahhh, I don't know, no one for sure," I stuttered.

"No, someone for sure. I'm sure! Thanks for the heads up about Sofi." Trent laughed as he turned and walked the other way. What did he know that I didn't know? Sofi was right, he did like to laugh at himself, and he liked to tease others! Sofi and Trent. Two forces to be reckoned with! Fun match.

When I got home from school I went to find Misty. She had been neglected over the past few months and was not the forgiving kind unless she was spoiled rotten as restitution. After feeding and brushing her, I picked her up to take her outside to the garden. I needed the calming waterfall to comfort the voices expressing a variety of opinions once again in my head. My efforts to live out loud and in color had neglected my introverted needs for alone time and order. As I opened the back door she leaped out of my arms to go pursue her own agenda. I watched her as she landed and sprinted toward the bushes. My eye was drawn to a lacrosse ball, a bright white sphere on the dark green grass. Then I saw another. Then another. In an arrow pattern. It pointed to the side yard where the beloved lacrosse goal stoically stood guard over a message spelled out in equally bright white balls . . .

PROM?

A bouquet of flowers was in the goal. The dot of the question mark was a hammer. Someone had let the elephant out of my car and into my backyard.

Cool! Unbelievable. Jason awesomely, monumentally asked me out. To Prom! The Mega Date. Yikes! What do I do now? Besides treat myself for shock. As I stared at the message I thought that I really should read up on the intricacies of modern dating. What was the appropriate response? Did it have to be clever? *Argh.*

I picked up a lacrosse ball, the hammer and the bouquet and went back inside. I cut the bottom of the flower stems and put them in a vase with water. It was a bright, colorful assortment of flowers and greenery. Gorgeous. I looked at the hammer and the ball and drew a blank.

I finally grabbed a black marker and wrote "Yep" on the white ball and went out in my backyard and tossed it over the fence toward his patio. Done. Now I had to figure out who to ask for help, what to wear, when to tell my dad to minimize the teasing, why I was so clueless and how I could go to a dance and not, actually, dance? Journalism 101. Again.

Then I heard. Music. Loud. From next door. My heart stopped. REO Speedwagon's "Can't Fight This Feeling." Really? REALLY.

The doorbell rang. I stood frozen in the kitchen. Then someone knocked on my back door. What is going on?

That's when Jason, Sofi, Sam and Gracie called from our back porch. "Open up Jett! It's time for your first dance lesson!"

You. Have got. To be kidding me. Panic. And then. Slowly. I felt a smile work its way up my cheeks. I blinked a couple of times. And that's when the goofballs started singing. Loudly. Horribly. Wonderfully.

I shook my head, started to laugh, and walked toward the wonderfully annoying noise.

It ended *(badly)* with Sam going falsetto and Jason howling and Sofi and Gracie trying *(emphasis on trying)* to harmonize. Painfully. Beautifully. I was back. Forever. From Nowhere. I had found the way. With help. I was home. And I went to let my life in.

"So I hear you got hammered! Ha ha! Just kidding! I'm soooooo relieved he asked you so I can talk about it! I was going crazy! I thought I was going to explode! And guess what? As if YOU will be surprised that is! Trent asked me! At track practice! He wrapped a note around a baton with a rubber band and had my relay time pass it up to me when we were working on our exchange timing! How fun is that! Oh my goodness! We need to go shopping!" Cyclone Sofi whipped in and spun her way to the kitchen. I followed in the aftermath. "Oh, look at the flowers! He listened to me! I told him to get a variety of colors and kinds. I can't believe he doesn't know your favorite color or favorite flower! Dudes!" she exclaimed. In one breath.

"Black," said Sam.

"What?"

"Her favorite color, it's black of course," Sam answered smugly.

"No, I think green? Like your eyes?" Jason asked me.

"Well at least you know the color of her eyes," Sofi snorted.

"He should, he can't stop staring into them," Gracie added dramatically with the perfect eye roll.

"I do not, back me up Sam," Jason said.

"Sorry bro, she's right."

"Thanks for nothing," Jason said.

"No problem, I've got your back," Sam teased.

"Long enough to grab and throw me under the bus," Jason said.

"Enough chatting it's time to get dancing," Sofi announced as she set her cell on the island. Wow, she successfully provided a bridge from one awkward moment to the next. I was appreciative and relieved for Jason, as it was a little awkward.

"She's right! Jason you dance with Joan, Sofi you get Sam," Gracie said.

"In her dreams," Sam smiled as he reached out his hand.

"More like my nightmares," Sofi laughed as she took it, adding, "Gracie put on a fast song first, something from the eighties."

"Why 80's?" I asked. Jason took my hand. And my attention.

"Because I'm the sophomore representative on the Prom Committee," Sofi said matter-of-factly.

"How did a mere "sofi-more" get to pick the theme?" Sam asked.

"Silly boy, never underestimate the power of this Force," Sofi said, flexing her impressive gymnastic bicep.

"Do you have a permit for those?" Sam asked.

"You betcha," Sofi said.

"Why did you pick the eighties theme?" Sam asked.

"To make amends, it's part of my probation," Sofi said, as she looked over her shoulder to wink at me.

That's when Madonna entered the room, in the form of "Cherish." Although it was a fast song, Jason still held my hand. In fact, he reached for my other one that had a death grip on the granite counter and gently pried it off.

"All right Jett, let's start with the swing dance," he said, as I stood planted.

"The Swing?" I groaned to buy myself some time.

"Yep. It's simple. Just watch my eyes, don't let go and count to three," he smiled. *How about we try for two out of three?* I thought to myself. *Because I think if I look into your eyes while holding your hands the ability to count will pretty much be out the window.*

"Watch – step – step – step, back step, step – step – step – back step, " he said as he gracefully moved from side to side, still holding my hands. As I stood glued to the floor. Still.

"Okay relax, now come with me, you're not going to dodge this," he coaxed. Strangely, escape hadn't even crossed my mind! Okay, here goes nothing. I picked up my foot and stepped into motion. It worked! I didn't fall down or explode or trip him! And we moved back and forth, in time with the music – then just as everything was working as prescribed he let go with one hand and lifted it out to the side, throwing me off balance. I stopped, still holding on to his other hand.

"I thought we weren't supposed to let go?" I asked.

"Don't worry, even if I let go, I'll find you again." He smiled as he reached for me.

"Some instructor you are. Leaving out important techniques. I may be forced to file a complaint with your dance studio," I said.

"Next song should be slow, Tunes Chairman," Sofi said.

"I'm already on it," Gracie replied. And then another Madonna hit, and I had to take a deep breath as "Crazy For You" played. Wow. Nailed it. Pretty much summed up how I felt.

Jason smiled and shifted my left hand to his shoulder and placed his right hand on my hip. But this time instead of freezing or retreating I exhaled slowly and looked up at him and smiled in return. All of the stress and worry about transitioning from teammate to Prom date was washed away by his easy-going attitude. Crush-mode shifted to comfort-zone. Again. At last!

"What did I tell you Jett? You're a natural!" Jason said. Then I stepped on his foot. *Oops.* We laughed and moved with the music. Nice. Really. *Really. Nice.*

After a few more songs, we were ready to launch a raid on the ice cream parlor. By now they all knew the "ice cream smells funny" trick so we called a cease-fire and ate in peace. It was a lot of fun hanging out with all of them. The three siblings teased each other mercilessly, and treated Sam like one of the family.

It felt good to be around them. It reminded me of being with Jon and my dad. Afterwards, we went back to my house and were hanging out in my backyard taking turns shooting at the goal. Sofi and Gracie picked up short sticks and tried to pass and catch. Jason, Sam and I took turns giving them pointers. Every once in awhile Jason would catch my eye and smile. Awesome.

It was getting late so Gracie, Sofi and Sam put away the lacrosse sticks and headed toward the gate. On the way out Sofi turned and asked if we could go shopping on Saturday morning at ten.

"Where do we go to get the stuff?" I attempted to casually ask.

"Stuff? Stuff? Seriously Joan, lacrosse is over. You definitely need girl time," she said. "We will start at the mall. That gives us a week to make all of the other preparations!"

"Other preparations?" I asked with dread.

"You know – hair, nails, make-up, pictures, dinner reservations, transportation . . . I am going to open a Facebook event that you need to join so we can all coordinate," she explained.

Ugh. Up to this point I had managed to be FB free. I agreed, and although secretly excited I feigned indifference. Jason lagged behind as the others let themselves out.

"Can we hang out Saturday after your excursion with Sofi? No teammates. No siblings. No Sam. Just the two of us?" said Jason.

"Think we can handle it?" I said, more flippant than I felt.

"Sure, it will be like last summer, without the workouts, tennis or running."

"I don't know. After a day of shopping with Sofi I may need to run away," I said.

"Well, you can let me know. If not, we can go to a movie or something," he said.

"Sounds kind of like a date." I teased, looking at him.

"That's because it is. Our first date," he answered, *way too seriously!*

"Ummmm. Good. Great. That sounds fun," I sputtered.

"Okay then, see you later."

I'm not sure how long I stood there in the dark. I awoke from my reverie when my dad flipped on a light inside, and followed the glow in. I felt warm. And safe. And happy. He looked at me and smiled.

The week flew by. Teachers tried to cram as much information in us as possible to get us ready for finals before spring fever set in. *(Good luck with that.)*

Saturday morning Sofi was on my doorstep at nine forty five so we could get to the mall when it opened. She was not sure about what color I should look for, but she was definitely going for a shiny teal.

She flipped through the dress racks like a speed-reader devouring a novel. I hadn't a clue what I liked or wanted. Still reeling from the idea I was going with Jason to Prom, and more imminently, out on our first date tonight.

Sophie woke me up from my daydream to tell me to grab something to try on as she maneuvered through the aisle towards the fitting rooms with no less than ten dresses flowing over her shoulders. They all looked long, so I grabbed two, one black and one green, and followed in her wake. Neither worked for various reasons, so I put them back and sat in the couch near the three-panel mirror per Sofi's directive, to critique her runway modeling. She tried on all of them, ending up with a shimmering teal that looked incredible.

"Winner!" Sofi declared as she spun in front of the mirrors.

"It looks great," I added.

"I love it!" she said, bubbling over with enthusiasm. "You're next!" We went to a few more stores but nothing "wowed me" –

which apparently was the intent, so we grabbed a bite to eat and then continued our quest.

Since failure wasn't an option and I wanted to get out of the mall I doubled my effort. Finally in the hundredth store *(slight exaggeration perhaps)*, a glimmer of bronze caught my eye, and I dove into the rack and pulled out a stunning, slender, long dress. It was beautiful. Liquid bronze. And my size. Sofi squealed when she saw it.

"Go. Now. Put it on. I have to see it on," she commanded. I did. *It wowed me.* Winner. I bought it and headed towards the door.

"Not so fast! We have to get shoes and jewelry." Sofi ordered. I looked down at my kicks. The dress would cover my feet.

"No, I'm good. I've got something in mind and no one will have it here, and I already have earrings and a necklace," I said without breaking stride to make my escape.

"Okay, I see you are anxious to get home for your date so I'll let you off the hook for now," Sofi sighed as I exited the store and headed toward my Jeep. On the way home she agonized over who she could set up with Shelley so she could join "our group." Which was a combination of track and lacrosse players. "Duh! I can't believe I didn't think of him sooner!"

"I'll bite, who's the lucky guy?" I asked.

"Sam!" she replied. "They will have a blast and I already know she thinks he's fun. He won't get off his butt and ask anyone until the ridiculously last minute so I think we should just assign him. He'll probably be relieved and thrilled he doesn't have to be creative or fork out bucks for a bouquet to ask her," she continued.

I seized the air space as she finally paused to take a breath.

"I leave that up to you. Thanks for going with me today. I don't know how I would have done this without you." I looked over at her. She smiled and thought for a moment.

"You are totally welcome. That's what friends do, now go figure out what to wear on your 'date.' BTDubs, Jason's favorite color is golden yellow. Like a dandelion. What's yours?"

"My what?" I asked, lost in thought.

"Favorite color!" she answered.

"All of them," I responded.

"Of course they are!" She charged up to their front door.

I hung up the dress, opened my laptop and searched for the shoes I had in mind. Done. It was time to get ready for my date. What to wear? Not too dressy. One, because that would be awkward if he were dressed super casual. Two, because it would look like I was making a big deal about it. Three, because I don't really having anything dressy to wear. Simple as that.

(jason gb)
Did you survive?

(me)
Barely

(jason gb)
Pick you up at seven?

(me)
Doubt you can lift me

(jason gb)
Ha ha

(me)
Seven is good

(jason gb)
You bet I am!

(me)
Ugh. Ha ha. Modest too

I ended up putting on a white tee, blue jeans and classic black low top kicks. I looked up on the shelf and the yellow gold sweatshirt Dad had bought me in Boulder caught my eye. Looked dan-de-lion to me. I grabbed it and tied it around my waist. Of course the doorbell rang at exactly seven. I had told Dad we were "going on a date" and he was thrilled. And of course he was predictably annoying. Teasing. Interrogating. And joyful. He even raced me to answer the door. Argh. He got there first. *(He had a head start.)* He welcomed Jason in and shook his hand.

"Going just a little overboard there Dad?" I said as I walked around and headed out the door.

"Just wait until Prom!" he laughed as he blew me a kiss. I caught it and returned it, then had to roll my eyes as he did jazz hands as Jason opened the car door for me so I could get in. I pretended to be annoyed, but it was great to see him so happy.

"So Sofi said you got a dress but she wouldn't tell me anything about it," Jason said as soon as he was in and buckled up.

"Why not?"

"She wants me to be surprised."

"It's long, bronze and shiny."

"She's going to mad you told me! But I need to know what kind of corsage to get you."

"You don't have to get me a corsage."

"How about a wrist thingy?"

"Not necessary."

"Well, I want to get you some flowers since it is a formal event."

"All right, how about one long stem red rose wrapped in a bronze ribbon, and since you insist, Dad said that I'm supposed to get you the same kind to pin on your jacket, that is, if you are wearing a jacket."

"I'm wearing a black tux, white shirt and black bow tie. Do you want me to wear a bronze vest?"

"You decide. Oh. One more thing. I don't do heels, so I hope you don't mind if I wear comfortable flat shoes that are a little crazy. You won't be able to see them because the dress is long."

"I don't care if you wear running shoes, as long as you can dance in them!"

"Actually they aren't good to run in, not enough arch or padding, and as you know I'm not much of a dancer, but the toes are rounded so they shouldn't do too much damage when I step on you," I said, and asked, "What are we going to do tonight?"

"I was thinking we could go to a movie that just came out," Jason responded as he drove us out of out neighborhood.

"What's it about?"

"I'm not going to tell you, I don't want to ruin it."

"By NOT telling me you are in essence ruining it."

"What do you mean, don't you want to be surprised?"

"Nope. Never. Uh-ah. Don't like surprises."

"You're kidding."

"Nope. Totally serious."

"You're not one of those people who reads the ending of a book first are you?" he asked suspiciously.

"Sometimes. If the visual on the cover and the synopsis doesn't give it away," I admitted.

"That's cheating!"

"No, not really, it lets me know if it's worth my time."

"But then you know how it's going to end!"

"Yes, but it's the *how* the author gets me *there* that interests me more than the actual *there* where they take me," I explained.

"Now that I won't argue with. Don't move," he said as he pulled the car into a parking space.

"Why?" I asked, as I looked around.

"Because after a captivating journey we are *there*, and I'm going to open your door," he explained with a smile as he got out and walked around to my side. As we got up to the ticket counter I reached into my purse. "I've got this, I get a military discount."

"Okay, then, I'll buy the treats because I get a bulk rate discount. I eat a lot when I don't know what is going to happen."

He didn't argue as he realized this was yet another battle that he was not going to win. We found seats, watched the previews and discussed whether Milk Duds or red licorice went better with popcorn. As the main feature started up he whispered, "I hope you enjoy the movie."

"I can't," I whispered back.

"Why?" he asked and looked at me all serious-like.

"Because I don't know how it ends," I answered, not looking at him so I wouldn't spew soda through my nose.

"I hope you at least like suspense," he said.

"Is this a scary movie?" I asked. The screen went black and someone screamed. I shoved the popcorn into his hands and covered my ears and squeezed my eyes shut. And started to hum. I'd sneak a peek now and then so I could follow the story line. It was actually more of a "who done it" rather than how horrifically it was done so I could watch most of it.

Afterwards, Jason was somewhat concerned that he had made a mistake choosing it, judging by my actions and reactions, but I assured him it was a form of "interpretive dance movie watching." And that it would be better the second time. When I knew what was going to happen. He groaned and shook his head.

After we were safely in the car *(and had locked the doors)* he turned to me and asked, "What's with covering your ears?"

"That's so I can't hear the soundtrack that intensifies the terror."

"And the humming?"

"Oops. Ditto. Didn't realize it was so loud. It counters the surround sound vibrations," I said. "Music is key to the setting. After seeing, or more appropriately, not seeing – just hearing the 'Don Don – Don Don – Don Don – Don Don' beating of *Jaws* or the screams behind the crate at the beginning of *Jurassic Park* is enough to cause nightmares and irreparable damage."

"What scary movies have you seen?"

"Seen?"

"Been to at least," he amended.

"The original *Alien*, which wasn't scary after the alien burst out of that guy's stomach," I said. "Oh, and I also went to *The Amityville Horror.*"

"The one where they go down into the basement, which was literally hell, to look for a dog?"

"Yes! How crazy was that?" I practically screamed.

"Okay Jett, we have to get something straight. You can run. Fast. So I hope you don't hold it against me that if we ever find ourselves in a haunted mansion, and there are all these creepy sounds and then an eerie silence behind the door and you go to open it . . . "

"Let me interrupt right there. If I do something that is so incredibly stupid, you have my blessing to hightail it out of there and let Darwin determine my outcome."

"That being said, if you are injured and cannot run, and don't do anything dumb, I won't leave you hanging. I'd throw you over my shoulder and get the heck out of Dodge," he offered.

"Fair enough. And hopefully enough adrenaline would kick in so I could do the same." I accepted and countered.

"Deal. Any other horror flicks? Did you ever attempt *The Exorcist*?"

"Nope."

"*The Omen*?"

"Nope."

"*Pet Cemetery*?"

"Nope." I shivered.

"*Silence of the Lambs*?" he snickered.

"Heck no, are you kidding me?" I said, assuming the eyes squeezed shut, ears covered and humming.

He tapped me on my shoulder.

"You know it's not real, why does it bother you so much?"

"My dad told me I was much too sensitive to negative stimuli. If I read, or see, or hear something scary before I go to sleep I create a whole movie in my head. We're talking color, sounds, smells, action and camera angles. Not real conducive to restful sleep."

"Okay then, what kind of movies do you enjoy?"

"The ones I know the ending to, duh." I laughed.

"I mean *types* of movies," he clarified.

"Action. Intrigue. Some comedies. Some chick flicks."

"Next time you can pick a movie, okay?" he offered.

"Sounds good to me," I accepted. Really. *Really.* Good.

We drove around town and ended up at the school overlooking the football stadium. We parked his mom's car where I used to park my mom's Jeep and walked down the hill to the track. And walked. Around and around. Counter-clockwise. And talked. About anything. Everything. It was comfortable. Ordinary. But magical too. And when he took me home and walked me to my door, we felt it was necessary to review all first five kisses, sans audience. And then we ended with the Official First Date First Kiss. Which I shared with Jason. And no one else.

26

"Hero"

Leading up to Prom was another spirit week of fun daily themes. Monday kicked it off with workout outfits of the 80's so everyone was wearing their interpretation of parachute pants, leg warmers and sweatshirts with the neck seam cut out so it draped over the shoulder. *Très chic.* But distracting as the school year was ending soon and reviews for finals would be next week.

Teachers didn't expect much homework to be done so they heaped on in-class assignments. Daily announcements reminded students to get their tickets to the dance and After Prom in advance, to order flowers for their dates and remember to go online to nominate seniors for Prom Queen and King. I got to Psych class early to talk to Trent.

"I see you joined the Prom FB," Trent said as I turned to chat.

"Thanks to your date."

"I need to figure out her corsage but she won't tell me what color she is wearing, wants to be a surprise, and she has sworn her friends to secrecy so I'm suppose to read her mind?"

"What with the Halsted surprise thing? Must be genetic. I have a picture of her dress on my phone. I can show you but not tell."

"Deal. Let me see."

I dug in my backpack for my phone, pulled the picture up and zoomed in so the color filled the screen. With my mouth firmly shut I held the phone out for him to see. He nodded and pretended to zip his lips as Chelsea arrived to claim her seat in between us.

"What's the secret?" she asked, looking from Trent to me.

"It's a surprise," Trent said.

"Ohhhh, I love surprises! I can't wait to hear my name being announced as a nominee for Queen, again." She gushed.

"Since you're nominated it won't be a surprise," Trent said.

"I guess. It's pretty much guaranteed that I would be, Joan on the other hand, now that would be a surprise!" she said.

"More like a nightmare. Unlike you, I don't like surprises and definitely don't want to be queen of the ball or anything else," I added, entering into the conversation to my surprise. Chelsea turned to study me for a moment.

"Good thing, not even a fairy godmother could pull that off," she said, with a little less conviction than normal.

"Maybe not, but I do think a certain fairy *godsister* could!" Trent laughed and winked at me. *Don't. You. Dare.* Was the mental message I sent him, which probably egged him on.

The rest of the week Facebook messages bounced around regarding Prom logistics. It was hard not to get caught up in it so I jumped on a raft and went with the flow. Until Friday, when the morning announcements brought the anticipated results and also an unexpected and unwanted logjam.

I was a nominee. Along with Chelsea, Jill, Jason, Will, Sam and a few others that I didn't know. We were supposed to cast our votes in the last period of the day. Oh boy. Psych. Before I could get my hands on Trent he met me in the hallway denying that he had said a word about it to Sofi, and hadn't nominated me either. We went in together. Chelsea was seething in her seat and fixed an icy stare at us both as we entered.

"Nice act Bennett, almost had me convinced," she growled as I sat down and faced the board.

Nothing I could say would change her mind so I said nothing at all. At the end of class, the teacher passed out slips with the nominated seniors' names and the instructions to circle one female and one male and turn it in. I looked at all of the names, then took out a red pen and quickly circled *Jason* and after more deliberate contemplation I slowly circled *Chelsea*. I folded the ballot slip and dropped it into the box on the teacher's desk as I left the room.

Sofi met me at the car and looked worried. "It wasn't me Joan, honest, not that I don't think you should be, because it would awesome if you and Jason could be, you know, crowned, but I know you would probably implode from being the center of attention, or disappear like a magician and never be heard from again. I really don't know who did put you in, but it wasn't any of us," she purged.

"Forget it. No worries. It was probably a joke. Let's get home, I'm expecting my shoes in the mail today and if they don't come in we may have to go on an emergency quest." The shoes did come. And they were incredible. Custom high top Converse in a leopard print on the outside panel and zebra on the inside, with red tongue, eyelets and back stripe and chocolate laces. I slipped them on. Perfect! A party on my feet! The doorbell rang, and I figured it was Sophie coming to check to see if we had to make another mad mall dash. I opened up the door to show her, but it was Jason. He looked down and cracked up!

"Are those your Prom shoes?" he laughed.

"Yes . . . too weird? I asked, a little concerned.

"Too awesome! Gracie is going to flip when she sees them. She'll bug Mom for a pair before we are out the door after pictures! You up for a run after dinner?"

"Sure, that sounds great, is seven okay?" I asked.

"I'm more than okay," he teased.

"A legend in your own mind," I said.

❁

The next morning Sophie called at nine to give me our Prom Day Schedule. It had begun. Hair. Nails. Make up. I insisted on keeping it simple. Liner. Pearl eye shadow. Mascara. My pale skin and freckles actually complemented the bronze dress well. At the last second Sophie moved that I add red lipstick. And Gracie seconded the motion. Following discussion, the motion carried.

"Joan, you look stunning," Jason's mom said as she stopped to check on us and tell me that my dad had come over to take pictures. Of course, Sofi was amazing in chiffon petals of teal with her blonde hair swept up, and Shelley's dark eyes and hair were striking with her tan complexion and beautiful hot pink dress.

We went downstairs to meet up with the guys. Jason smiled when he saw me. He was standing there all tall, tan and handsome, of course, in his tuxedo, bow tie and black low top Converse. *(A fun surprise that I didn't mind.)* Trent was speechless for a change as Sofi struck a dramatic pose and then elegantly descended like a princess. The girl definitely knew how to make an entrance.

Shelley walked carefully down in her strappy high heels, then twirled and jumped into Sam's outstretched arms. Yep. Match made in an amusement park. Sam and Trent both wore black low top Converse as well. Dad took some goofy Prom pictures. And the evening started out and continued to be, way too much fun. How could it not?

It turned out most of the lacrosse guys, including Will, had on black low top Converse shoes with their black tuxes. Jason had put the word out Friday night after seeing my shoes. What a riot. Everyone thought it was hysterical. *(Well, except for one person, who made it very clear a little later.)*

After awhile we all had to be quiet so they could announce the royal court. Chelsea earned her second tiara, and was crowned Queen, and Will was hysterical as he hammed it up when he was declared King. First he gushed. And he pretended to cry. And blew kisses to the crowd. And then made a declaration that all he really wanted was World Peace for the Pride Lands.

Chelsea wasn't amused. But we were. To make matters worse

for her, in the middle of the Prom Royalty Theme Slow Song someone screamed, "Let's Dance!" all *Footloose*-like and the music changed to the fast paced movie theme song as confetti fell from the ceiling and the crowd rushed the floor. And in the middle of it, of course, were Jason and Sam doing the Kevin Bacon / Chris Penn dance. Hysterical. I even joined in. Who'd have thought?

After that dance frenzy it was a billion degrees so Sofi and I went to get some air and go to the restroom. She was in the stall as I was alone at the sinks. I looked into the mirror to reapply my red lipstick. For a moment, starring into my eyes, I saw my mom looking back at me. And I smiled. Then the Queen arrived with her entourage.

"Well, if it isn't our shoe trend-setting Jetting Joan, all alone, what a surprise," her majesty shared. I finished applying the lipstick, inhaled and turned to her Excellency.

"Congratulations Chelsea. I hope it is everything you wished for," I tried to say sincerely, but to be honest it sounded a lot snottier than I had intended. Really. Really.

"Give it up Joan. Your goody two tennis shoes act doesn't fly with me," she snarled.

"Believe it or not Chelsea, I voted for you. I'm happy for Will too. It's nice you can share it with your boyfriend," I said.

"Will is an idiot. He proved it on the stage and following your silly friends' crass low life shoe fashion," Chelsea said.

That's when the stall door slammed open.

"Your ladyship doth protest too much, if King William willfully asked you to this festivity, and an idiot he be, what doth that sayeth about the Queen?" Sofi eloquently joked.

"Excuse me? Sophomore? You have nerve!" Chelsea ranted.

"No. Not some. A lot. And it's about time I showed it," Sofi said, dropping the Shakespeare speak.

"You better watch yourself. Cheer tryouts are next week, and I'm one of the judges," Chelsea threatened.

"One is such a lonely number. Your reign of terror is over. There's a new sheriff in town," Sofi said, glancing through the mirror at Chelsea, "and you're looking at her. As for Joan, she has more class in one of her shoes then you can ever hope for. And truer friends than you could ever imagine. You better watch out, that tiara might actually be a cursed diadem – don't go splitting your soul over it. Come on Joan, let's dance!"

And with that we exited into the hallway.

"Well said Sheriff. Thanks for coming to my rescue. Probation over. We're even," I said to Sofi.

"You're forever welcome! It felt so good to get out from under that shadow. Did you really, truly vote for her?"

"Yep. Under all of the fluff and resentment I felt it was important to her. That, and since I don't want it, a vote for her cancels out one for me, if I get one."

When we got back to the guys we saw them talking to Will. Sofi shouted, "All hail King William!"

"Hail yes!"said Sam.

"Thank you. Thank you. It is good to be the King!" Will hammed it up. "Actually it should have been Jason. And Joan. I nominated you guys and all of the lacrosse team voted for you! Unfortunately, Chelsea's highly skilled political machine was too much for our grass roots efforts!"

"Fortunately for me is more like it! However, I hope she doesn't know, or you and your head may soon be parting company," I warned.

"Oh she knows, I told her after she flipped out at my not formal footwear. At midnight when I drop her off, this carriage is turning back into a pumpkin in time to kick your butts on the volleyball court at After Prom!"

That's when we heard a few notes of the next song. A sweet, classic, slow one. Jason took my hand, and we disappeared into the crowd.

❂

Cheer tryouts. Sofi made it and was voted a co-captain. Finals. The last day of school. Check out and Senior Sunset. Strange how hard it was to leave the halls that I had haunted. Graduation. After the ceremony, and pictures with friends and family, Jon, Dad and I went out to lunch.

"Well Joan, have you decided which college gets the privilege of kicking you out?" Jon asked.

"Yep."

"Well, aren't you going to tell me?"

"Nope. It's a surprise," I said slyly.

"You know I don't like surprises."

"Yep," I teased.

"One of the reasons I ask, is because awhile back I *might* have told our lovable lacrosse coach you *might* be thinking of heading out west, and he *might* have made a call to the new women's lacrosse coach at CU before Jacket Day," he counter-teased.

"You!" I yelled.

"Yep. And they *might* be looking for a newb who thinks she can play with the big girls, now that she's cut her teeth on the little boys' game," Jon said.

"You don't know my life. Are you ever going to let me live it for myself without butting in?"

"Nope." He shook his head, and grinned across the table at Dad, who was smiling back at the two of us.

❂

Eyelash Lady greeted Jason and me with enthusiasm when we walked through her door later that night. "Congratulations Graduates! This one is on me! What will you have?"

"Go ahead. I'm thinking," I told Jason as my eyes reviewed the line of ice cream containers standing at attention in the freezer. He ordered his usual. Vanilla, on a sugar cone. With sprinkles. Eyelash Lady laughed and went to get it for him. My turn. I ordered.

"Glad you finally figured it out," she said slyly.

"My combo? It's pretty much the same as always," I said.

"No, him. You. Together. Took you long enough," she said coyly.

"Oh. Well. Maybe. We'll see. Enjoying the moment." I looked over at Jason waiting patiently for me to get my treat before he started on his.

"You do that sugar. Savor the sweetness." She winked.

It had been a long emotional day. We called it an early night and I went in to talk with Dad. He told me for the zillionth time how proud he was of me. Of all I had accomplished on my own. And how much he wished Mom could have been there for me. I assured him that he and Jon had given me more support than I could ever have asked for, even though I had never thought to ask.

I went to bed, but couldn't sleep. It was late when it dawned on me. The more conversations I was now having outside of my head with others, the less I was conversing inside, with myself. For a brief moment I was afraid I had lost something. Someone. Who? *Me*? Or *Mom*? I shut my eyes. Tears filled the black screen on my eyelids and the motion picture started, blurry, as before, but then became clearer. The two of us spinning. Copper penny swirls. The sound of her laughter. The smell of her shampoo. The lessons being carefully taught. The lessons being faithfully learned. They weren't lost. They were still there. *She* was still here. With *me*.

27

"Holding On To Heaven"

I was in eighth grade. Time was not on our side. Mom was losing her strength and could only manage short outings. But staying in bed in her room was not an option. "These walls are going to drive me crazy! And we all know what a short trip that is!" She would laugh. So we drove to the park. And I took her to the lake to feed the ducks. On our way down to the bench a jogger came by, looked at us and then stopped. "Helen? Helen Bennett? Is that you?" the woman asked. My mom looked at her and nodded.

"Yes Silvia. How are you doing? Great day for a run."

"I heard about your illness. I'm so sorry," the woman whispered.

"Thank you, but it's not that bad," Mom said as she smiled.

"You take care. I'll be praying for you," the woman said.

"Thank you. Enjoy your run."

It took a few minutes to reach the bench and sit down.

"I'm having a hard time praying," I sighed. "Knowing what to say. How to pray."

She thought for a moment, "Prayer may be difficult, but it was never meant to be hard. It can be soft. Like a whisper. Or loud. Like a shout. It can be like opening your clenched fists and letting your thoughts flow. Or searching your heart for an explanation. It's an open conversation. Or an honest apology. It's a praise for a blessing. Or a plea for strength. It's not a punishment, a rationalization or excuse. It has given me more comfort, confidence, and companionship than I can ever express. Yes, it may be difficult at times, especially when you are angry or hurt or afraid. That's when it's best to channel the negative into something productive and then let it go. Otherwise, it will take your joy and leave you bitter and alone. And being alone can be very, very hard. But prayer was never meant to be."

Summer. "Because We Can" by Jon Bon Jovi playing on the radio. Tennis matches with the loser buying ice cream. Running in the rain. Riding in the Jeep. Kisses, lots of kisses. Too numerous to describe or name. Nothing more, nothing less. Perfect. Heroic. *Perfectly heroic.* And exactly because of this, it allowed us to go our separate ways with no regrets, with luggage, but no baggage.

> (jason gb)
> You all set?
>
> (me)
> Pretty much. You?
>
> (jason gb)
> Yep. How does a quick run sound?
>
> (me)
> Zoom?
>
> (jason gb)
> Hilarious. Three miles on the trail?
>
> (me)
> Sure. Meet you out front in ten

I was going through all of the motions of leaving but couldn't figure out how to let go. Excited at the thought of there, dreading the idea of leaving here. Him. The Golden Boy that brought me home. I acted flippant. And joked. But lived in fear. Again.

At least I was living. Out loud and in color. Of course I needed to move on. The reality was we were only eighteen and needed to go out and invent ourselves. Be comfortable and content and jazzed about who we were, and who we could become.

However, the desire to not let go of this magical moment was overwhelming. Of being able to be yourself with someone, or be a better self because of that someone. I won't regret meeting Jason so young. He was sent to me for a reason. And now I had to let him go. But I didn't know how. So I put on my running shoes. To go face my fears. Because that's who I am. Now.

"Hey." Jason smiled.

"Hey yourself." I grinned back. And we were off.

The evenings had gotten cooler. The rhythm of our footsteps comforted me as we ran our familiar route and ended up back at the playground. We slowed to a walk and stretched a bit, and then automatically went to the swings. Both of us took one and kicked off; neither of us put too much effort in the motion or conversation. Comfortable yet on edge.

It's started to get dark so we slowed to a stop and retrieved the hoodies we'd dropped at the trail head. As I slipped mine on, Jason reached out and grabbed the back of my hood and pulled me over to him with his arm across my shoulders. We walked in silence back to my house. Bittersweet, but still sweet. Automatically, naturally, we went into my back yard. One more block to check. We picked up sticks and started to pass and catch. *Together.*

After a while, a slow painful conclusion reached us, and we put away the sticks.

"It's about that time," Jason quietly said. I bit my lip and blinked. And nodded. He reached out and I fell in. My forehead on his chest.

I inhaled.

"I smell like sweat," he confessed.

"You smell like you."

"Well that's a relief," he laughed.

"So is the fact that your mom washed your sweatshirt," I teased.

He inhaled, "You smell like fresh air and rain and shampoo."

I thought of my mom. I looked up at him. I stopped smiling.

"I'm not good at this," I whispered.

"That's okay, you're good at everything else," he whispered.

I studied his face. Took a mental photograph. Sighed.

"You'll be fine. We'll be fine. It's not forever. It's just see you later," he smiled. "Now close your eyes."

"You know I don't close my eyes when I kiss." I reminded him.

"Who says you're going to get kissed?" he asked.

"A girl can dream," I said.

"Well pretend you're asleep then and shut your eyes. I promise to keep mine open."

"Well how will I know that you do if mine are shut?"

"I guess you'll just have to trust me," he said.

"I was afraid you'd say that." I sighed, and shut my eyes.

After a moment he softly kissed my left eyelid, and then my right, squeezed my shoulders and said, "See you."

And I knew he could. And I believed he would. And I stood there in the dark, with my eyes closed, until I heard the gate shut. Then the porch light came on. Enlightened, I went in to say good night to my dad and Misty and try to get some sleep.

Early the next morning I jumped into my *topless* Jeep wearing a gold CU Go Buff tee shirt, with all of my belongings strapped down and the music turned up. With "Wide Open Spaces" blasting on the radio, I looked back to see Dad mouth the lyrics, "check the oil." He kissed his fist and threw it to me. I caught it; double fist bumped over my heart, kissed my fist, and released it up to Mom in the blue sky above. Driving west to the mountains, I knew that Jason was flying east to The Ohio State University. He'd accepted a ROTC Scholarship and would be a Buckeye in Columbus.

When I knew he was airborne I sent up a prayer for safe travels, willed his pilot not fly too close to the sun, and to deliver my hero to his next, great adventure ...

The end . . . ?

No, it's only the beginning!

Joan & Jason's story continues

in the award-winning second,

and final third novel of the Hero Series:

I WISH MY WORDS TASTED BETTER and

MY WINGS AREN'T READY TO FLY

Ruptured Appendix

As promised, here are the trivia answers,
explanations, and inside jokes!

p 1   "Total Eclipse of the Heart": Bonnie Tyler, 1983
        A great uplifting song, unless you actually listen to the
        words.

p 1   Icarus and Daedalus: In Greek mythology Icarus was the
        son of Daedalus, a skillful craftsman and artist.

p 2   *Caddy Shack* and *Animal House*: Ah yes, two movies
        that are perfect for the entire family to watch. Unless
        are between the ages of 1-14 or 25 -100, or have an IQ greater
        than 60. In short, two perfect teen-age boy movies.

p 2   *Princess Bride*: is a great movie for everybody. Not to
        see this movie would be . . . well, *inconceivable.*

p 2   *Role Models*: Us older folks instantly recognize the spoof of
        the lyrics from the rock band KISS: "I wanna rock and roll
        all night and party every day" instead of "*part of* every day"
        as used in the *Role Models* scene, 2008. Check out Kiss –
        70's, 80's and 90's band, their early on black and white face
        paint was unique at the time.

p 3   Jon Bon Jovi: John Francis Bongiovi, Jr. *(born March 2,
        1962)*, known as Jon Bon Jovi, is an American singer-
        songwriter, record producer, philanthropist, and actor,
        best known for having great hair and as the founder and
        frontman of rock band Bon Jovi, which was formed in 1983.

p 4   "Close To You": The Carpenters, 1970.

p 4   Kevin Bacon: adorable and talented 80's movie and tv star
        married to the equally adorable and talented movie and tv

star Kyra Sedgwick *(I want them to play Jason's parents in the movie so they can chaperone Prom . . . a girl can dream!).*

p 5   Jason Bourne: a character created by Robert Ludlum in the spy movie series *Bourne Identity* played by Matt Damon. Highly recommended . . . note his getaway car is a red Mini Cooper.

p 5   *Jason and the Argonauts*: epic black & white movie about a Hero and his posse of dancing skeletons.

p 5   Newb: pronounced "noob," meaning new at something, a novice. But seriously, if you don't   already know what it is, you are one.

p 7   Jane Austen: 1775 – 1817, was an English novelist whose works of romantic fiction earned her a place as one of the most widely read writers in English literature. She was a front runner in creating romantic leads like Jason – men who appreciated rather than feared intelligent, witty, women. Bravo! Well done! Spot on!

p 9   "Wind Beneath My Wings": Bette Midler, 1988.

p 9   "I Love Rock n Roll": Joan Jett, 1981.

p 13   "Because You Loved Me": Celine Dion, 1996.

p 14   Invisibility cloak: duh, "Harry Potter" book series of course, by the amazing J.K. Rowling.

p 15   "I Hope You Dance": Lee Anne Womack, 2000. Profoundly inspirational tune.

p 19   Functional Fit: Current work out craze that uses one's body weight for resistance training.

p 19   *Twilight Zone*: Horror/Sci Fi TV show in the 1959-1964.

p 22   "Hit Me With Your Best Shot": written by Canadian singer songwriter Eddie Schwartz and by American singer Pat Benatar, 1980.

p 22   *Pretty in Pink, Sixteen Candles, Breakfast Club* and
        Flash Dance: Molly Ringwald and Jennifer Beals
        totally rocked the '80s movie scene.

p 22   *Footloose*: really fun dance movie in the 1980s, could not
        bring myself to see the new one. Kevin Bacon rocks forever.
        If it's not broken, don't fix it.

p 23   LSM is short for Long Stick Middie: a player who plays with
        a "Pole" but as a Midfielder. LSMs are used on face-offs and
        during defensive situations.

p 23   Stick-check: refers to a player using his/her stick to stop an
        opposing player, often by hitting the opposing player's
        stick with your own.

p 26   Musical *Annie*: Original Broadway, 1977.
        Another fictional copper penny curly haired girl.

p 27   Vanilla Ace: What you get when you cross the rapper
        Vanilla Ice with an un-returnable serve in tennis.

p 27   Adonis: the Greek mythological god of beauty and desire.

p 27   Sir Lancelot: King Arthur of The Round Table fame's right
        hand "go to guy" knight.

p 30   "Misty": song originally by Leslie Gore, 1963. Covered by
        Johnny Mathis, 1990.

p 34   Roger Federer: One of the greatest – if not the greatest –
        tennis player from around 2005 to 2014.

p 34   Einstein: of the genius scientist Albert variety.

p 36   *Hercules*: Zero to Hero! Roman name for demigod Zeus' son
        who got his own animated film released by Walt Disney
        Pictures, 1997.

p 38   "Firework": Katy Perry, 2010.

p 38   Mount Olympus: Mythical residence of Greek gods.

p 38   Number of men it takes to change a roll of toilet paper?:
        No one knows, it has never happened. Ha ha.

p 38   "1812 Overture": Tchaikovsky's musical score often played
        during fireworks displays, 1882.

p 39   "Hallelujah Chorus": Stand and absorb the glory.
        From Georg Friedrich Handel's Messiah, 1741.

p 39   "Just The Way You Are": Billy Joel, 1977 and Bruno Mars,
        2010.

p 39   Whirly Pop: Best popcorn ever. Toss in a little sea salt. Yum.

p 39   *The Little Mermaid*: Sing along with the Jamaican crab!
        Animated movie released by Walt Disney Pictures, 1989.

p 43   Renaissance: A cultural movement period, through the
        14th to the 17th century.

p 47   Just Do It: Slogan for Nike of course.

p 50   Ansel Adams: Famous Photographer, (1902-1984)
        Incredibly beautiful work. Look it up, right now.

p 50   Law of Attraction: name given to the belief that "like
        attracts like" and by focusing on positive or negative
        thoughts, one can bring about positive or negative results.

p 54   *Dr. Jekyll and Mr. Hyde*: Scary movie, 1931, about two
        personalities inhibiting one body, one good and
        one evil, based on the original novella written by the
        Scottish author Robert Louis Stevenson that was
        first published in 1886.

p 59   "Amazing Grace": Jadon Lavik, 2008 Upbeat and groovy
        version of the Christian hymn with words written by the
        English poet and clergyman John Newton (1725–1807),
        published in 1779.

p 59   Michael Sullivan's "Riyria Revelations": amazing book
        series that I highly recommend, as does my teenage son.

p 60   "I meant what I said and I said what I meant, an elephant's
        faithful one hundred percent.": "Horton Hatches An Egg"
        by the incredible Dr. Suess.

p 62   "Fortune favors the Brave.": something my teenager says a
        million times a day.

p 66   "Maneater": is a single recorded by American duo Hall &
        Oates from their 1982 album H2O.

p 66   Liars and tyrants and stares, oh my: *Wizard of Oz* reference.

p 66   Theseus: Greek mythology, the hero who led youth through a
        maze-like labyrinth and battled the half man and half bull
        Minotaur to help them escape.

p 67   "Calvin and Hobbes": cartoon series by William Boyd
        Watterson II.

p 67   Take off of the movie *Close Encounters of the Third Kind*,
        1977.

p 68   Sir Isaac Newton: (1643-1727), explained gravity.

p 71   *ESPN*: Entertainment and Sports Programming Network.

p 72   Mr. Heisman: referring to the Heisman trophy, awarded to
        the outstanding college football player. Classic pose depicts
        a football player sidestepping and straight-arming a tackler.

p 73   *Compadre*: a friend or companion.

p 75   "Fire and Rain": James Taylor, 1970 good chill'n tune.

p 77   Gauntlet: a glove worn with medieval armor. Throwing
        down the gauntlet is equivalent to issuing a challenge.

p 79   Donkey Kong: an arcade game produced by Nintendo in the
        80's that is no longer around, thus the phrase.

p 82   "Singing in the Rain" Gene Kelly, 1952. Amazing tap dance
        scene in the rain. Check it out on YouTube. Too much fun.

p 87   Chaos Theory: made famous in the entertaining dinosaur

movie Jurassic Park, 1993, that I confess I only saw
half of when I went to see it in the theater and spent a good
portion of the experience tucked up on my back with my
eyes shut and ears covered. Sounds effects were awesome,
thank you Sir Stephen Spielberg. Ian Malcolm, character
played by actor Jeff Goldblum,"You've never heard of Chaos
Theory? Non-linear equations? Strange attractions?"

p 88   "Mean": Taylor Swift 2010.

p 89   Land line: Before cell phones telephones were actually
          connected with wires! No way! Way!

p 97   "Impossible": Shontelle, 2010.

p 99   Dr. Seuss' *How the Grinch Stole Christmas*: film based on the
          1957 book. Classic redemption flick. Love the Whos, love
          Max the reindeer pup, love Cindy Lou Who, who was
          no more than two, and don't get me started on the Jing
          Tinglers and the Flu Floopers.

p 100   Blindsided: referring to being surprised or caught off guard.

p 102   "Forever and Ever, Amen": by Paul Overstreet. Sung by
          Randy Travis, 1987.

p 105   Friendly fire: is an attack by a military force on their own
          forces while attempting to attack the enemy

p 105   Collateral damage: is damage to things that are incidental
          to the intended target.

p 109   Professor Snape: Tragic hero of Harry Potter fame. Spoiler
          alert! I knew he would ultimately sacrifice himself
          for Harry.

p 109   Wednesday: Daughter in The Addams Family movie, 1991,
          and earlier TV series, 1964, who had a wicked dark
          sense of humor.

p 117   "Eye of The Tiger": Survivor, 1982.

p 117   Witness Protection: is protection of a threatened witness
         or any person involved in the justice system. Witnesses
         and their families typically get new identities
         with authentic documentation.

p 134   Protégé: a person who is guided and supported by an older
         and more experienced or influential person.

p 134   Deflector shield: In Gene Roddenberry's Star Trek's
         fictional television universe, shields refer to a 23rd and
         24th century technology that provides starships and
         planets with limited protection against damage.

p 143   "You Give Love a Bad Name": Jon Bon Jovi, 1986 Habit for
         Humanity, Extraordinary dude, you've got to love him.

p 154   "Point of Light": Randy Travis, 1991. By Don Schlitz and
         Thom Schuyler.

p 160   BTW or BTdubs: By the way.

p 161   ROTC: Reserve Officers' Training Corps.

p 162   Longfellow: Henry Wadsworth Longfellow (February 27,
         1807 – March 24, 1882) was an American poet.

p 163   *A journey* . . . : English translation of quotation is from
         Chapter 64 of the Tao Te Ching ascribed to Laozi.

p 165   "Roar": Katy Perry, 2013.

p 170   "Name of the Game": is a 1977 song by Swedish pop group
         ABBA, and was released as the first single from the
         group's fifth studio album, The Album. Also sung by
         Amanda Seyfried, 2008, in the Universal Pictures musical
         film *Mamma Mia*!

p 176   Amazon: Tribe of women warriors. Not the website.

p 178   "Larger Than Life": Backstreet Boys, 1999.

p 181   Lady Gaga: Eccentric singer released "Poker Face," 2008.

p 181   Witch's guards: From *The Wizard of Oz*, 1939 movie
         produced by Metro-Goldwyn-Mayer based on the 1900 novel
         "The Wonderful Wizard of Oz" by L. Frank Baum.

p 186   Samson: Muscle bound man who lost his strength when
         Delilah tricked him into cutting his hair off. Lesson
         to be learned here is don't take fashion advice from
         anyone named Delilah.

p 189   "I'll Make a Man out of You": composed by Matthew Wilder,
         lyrics by David Aippek, sung in the Disney film *Mulan* by
         Donny Osmond, 1998.

p 197   G2G: Good to go – got everything covered.

p 199   "My Guy": Mary Wells, 1964.

p 199   Larry, Moe and Curly: The Three Stooges numerous silly
         short films specializing in physical farce and slapstick
         humor, 1938 and other years . . . .

p 199   Mini Me: Of Austin Power's fame, Mike Myers really funny,
         sometimes inappropriate for young audiences movies
         series, but hysterical none the less.

p 204   Diddly squat : nothing, *nada*, nil, zero.

p 212   Storm Troopers, Princess Leia, Jedi Knights, Han Solo,
         Chewbacca, Lando and Death Star: *Star Wars* Phenomena,
         started in 1977, continues forever, and ever.

p 214   "U Can't Touch This": written, produced and performed
         by MC Hammer, 1990.

p 227   Light me up: to knock down a player *(me)* causing them to
         see stars revolving around their head like in cartoons.

p 229   Humpty Dumpty: a good egg, but clumsy.

p 234   "This Kiss": Faith Hill, 1998.

p 237   Peace Out sign: OG, Original Gangster for all you newbs.

p 240   *Mulan*: American animated movie produced by Walt Disney. Feature Animation based on the Chinese legend of Hua Mulan, 1998. The girl had crazy mad skills.

p 240   Boots are made for walking: "These Boots Are Made for Walkin'" is a pop song written by Lee Hazlewood and recorded by Nancy Sinatra, 1966, then covered by Jessica Simpson, 2005.

p 240   "Anybody want a peanut?": Dialogue from *The Princess Bride,* a movie based on a book by William Goldman that is filled with the best one-liners ever.

p 241   Pterosaur: a flying dinosaur – seriously people, download some "Magic School Bus" episodes and learn something for a change will you?

p 242   Force, droids, Obi Wan: Awesome Star Wars jargon again.

p 248   "When We Stand Together": Nickelback, 2011.

p 250   *Touché*: acknowledgement of a hit by an opponent.

p 251   Density of Plutonium: the heaviest primordial element.

p 254   Sudden victory: is a form of competition where play ends as soon as one competitor is ahead of the others, with that competitor becoming the winner.

p 259   Et tu Brute?: is a Latin phrase meaning "and you, Brutus?" or "and you too, Brutus?" or "Brutus – bro – what's with the blade?" The phrase is often used poetically to represent the last words of the Roman dictator Julius Caesar to his friend Marcus Brutus at the moment of his assassination.

p 266   Warp 8: Star Trek term for speed, really really fast.

p 267   Four-hole: bottom left corner of goal.

p 270   *Sharknado*, a 2013 made-for-television disaster horror B movie about a waterspout that lifts sharks

out of the ocean and deposits them in Los Angeles. And we
have to include Sharknado 2, The Second One,
which takes place in New York City! Released 2014.

p 270   *Gladiator*: one of Russell Crowe's finest flicks. "Are you not
entertained?"

p 272   "Something to Talk About": written by Canadian singer-
songwriter Shirley Eikhard and recorded by Bonnie Raitt,
1990.

p 273   Dame Jane Morris Goodall: considered to be the world's
foremost expert on chimpanzees.

p 275   "Can't Fight This Feeling": REO Speedwagon, 1985.

p 277   "Cherish": Madonna, 1989, by Sire Records.

p 278   "Crazy For You": is a song by American recording artist
Madonna for the 1985 film Vision Quest.

p 285   *Jaws*: is a 1975 American thriller film directed by Steven
Spielberg and based on Peter Benchley's novel.

p 285   *Jurassic Park*: is a 1993 American science fiction/
adventure film, which incorporates some elements
of horror as well.

p 286   *Alien*: is a 1979 American science-fiction horror film
directed by Ridley Scott. The film's title refers to a highly
aggressive extraterrestrial creature that stalks and kills
the crew of a spaceship.

p 286   *The Amityville Horror*: 1979 American film, directed by
Stuart Rosenberg, and based on the novel by Jay Anson,
1977.

p 286   Darwin: referring to "The Darwin Awards," book that
explains when people do something so dumb they are
eliminated before they have the chance to reproduce
and weaken the human species.

p 286   *The Exorcist*: is a 1973 American supernatural horror film. Directed by William Friedkin, adapted by William Peter Blatty from his 1971 novel of the same name. The movie deals with the demonic possession of a 12 year old girl and her mother's desperate attempts to win back her child through an exorcism conducted by two priests.

p 286   *The Omen*: is an 1976 British/American suspense horror film directed by Richard Donner.

p 286   *Pet Cemetary*: Behind a young family's home in Maine is a terrible secret that holds the power of life after death. When tragedy strikes, the threat of that power soon becomes undeniable. Director: Mary Lambert Writer: Stephen King *(novel)*, Stephen King *(screenplay)*.

p 286   *Silence of the Lambs*: a 1991 American thriller film that blends elements of the crime and horror genres.

p 288   "Hero": is a song by American singer-songwriter Mariah Carey, 1993 by Columbia Records.

p 288   *Très chic*: in style.

p 291   Pride Lands: From *The Lion King*, a 1994 American animated film produced by Walt Disney Feature Animation and released by Walt Disney Pictures.

p 292   "Footloose": Kenny Loggins, 1984.

p 292   Shakespeare speak: referring to William Shakespeake, an English poet, playwright and actor, baptised 1564.

p 293   Diadem: In "Harry Potter" series Voldemort split his soul into it as his fifth horcrux.

p 296   "Holding On To Heaven": Nickleback, 2011.

p 297   "Because We Can": Bon Jovi, , 2013.

p 298   "Wide Open Spaces": Dixie Chicks, 1998.

Fade to **Black** & White

Book Club Questions

1. Would you have chosen a different treatment than Joan's mother?

2. Why did Joan change her hair color?

3. Do you know anyone similar to any of these characters?

4. Which character(s) did you identify with most and why?

5. What did you think of Joan's relationships with her father and Jon?

6. What problems/challenges do the characters face?

7. How did Joan's sense of humor play a part in her recovery?

8. How do character decisions affect their lives and the lives of others?

9. Who was your favorite character? Why?

10. Is the book believable?

11. Who were "The Nakeds" and why were they relevant?

12. Are conflicts neatly resolved or are they left undecided?

13. Can you identify examples of light vs. dark in the book?

14. What is the significance of the phoenix illustration on the title page?

15. Is the theme relevant today?

16. What do you think will happen between Joan and Jason?

17. Did the playlist add or detract from the story?

18. Did you read the Ruptured Appendix as you read the novel, or after?

19. Would you recommend this book to someone else?

20. Would you like to read the next book in the Hero series?

About the author

Kris is a graphic designer and author/ illustrator of multiple picture books. Substitute teaching inspired her young adult Hero series, including award-winning I WISH MY WORDS TASTED BETTER. Originally from Illinois, she and her husband Mike have moved coast to coast and many states in between *with* a herd of animals and *for* visits from their three sons, two daughters-in-law, two grandkids and friends near and far. Diagnosed with breast cancer in 2001 and a benign brain tumor in 2022, she advocates early detection, aggressive treatments and thriving happily ever after.

Picture books written and/or illustrated by Kris Abel-Helwig:

"I love you I love you I love you I do. If you were a sock . . . then I'd be your shoe." (Available in English and Spanish)

"I love you I love you I love you I do. If you were purple . . . then I'd be blue."

"We love you We love you We love you We do. If you were a pirate . . . then we'd be your crew."

"Any color in the rainbow, and then some . . ."

"Any dinosaur that's been discovered, and then some . . ."

"Any place you've ever imagined, and then some . . ."

"The wifful wafful difle daffle sniffle snaffle snorful dorful waffle" by Grandma Helwig • Art & Design by Kris Abel-Helwig

"I wish I were a firefigher instead of a little girl" by Connie Kotnik-Abel • Art & Design by Kris Abel-Helwig

Follow Kris for updates :-) https://kahcreative.com

FB: @krisabelhelwig.author.illustrator • T/I: @krisabelhelwig